An Armada Three-in-One

The Katy Trilogy

D1369216

ARMADA

Famous stories available in Armada

What Katy Did
What Katy Did at School
What Katy Did Next

Susan M. Coolidge

ARMADA

This Armada *Katy Three-in-One* was
first published in the U.K. in Armada in 1988
by William Collins Sons & Co. Ltd

Armada is an imprint of
the Children's Division, part of
the Collins Publishing Group,
8 Grafton Street, London W1X 3LA

Printed and bound in Great Britain by
William Collins Sons & Co. Ltd, Glasgow

What Katy Did

What Katy Did was
first published in this edition in the U.K. in a single volume
in 1963 by William Collins Sons & Co. Ltd,
and in Armada in 1967

Contents

CHAPTER ONE

The Little Carrs

I WAS SITTING in the meadows one day, not long ago, at a place where there was a small brook. It was a hot day. The sky was very blue, and white clouds, like great swans, went floating over it to and fro. Just opposite me was a clump of green rushes, with dark velvety spikes, and among them one single tall, red cardinal flower, which was bending over the brook as if to see its own beautiful face in the water. But the cardinal did not seem to be vain.

The picture was so pretty that I sat a long time enjoying it. Suddenly, close to me, two small voices began to talk—or to sing, for I couldn't tell exactly which it was. One voice was shrill; the other, which was a little deeper, sounded very positive and cross. They were evidently disputing about something, for they said the same words over and over again. These were the words—"Katy did." "Katy didn't." "She did." "She didn't." "She did." "She didn't." "Did." "Didn't." I think they must have repeated them at least a hundred times.

I got from my seat to see if I could find the speakers, and sure enough, there on one of the cat-tail bulrushes I spied two tiny pale-green creatures. Their eyes seemed to be weak, for they both wore black goggles. They had six

9

legs apiece,—two short ones, two not so short, and two very long. These last legs had joints like the springs to buggy-tops; and as I watched, they began walking up the rush, and then I saw that they moved exactly like an old-fashioned gig. In fact, if I hadn't been too big, I *think* I should have heard them creak as they went along. They didn't say anything so long as I was there, but the moment my back was turned they began to quarrel again, and in the same old words—"Katy did." "Katy didn't." "She did." "She didn't."

As I walked home I fell to thinking about another Katy —a Katy I once knew, who planned to do a great many wonderful things, and in the end did none of them, but something quite different—something she didn't like at all at first, but which, on the whole, was a great deal better than any of the doings she had dreamed about. And as I thought, this story grew in my head, and I resolved to write it down for you. I have done it; and, in memory of my two little friends on the bulrush, I give it their name. Here it is—the story of What Katy Did.

KATY'S NAME WAS Katy Carr. She lived in the town of Burnet, which wasn't a very big town, but was growing as fast as it knew how. The house she lived in stood on the edge of town. It was a large square house. white, with green blinds. and had a porch in front, over which roses and clematis made a thick bower. Four tall locust-trees shaded the gravel path which led to the front gate. On one side of the house was an orchard: on the other side were wood piles and barns, and an ice-house. Behind was a kitchen garden sloping to the south; and behind that a pasture with a brook in it, and butternut trees, and four cows—two red ones, a yellow one with sharp horns tipped with tin, and a dear little white one named Daisy.

There were six of the Carr children—four girls and two boys. Katy, the eldest, was twelve years old; little Phil. the youngest, was four, and the rest fitted in between.

Dr. Carr, their papa, was a dear, kind, busy man, who was away from home all day, and sometimes all night too, taking care of sick people. The children hadn't any mamma. She had died when Phil was a baby, four years before my story began. Katy could remember her pretty well; to the rest she was but a sad, sweet name, spoken on Sunday, and at prayer-times, or when papa was specially gentle and solemn.

In place of this mamma, whom they recollected so dimly, there was Aunt Izzie, papa's sister, who came to take care of them when mamma went away on that long journey, from which, for so many months, the little ones kept hoping she might return. Aunt Izzie was a small woman, sharp-faced and thin, rather old-looking, and very neat and particular about everything. She meant to be kind to the children, but they puzzled her much, because they were not a bit like herself when she was a child. Aunt Izzie had been a gentle, tidy little thing, who loved to sit, as Curly Locks did, sewing long seams in the parlour, and to have her head patted by older people, and be told that she was a good girl; whereas Katy tore her dress every day, hated sewing, and didn't care a button about being called "good," while Clover and Elsie shied off like restless ponies when anyone tried to pat their heads. It was very perplexing to Aunt Izzie, and she found it quite hard to forgive the children for being so "unaccountable," and so little like the good boys and girls in Sunday-school memoirs, who were the young people she liked best, and understood most about.

Then Dr. Carr was another person who worried her. He wished to have the children hardy and bold, and encouraged climbing and rough plays, in spite of the bumps and ragged clothes which resulted. In fact, there was just one half-hour of the day when Aunt Izzie was really satisfied about her charges, and that was the half-hour before break-fast, when she had made a law that they were all to sit in their little chairs and learn the Bible verse for the day. At this time she looked at them with pleased eyes; they were all so spick and span, with such nicely-brushed jackets and such neatly-combed hair. But the moment the bell rang her comfort was over. From that time on, they were what she called "not fit to be seen." The neighbours pitied her very much. They used to count the sixty stiff white pantalette legs hung out to dry every Monday morning, and say to each other what a sight of washing those children made, and what a labour it must be for poor Miss Carr to keep them so nice. But poor Miss Carr didn't think them at all nice; that was the worst of it.

"Clover, go upstairs and wash your hands! Dorry, pick your hat off the floor and hang it on the nail! Not that nail —the third nail from the corner! " These were the kind of things Aunt Izzie was saying all day long. The children minded her pretty well, but they didn't exactly love her, I fear. They called her "Aunt Izzie" always, never "Aunty." Boys and girls will know what *that* meant.

I want to show you the little Carrs, and I don't know that I could ever have a better chance than one day when five out of six were perched on the top of the ice-house, like chickens on a roost. This ice-house was one of their favourite places. It was only a low roof set over a hole in the ground, and, as it stood in the middle of the side-yard, it always seemed to the children that the shortest road to every place was up one of its slopes and down the other. They also liked to mount to the ridge-pole, and then, still keeping the sitting position, to let go, and scrape slowly down over the warm shingles to the ground. It was bad for their shoes and trousers, of course: but what of that? Shoes and trousers, and clothes generally, were Aunt Izzie's affair; theirs was to slide and enjoy themselves.

Clover, next in age to Katy, sat in the middle. She was a fair sweet dumpling of a girl, with thick pig-tails of light brown hair, and short-sighted blue eyes, which seemed to hold tears, just ready to fall from under the blue. Really Clover was the jolliest little thing in the world: but these eyes, and her soft cooing voice, always made people feel like petting her and taking her part. Once, when she was very small, she ran away with Katy's doll, and when Katy pursued, and tried to take it from her, Clover held fast and would not let go. Dr. Carr who wasn't attending particularly, heard nothing but the pathetic tone of Clover's voice, as she said; "Me won't! Me want Dolly!" and, without stopping to inquire, he called out sharply; "For shame, Katy! give your sister *her* doll at once!" which Katy, much surprised, did; while Clover purred in triumph, like a satisfied kitten. Clover was sunny and sweet-tempered, a little indolent, and very modest about herself, though, in fact, she was particularly clever in all sorts of games, and extremely droll and funny in a quiet way. Everybody loved her, and she loved everybody, especially Katy, whom she looked up to as one of the wisest people in the world.

Pretty little Phil sat next on the roof to Clover, and she held him tight with her arm. Then came Elsie, a thin, brown child of eight, with beautiful dark eyes, and crisp, short curls covering the whole of her small head. Poor little Elsie was the "odd one" among the Carrs. She didn't seem to belong exactly to either the older or the younger children. The great desire and ambition of her heart was to be allowed to go about with Katy and Clover and Cecy Hall, and to know their secrets, and be permitted to put notes into the little post-offices they were for ever establishing in all sorts of hidden places. But they didn't want Elsie, and used to tell her to "run away and play with the children," which hurt her feelings very much. When she wouldn't run away, I am sorry to say they ran away from her, which, as their legs were longer, it was easy to do. Poor Elsie, left behind, would cry bitter tears, and, as she was too proud to play much with Dorry and John, her principal comfort was tracking the older ones about, and discovering their mysteries, especially the post-offices, which were her greatest grievance. Her eyes were bright and quick as a bird's. She would peep and peer, and follow and watch, till at last, in some odd, unlikely place, the crotch of a tree, the middle of the asparagus bed, or, perhaps, on the very top step of the scuttle ladder, she spied the little paper box, with its load of notes, all ending with "Be sure and not let Elsie know." Then she would seize the box, and, marching up to wherever the others were, she would throw it down, saying defiantly: "There's your old post-office!" but feeling all the time just like crying. Poor little Elsie! In almost every large family, there is one of these unmated, left-out children. Katy, who had the finest plans in the world for being "heroic," and of use, never saw, as she drifted on her heedless way, that here, in this lonely little sister, was the very chance she wanted for being a comfort to somebody who needed comfort very much. She never saw it, and Elsie's heavy heart went uncheered.

Dorry and Joanna sat on the two ends of the ridge-pole. Dorry was six years old; a pale, pudgy boy, with rather a solemn face, and smears of molasses on the sleeve of his jacket. Joanna, whom the children called "John," and "Johnnie," was a square, splendid child, a year younger than Dorry; she had big grave eyes, and a wide rosy mouth, which always looked ready to laugh. These two were great friends, though Dorry seemed like a girl who had got into boy's clothes by mistake, and Johnnie like a boy who, in a fit of fun, had borrowed his sister's frock. And now, as they all sat there chattering and giggling, the window above opened, a glad shriek was heard, and Katy's head appeared. In her hand she held a heap of stockings, which she waved triumphantly.

"Hurray!" she cried, "all done, and Aunt Izzie says we may go. Are you tired of waiting? I couldn't help it, the holes were *so* big, and took so long. Hurry up, Clover, and get the things! Cecy and I will be down in a minute."

The children jumped up gladly, and slid down the roof. Clover fetched a couple of baskets from the wood-shed. Elsie ran for her kitten. Dorry and John loaded themselves with two great faggots of green boughs. Just as they were ready the side-door banged, and Katy and Cecy Hall came into the yard.

I must tell you about Cecy. She was a great friend of the

14

children's, and lived in a house next door. The yards of
the houses were only separated by a green hedge, with no
gate, so that Cecy spent two-thirds of her time at Dr.
Carr's, and was exactly like one of the family. She was a
neat, dapper, pink-and-white-girl, modest and prim in
manner, with light shiny hair which always kept smooth,
and slim hands which never looked dirty. How different
from my poor Katy! Katy's hair was forever in a tangle:
her gowns were always catching on nails and "tearing
themselves"; and, in spite of her age and size, she was as
heedless and innocent as a child of six. Katy was the
longest girl that was ever seen. What she did to make herself grow so, nobody could tell; but there she was—up
above papa's ear, and half a head taller than poor Aunt
Izzie. Whenever she stopped to think about her height she
became very awkward, and felt as if she were all legs and
elbows, and angles and joints. Happily, her head was so
full of other things, of plans and schemes, and fancies of all
sorts that she didn't often take time to remember how tall
she was. She was a dear, loving child, for all her careless
habits, and made bushels of good resolutions every week
of her life, only unluckily she never kept any of them. She
had fits of responsibility about the other children, and
longed to set them a good example, but when the chance
came, she generally forgot to do so. Katy's days flew like
the wind; for when she wasn't studying lessons, or sewing
and darning with Aunt Izzie, which she hated extremely,
there were always so many delightful schemes rioting in
her brains, that all she wished for was ten pairs of hands
to carry them out. These same active brains got her into
perpetual scrapes. She was fond of building castles in the
air, and dreaming of the time when something she had done
would make her famous, so that everybody would hear
of her, and want to know her. I don't think she had made
up her mind what this wonderful thing was to be; but
while thinking about it she often forgot to learn a lesson,
or to lace her boots, and then she had a bad mark, or a
scolding from Aunt Izzie. At such times she consoled her-

15

self with planning how, by-and-by, she would be beautiful and beloved, and amiable as an angel. A great deal was to happen to Katy before that time came. Her eyes, which were black, were to turn blue; her nose was to lengthen and straighten, and her mouth, quite too large at present to suit the part of a heroine, was to be made over into a sort of rosy button. Meantime, and until these charming changes should take place, Katy forgot her features as much as she could, though still, I think, the person on earth whom she most envied was that lady on the big posters with the wonderful hair which sweeps the ground.

CHAPTER TWO

Paradise

THE PLACE to which the children were going was a sort of marshy thicket at the bottom of a field near the house. It wasn't a big thicket, but it looked big, because the trees and bushes grew so closely that you could not see just where it ended. In the winter the ground was damp and boggy, so that nobody went there, excepting cows, who didn't mind getting their feet wet; but in summer the water dried away, and then it was all fresh and green, and full of delightful things wild roses, and sassafras, and birds' nests. Narrow, winding paths ran here, and there, made by the cattle as they wandered to and fro. This place the children called "Paradise," and to them it seemed as wide and endless and full of adventure as any forest of fairyland.

The way to Paradise was through some wooden bars. Katy and Cecy climbed these with a hop, skip, and jump, while the smaller ones scrambled underneath. Once past the bars they were fairly in the field, and, with one consent, they all began to run till they reached the entrance of the wood. Then they halted, with a queer look of hesitation on their faces. It was always an exciting occasion to go to Paradise for the first time after the long winter.

Who knew what the fairies might not have done since any of them had been there to see?

"Which path shall we go in by?" asked Clover, at last.

"Suppose we vote," said Katy. "I say by the Pilgrim's Path and the Hill of Difficulty."

"So do I!" chimed in Clover, who always agreed with Katy.

"The Path of Peace is nice," suggested Cecy.

"No, no! We want to go by Sassafras Path!" cried John and Dorry.

However, Katy, as usual, had her way. It was agreed that they should first try Pilgrim's Path, and afterward make a thorough exploration of the whole of their little kingdom, and see all that happened, since last they were there. So in they marched, Katy and Cecy heading the procession, and Dorry, with his great trailing bunch of boughs, bringing up the rear.

"Oh, there is the dear rosary, all safe!" cried the children, as they reached the top of the Hill of Difficulty, and came upon a tall stump, out of the middle of which waved a wild rose-bush budded over with fresh green leaves. This "rosary" was a fascinating thing to their minds. They were always inventing stories about it, and were in constant terror lest some hungry cow should take a fancy to the rose-bush and eat it up.

"Yes," said Katy, stroking a leaf with her finger, "it was in great danger one night last winter, but it escaped."

"Oh! how? Tell us about it!" cried the others, for Katy's stories were famous in the family.

"It was Christmas Eve," continued Katy, in a mysterious tone. "The fairy of the rosary was quite sick. She had taken a dreadful cold in her head, and the poplar-tree fairy, just over there, told her that sassafras tea is good for colds. So she made a large acorn-cup full, and then cuddled herself in where the wood looks so black and soft, and fell asleep. In the middle of the night, when she was snoring soundly, there was a noise in the forest, and a dreadful black bull with fiery eyes galloped up. He saw our poor Rosy Posy,

18

and, opening his big mouth, he was just going to bite her in two; but at that minute a little fat man, with a wand in his hand, popped out from behind the stump. It was Santa Claus, of course. He gave the bull such a rap with his wand that he moo-ed dreadfully, and then put up his forepaw, to see if his nose was on or not. He found it was, but it hurt him so that he moo-ed again, and galloped off as fast as he could into the woods Then Santa Claus woke up the fairy, and told her that if she didn't take better care of Rosy Posy he should put some other fairy into her place, and set her to keep guard over a prickly, scratchy, blackberry bush."

"Is there really any fairy?" asked Dorry, who had listened to his narrative with open mouth.

"Of course," answered Katy. Then bending down toward Dorry, she added in a voice intended to be of wonderful sweetness: "I am a fairy, Dorry! "

"Pshaw! " was Dorry's reply; "you're a giraffe—pa said so! "

The Path of Peace got its name because of its darkness and coolness. High bushes almost met over it, and trees kept it shady, even in the middle of the day. A sort of white flower grew there, which the children called Pollypods, because they didn't know the real name. They stayed a long while picking bunches of these flowers, and then John and Dorry had to grub up an armful of sassafras roots; so that before they had fairly gone through Toadstool Avenue, Rabbit Hollow, and the rest, the sun was just over their heads, and it was noon.

"I'm getting hungry," said Dorry.

"Oh, no, Dorry, you mustn't be hungry till the bower is ready! " cried the little girls, alarmed, for Dorry was apt to be disconsolate if he was kept waiting for his meals. So they made haste to build the bower. It did not take long, being composed of boughs hung over skipping-ropes, which were tied to the very poplar tree where the fairy lived who had recommended sassafras tea to the fairy of the rose.

19

When it was done they all cuddled in underneath. It was a very small bower—just big enough to hold them, and the baskets, and the kitten. I don't think there would have been room for anybody else, not even another kitten. Katy, who sat in the middle, untied and lifted the lid of the largest basket, while all the rest peeped eagerly to see what was inside.

First came a great many ginger cakes. These were carefully laid on the grass to keep till wanted; buttered biscuit came next—three apiece, with slices of cold lamb laid in between; and last of all were a dozen hard-boiled eggs, and a layer of thick bread and butter sandwiched with corned-beef. Aunt Izzie had put up lunches for Paradise before, you see, and knew pretty well what to expect in the way of appetite.

Oh, how good everything tasted in that bower, with the fresh wind rustling the poplar leaves, sunshine and sweet wood-smells about them, and birds singing overhead! No grown-up dinner-party ever had half so much fun. Each mouthful was a pleasure; and when the last crumb had vanished, Katy produced the second basket, and there—oh, delightful surprise!—were seven little pies—molasses pies, baked in saucers—each with a brown top and crisp, candified edge, which tasted like toffee and lemon-peel, and all sorts of good things mixed up together.

There was a general shout. Even demure Cecy was pleased, and Dorry and John kicked their heels on the ground in a tumult of joy. Seven pairs of hands were held out at once toward the basket; seven sets of teeth went to work without a moment's delay. In an incredibly short time every vestige of pie had disappeared, and a blissful stickiness pervaded the party.

"What shall we do now?" asked Clover, while little Phil tipped the baskets upside down, as if to make sure there was nothing left that could possibly be eaten.

"I don't know," replied Katy, dreamily. She had left her seat, and was half-sitting, half-lying on the low crooked bough of a butternut-tree, which hung almost over the children's heads.

"Let's play we're grown up," said Cecy, "and tell what we mean to do?"

"Well," said Clover, "you begin. What do you mean to do?"

"I mean to have a black silk dress, and pink roses in my bonnet, and a white muslin long-shawl," said Cecy; "and I mean to look *exactly* like Minerva Clark! I shall be very good, too; as good as Mrs. Bedell, only a great deal prettier. All the young gentlemen will want me to go and ride, but I shan't notice them at all, because you know I shall always be teaching in Sunday-school, and visiting the poor. And some day, when I am bending over an old woman, and feeding her with currant jelly, a poet will come along and see me, and he'll go home and write a poem about me," concluded Cecy, triumphantly.

"Pooh!" said Clover. "I don't think that would be nice at all. *I'm* going to be a beautiful lady—the most beautiful lady in the world! And I'm going to live in a yellow castle, with yellow pillars to the portico, and a square thing on top, like Mr. Sawyer's. My children are going to have a play-house up there. There's going to be a spy-glass in the window to look out of. I shall wear gold dresses and silver dresses every day, and diamond rings, and have white satin aprons to tie on when I'm dusting, or doing anything dirty. In the middle of my backyard there will be a pond full of scent, and whenever I want any I shall just go out and dip a bottle in. And I shan't teach in Sunday-schools, like Cecy, because I don't want to; but every Sunday I'll go and stand by the gate, and when her scholars go by on their way home I'll put some scent on their handkerchiefs."

"I mean to have just the same," cried Elsie, whose imagination was fired by this gorgeous vision, "only my pond will be the biggest. I shall be a great deal beautifuller, too," she added.

21

"You can't," said Katy from overhead. "Clover is going to be the most beautiful lady in the world."

"But I'll be *more* beautiful than the most beautiful," persisted poor little Elsie; "and I'll be big, too, and know everybody's secrets. And everybody'll be kind then, and never run away and hide; and there won't be any post-offices, or anything disagreeable."

"What'll you be, Johnnie?" asked Clover anxiously to change the subject, for Elsie's voice was growing plaintive.

But Johnnie had no clear idea as to her future. She laughed a great deal, and squeezed Dorry's arm very tight, but that was all. Dorry was more explicit.

"I mean to have turkey every day," he declared, "and batter-puddings; not boiled ones, you know, but little baked ones, with brown shiny tops, and a great deal of pudding-sauce to eat on them. And I shall be so big then that nobody will say, 'Three helps is quite enough for a little boy.'"

"Oh, Dorry, you pig!" cried Katy, while the others screamed with laughter.

Dorry was much affronted.

"I shall just go and tell Aunt Izzie what you called me," he said, getting up in a great pet.

But Clover, who was a born peacemaker, caught hold of his arm, and her coaxing and entreaties consoled him so much that he finally said he would stay; especially as the others were quite grave now, and promised that they wouldn't laugh any more.

"And now, Katy, it's your turn," said Cecy; "tell us what you're going to be when you grow up."

"I'm not sure about what I'll be," replied Katy, from overhead; "beautiful, of course, and good if I can, only not so good as you, Cecy, because it would be nice to go and ride with the young gentlemen *sometimes*. And I'd like to have a large house and splendiferous garden, and then you could all come and live with me, and we would play in the garden, and Dorry should have turkey five times a day if he liked. And we'd have a machine to darn the stockings, and another machine to put the bureau drawers in order, and we'd never sew or knit garters, or do anything we didn't want to. That's what I'd like to *be*. But now I'll tell you what I mean to *do*."

"Isn't it the same thing?" asked Cecy.

"Oh, no!" replied Katy, "quite different; for you see I mean to *do* something grand. I don't know what yet; but when I'm grown up I shall find out." (Poor Katy always said "when I'm grown up," forgetting how very much she had grown already.) "Perhaps," she went on, "it will be rowing out in boats, and saving peoples' lives, like that girl in the book. Or perhaps I shall go and nurse in the hospital, like Miss Nightingale. Or else I'll head a crusade and ride on a white horse, with armour and a helmet on my head and carry a sacred flag. Or if I don't do that, I'll paint pictures, or sing, or scalp—sculp—what is it? you know—make figures in marble. Anyhow it shall be *something*. And when Aunt Izzie sees it, and reads about me in newspapers, she will say, 'The dear child! I always knew she would turn out an ornament to the family.' People very often say afterward that they 'always knew,'" concluded Katy, sagaciously.

"Oh, Katy! how beautiful it will be!" said Clover, clasping her hands. Clover believed in Katy as she did in the Bible.

"I don't believe the newspapers would be so silly as to print things about *you*, Katy Carr," put in Elsie vindictively.

"Yes, they will!" said Clover, and gave Elsie a push.

By-and-bye John and Dorry trotted away on mysterious errands of their own.

"Wasn't Dorry funny with his turkey?" remarked Cecy; and they all laughed again.

"If you won't tell," said Katy, "I'll let you see Dorry's journal. He kept it once for almost two weeks, and then gave it up. I found the book this morning in the nursery closet."

All of them promised, and Katy produced it from her pocket. It began thus:

"*March* 12.—Have resolved to keep jurnal.

"*March* 13.—Had rost befe for dinner, and cabage, and potato and appel sawse, and rice-puding. I do not like rice-puding when it is like ours. Charley Slack's kind is rele good. Mush and sirup for tea.

"*March* 19.—Forgit what did. John and me saved our pie to take to scule.

March 21.—Forgit what did. Gridel cakes for brekfast. Debby didn't fry enuff.

"*March* 24.—This is Sunday. Corn-befe for dinnir. Studdied my Bibel leson. Aunt Issy said I was gredy. Have resollved not to think so much about things to ete. Wish I was a beter boy. Nothing partikeler for tea.

"*March* 25.—Forgit what did.

"*March* 27.—Forgit what did.

"*March* 29.—Played.

"*March* 31.—Forgit what did.

"*April* 1.—Have dissided not to kepe a jurnal enny more."

Here ended the extracts; and it seemed as if only a minute had passed since they stopped laughing over them, before the long shadows began to fall, and Mary came to say that all of them must come in to get ready for tea. It was dreadful to have to pick up the empty baskets and go home, feeling that the long, delightful Saturday was over, and that there wouldn't be another for a week. But it was comforting to remember that Paradise was always there; and that at any moment when Fate and Aunt Izzie were willing they had only to climb a pair of bars—very easy ones, and without any fear of an angel with flaming sword to stop the way—enter it, and take possession of their Eden.

24

CHAPTER THREE

The Day of Scrapes

MRS. KNIGHT'S school, to which Katy and Clover and Cecy went, stood quite at the other end of the town from Dr. Carr's. It was a low, one-storey building, and had a yard behind it, in which the girls played at recess. Unfortunately, next door to it was Miss Miller's school, equally large and popular, and with a yard behind it also. Only a high board fence separated the two playgrounds.

Mrs. Knight was a stout, gentlewoman, who moved slowly, and had a face which made you think of an amiable and well-disposed cow. Miss Miller, on the contrary, had black eyes, with black corkscrew curls waving about them, and was generally brisk and snappy. A constant feud raged between the two schools as to the respective merits of the teachers and the instruction. The Knight girls, for some unknown reason, considered themselves genteel and the Miller girls vulgar, and took no pains to conceal this opinion; while the Miller girls, on the other hand, retaliated by being as aggravating as they knew how. They spent their recesses and intermissions mostly in making faces through the knot-holes in the fence, and over the top of it, when they could get there, which wasn't an easy thing to do, as the fence was pretty high. The Knight girls could make faces too, for all their gentility. Their yard had one great advantage over the other: it possessed a wood-shed, with a climbable roof, which commanded Miss Miller's premises, and upon this the girls used to sit in rows, turning up their noses at the next yard, and irritating the foe by jeering remarks. "Knights" and "Millerites" the two schools called each other; and the feud raged so high that sometimes it was hardly safe for a Knight to meet a Millerite in the street; all of which, as may be imagined was exceedingly improving both to the manners and morals of the young ladies concerned.

One morning, not long after the day in Paradise, Katy was late. She could not find her things. Her algebra, as she expressed it, had "gone and lost itself," her slate was missing. and the string was off her sun-bonnet. She ran about, searching for these articles and banging doors, till Aunt Izzie was out of patience.

"As for your algebra," she said, "if it is that very dirty book with only one cover, and scribbled all over the leaves, you will find it under the kitchen table. Philly was playing before breakfast that it was a pig; no wonder, I'm sure, for it looks good for nothing else. How you do manage to spoil your school-books in this manner, Katy, I cannot imagine. It is less than a month since your father got you a new algebra, and look at it now—not fit to be carried about. I do wish you'd realise what books cost!"

"About your slate," she went on, "I know nothing; but here is the bonnet-string;" taking it out of her pocket.

"Oh, thank you!" said Katy, hastily sticking it on with a pin.

"Katy Carr!" almost screamed Miss Izzie, "what *are* you about? Pinning on your bonnet string! Mercy on me! what shiftless thing will you do next? Now stand still and don't fidget! You shan't stir till I have sewed it on properly."

It wasn't easy to "stand still and not fidget," with Aunt Izzie fussing away and lecturing, and now and then, in a moment of forgetfulness, sticking her needle into one's

26

chin. Katy bore it as well as she could, only shifting perpetually from one foot to the other, and now and then uttering a little snort, like an impatient horse. The minute she was released she flew into the kitchen, seized the algebra, and rushed like a whirlwind to the gate, where good little Clover stood patiently waiting, though all ready herself, and terribly afraid she should be late.

"We shall have to run," gasped Katy, quite out of breath. "Aunt Izzie kept me. She has been so horrid!"

They did run as fast as they could, but time ran faster. And before they were half-way to school the town clock struck nine, and all the hope was over. This vexed Katy very much; for, though often late, she was always eager to be early.

"There," she said, stopping short, "I shall just tell Aunt Izzie that it was her fault. It is *too* bad." And she marched into school in a very cross mood.

A day begun in this manner is pretty sure to end badly, as most of us know. All the morning through things seemed to go wrong. Katy missed twice in her grammar lesson, and lost her place in the class. Her hand shook so when she copied her composition, that the writing, not good at best, turned out almost illegible, so that Mrs. Knight said it must be all done over again. This made Katy crosser than ever; and, almost before she thought, she had whispered to Clover, "How hateful!" And then, when just before recess all who had been speaking were requested to stand up, her conscience gave such a twinge that she was forced to get up with the rest, and see a black mark put against her name on the list. The tears came into her eyes from vexation; and, for fear the other girls would notice them, she made a bolt for the yard as soon as the bell rang, and mounted up all alone to the wood-house roof, where she sat with her back to the school, fighting with her eyes, and trying to get her face in order before the rest should come.

Miss Miller's clock was about four minutes slower than Mrs. Knight's, so the next playground was empty. It was a warm, breezy day, and as Katy sat there, suddenly a gust of wind came, and seizing her sun-bonnet, which was only half tied on, whirled it across the roof. She clutched after it as it flew, but too late. Once, twice, thrice it flapped, then it disappeared over the edge, and Katy, flying after, saw it lying a crumpled lilac heap in the very middle of the enemy's yard.

This was horrible! Not merely losing the bonnet, for Katy was comfortably indifferent as to what became of her clothes, but to lose it *so*. In another minute the Miller girls would be out. Already she seemed to see them dancing war-dances round the unfortunate bonnet, pinning it on a pole, using it as a football, waving it over the fence, and otherwise treating it as Indians treat a captive taken in war. Was it to be endured? Never! Better die first! And with very much the feeling of a person who faces destruction rather than forfeit honour, Katy set her teeth, and, sliding rapidly down the roof, seized the fence, and with one bold leap vaulted into Miss Miller's yard.

Just then the recess bell tinkled; and a little Millerite who sat by the window, and who, for two seconds, had been dying to give the exciting information, squeaked out to the others:

"There's Katy Carr in our backyard!"

Out poured the Millerites, big and little. Their wrath and indignation at this daring invasion cannot be described. With a howl of fury they precipitated themselves upon Katy, but she was quick as they, and holding the rescued bonnet in her hand, was already half-way up the fence.

There are moments when it is a fine thing to be tall. On this occasion Katy's long legs and arms served her an excellent turn. Nothing but a Daddy Longlegs ever climbed so fast or so wildly as she did now. In one second she had gained the top of the fence. Just as she went over a Miller-ite seized her by the last foot, and almost dragged her boot off.

Almost, not quite, thanks to the stout thread with which Aunt Izzie had sewed on the buttons. With a frantic kick

Katy released herself, and had the satisfaction of seeing her assailant go head over heels backwards, while. with a shriek of triumph and fright, she herself plunged headlong into the midst of a group of Knights. They were listening with open mouths to the uproar, and now stood transfixed at the astonishing spectacle of one of their number abso lutely returning alive from the camp of the enemy.

I cannot tell you what a commotion ensued. The Knights were beside themselves with pride and triumph. Katy was kissed and hugged, and made to tell her story over and over again. while rows of exulting girls sat on the wood· house roof to crow over the discomfited Millerites: and when. later, the foe rallied and began to retort over the fence, Clover, armed with a tack hammer, was lifted up in the arms of one of the tall girls to rap the intruding knuckles as they appeared on the top. This she did with such goodwill that the Millerites were glad to drop down again, and mutter vengeance at a safe distance. Altogether it was a great day for the school, a day to be remembered As time went on, Katy, what with the excitement of her adventure and of being praised and petted by the big girls, grew perfectly reckless, and hardly knew what she said or did.

A good many of the scholars lived too far from school to go home at noon, and were in the habit of bringing their lunches in baskets, and staying all day. Katy and Clover were of this number. This noon, after the dinners were eaten, it was proposed that they should play something in the school-room, and Katy's unlucky star put it into her head to invent a new game, which she called the Game of Rivers.

It was played in the following manner: —Each girl took the name of a river, and laid out for herself an appointed path through the room, winding among the desks and benches, and making a low, roaring sound, to imitate the noise of water. Cecy was the Plate: Marianne Brooks, a tall girl, the Mississippi; Alice Blair, the Ohio; Clover, the Penobscot; and so on. They were instructed to run into each other once in a while, because, as Katy said, "rivers do." As for Katy herself, she was "Father Ocean," and, growling horribly, raged up and down the platform where Mrs. Knight usually sat. Every now and then, when the others were at the far end of the room, she would suddenly cry out, "Now for a meeting of the waters!" whereupon all the rivers bouncing, bounding, scrambling, screaming, would turn and run toward Father Ocean, while he roared louder than all of them put together, and made short rushes up and down, to represent the movement of waves on a beach.

Such a noise as this beautiful game made was never heard in the town of Burnet before or since. It was like the bellowing of the bulls of Basham, the squeaking of pigs, the cackle of turkey-cocks, and the laugh of wild hyenas all at once; and, in addition, there was a great banging of furniture and scraping of many feet on an uncarpeted floor. People going by stopped and stared, children cried, an old lady asked why someone didn't run for a policeman; while the Miller girls listened to the proceedings with malicious pleasure, and told everybody that it was the noise that Mrs. Knight's scholars "usually made at recess."

Mrs. Knight, coming back from dinner, was much amazed to see a crowd of people collected in front of her school. As she drew near, the sounds reached her, and then she became really frightened, for she thought somebody was being murdered on her premises. Hurrying in, she threw open the door and there, to her dismay, was the whole room in a frightful state of confusion and uproar; chairs flung down, desks upset, ink streaming on the floor; while, in the midst of the ruin, the frantic rivers raced and screamed, and old Father Ocean, with a face as red as fire, capered like a lunatic on the platform.

"What *does* this mean?" gasped poor Mrs. Knight, almost unable to speak for horror.

At the sound of her voice the Rivers stood still; Father Ocean brought his prances to an abrupt close, and slunk down from the platform. All of a sudden, each girl seemed to realise what a condition the room was in, and what a horrible thing she had done. The timid ones cowered behind their desks, the bold ones tried to look unconscious, and, to make things look worse, the scholars who had gone home to dinner began to return, staring at the scene of disaster, and asking, in whispers, what had been going on?

Mrs. Knight rang the bell. When the school had come to order, she had the desks and chairs picked up, while she herself brought wet cloths to sop the ink from the floor. This was done in profound silence; and the expression of Mrs. Knight's face was so direful and solemn that a fresh damp fell upon the spirits of the guilty Rivers, and Father Ocean wished himself thousands of miles away.

When all was in order again, and the girls had taken their seats, Mrs. Knight made a short speech. She said she never was so shocked in her life before: she had supposed that she could trust them to behave like ladies when her back was turned. The idea that they could act so disgracefully, make such an uproar and alarm people going by, had never occurred to her, and she was deeply pained. It was setting a bad example to all the neighbourhood—by which Mrs. Knight meant the rival school. Miss Miller having just sent over a little girl, with her compliments, to ask if any one was hurt, and could *she* do anything? which was naturally aggravating! Mrs. Knight hoped they were sorry; she thought they must be--sorry and ashamed. The exercises could now go on as usual. Of course, some punishment would be inflicted for the offence. but she should have to reflect before deciding what it ought to be. Meanwhile, she wanted them all to think it over seriously; and if any one felt that she was more to blame than the others, now was the moment to rise and confess it.

Katy's heart gave a great thump. but she rose bravely: "I made up the game, and I was Father Ocean," she said to the astonished Mrs. Knight, who glared at her for a minute, and then replied solemnly, "Very well, Katy—sit down;" which Katy did, feeling more ashamed than ever.

31

but somehow relieved in her mind. There is a saving grace in truth which helps truth-tellers through the worst of their troubles, and Katy found this out now.

The afternoon was long and hard. Mrs. Knight did not smile once; the lessons dragged: and Katy, after the heat and excitement of the forenoon, began to feel miserable. She had received more than one hard blow during the meetings of the waters, and had bruised herself almost without knowing it against the desks and chairs. All these places now began to ache; her head throbbed so that she could hardly see, and a lump of something heavy seemed to be lying on her heart.

When school was over, Mrs. Knight rose and said: "The young ladies who took part in the game this afternoon are requested to remain." All the others went away, and shut the door behind them. It was a horrible moment: the girls never forgot it, or the hopeless sound of the door as the last departing scholar clapped it after her as she left.

I can't begin to tell you what it was that Mrs. Knight said to them: it was very affecting, and before long most of the girls began to cry. The penalty for their offence was announced to be the loss of recess for three weeks; but that wasn't half so bad as seeing Mrs. Knight so "religious and afflicted," as Cecy told her mother afterwards. One by one the sobbing sinners departed from the schoolroom.

When most of them were gone, Mrs. Knight called Katy up to the platform, and said a few words to her specially. She was not really severe, but Katy was too penitent and worn out to bear much, and before long was weeping like a waterspout, or like the ocean she had pretended to be.

At this, tender-hearted Mrs. Knight was so much affected that she let her off at once, and even kissed her in token of forgiveness, which made poor Ocean sob harder than ever. All the way home she sobbed; faithful little Clover, running along by her side in great distress, begging her to stop crying, and trying in vain to hold up the fragments of her dress, which was torn in at least a dozen places. Katy could not stop crying, and it was fortunate that Aunt Izzie happened to be out, and that the only person who saw her in this piteous plight was Mary, the nurse, who doted on the children and was always ready to help them out of their troubles.

On this occasion she petted and cosseted Katy exactly as if it had been Johnnie or little Phil. She took her on her lap, bathed the hot head, brushed the hair, put arnica on the bruises, and produced a clean frock, so that by tea-time the poor child, except for her red eyes, looked like herself again, and Aunt Izzie didn't notice anything unusual.

For a wonder Dr. Carr was at home that evening. It was always a great treat to the children when this happened, and Katy thought herself happy when, after the little ones had gone to bed, she got Papa to herself, and told him the whole story.

"Papa," she said, sitting on his knee, which, big girl as she was, she liked very much to do, "what is the reason that makes some days so lucky and other days so unlucky? Now to-day began all wrong, and everything that happened in it was wrong; and on other days I begin right, and all goes right straight through. If Aunt Izzie hadn't kept me in the morning I shouldn't have lost my mark, and then I shouldn't have been cross, and then *perhaps* I shouldn't have got in my other scrapes."

"But what made Aunt Izzie keep you, Katy?"

"To sew on the string of my bonnet, Papa."

"But how did it happen that the string was off?"

"Well," said Katy reluctantly, "I am afraid that was *my* fault, for it came off on Tuesday, and I didn't fasten it on."

"So you see we must go further back than Aunt Izzie for the beginning of this unlucky day of yours, Childie. Did you ever hear the old saying about 'For the want of a nail the shoe was lost?'"

"No, never—tell it to me!" cried Katy, who loved stories as well as when she was three years old.

So Dr. Carr repeated:

"For the want of a nail the shoe was lost,
For the want of a shoe the horse was lost,
For the want of a horse the rider was lost,
For the want of the rider the battle was lost,
For the want of the battle the kingdom was lost,
And all for the want of a horse-shoe nail."

"Oh, Papa!" exclaimed Katy, giving him a great hug as she got off his knee, "I see what you mean! Who would have thought such a little speck of a thing as not sewing on my string could make a difference? But I don't believe I shall get in any more scrapes, for I shan't ever forget:

'For the want of a nail the shoe was lost.'"

CHAPTER FOUR

Kikeri

BUT I am sorry to say that my poor, thoughtless Katy *did* forget, and did get into another scrape, and that no later than the very next Monday.

Monday was apt to be rather a stormy day at the Carr's. There was a big wash to be done, and Aunt Izzie always seemed a little harder to please and the servants a good deal crosser than on common days. But I think it was also, in part, the fault of the children, who, after the quiet of Sunday, were specially frisky and uproarious, and readier than usual for all sorts of mischief.

To Clover and Elsie, Sunday seemed to begin at Saturday's bed-time, when their hair was wet and screwed up in papers that it might curl next day. Elsie's waved naturally, so Aunt Izzie didn't think it necessary to pin her papers very tight; but Clover's thick, straight locks required to be pinched hard before they would give even the least twirl, and so her Saturday night was one of misery. She would lie tossing and turning, and trying first one side of her head and then the other; but whichever way she placed herself the hard knobs and the pins stuck out and hurt her; so when at last she fell asleep, it was face down, with her small nose buried in the pillow, which was not comfortable, and gave her bad dreams.

In consequence of these sufferings Clover hated curls, and when she "made up" stories for the younger children they always commenced: "The hair of the beautiful princess was as straight as a yardstick, and she never did it up in papers—never!"

Sunday always began with a Bible story, followed by a breakfast of baked beans, which two things were much tangled up together in Philly's mind. After breakfast the children studied their Sunday-school lessons, and then the big carry-all came round, and they drove to church, which was a good mile off. It was a large, old-fashioned church, with galleries, and long pews with high, red-cushioned seats.

The choir sat at the end, behind a low, green curtain, which slipped from side to side on rods. When the sermon began they would draw the curtain aside and show themselves, all ready to listen, but the rest of the time they kept it shut. Katy always guessed that they must be having good times behind the green curtain—eating orange-peel, perhaps, or reading the Sunday-school books—and she often wished she might sit up there among them.

The seat in Dr. Carr's pew was so high that none of the children, except Katy, could touch the floor, even with the point of a toe. This made their feet go to sleep; and when they felt the queer little pin-pricks which drowsy feet use to rouse themselves with, they would slide off the seat, and sit on the benches to get over it. Once there, and well hidden from view, it was almost impossible not to whisper.

Aunt Izzie would frown and shake her head, but it did little good, especially as Phil and Dorry were sleeping with their heads on her lap, and it took both her hands to keep them from rolling off into the bottom of the pew. When good old Dr. Stone said, "Finally, my brethren," she would begin waking them up. It was hard work sometimes, but generally she succeeded, so that during the last hymn the two stood together on the seat, quite brisk, and refreshed, sharing a hymn-book, and making believe to sing like the older people.

After church came Sunday-school, which the children liked very much, and then they went home to dinner, which was always the same on Sunday—cold corned-beef, baked potatoes, and rice-pudding. They did not go to church in the afternoon unless they wished, but were pounced upon by Katy instead, and forced to listen to the reading of *The Sunday Visitor*, a religious paper, of which she was the editor. This paper was partly written, partly printed, on a large sheet of foolscap and had at the top an ornamental device in lead pencil, with "Sunday Visitor" in the middle of it. The reading part began with a dull little piece of the kind which grown people call an editorial, about "Neatness," or "Obedience," or "Punctuality."

The children always fidgeted when listening to this— partly, I think, because it aggravated them to have Katy recommending on paper as very easy the virtues which she herself found it so hard to practise in real life. Next came anecdotes about dogs and elephants and snakes, taken from the Natural History book, and not very interesting, because the audience knew them by heart already. A hymn or two followed, or a string of original verses, and, last of all, a chapter of "Little Maria and Her Sisters," a dreadful tale, in which Katy drew so much moral, and made such personal allusions to the faults of the rest, that it was almost more than they could bear. In fact, there had just been a nursery rebellion on the subject. You must know that for some weeks back Katy had been too lazy to prepare any fresh *Sunday Visitors*, and so had forced the children to sit in a row and listen to the back numbers, which she read aloud from the very beginning! "Little Maria" sounded much worse when taken in these large doses, and Clover and Elsie, combining for once, made up their minds to endure it no longer. So, watching their chance, they carried off the whole edition, and poked it into the kitchen fire, where they watched it burn with a mixture of fear and delight which it was comical to witness. They dared not confess the deed, but it was impossible not to look conscious when Katy was flying about and rummaging after her lost treasure, and she suspected them, and was very irate in consequence.

The evenings of Sunday were always spent in repeating hymns to Papa and Aunt Izzie. This was fun, for they all took turns, and there was quite a scramble as to who should secure the favourites, such as "The west hath shut its gate of gold," and "Go when the morning shineth." On the whole, Sunday was a sweet and pleasant day, and the children thought so; but from its being so much quieter than other days, they always got up on Monday full of life and mischief, and ready to fizz over at any minute, like champagne bottles with the wires just cut.

This particular Monday was rainy, so there couldn't be any out-door play, which was the usual vent for over-high spirits. The little ones, cooped up in the nursery all the afternoon, had grown perfectly riotous. Philly was not quite well, and had been taking medicine. The medicine was called Elixir Pro. It was a great favourite with Aunt Izzie, who kept a bottle of it always on hand. The bottle was large and black, with a paper label tied round its neck, and the children shuddered at the sight of it.

After Phil had stopped roaring and spluttering, and play had begun again, the dolls, as was only natural, were taken ill also, and so was "Pikery," John's little yellow chair which she always pretended was a doll too. She kept an old apron tied on his back, and generally took him to bed with her—not *into* bed, that would have been troublesome; but close by, tied to the bed-post. Now, as she told the others, Pikery was very sick indeed. He must have some medicine just like Philly.

"Give him some water," suggested Dorry.

"No," said John, decidedly, "it must be black and out of a bottle, or it won't do any good."

After thinking a moment, she trotted quietly across the

passage into Aunt Izzie's room. Nobody was there, but John knew where the Elixir was kept—in the closet on the third shelf. She pulled one of the drawers out a little, climbed up, and reached it down. The children were enchanted when she marched back, the bottle in one hand, the cork in the other, and proceeded to pour a liberal dose on to Pikery's wooden seat, which John called his lap.

"There! there! my poor boy," she said, patting his shoulder—I mean his arm—"swallow it down; it'll do you good."

Just then Aunt Izzie came in, and to her dismay saw a long trickle of something dark and sticky running down on to the carpet. It was Pikery's medicine, which he had refused to swallow.

"What is that?" she asked sharply.

"My baby is sick," faltered John, displaying the guilty bottle.

Aunt Izzie rapped her over the head with a thimble, and told her that she was a very naughty child, whereupon Johnnie pouted, and cried a little. Aunt Izzie wiped up the slop, and taking away the Elixir retired with it to her closet, saying that she "never knew anything like it—it was always so on Mondays."

What further pranks were played in the nursery that day I cannot pretend to tell. But late in the afternoon a dreadful screaming was heard, and when people rushed from all parts of the house to see what was the matter, behold, the nursery door was locked and nobody could get in.

Aunt Izzie called through the keyhole to have it opened, but the roars were so loud that it was long before she could get an answer. At last Elsie, sobbing violently, explained that Dorry had locked the door, and now the key wouldn't turn, and they couldn't open it. *Would* they have to stay there always, and starve?

"Of course you won't, you foolish child," exclaimed Aunt Izzie. "Dear, dear, what on earth will come next?

Stop crying, Elsie—do you hear me? You shall all be got out in a few minutes."

And sure enough, the next thing came a rattling at the blinds, and there was Alexander, the hired man, standing outside on a tall ladder and nodding his head at the children. The little ones forgot their fright. They flew to open the window, and frisked and jumped about Alexander as he climbed in and unlocked the door. It struck them as being such a fine thing to be let out in this way, that Dorry began to rather plume himself for fastening them in.

But Aunt Izzie didn't take this view of the case. She scolded them well, and declared they were troublesome children, who couldn't be trusted one moment out of sight and that she was more than half sorry she had promised to go to the lecture that evening. "How do I know," she concluded, "that before I come home, you won't have set the house on fire, or killed somebody?"

"Oh, no, we won't! No, we won't!" whined the children, quite moved by this frightful picture. But, bless you. ten minutes afterward they had forgotten all about it.

All this time Katy had been sitting on the ledge of the bookcase in the library, poring over a book. It was called Tasso's *Jerusalem Delivered*. The man who wrote it was an Italian, but somebody had turned the story into English. It was rather a queer book for a little girl to take a fancy to, but somehow Katy liked it very much. It told about knights, and ladies, and giants, and battles, and made her feel hot and cold by turns as she read, and as if she must rush at something, and shout and strike blows.

Katy was naturally fond of reading. Papa encouraged it. He kept a few books locked up, and then turned her loose in the library. She read all sorts of things; travels, and sermons, and old magazines. Nothing was so dull that she couldn't get through with it. Anything really interesting absorbed her so that she never knew what was going on about her. The little girls to whose houses she went visiting had found this out, and always hid away their story-books, when she was expected to tea. If they didn't do this, she was sure to pick one up and plunge in, and then it was no use to call her or tug at her dress, for she neither saw nor heard anything more till it was time to go home.

This afternoon she read the "Jerusalem" till it was too dark to see any more. On her way upstairs she met Aunt Izzie, with bonnet and shawl on.

"Where *have* you been?" she said. "I have been calling you for the last half-hour."

"I didn't hear you, ma'am."

"But where were you?" persisted Miss Izzie.

"In the library, reading," replied Katy.

Her aunt gave a sort of sniff, but she knew Katy's ways, and said no more.

"I'm going out to drink tea with Mrs. Hall and attend the evening lecture," she went on. "Be sure that Clover gets her lesson, and if Cecy comes over as usual, you must send her home early. All of you must be in bed by nine."

"Yes'm," said Katy; but I fear she was not attending much, but thinking in her secret soul, how jolly it was to have Aunt Izzie go out for once. Miss Carr was very faithful to her duties: and seldom left the children, even for an evening; so whenever she did, they felt a certain sense of novelty and freedom, which was dangerous as well as pleasant.

Still, I am sure that on this occasion Katy meant no mischief. Like all excitable people, she seldom did *mean* to do wrong; she just did it when it came into her head. Supper passed off successfully, and all might have gone well had it not been that after the lessons were learned and Cecy had come in, they fell to talking about "Kikeri."

Kikeri was a game which had been very popular with them a year before. They had invented it themselves, and chosen for it this queer name out of an old fairy story. It was a sort of mixture of Blindman's Buff and Tag—only, instead of any one's eyes being bandaged, they all played in the dark. One of the children would stay out in the hall, which was dimly lighted from the stairs, while the others hid themselves in the nursery. When they were all hidden they would call out "Kikeri!" as a signal for the one in the hall to come in and find them. Of course, coming from the light he could see nothing, while the others could see only dimly. It was very exciting to stand crouching up in a corner and watch the dark figure stumbling about and feeling to right and left, while every now and then somebody, just escaping his clutches, would slip past and gain the hall- which was "Freedom Castle,"- with a joyful shout of "Kikeri, Kikeri, Kikeri, Ki!" Whoever was caught had to take the place of the catcher. For a long time this game was the delight of the Carr children; but so many scratches and black-and-blue spots came of it, and so many of the nursery things were thrown down and broken, that at last Aunt Izzie issued an order that it should not be played any more. This was almost a year since; but talking of it now put it into their heads to want to try it again.

"After all, we didn't promise," said Cecy.

"No, and *Papa* never said a word about our not playing it," added Katy, to whom "Papa" was authority, and must always be minded, while Aunt Izzie might now and then be defied.

So they all went upstairs. Dorry and John, though half undressed, were allowed to join the game. Philly was fast asleep in another room.

It was certainly splendid fun. Once Clover climbed up on the mantelpiece and sat there, and when Katy, who was finder, groped about a little more wildly than usual, she caught hold of Clover's foot, and couldn't imagine where it came from. Dorry got a hard knock, and cried, and at another time Katy's dress caught on the bureau handle and was frightfully torn: but these were too much affairs of every day to interfere in the least with the pleasures of Kikeri. The fun and frolic seemed to grow greater the longer they played. In the excitement time went on so much faster than any of them dreamed. Suddenly, in the midst of the noise, came a sound—the sharp distinct slam of the carry-all door at the side entrance. Aunt Izzie had returned from her lecture!

The dismay and confusion of that moment! Cecy slipped downstairs like an eel, and fled on the wings of fear along the path which led to her home. Mrs. Hall, as she bade Aunt Izzie good-night, and shut Dr. Carr's front door behind her with a bang, might have been struck with the singular fact that a distant bang came from her own front door like a sort of echo. But she was not a suspicious woman; and when she went upstairs there were Cecy's clothes neatly folded on a chair, and Cecy herself in bed, fast asleep, only with a little more colour than usual in her cheeks.

Meantime, Aunt Izzie was on *her* way upstairs, and such a panic as prevailed in the nursery! Katy felt it, and basely scuttled off to her own room, where she went to bed with all possible speed. But the others found it much harder to go to bed; they were so many of them, all getting into each other's way, and with no lamp to see by. Dorry and John popped under the clothes half undressed, Elsie disappeared, and Clover, too late for either, and hearing Aunt Izzie's step in the hall, did this horrible thing—fell on her knees with her face buried in a chair, and began to say her prayers very hard indeed.

Aunt Izzie coming in with a candle in her hand, stood in the doorway, astonished at the spectacle. She sat down and waited for Clover to get through, while Clover, on her part, didn't dare to get through, but went on repeating "Now I lay me" over and over again, in a sort of despair. At last Aunt Izzie said very grimly: "That will do, Clover, you can get up! " and Clover rose, feeling like a culprit, which she was, for it was much naughtier to pretend to be praying than to disobey Aunt Izzie and be out of bed after ten o'clock, though I think Clover hardly understood this then.

Aunt Izzie began at once to undress her, and while doing so asked so many questions, and before long she had got at the truth of the whole matter. She gave Clover a sharp

43

scolding; and, leaving her to wash her tearful face, she went to the bed where John and Dorry lay fast asleep. and snoring as conspicuously as they knew how. Something strange in the appearance of the bed made her look more closely; she lifted the clothes, and there, sure enough, they were—half dressed, and with their school boots on.

Such a shake as Aunt Izzie gave the little scamps at this discovery would have roused a couple of dormice. Much against their will, John and Dorry were forced to wake up, and be slapped and scolded, and made ready for bed, Aunt Izzie standing over them all the while, like a dragon. She had just tucked them warmly in, when for the first time she missed Elsie.

"Where is my poor little Elsie?" she exclaimed.

"In bed," said Clover, meekly.

"In bed!" repeated Aunt Izzie, much amazed. Then stooping down she gave a vigorous pull. The trundle-bed came into view, and, sure enough, there was Elsie, in full dress, shoes and all, but so fast asleep that not all Aunt Izzie's shakes and pinches and calls were able to rouse her Her clothes were taken off, her boots unlaced, her night-gown put on: but through it all Elsie slept, and she was the only one of the children who did not get the scolding she deserved that dreadful night.

Katy did not even pretend to be asleep when Aunt Izzie went to her room. Her tardy conscience had waked up, and she was lying in bed, very miserable at having drawn the others into a scrape as well as herself, and at the failure of her last set of resolutions about "setting an example to the younger ones." So unhappy was she, that Aunt Izzie's severe words were almost a relief; and though she cried herself to sleep, it was rather from the burden of her own thoughts than because she had been scolded.

She cried even harder the next day, for Dr. Carr talked to her more seriously than he had ever done before. He reminded her of the time when her Mamma died, and of how she said, "Katy must be a Mamma to the little ones, when she grows up." And he asked her if she didn't think the time was come for beginning to take this dear place towards the children. Poor Katy! She sobbed as if her heart would break at this, and though she made no promises, I think she was never so thoughtless again after that day.

As for the rest, Papa called them together and made them distinctly understand that "Kikeri" was never to be played any more. It was so seldom that Papa forbade any games, however boisterous, that this order really made an impression on the unruly brood, and they never have played Kikeri again from that day to this.

CHAPTER FIVE

In the Loft

"I DECLARE," said Miss Petingill, laying down her work, "if them children don't beat all! What on airth *are* they going to do now?"

Miss Petingill was sitting in the little room in the back building, which she always had when she came to the Carr's for a week's mending and making over. She was the dearest, funniest old woman who ever went out sewing by the day. Her face was round, and somehow made you think of a very nice baked apple, it was so crisscrossed, and lined by a thousand good-natured puckers. She was small and wiry, and wore caps and a false front, which was just the colour of a dusty Newfoundland dog's back. Her eyes were dim, and she used spectacles; but for all that, she was an excellent worker. Everyone liked Miss Petingill, though Aunt Izzie *did* once say that her tongue "was hung in the middle." Aunt Izzie made this remark when she was in a temper, and was by no means prepared to have Phil walk up at once and request Miss Petingill to "stick it out," which she obligingly did; while the rest of the children crowded to look. They couldn't see that it was different from other tongues, but Philly persisted in finding something curious about it; there must be, you know—since it was hung in that queer way!

46

Wherever Miss Petingill went all sorts of treasures went with her. The children liked to have her come, for it was as good as a fairy story or the circus, to see her things unpacked. Miss Petingill was very much afraid of burglars; she lay awake half the night listening for them, and nothing on earth would have persuaded her to go anywhere, leaving behind what she called her "Plate." This stately word meant six old tea-spoons, very thin and bright and sharp, and a butterknife, whose handle set forth that it was "A testimonial of gratitude, for saving the life of Ithuriel Jobson, aged seven, on the occasion of his being attacked with quinsy sore throat." Miss Petingill was very proud of her knife. It and the spoons travelled about in a little basket which hung on her arm, and was never allowed to be out of her sight, even when the family she was sewing for were the most honest people in the world.

Then, beside the plate-basket, Miss Petingill never stirred without Tom, her tortoiseshell cat. Tom was a beauty, and knew his power; he ruled Miss Petingill with a rod of iron, and always sat in the rocking-chair when there was one. It was no matter where *she* sat, Miss Petingill told people, but Tom was delicate, and must be made comfortable. A big family Bible always came too, and a special red merino pin-cushion, and some "shade pictures" of old Mr. and Mrs. Petingill and Peter Petingill, who was drowned at sea, and photographs of Mrs. Porter, who used to be Marcia Petingill, and Mrs. Porter's husband, and all the Porter children. Many little boxes and jars came also, and a long row of phials and bottles filled with home-made physics and herb teas. Miss Petingill could not have slept without having them beside her, for, as she said, how did she know that she might not be "took sudden" with something, and die for want of a little ginger-balsam or pennyroyal?

The Carr children always made so much noise, that it required something unusual to make Miss Petingill drop her work, as she did now, and fly to the window. In fact there *was* a tremendous hubbub, hurrahs, from Dorry.

stamping of feet, and a great outcry of shrill, glad voices. Looking down, Miss Petingill saw the whole six—no seven, for Cecy was there too—stream out of the wood-house door—which wasn't a door, but only a tall open arch—and rush noisily across the yard. Katy was at the head, bearing a large black bottle without any cork in it, while the others carried in each hand what seemed to be a cookie.

"Katherine Carr! Kather-*ine*!" screamed Miss Petingill, tapping loudly on the glass. "Don't you see that it's raining? You ought to be ashamed to let your little brothers and sisters go out and get wet in such a way!" But nobody heard her, and the children vanished into the shed, where nothing could be seen but a distant flapping of pantalettes and frilled trousers, going up what seemed to be a ladder, farther back in the shed. So, with a dissatisfied cluck, Miss Petingill drew back her head, perched the spectacles on her nose, and went to work again on Katy's plaid alpaca, which had two immense zigzag rents across the middle of the front breadth. Katy's frocks, strange to say, always tore exactly in that place.

If Miss Petingill's eyes could have reached a little farther, they would have seen that it wasn't a ladder up which the children were climbing but a tall wooden post, with spikes driven into it about a foot apart. It required quite a stride to get from one spike to the other; in fact, the little ones couldn't have managed it at all had it not been for Clover and Cecy pushing very hard from below, while Katy, making a long arm, clawed from above. At last they were all safely up, and in the delightful retreat which I am about to describe.

Imagine a low, dark loft without any windows, and with only a very little light coming in through the square hole in the floor, to which the spikey post led. There was a strong smell of corn-cobs, though the corn had been taken away; a great deal of dust and spider-web in the corners, and some wet spots on the boards, for the roof always leaked a little in rainy weather.

This was the place, which for some reason I have never been able to find out, the Carr children preferred to any other on rainy Saturdays when they could not play outdoors. Aunt Izzie was as much puzzled at this fancy as I am. When she was young (a vague, far-off time, which none of her nieces and nephews believed in much), she had never had any of these queer notions about getting off into holes and corners and poke-away places. Aunt Izzie would gladly have forbidden them to go to the loft, but Dr. Carr had given his permission, so all she could do was to invent stories about children who had broken their bones in various dreadful ways by climbing posts and ladders. But these stories made no impression on any of the children except little Phil, and the self-willed brood kept on their way, and climbed their spiked posts as often as they liked.

"What's in the bottle?" demanded Dorry, the minute he was fairly landed in the loft.

"Don't be greedy," replied Katy, severely, "you will know when the time comes. It is something *delicious*, I can assure you.

"Now," she went on, having thus quenched Dorry, "all of you had better give me your cookies to put away: if you don't they'll be sure to be eaten up before the feast, and then you know there wouldn't be anything to make a feast of."

So all of them handed over their cookies. Dorry, who had begun his as he came up the ladder, was a little unwilling, but he was too much in the habit of minding Katy to dare to disobey. The big bottle was set in a corner, and a stack of cookies built up around it.

"That's right," proceeded Katy, who, as oldest and biggest, always took the lead in their plays. "Now if we're fixed and ready to begin, the fête (Katy pronounced it *feet*) can commence. The opening exercise will be 'A Tragedy of the Alhambra,' by Miss Hall."

"No," cried Clover; "first 'The Blue Wizard, or Edwitha of the Hebrides,'—you know, Katy."

49

"Didn't I tell you," said Katy, "a dreadful accident has happened to that?"

"Oh, what?" cried all the rest, for Edwitha was rather a favourite with the family. It was one of the many serial stories which Katy was forever writing, and was about a lady, a knight, a blue wizard, and a poodle named Bop. It had been going on for so many months now that everybody had forgotten the beginning, and nobody had any particular hope for living to hear the end, but still the news of its untimely fate was a shock.

"I'll tell you," said Katy. "Old Judge Kirby called this morning to see Aunt Izzie; I was studying in the little room, but I saw him come in, and pull out the big chair and sit down, and I almost screamed out 'Don't.'"

"Why?" cried the children.

"Don't you see? I had stuffed 'Edwitha' down between the back and the seat. It was a *beau*tiful hiding-place, for the seat goes back ever so far; but Edwitha was such a fat bundle, and old Judge Kirby takes up so much room, that I was afraid there would be trouble. And sure enough, he had hardly dropped down before there was a great crackling of paper, and he jumped up again and called out, 'Bless me! what is that?' And then he began poking and poking, and just as he had poked out the whole bundle, and was putting on his spectacles to see what it was, Aunt Izzie came in."

"Well, what next?" cried the children, immensely tickled.

"Oh!" continued Katy, "Aunt Izzie put on her glasses too, and screwed up her eyes—you know the way she does—and she and the judge read a little of it; that part at the first, you remember, where Bop steals the blue-pills, and the Wizard tries to throw him into the sea. You can't think how funny it was to hear Aunt Izzie reading 'Edwitha' out loud"—and Katy went into convulsions at the recollection—"where she got to 'Oh, Bop—my angel Bop—' I just rolled under the table, and stuffed the table-cover in my mouth to keep from screaming right out. By-and-by I heard her call Debby, and give her the papers, and say: 'Here is a mass of trash which I wish you to put at once into the kitchen fire.' And she told me afterward that she thought I would be in an insane asylum before I was twenty. It was too bad," ended Katy, half laughing and half crying, "to burn up the new chapter and all. But there's one good thing—she didn't find 'The Fairy of the Dry-Goods Box,' that was stuffed farther back in the seat."

"And now," continued the mistress of ceremonies, "we will begin. Miss Hall will please rise."

"Miss Hall," much flustered at her fine name, got up with very red cheeks.

"It was once upon a time," she read. "Moonlight lay on the halls of the Alhambra, and the knight, striding impatiently down the passage, thought she would never come."

"Who, the moon?" asked Clover.

"No, of course not," replied Cecy, "a lady he was in love with. The next verse is going to tell about her, only you interrupted.

"She wore a turban of silver, with a jewelled crescent. As she stole down the corregidors the beams struck it, and it glittered like stars.

" 'So you are come, Zuleika?'

" 'Yes, my lord.'

"Just then a sound as of steel smote upon the ear, and Zuleika's mail-clad father rushed in. He drew his sword, so did the other. A moment more, and they both lay dead and stiff in the beams of the moon. Zuleika gave a loud shriek, and threw herself upon their bodies. She was dead, too! And so ends the 'Tragedy of the Alhambra.' "

"That's lovely," said Katy, drawing a long breath, "only very sad! What beautiful stories you do write, Cecy! but I wish you wouldn't always kill the people. Why couldn't the knight have killed the father, and—no, I suppose Zuelika wouldn't have married him then. Well, the father might have—oh, bother! why must anybody be killed, anyhow? why not have them fall on each other's neck, and make up?"

"Why, Katy!" cried Cecy, "it wouldn't have been a tragedy then. You know the name was 'A *Tragedy* of the Alhambra.' "

"Oh, well," said Katy, hurriedly, for Cecy's lips were beginning to pout, and her fair, pinkish face to redden, as if she were about to cry; "perhaps it *was* prettier to have them all die; only your ladies and gentlemen always do die, and I thought, for a change, you know! —What a lovely word that was—'corregidor'—what does it mean?"

"I don't know," replied Cecy, quite consoled. "It was in the *Conquest of Granada.* Something to walk over, I believe."

"The next," went on Katy, consulting her paper, "is 'Yap,' a Simple Poem, by Oliver Carr."

All the children giggled, but Clover got up composedly, and recited the following verses:

> "Did you ever know Yap?
>   The best little dog
>   Who e'er sat on a lap
>   Or barked at a frog.
>
> His eyes were like beads,
>   His tail like a mop,
> And it wagged as if
>   It would never stop.
>
> His hair was like silk
>   Of the glossiest sheen,
> He always ate milk,
>   And once the cold-cream
>
> Off the nursery bureau
>   (That line is too long)!
> It made him quite ill,
>   So endeth my song.

For Yappy he died
        Just two months ago,
        And we oughtn't to sing
        At a funeral, you know."

The "Poem" met with immense applause; all the children laughed and shouted and clapped, till the loft rang again.

But Clover kept her face perfectly, and sat down as demure as ever, except that the little dimples came and went at the corners of her mouth; dimples, partly natural, and partly, I regret to say, the result of a pointed slate-pencil, with which Clover was in the habit of deepening them every day while she studied her lessons.

"Now," said Katy, after the noise had subsided, "now comes 'Scripture Verse,' by Miss Elsie and Joanna Carr. Hold up your head, Elsie, and speak distinctly; and oh, Johnnie, you *mustn't* giggle in that way when it comes your turn!"

But Johnnie only giggled the harder at this appeal, keeping her hands very tight across her mouth, and peeping out over her fingers.

Elsie, however, was solemn as a little judge, and with great dignity began:

        "An angel with a fiery sword
        Came to send Adam and Eve abroad;
        And as they journeyed through the skies
        They took one look at Paradise.
        They thought of all the happy hours
        Among the birds and fragrant bowers,
        And Eve, she wept and Adam bawled,
        And both together loudly squalled."

Dorry snickered at this, but sedate Clover hushed him. "You mustn't," she said, "it's about the Bible, you know. Now, John, it's your turn."

But Johnnie would persist in holding her hands over

her mouth, while her fat little shoulders shook with laughter. At last, with a great effort, she pulled her face straight, and speaking as fast as she possibly could, repeated, in a sort of burst:

> "Balaam's donkey saw the Angel,
>   And stopped short in fear.
> Balaam didn't see the Angel,
>   Which is very queer."

After which she took refuge behind her fingers, while Elsie went on:

> "Elijah by the creek,
>   He by ravens fed,
> Took from their horny beak
>   Pieces of meat and bread."

"Come, Johnnie," said Katy; but the incorrigible Johnnie was shaking again, and all they could make out was:

> "The bears came down, and ate——and ate,"

These "verses" were a part of a grand project on which Clover and Elsie had been busy for more than a year. It was a sort of rearrangement of Scripture for infant minds; and when it was finished they meant to have it published, bound in red, with daguerreotypes of the two authoresses on the cover. *The Youth's Poetical Bible* was to be the name of it. Papa, much tickled with the scraps which he overheard, proposed, instead, *The Trundle-Bed Book*, as having been composed principally in that spot; but Elsie and Clover were highly indignant, and would not listen to the idea for a moment.

After the "Scripture Verses," came Dorry's turn. He had been allowed to choose for himself, which was unlucky, as his taste was peculiar, not to say gloomy. On this

54

occasion he had selected that cheerful hymn which begins:

> "Hark! from the tombs a doleful sound."

And he now began to recite it in a lugubrious voice and with great emphasis, smacking his lips, as it were, over such lines as:

> "Princess, this clay *shall* be your bed,
> In spite of all your towers."

The older children listened with a sort of fascinated horror, rather enjoying the cold chills which ran down their backs, and huddling close together, as Dorry's hollow tones echoed from the dark corners of the loft. It was too much for Philly, however. At the close of the piece he was found to be in tears.

"I don't want to st-a-a-y up here and be groaned at," he sobbed.

"There, you bad boy!" cried Katy, all the more angry because she was conscious of having enjoyed it herself, "that's what you do with your horrid hymns, frightening us to death and making Phil cry!" And she gave Dorry a little shake. He began to whimper, and as Phil was still sobbing, and Johnnie had begun to sob too, out of sympathy with the others, the *feet* in the loft seemed likely to come to a sad end.

"I'm going to tell Aunt Izzie that I don't like you," declared Dorry, putting one leg through the opening in the floor.

"No, you aren't," said Katy, seizing him, "you are going to stay, because *now* we are going to have the feast! Do stop, Phil; and Johnnie, don't be a goose, but come and pass round the cookies."

The word "feast" produced a speedy effect on the spirits of the party. Phil cheered at once, and Dorry changed his mind about going. The black bottle was solemnly set in the midst, and the cookies were handed about by Johnnie, who was now all smiles. The cookies had scalloped edges and caraway seeds inside, and were very nice. There were two apiece; and as the last was finished, Katy put her hand in her pocket, and, amid great applause, produced the crowning addition to the repast —seven long brown sticks of cinnamon.

"Isn't it fun?" she said. "Debby was real good-natured to-day, and let me put my own hand into the box, so I picked out the longest sticks there were. Now, Cecy, as you're company, you shall have the first drink out of the bottle."

The "something delicious" proved to be weak vinegar-and-water. It was quite warm, but somehow, drunk up there in the loft, and out of a bottle, it tasted very nice. Besides, they didn't *call* it vinegar-and-water- of course not! Each child gave his or her swallow a different name, as if the bottle were like Signor Blitz's and could pour out a dozen things at once. Clover called her share "Raspberry Shrub," Dorry christened his "Ginger Pop," while Cecy, who was romantic, took her three sips under the name of "Hydomel," which she explained was something nice, made, she believed, of beeswax.

The last drop gone, and the last bit of cinnamon crunched, the company came to order again, for the purpose of hearing Philly repeat his one piece:

"Little drops of water,"

which exciting poem he had said every Saturday as far back as they could remember. After that, Katy declared the literary part of the *feet* over, and they fell to playing "Stage-coach," which in spite of close quarters and an occasional bump from the roof was such good fun that a general "Oh dear!" welcomed the ringing of the tea-bell. I suppose cookies and vinegar had taken away their appetites, for none of them were hungry, and Dorry astonished Aunt Izzie very much by eyeing the table in a disgusted way, and saying: "Pshaw! *only* plum sweet-meats and sponge cake and hot biscuit! I don't want any supper."

"What ails the child? he must be sick," said Dr. Carr; but Katy explained.

"Oh, no, Papa, it isn't that—only we've been having a feast in the loft."

"Did you have a good time?" asked Papa, while Aunt Izzie gave a dissatisfied groan. And all the children answered at once: "Splendiferous!"

CHAPTER SIX

Intimate Friends

"Aunt Izzie, may I ask Imogen Clark to spend the day here on Saturday?" cried Katy, bursting in one afternoon.

"Who on earth is Imogen Clark? I never heard the name before," replied her aunt.

"Oh, the *loveliest* girl! She hasn't been going to Mrs. Knight's school but a little while, but we're the greatest friends. And she's perfectly beautiful, Aunt Izzie. Her hands are just as white as snow, and no bigger than *that*. She's got the littlest waist of any girl in the school, and she's real sweet, and so self-denying and unselfish! I don't believe she has a bit good times at home, either. Do let me ask her!"

"How do you know she's so sweet and self-denying if you've known her such a short time?" asked Aunt Izzie, in an unpromising tone.

"Oh, she tells me everything! We always walk together at recess now. I know all about her, and she's just lovely! Her father used to be real rich, but they're poor now, and Imogen had to have her boots patched twice last winter. I guess she's the flower of her family. You can't think how I love her!" concluded Katy, sentimentally.

"No, I can't," said Aunt Izzie. "I never could see into these sudden friendships of yours, Katy, and I'd rather you wouldn't invite this Imogen, or whatever her name is, till I've had a chance to ask somebody about her."

Katy clasped her hands in despair. "Oh, Aunt Izzie!" she cried, "Imogen knows that I came in to ask you, and she's standing at the gate at this moment, waiting to hear what you say. Please let me just this once! I shall be so dreadfully ashamed not to."

"Well," said Miss Izzie, moved by the wretchedness of Katy's face, "if you've asked her already it's no use my saying no, I suppose. But recollect, Katy, this is not to happen again. I can't have you inviting girls, and then coming for my leave. Your father won't be at all pleased. He's very particular about whom you make friends with. Remember how Mrs. Spenser turned out."

Poor Katy! Her propensity to fall violently in love with new people was always getting her into scrapes. Ever since she began to walk and talk "Katy's intimate friends" had been one of the jokes of the household.

Papa once undertook to keep a list of them, but the number grew so great that he gave it up in despair. First on the list was a small Irish child, named Marianne O'Riley. Marianne lived in a street which Katy passed on her way to school. It was not Mrs. Knight, but an A B C school, to which Dorry and John now went. Marianne used to be always making sand-pies in front of her mother's house, and Katy, who was about five years old, often stopped to help her. Over this mutual pastry they grew so intimate that Katy resolved to adopt Marianne as her own little girl, and bring her up in a safe and hidden corner.

She told Clover of this plan, but nobody else. The two children, full of their delightful secret, began to save pieces of bread and cookies from their supper every evening. By degrees they collected a great heap of dry crusts, and other refreshments, which they put safely away in the garret. They also saved the apples which were given them for two weeks, and made a bed in a big empty box, with cotton quilts, and the doll's pillows out of the babyhouse. When all was ready Katy broke her plan to her beloved Marianne, and easily persuaded her to run away and take possession of this new home.

"We won't tell Papa and Mamma till she's quite grown up," Katy said to Clover; "then we'll bring her downstairs, and *won't* they be surprised! Don't let's call her Marianne any longer, either. It isn't pretty. We'll name her Susquehanna instead—Susquehanna Carr. Remember, Marianne, you mustn't answer if I call you Marianne—only when I say Susquehanna."

"Yes'm," replied Marianne, very meekly.

For a whole day all went on delightfully. Susquehanna lived in her wooden box, ate all the apples and the freshest cookies, and was happy. The two children took turns to steal away and play with the "Baby," as they called Marianne, though she was a great deal bigger than Clover. But when night came on and nurse swooped on Katy and Clover and carried them off to bed, Miss O'Riley began to think that the garret was a dreadful place. Peeping out of her box she could see black things standing in corners which she did not recollect seeing in the day-time. They were really trunks and brooms and warming-pans, but somehow in the darkness they looked different— big and awful. Poor little Marianne bore it as long as she could but when at last a rat began to scratch in the wall close beside her her courage gave way entirely, and she screamed at the top of her voice.

"What is that?" said Dr. Carr, who had just come in, and was on his way upstairs.

"It sounds as if it came from the attic," said Mrs. Carr (for this was before Mamma died). "Can it be that one of the children has got out of bed and wandered upstairs in her sleep?"

No, Katy and Clover were safe in the nursery, so Dr. Carr took a candle and went as fast as he could to the attic, where the yells were growing terrific. When he reached the top of the stairs the cries ceased. He looked about. Nothing was to be seen at first, then a little head appeared over the edge of a big wooden box, and a piteous voice sobbed out:

"Ah, Miss Katy, and indeed I can't be staying any longer. There's rats in it!"

"Who on earth are *you*?" asked the amazed Doctor.

"Sure, I'm Miss Katy's and Miss Clover's Baby. But I don't want to be a baby any longer. I want to go home and see my mother." And again the poor little midge lifted up her voice and wept.

I don't think Dr. Carr ever laughed so hard in his life as when he finally got to the bottom of the story, and found that Katy and Clover had been "adopting" a child. But he was very kind to poor Susquehanna, and carried her downstairs in his arms to the nursery. There, in a bed close to the other children, she soon forgot her troubles and fell asleep.

The little sisters were much surprised when they waked up in the morning, and found their baby asleep beside them. But their joy was speedily turned to tears. After breakfast Dr. Carr carried Marianne home to her mother. who was in a great fright over her disappearance, and explained to the children that the garret plan must be given up. Great was the mourning in the nursery; but as Marianne was allowed to come and play with them now and then. they gradually got over their grief. A few months later Mr. O'Riley moved away from Burnet, and that was the end of Katy's first friendship.

The next was even funnier. There was a queer old black woman who lived all alone by herself in a small house near the school. This old woman had a very bad temper. The neighbours told horrible stories about her, so that the children were afraid to pass the house. They used to turn always just before they reached it, and cross to the other side of the street. This they did so regularly that their feet had worn a path in the grass. But for some reason Katy found a great fascination in the little house. She liked to

61

dodge about the door, always holding herself ready to turn and run in case the old woman rushed out upon her with a broomstick. One day she begged a large cabbage off Alexander, and rolled it in at the door of the house. The old woman seemed to like it, and after this Katy always stopped to speak when she went by. She even got so far as to sit on the step and watch the old woman at work. There was a sort of perilous pleasure in doing this. It was like sitting at the entrance of a lion's cage, uncertain at what moment his majesty might take it into his head to give a spring and eat you up.

After this, Katy took a fancy to a couple of twin sisters, daughters of a German jeweller. They were quite grown-up, and always wore dresses exactly alike. Hardly any one could tell them apart. They spoke very little English, and as Katy didn't know a word of German, their intercourse was confined to smiles, and to the giving of bunches of flowers, which Katy used to tie up and present to them whenever they passed the gate. She was too shy to do more than just put the flowers in their hands and run away; but the twins were evidently pleased, for one day, when Clover happened to be looking out of the window, she saw them open the gate, fasten a little parcel to a bush, and walk rapidly off.

Of course she called Katy at once, and the two children flew out to see what the parcel was. It held a bonnet—a beautiful doll's bonnet of blue silk, trimmed with artificial flowers; upon it was pinned a slip of paper, with these words, in an odd foreign hand:

"To the nice little girl who was so kindly to give us some flowers." You can judge whether Katy and Clover were pleased or not.

This was when Katy was six years old. I can't begin to tell you how many different friends she had set up since then. There was an ash-man, and a steamboat captain. There was Mrs. Sawyer's cook, a nice old woman, who gave Katy lessons in cooking, and taught her to make soft custard and sponge cake. There was a bonnet-maker, pretty and dressy, whom, to Aunt Izzie's great indignation, Katy persisted in calling "Cousin Estelle!" There was a thief in the town jail, under whose window Katy used to stand, saying, "I'm so sorry, poor man!" and "Have you got any little girls like me?" in the most piteous way. The thief had a piece of string which he let down from the window. Katy would tie rose-buds and cherries to this string, and the thief would draw them up. It was so interesting to do this that Katy felt dreadfully when they carried the man off to the State prison. Then followed a short interval of Cornelia Perham, a nice, good-natured girl, whose father was a fruit-merchant. I am afraid Katy's liking for prunes and white grapes played a part in this intimacy. It was splendid fun to go with Cornelia to her father's big shop, and have whole boxes of raisins and drums of figs opened for their amusement, and be allowed to ride up and down in the elevator as much as they liked.

But of all Katy's queer acquaintances, Mrs. Spenser, to whom Aunt Izzie had alluded, was the queerest.

Mrs. Spenser was a mysterious lady whom nobody ever saw. Her husband was a handsome, rather bad-looking man, who had come from parts unknown, and rented a small house in Burnet. He didn't seem to have any particular business, and was away from home a great deal. His wife was said to be an invalid, and people, when they spoke of him, shook their heads and wondered how the poor woman got on all alone in the house while her husband was absent.

Of course Katy was too young to understand these whispers, or the reasons why people were not disposed to think well of Mr. Spenser. The romance of the closed door and the lady whom nobody saw interested her very much. She used to stop and stare at the windows, and wonder what was going on inside till at last it seemed as if she *must* know. So one day she took some flowers and Victoria, her favourite doll, and boldly marched into the Spensers' yard.

She tapped at the front door, but nobody answered.

Then she tapped again. Still nobody answered. She tried the door. It was locked. So shouldering Victoria, she trudged round to the back of the house. As she passed the side-door she saw that it was open a little way. She knocked for the third time; and as no one came, she went in, and, passing through the little hall, began to tap at all the inside doors.

There seemed to be no people in the house. Katy peered into the kitchen first. It was bare and forlorn. All sorts of dishes were standing about.

There was no fire in the stove. The parlour was not much better. Mr. Spenser's boots lay in the middle of the floor. There were dirty glasses on the table. On the mantelpiece was a platter with bones of meat upon it. Dust lay thick over everything, and the whole house looked as if it hadn't been lived in for at least a year.

Katy tried several other doors, all of which were locked, and then she went upstairs. As she stood on the top step, grasping her flowers, and a little doubtful what to do next, a feeble voice from a bedroom called out:

"Who is there?"

This was Mrs. Spenser. She was lying on her bed, which was very tossed and tumbled, as if it hadn't been made up that morning. The room was as disorderly and dirty as all the rest of the house, and Mrs. Spenser's wrapper and night-cap were by no means clean, but her face was sweet, and she had beautiful curling hair, which fell over the pillow. She was evidently very sick, and altogether Katy felt sorrier for her than she had ever done for anybody in her life.

"Who are you, child?" asked Mrs. Spenser.

"I'm Dr. Carr's little girl," answered Katy, going straight up to the bed. "I came to bring you some flowers." And she laid the bouquet on the dirty sheet.

Mrs. Spenser seemed to like the flowers. She took them up and smelled them for a long time, without speaking.

"But how did you get in?" she said, at last.

"The door was open," faltered Katy, who was beginning to feel scared at her own daring, "and they said you were sick, so I thought perhaps you would like me to come and see you."

"You are a kind little girl," said Mrs. Spenser, and gave her a kiss.

After this Katy used to go every day. Sometimes Mrs. Spenser would be up and moving feebly about; but more often she was in bed, and Katy would sit beside her. The house never looked a bit better than it did that first day, but after a while Katy used to brush Mrs. Spenser's hair, and wash her face with the corner of a towel.

I think her visits were a comfort to the poor lady, who was very ill and lonely. Sometimes when she felt pretty well, she would tell Katy stories about the time when *she* was a little girl and lived with her father and mother. But she never spoke of Mr. Spenser, and Katy never saw him except once, when she was so frightened that for several days she dared not go near the house. At last Cecy reported that she had seen him go off in the stage with his carpet-bag, so Katy ventured in again. Mrs. Spenser cried when she saw her.

"I thought you were never coming any more," she said.

Katy was touched and flattered at having been missed, and after that she never lost a day. She always carried the prettiest flowers she could find, and if any one gave her a specially nice peach or a bunch of grapes she saved it for Mrs. Spenser.

Aunt Izzie was much worried at all this. But Dr. Carr would not interfere. He said it was a case where grown people could do nothing, and if Katy was a comfort to the poor lady he was glad. Katy was glad too, and the visits did her as much good as they did Mrs. Spenser, for the intense pity she felt for the sick woman made her gentle and patient as she had never been before.

One day she stopped, as usual, on her way home from school. She tried the side-door—it was locked; the back-door—it was locked too. All the blinds were shut tight. This was very puzzling.

As she stood in the yard a woman put her head out of the window of the next house. "It's no use knocking," she said; "all the folks have gone away."

"Gone away where?" asked Katy.

"Nobody knows," said the woman; "the gentleman came back in the middle of the night, and this morning, before light, he had a wagon at the door, and just put in the trunks and the sick lady, and drove off. There's been more than one a-knocking besides you since then. But Mr. Pudgett, he's got the key, and nobody can get in without goin' to him."

It was too true. Mrs. Spenser was gone, and Katy never saw her again. In a few days it came out that Mr. Spenser was a very bad man, and had been making false money—*counterfeiting*, as grown people call it. The police were searching for him, to put him in gaol; and that was the reason he had come back in such a hurry and carried off his poor sick wife. Aunt Izzie cried with mortification when she heard this. She said she thought it was a disgrace that Katy should have been visiting in a counterfeiter's family. But Dr. Carr only laughed. He told Aunt Izzie that he didn't think that kind of crime was catching; and as for Mrs. Spenser, she was much to be pitied. But Aunt Izzie could not get over her vexation, and every now and then, when she was vexed, she would refer to the affair, though this all happened so long ago that most people had forgotten all about it, and Philly and John had stopped playing at "Putting Mr. Spenser in Gaol," which for a long time was one of their favourite games.

Katy always felt badly when Aunt Izzie spoke unkindly of her poor sick friend. She had tears in her eyes now as she walked to the gate, and looked so very sober that Imogen Clark, who stood there waiting, clasped her hands and said:

"Ah, I see! Your aristocratic aunt refuses."

Imogen's real name was Elizabeth. She was rather a pretty girl, with a screwed-up, sentimental mouth, shiny brown hair, and a little round curl on each of her cheeks.

These curls must have been fastened on with glue or tin-tacks, one would think, for they never moved however much she laughed or shook her head. Imogen was a bright girl naturally, but she had read so many novels that her brain was completely turned. It was partly this which made her so attractive to Katy, who adored stories, and thought Imogen was a real heroine of romance.

"Oh no, she doesn't," she replied, hardly able to keep from laughing at the idea of Aunt Izzie's being called an "aristocratic relative"—"she says she shall be very hap—" But here Katy's conscience gave a prick, and the sentence ended in "um, um, um——" "So you'll come, won't you, darling? I'm so glad!"

"And I!" said Imogen, turning up her eyes, theatrically.

From this time on till the end of the week the children talked of nothing but Imogen's visit, and the nice time they were going to have. Before breakfast on Saturday morning, Katy and Clover were at work building a beautiful bower of asparagus boughs under the trees. All the playthings were set out in order. Debby baked them some cinnamon cakes; the kitten had a pink ribbon tied round her neck; and the dolls, including "Pikery," were arrayed in their best clothes.

About half-past ten Imogen arrived. She was dressed in a light-blue barège, with low neck and short sleeves, and wore coral beads in her hair, white satin slippers, and a pair of yellow gloves. The gloves and slippers were quite dirty, and the barège was old and darned; but the general effect was so very gorgeous that the children, who were dressed for play, in gingham frocks and white aprons, were quite dazzled at the appearance of their guest.

"Oh, Imogen, you look just like a young lady in a story!" said simple Katy; whereupon Imogen tossed her head and rustled her skirts about her more than ever.

Somehow, with these fine clothes, Imogen seemed to have put on a fine manner, quite different from the one she used every day. You know some people always do when they go out visiting. You would almost have supposed that this was a different Imogen, who was kept in a box most of the time, and taken out for Sundays and grand occasions. She turned herself about, and tittered, and lisped, and looked at herself in the glass, and was generally grown-up and airy. When Aunt Izzie spoke to her, she fluttered and behaved so queerly that Clover almost laughed; and even Katy, who could see nothing wrong in people she loved, was glad to carry her away to the playroom.

"Come out to the bower," she said, putting her arm round the blue barège waist.

"A bower!" cried Imogen. "How sweet!" But when they reached the asparagus boughs her face fell. "Why it hasn't any roof, or pinnacles, or any fountain!" she said.

"Why no, of course not," said Clover, staring; "we made it ourselves."

"Oh!" said Imogen. She was evidently disappointed. Katy and Clover felt fortified; but as their visitor did not care for the bower, they tried to think of something else.

"Let us go to the loft," they said.

So they all crossed the yard together. Imogen picked her way daintily in the white satin slippers, but when she saw the spiked post she gave a scream.

"Oh, not up there, darling, not up there!" she cried; "never, never!"

"Oh, do try! It's just as easy as can be," pleaded Katy, going up and down half a dozen times in succession to show how easy it was. But Imogen wouldn't be persuaded.

"Do not ask me," she said, affectedly; "my nerves would never stand such a thing! And besides—my dress!"

"What made you wear it?" said Philly, who was a plain-spoken child, and given to questions. While John whispered to Dorry, "That's a real stupid girl. Let's go off somewhere and play by ourselves."

So one by one the small fry crept away, leaving Katy and Clover to entertain the visitor by themselves. They tried dolls, but Imogen did not care for dolls. Then they proposed to sit down in the shade, and cap verses—a game they all liked. But Imogen said that though she adored poetry, she never could remember any. So it ended in their going to the orchard; where Imogen ate a great many plums and early apples, and really seemed to enjoy herself. But when she could eat no more a dreadful dullness fell over the party. At last Imogen said:

"Don't you ever sit in the drawing-room?"

"The what?" asked Clover.

"The drawing-room," repeated Imogen.

"Oh, she means the parlour!" cried Katy. "No, we don't sit there except when Aunt Izzie has company to tea. It is all dark and poky, you know. Besides, it's so much pleasanter to be out-doors. Don't you think so?"

"Yes, sometimes," replied Imogen, doubtfully; "but I think it would be pleasant to go in and sit there for a while now. My head aches dreadfully, being out here in this horrid sun."

Katy was at her wit's end to know what to do. They scarcely ever went into the parlour, which Aunt Izzie regarded as a sort of sacred place. She kept cotton petticoats over all the chairs for fear of dust, and never opened the blinds for fear of flies. The idea of children with dusty boots going in there to sit! On the other hand, Katy's natural politeness made it hard to refuse a visitor anything she asked for. And besides, it was dreadful to think that Imogen might go away and report, "Katy Carr isn't allowed to sit in the best room, even when she has company!" With a quaking heart she led the way to the parlour. She dared not open the blinds, so the room looked very dark. She could just see Imogen's figure as she sat on the sofa, and Clover twirling uneasily about on the piano-stool. All the time she kept listening to hear if Aunt Izzie were not coming, and altogether the parlour was a dismal place to her; not half so pleasant as the asparagus bower, where they felt perfectly safe.

But Imogen, who for the first time seemed comfortable, began to talk. Her talk was about herself. Such stories she told about the things which happened to her! All the young ladies in "The Ledger" put together never had stranger adventures. Gradually, Katy and Clover got so interested that they left their seats and crouched down close to the sofa, listening with open mouths to these stories. Katy forgot to listen for Aunt Izzie. The parlour door swung open, but she did not notice it. She did not even hear the front door shut when Papa came home to dinner.

Dr. Carr, stopping in the hall to glance over his newspaper, heard the high-pitched voice running on in the parlour. At first he hardly listened: then these words caught his ear:

"Oh, it was lovely, girls, perfectly delicious! I suppose I did look well, for I was all in white with my hair let down, and just one rose, you know, here on top. And he leaned over me and said in a low, deep tone: 'Lady, I am a Brigand, but I feel the enchanting power of beauty. You are free!' "

Dr. Carr pushed the door open a little farther. Nothing was to be seen but some indistinct figures, but he heard Katy's voice in an eager tone:

"Oh, *do* go on. What happened next?"

"Who on earth have the children got in the parlour?" he asked Aunt Izzie, whom he found in the dining-room.

"The parlour! " cried Miss Izzie, wrathfully; "why, what are they there for?" Then going to the door she called out, "Children, what are you doing in the parlour? Come get right away. I thought you were playing out-doors."

"Imogen had a headache," faltered Katy. The three girls came out into the hall; Clover and Katy looked scared, and even the Enchanter of the Brigand quite crestfallen, "Oh," said Aunt Izzie grimly, "I am sorry to hear that. Probably you are bilious. Would you like some camphor or anything?"

"No, thank you," replied Imogen, meekly. But afterwards she whispered to Katy:

"Your aunt isn't very nice, I think. She's just like

Jackima, that horrid old woman I told you about, who lived in the Brigand's Cave and did the cooking."

"I don't think you're a bit polite to tell me so," retorted Katy, very angry at this speech.

"Oh, never mind, dear, don't take it to heart!" replied Imogen sweetly. "We can't help having relations that ain't nice, you know."

The visit was evidently not a success. Papa was very civil to Imogen at dinner, but he watched her closely, and Katy saw a comical twinkle in his eye which she did not like. Papa had very droll eyes. They saw everything, and sometimes they seemed to talk almost as distinctly as his tongue.

Katy began to feel low-spirited. She confessed afterward that she should never have got through the afternoon if she hadn't run upstairs two or three times, and comforted herself by reading a little in *Rosamond*.

"Aren't you glad she's gone?" whispered Clover, as they stood at the gate together watching Imogen walk down the street.

"Oh, Clover! how can you?" said Katy. But she gave Clover a great hug, and I think in her heart she *was* glad.

"Katy," said Papa, next day, "you came into the room then, exactly like your new friend Miss Clark."

"How? I don't know what you mean," answered Katy, blushing deeply.

"*So*," said Dr. Carr; and he got up, raising his shoulders and squaring his elbows, and took a few mincing steps across the room. Katy couldn't help laughing, it was so funny, and so like Imogen. Then Papa sat down again and drew her close to him.

"My dear," he said, "you're an affectionate child, and I'm glad of it. But there is such a thing as throwing away one's affection. I didn't fancy that little girl at all yesterday. What makes you like her so much?"

"I didn't like her so much yesterday," admitted Katy, reluctantly. "She's a great deal nicer than that at school, sometimes."

71

"I'm glad to hear it," said her father. "For I should be sorry to think that you really admired such silly manners. And what was that nonsense I heard her telling you about Brigands?"

"It really hap——" began Katy. Then she caught Papa's eye, and bit her lip, for he looked very quizzical. "Well," she went on laughing, "I suppose it didn't really all happen;—but it was ever so funny, Papa, even if it was a make-up. And Imogen's just as good-natured as can be. All the girls like her."

"Make-ups are all very well," said Papa, "as long as people don't try to make you believe they are true. When they do that, it seems to me it comes too near the edge of falsehood to be very safe or pleasant. If I were you, Katy, I'd be a little shy of swearing eternal friendship for Miss Clark. She may be good-natured, as you say, but I think two or three years hence she won't seem so nice to you as she does now. Give me a kiss, Chick, and run away, for there's Alexander with the gig."

CHAPTER SEVEN

Cousin Helen's Visit

A LITTLE KNOT of the schoolgirls were walking home to-gether one afternoon in July. As they neared Dr. Carr's gate, Maria Fiske exclaimed, at the sight of a pretty bunch of flowers lying in the middle of the sidewalk:

"Oh, my!" she cried, "see what somebody's dropped! I'm going to have it." She stooped to pick it up. But just as her fingers touched the stems, the nosegay, as if be-witched, began to move. Maria made a bewildered clutch. The nosegay moved faster, and at last vanished under the gate, while a giggle sounded from the other side of the hedge.

"Did you see that?" shrieked Maria; "those flowers ran away of themselves."

"Nonsense," said Katy, "it's those absurd children." Then, opening the gate, she called: "John! Dorry! come out and show yourselves." But nobody replied, and no one could be seen. The nosegay lay on the path, how-ever, and picking it up, Katy exhibited to the girls a long end of black thread tied to the stems.

"That's a very favourite trick of Johnny's," she said; "she and Dorry are always tying up flowers, and putting them out on the walk to tease people. Here, Maria, take

73

them if you like. Though I don't think John's taste in bouquets is very good."

"Isn't it splendid to have vacation come?" said one of the bigger girls. "What are you all going to do? We're going to the sea-side."

"Pa says he'll take Susie and me to Niagara," said Maria.

"I'm going to make my Aunt a visit," said Alice Blair. "She lives in a real lovely place in the country, and there's a pond there; and Tom (that's my cousin) says he'll teach me to row. What are you going to do, Katy?"

"Oh, I don't know; play round and have splendid times," replied Katy, throwing her bag of books into the air, and catching it again. But the other girls looked as if they didn't think this good fun at all, and as if they were sorry for her; and Katy felt suddenly that her vacation wasn't going to be so pleasant as that of the rest.

"I wish Papa *would* take us somewhere," she said to Clover, as they walked up the gravel path. "All the other girls' Papas do."

"He's too busy," replied Clover. "Besides, I don't think any of the rest of the girls have half such good times as we. Ellen Roberts says she'd give a million of dollars for such nice brothers and sisters as ours to play with. And, you know, Maria and Susie have *awful* times at home, though they do go to places. Mrs. Fiske is so particular. She always says 'Don't'; and they haven't got any yard to their house, or anything. I wouldn't change."

"Nor I," said Katy, cheering up at these words of wisdom. "Oh! isn't it lovely to think there won't be any school to-morrow? Vacations are just splendid! " and she gave her bag another toss. It fell to the ground with a crash.

"There, you've cracked your slate," said Clover.

"No matter, I shan't want it again for eight weeks," replied Katy, comfortably, as they ran up the steps.

They burst open the front door and raced upstairs, crying, "Hurrah! hurrah! vacation's begun. Aunt Izzie, vacation's begun!" Then they stopped short, for lo! the upper hall was all in confusion. Sounds of beating and dusting came from the spare room. Tables and chairs were standing about; and a cot-bed, which seemed to be taking a walk all by itself, had stopped short at the head of the stairs, and barred the way.

"Why, how queer," said Katy, trying to get by. "What *can* be going to happen? Oh, there's Aunt Izzie! Aunt Izzie, who's coming? What *are* you moving the things out of the Blue-room for?"

"Oh, gracious! is that you?" replied Aunt Izzie, who looked very hot and flurried. "Now, children, it's no use for you to stand there asking questions; I haven't got time to answer them. Let the bedstead alone, Katy, you'll push it into the wall. There, I told you so!" as Katy gave an impatient shove, "you've made a bad mark on the paper. What a troublesome child you are! Go right downstairs, both of you, and don't come up this way again till after tea. I've just as much as I can possibly attend to till then."

"Just tell us what's going to happen, and we will," cried the children.

"Your Cousin Helen is coming to visit us," said Miss Izzie, curtly, and disappeared, into the Blue-room.

This was news indeed. Katy and Clover ran downstairs in great excitement, and, after consulting a little, retired to the loft to talk it over in peace and quiet. Cousin Helen coming! It seemed as strange as if Queen Victoria, gold crown and all, had invited herself to tea; or as if some character out of a book, Robinson Crusoe, say, or "Amy Herbert," had driven up with a trunk and announced the intention of spending a week. For the imaginations of the children, Cousin Helen was as interesting and unreal as anybody in the fairy tales: Cinderella, or Blue Beard, or dear Red Riding-Hood herself. Only there was a sort of mixture of Sunday-school book in their idea of her, for Cousin Helen was very, very good.

None of them had ever seen her. Philly said he was sure she hadn't any legs, because she never went away from

75

home, and lay on a sofa all the time. But the rest knew that this was because Cousin Helen was ill. Papa always went to visit her twice a year, and he liked to talk to the children about her, and tell how sweet and patient she was, and what a pretty room she lived in. Katy and Clover had "played Cousin Helen" so long, that now they were frightened as well as glad at the idea of seeing the real one.

"Do you suppose she will want us to say hymns to her *all* the time?" asked Clover.

"Not all the time," replied Katy, "because you know she'll get tired, and have to take naps in the afternoons. And then, of course, she reads the Bible a great deal. Oh dear, how quiet we shall have to be! I wonder how long she's going to stay?"

"What do you suppose she looks like?" went on Clover.

"Something like 'Lucy' in Mrs. Sherwood's story, I guess, with blue eyes, and curls, and a long, straight nose. And she'll keep her hands clasped *so* all the time, and wear 'frilled wrappers,' and lie on the sofa perfectly still and never smile, but just look patient. We'll have to take off our boots in the hall, Clover, and go upstairs in stocking feet, so as not to make a noise, all the time she stays."

"Won't it be funny! " giggled Clover, her sober little face growing bright at the idea of this variation on the hymns.

The time seemed very long till the next afternoon, when Cousin Helen was expected. Aunt Izzie, who was in a great excitement, gave the children many orders about their behaviour. They were to do this and that, and not to do the other. Dorry at last announced that he wished Cousin Helen would just stay at home. Clover and Elsie, who had been thinking pretty much the same thing in private, were glad to hear that she was on her way to a water cure, and would stay only four days.

Five o'clock came. They all sat on the steps waiting for the carriage. At last it drove up. Papa was on the box. He motioned the children to stand back. Then he helped out a nice-looking young woman, who, Aunt Izzie told them

76

was Cousin Helen's nurse, and then very carefully lifted Cousin Helen in his arms and brought her in.

"Oh, there are the chicks! " were the first words the children heard, in *such* a gay, pleasant voice. "Do set me down somewhere, Uncle. I want to see them so much! "

So Papa put Cousin Helen on the hall sofa. The nurse fetched a pillow, and when she was made comfortable, Dr. Carr called to the little ones.

"Cousin Helen wants to see you," he said.

"Indeed I do," said the bright voice. "So this is Katy? Why, what a splendid tall Katy it is! And this is Clover," kissing her; "and *this* dear little Elsie. You all look as natural as possible—just as if I had seen you before." And hugged them all round, not as if it was polite to like them because they were relations, but as if she had loved them and wanted them all her life.

There was something in Cousin Helen's face and manner which made the children at home with her at once. Even Philly, who had backed away with his hands behind him, after staring hard for a minute or two, came up with a sort of rush to get his share of kissing.

Still, Katy's first feeling was one of disappointment. Cousin Helen was not at all like "Lucy," in the story. Her nose turned up the least bit in the world. She had brown hair, which didn't curl, a brown skin, and bright eyes which danced when she laughed or spoke. Her face was thin, but except for that you wouldn't have guessed that she was sick. She didn't fold her hands, and she didn't look patient, but absolutely glad and merry. Her dress wasn't a "frilled wrapper," but a sort of loose travelling thing of pretty grey stuff, with a rose-coloured bow, and bracelets, and a round hat, trimmed with a grey feather. All Katy's dreams about the "saintly invalid" seemed to take wings and fly away. But the more she watched Cousin Helen the more she seemed to like her, and to feel as if she were nicer than the imaginary person which she and Clover had invented.

"She looks just like other people, don't she?" whispered Cecy, who had come over to have a peep at the new arrival.

"Y-e-s," replied Katy, doubtfully, "only a great, great deal prettier."

By-and-by Papa carried Cousin Helen upstairs. All the children wanted to go too, but he told them she was tired, and must rest. So they went out-doors to play till tea-time.

"Oh, do let me take up the tray," cried Katy at the tea table, as she watched Aunt Izzie getting ready Cousin Helen's supper. Such a nice supper! Cold chicken, and raspberries and cream, and tea in a pretty pink-and-white china cup. And such a snow-white napkin as Aunt Izzie spread over the tray!

"No, indeed," said Aunt Izzie. "You'll drop it the first thing." But Katy's eyes begged so hard, that Dr. Carr said, "Yes, let her, Izzie; I like to see the girls useful."

So Katy, proud of the commission, took the tray and carried it carefully across the hall. There was a bowl of flowers on the table. As she passed she was struck with a bright idea. She set down the tray, and picking out a rose, laid it on the napkin beside the saucer of crimson raspberries. It looked very pretty, and Katy smiled to herself with pleasure.

"What are you stopping for?" called Aunt Izzie, from the dining-room. "*Do* be careful, Katy; I really think Bridget had better take it."

"Oh, no, no!" protested Katy, "I'm most up already." And she sped upstairs as fast as she could go. Luckless speed! She had just reached the door of the Blue-room when she tripped over her bootlace, which, as usual, was dangling, made a mis-step, and stumbled. She caught at the door to save herself; the door flew open; and Katy, with the tray, cream, raspberries, rose and all, descended in a confused heap upon the carpet.

"I told you so!" exclaimed Aunt Izzie from the bottom of the stairs.

Katy never forgot how kind Cousin Helen was on this occasion. She was in bed, and was of course a good deal startled at the sudden crash and tumble on her floor. But after one little jump, nothing could have been sweeter than the way in which she comforted poor crestfallen Katy, and made so merry over the accident that even Aunt Izzie almost forgot to scold. The broken dishes were piled up, and the carpet made clean again, while Aunt Izzie prepared another tray just as nice as the first.

"Please let Katy bring it up!" pleaded Cousin Helen, in her pleasant voice; "I am sure she will be careful this time. And Katy, I want just such another rose on the napkin. I guess that was your doing—wasn't it?"

Katy *was* careful. This time all went well. The tray was placed safely on a little table beside the bed, and Katy sat watching Cousin Helen eat her supper with a warm, loving feeling at her heart. I think we are scarcely ever so grateful to people as when they help us to get back our own self-esteem.

Cousin Helen hadn't much appetite, though she declared everything was delicious. Katy could see that she was very tired.

"Now," she said, when she had finished, "if you'll shake up this pillow, *so*—and move this other pillow a little, I think I will settle myself to sleep. Thanks—that's just right. Why, Katy dear, you are a born nurse. Now kiss me. Good-night! To-morrow we will have a nice talk."

Katy went downstairs very happy. "Cousin Helen's perfectly lovely," she told Clover. "And she's got on the most *beautiful* night-gown, all lace and ruffles. It's just like a night-gown in a book."

"Isn't it wicked to care about clothes when you're sick?" questioned Cecy.

"I don't believe Cousin Helen *could* do anything wicked," said Katy.

"I told Ma that she had on bracelets, and Ma said she feared your cousin was a worldly person," retorted Cecy, primming up her lips.

Katy and Clover were quite distressed at this opinion. They talked about it while they were undressing.

"I mean to ask Cousin Helen to-morrow," said Katy.

Next morning the children got up very early. They were so glad that it was vacation! If it hadn't been, they would have been forced to go to school without seeing Cousin Helen, for she didn't waken till late. They grew so impatient of the delay, and went upstairs so often to listen at the door, and see if she were moving, that Aunt Izzie finally had to order them off. Katy rebelled against this order a good deal, but she consoled herself by going into the garden and picking the prettiest flowers she could find, to give to Cousin Helen the moment she should see her.

When Aunt Izzie let her go up, Cousin Helen was lying on the sofa all dressed for the day in a fresh blue muslin, with blue ribbons, and cunning bronze slippers with rosettes on the toes. The sofa had been wheeled round with its back to the light. There was a cushion with a pretty fluted cover that Katy had never seen before, and several other things were scattered about, which gave the room quite a different air. All the house was neat, but somehow Aunt Izzie's rooms never were *pretty*. Children's eyes are quick to perceive such things, and Katy saw at once that the Blue-room had never looked like this.

Cousin Helen was white and tired, but her eyes and smile were as bright as ever. She was delighted with the flowers which Katy presented rather shyly.

"Oh, how lovely!" she said; "I must put them in water right away. Katy dear, don't you want to bring that little vase on the bureau and set it on this chair beside me? And please pour a little water into it first."

"What a beauty!" cried Katy, as she lifted the graceful white cup swung on a gilt stand. "Is it yours, Cousin Helen?"

"Yes, it is my pet vase. It stands on a little table beside me at home, and I fancied that the water cure would seem more home-like if I had it with me there, so I brought it along. But why do you look so puzzled, Katy? Does it seem queer that a vase should travel about in a trunk?"

"No," said Katy, slowly, "I was only thinking—Cousin Helen, is it worldly to have pretty things when you're sick?"

Cousin Helen laughed heartily.

"What put that idea into your head?" she asked.

"Cecy said so when I told her about your beautiful night-gown."

Cousin Helen smiled again.

"Well," she said, "I'll tell you what I think, Katy. Pretty things are no more 'worldly' than ugly ones, except when they spoil us by making us vain, or careless of the comfort of other people. And sickness is such a disagreeable thing in itself that, unless sick people take great pains, they soon grow to be eyesores to themselves and everybody about them. I don't think it is possible for an invalid to be too particular. And when one has the backache and the headache and the all-over-ache," she added, smiling, "there isn't much danger of growing vain because of a ruffle more or less on one's night-gown, or a bit of bright ribbon."

Then she began to arrange the flowers, touching each separate one gently, as if she loved it.

"What a queer noise!" she exclaimed, suddenly stopping.

It was queer—a sort of snuffling and snorting sound, as if a walrus or a sea-horse were promenading up and down in the hall. Katy opened the door. Behold! there were John and Dorry, very red in the face from flattening their noses against the keyhole, in a vain attempt to see if Cousin Helen were up and ready to receive company.

"Oh, let them come in!" cried Cousin Helen from her sofa.

So they came in, followed before long by Clover and Elsie. Such a merry morning as they had! Cousin Helen proved to possess a perfect genius for story-telling, and for suggesting games which could be played about her sofa, and did not make more noise than she could bear. Aunt Izzie, dropping in about eleven o'clock, found them having such a good time that, almost before she knew it, *she* was drawn into the game too. Nobody had ever heard of such a thing before! There sat Aunt Izzie on the floor, with three long paper quills stuck in her hair, playing 'I'm a genteel Lady, always genteel,' in the jolliest manner possible. The children were so enchanted at the spectacle that they could hardly attend to the game, and were always forgetting how many "horns" they had.

Clover privately thought that Cousin Helen must be a witch; and Papa, when he came home at noon, said almost the same thing.

"What have you been doing to them, Helen?" he inquired, as he opened the door and saw the merry circle on the carpet. Aunt Izzie's hair was half pulled down, and Philly was rolling over and over in convulsions of laughter. But Cousin Helen said she hadn't done anything, and pretty soon Papa was on the floor too, playing away as fast as the rest.

"I must put a stop to this," he cried, when everybody was tired of laughing, and everybody's head was stuck as full of paper quills as a porcupine's back. "Cousin Helen will be worn out. Run away, all of you, and don't come near this door again till the clock strikes four. Do you hear, chicks? Run—run! Shoo! shoo!"

The children scuttled away like a brood of fowls—all but Katy. "Oh, Papa, I'll be *so* quiet!" she pleaded. "Mightn't I stay just till the dinner-bell rings?"

"Do let her!" said Cousin Helen. So Papa said "Yes."

Katy sat on the floor holding Cousin Helen's hand, and listening to her talk with Papa. It interested her, though it was about things and people she did not know.

"How is Alex?" asked Dr. Carr, at length.

"Quite well, now," replied Cousin Helen, with one of her brightest looks. "He was run down and tired in the spring, and we were a little anxious about him; but Emma persuaded him to take a fortnight's vacation, and he came back all right."

"Do you see them often?"

"Almost every day. And little Helen comes every day, you know, for her lessons."

"Is she as pretty as she used to be?"

"Oh yes—prettier, I think. She is a lovely little creature. Having her so much with me is one of my greatest treats. Alex. tries to think that she looks a little as I used to. But that is a compliment so great I dare not appropriate it."

Dr. Carr stooped and kissed Cousin Helen as if he could not help it. "My *dear* child," he said. That was all; but something in the tone made Katy curious.

"Papa," she said after dinner, "who is Alex., that you and Cousin Helen were talking about?"

"Why, Katy? What makes you want to know?"

"I can't exactly tell—only Cousin Helen looked so; and you kissed her; and I thought perhaps it was something interesting."

"So it is," said Dr. Carr, drawing her on to his knee. "I've a mind to tell you about it, Katy, because you're old enough to see how beautiful it is, and wise enough, I hope, not to chatter or ask questions. Alex. is the name of somebody who long ago, when Cousin Helen was well and strong, she loved, and expected to marry."

"Oh, why didn't she?" cried Katy.

"She met with a dreadful accident," continued Dr. Carr. "For a long time they thought she would die. Then she grew slowly better, and the doctors told her that she might live a good many years, but that she would have to lie on her sofa always, and be helpless, and a cripple.

"Alex. felt dreadfully when he heard this. He wanted to marry Cousin Helen just the same, and be her nurse, and take care of her always; but she would not consent. She broke the engagement, and told him that some day she hoped he would love somebody else well enough to marry her. So, after a good many years he did, and now he and his wife live next door to Cousin Helen, and are her dearest friends. Their little girl is named 'Helen.' All their plans are talked over with her, and there is nobody in the world they think so much of."

"But doesn't it make Cousin Helen feel bad when she sees them walking about and enjoying themselves and she can't move?" asked Katy.

"No," said Dr. Carr, "it doesn't, because Cousin Helen is half an angel already, and loves other people better than herself. I'm very glad she could come here for once. She's an example to us all, Katy, and I couldn't ask anything better than to have my little girls take pattern after her."

"It must be *awful* to be sick," soliloquised Katy, after Papa was gone. "Why if I had to stay in bed a whole week—I should *die*, I know I should."

Poor Katy! It seemed to her, as it does to almost all young people, that there is nothing in the world so easy as to die the moment things go wrong!

This conversation with Papa made Cousin Helen doubly interesting to Katy's eyes. "It was just like something in a book," to be in the same house with the heroine of a love-story so sad and sweet.

The play that afternoon was much interrupted, for every few minutes somebody had to run and see if it wasn't four o'clock. The instant the hour came all six children galloped upstairs.

"I think we'll tell stories this time," said Cousin Helen.

So they told stories. Cousin Helen's were the best of all. There was one of them about a robber, which sent delightful chills creeping down all their backs. All but Philly. He was so excited that he grew warlike.

"I ain't afraid of robbers," he declared, strutting up and down. "When they come I shall just cut them in two with my sword which Papa gave me. They did come once. I did cut them in two—three, five, eleven of 'em. You'll see! "

But that evening, after the youngest children were gone

to bed, and Katy and Clover were sitting in the Blue-room, a lamentable howling was heard from the nursery. Clover ran to see what was the matter. Behold—there was Phil, sitting up in bed, and crying for help.

"There's robbers under the bed," he sobbed; "ever so many robbers."

"Why no, Philly!" said Clover, peeping under the valance to satisfy him; "there isn't anybody there."

"Yes there is, I tell you," declared Phil holding her tight. "I heard one. They were *chewing my india-rubbers.*"

"Poor little fellow!" said Cousin Helen, when Clover, having pacified Phil, came back to report. "It's a warning against robber stories. But this one ended so well that I didn't think of anybody's being frightened."

It was no use, after this, for Aunt Izzie to make rules about going into the Blue-room. She might as well have ordered flies to keep away from a sugar-bowl. By hook or by crook, the children *would* get upstairs. Whenever Aunt Izzie went in she was sure to find them there, just as close to Cousin Helen as they could get. And Cousin Helen begged her not to interfere.

"We have only three or four days to be together," she said. "Let them come as much as they like. It won't hurt me a bit."

Little Elsie clung with a passionate love to this new friend. Cousin Helen had sharp eyes. She saw the wistful look in Elsie's face at once, and took special pains to be sweet and tender to her. This preference made Katy jealous. She couldn't bear to share her cousin with anybody.

When the last evening came, and they went up after tea to the Blue-room, Cousin Helen was opening a box which had just come by express.

"It is a Good-bye Box," she said. "All of you must sit down in a row, and when I hide my hands behind me, *so,* you must choose in turn which you will take."

So they all chose in turn, "Which hand will you have, the right or the left?" and Cousin Helen, with the air of

85

a wise fairy, brought out from behind her pillow something pretty for each one.

First came a vase exactly like her own, which Katy had admired so much. Katy screamed with delight as it was placed in her hands.

"Oh, how lovely! how lovely!" she cried, "I'll keep it as long as I live and breathe."

"If you do, it'll be the first time you ever kept anything for a week without breaking it," remarked Aunt Izzie.

Next came a pretty purple pocket-book for Clover. It was just what she wanted, for she had lost her portemonnaie. Then a cunning little locket on a bit of velvet ribbon, which Cousin Helen tied round Elsie's neck.

"There's a piece of my hair in it," she said. "Why, Elsie, darling, what's the matter? Don't cry so!"

"Oh, you're s-o beautiful, and s-o sweet!" sobbed Elsie; "and you're go-o-ing away."

Dorry had a box of dominoes, and John a solitaire board. For Phil there appeared a book—*The History of the Robber Cat*.

"That will remind you of the night when the thieves came and chewed your india-rubbers," said Cousin Helen, with a mischievous smile. They all laughed, Phil loudest of all.

Nobody was forgotten. There was a note-book for Papa, and a set of ivory tablets for Aunt Izzie. Even Cecy was remembered. Her present was *The Book of Golden Deeds*, with all sorts of stories about boys and girls who had done brave and good things. She was almost too pleased to speak.

"Oh, thank you, Cousin Helen!" she said at last. Cecy wasn't a cousin, but she and the Carr children were in the habit of sharing their aunts and uncles and relations generally, as they did other good things.

Next day came the sad parting. All the little ones stood at the gate, to wave their pocket-handkerchiefs as the carriage drove away. When it was quite out of sight, Katy rushed off to "weep a little weep," all by herself.

"Papa said he wished we were all like Cousin Helen," she thought, as she wiped her eyes, "and I mean to try, though I don't suppose if I tried a thousand years I should ever get to be half so good. I'll study, and keep my things in order, and be ever so kind to the little ones. Dear me —if only Aunt Izzie was Cousin Helen, how easy it would be! Never mind—I'll think about her all the time, and I'll begin to-morrow."

CHAPTER EIGHT

To-morrow

"TO-MORROW I will begin," thought Katy, as she dropped asleep that night. How often we all do so! And what a pity it is that when morning comes and to-morrow is to-day we so frequently wake up feeling quite differently; careless or impatient, and not a bit inclined to do the fine things we planned overnight.

Sometimes it seems as if there must be wicked little imps in the world, who are kept tied up so long as the sun shines, but who creep into our bedrooms when we are asleep to tease us and ruffle our tempers. Else, why, when we go to rest good-natured and pleasant, should we wake up so cross? Now there was Katy. Her last sleepy thought was an intention to be an angel from that time on, and as much like Cousin Helen as she could; and when she opened her eyes, she was all out of sorts and as fractious as a bear! Old Mary said that she got out of bed on the wrong side.

I wonder, by the way, if anybody will ever be wise enough to tell us which side that is, so that we may always choose the other? How comfortable it would be if they could!

You know how, if we begin the day in a cross mood,

all sorts of unfortunate accidents seem to occur to add to our vexations. The very first thing Katy did this morning was to break her precious vase—the one Cousin Helen had given her.

It was standing on the bureau with a little cluster of blush-roses in it. The bureau had a swing-glass. While Katy was brushing her hair, the glass tipped a little so that she could not see. At a good-humoured moment this accident wouldn't have troubled her much. But being out of temper to begin with, it made her angry. She gave the glass a violent push. The lower part swung forward, there was a smash, and the first thing Katy knew, the blush-roses lay scattered all over the floor, and Cousin Helen's pretty present was ruined.

Katy just sat down on the carpet and cried as hard as if she had been Phil himself. Aunt Izzie heard her lamenting, and came in.

"I'm very sorry," she said, picking up the broken glass, "but it's no more than I expected, you're so careless, Katy. Now don't sit there in that foolish way! Get up and dress yourself. You'll be late to breakfast."

"What's the matter?" asked Papa, noticing Katy's red eyes as she took her seat at the table.

"I've broken my vase," said Katy, dolefully.

"It was extremely careless of you to put it in such a dangerous place," said her aunt. "You might have known that the glass would swing and knock it off." Then, seeing a big tear fall in the middle of Katy's plate, she added: "Really, Katy, you're too big to behave like a baby. Why Dorry would be ashamed to do so. Pray control yourself! "

This snub did not improve Katy's temper. She went on with her breakfast in sulky silence.

"What are you all going to do to-day?" asked Dr. Carr, hoping to give things a more cheerful turn.

"Swing! " cried John and Dorry both together. "Alexander's put us up a splendid one in the wood-shed."

"No you're not," said Aunt Izzie, in a positive tone,

"the swing is not to be used till to-morrow. Remember that, children. Not till to-morrow. And not then, unless I give you leave."

This was unwise of Aunt Izzie. It would have been better had she explained further. The truth was, that Alexander, in putting up the swing, had cracked one of the staples which fastened it to the roof. He meant to get a new one in the course of the day, and meantime, he had cautioned Miss Carr to let no one use the swing, because it really was not safe. If she had told this to the children all would have been right; but Aunt Izzie's theory was that young people must obey their elders without explanation.

John, and Elsie, and Dorry all pouted when they heard this order. Elsie recovered her good-humour first.

"I don't care," she said, " 'cause I'm going to be very busy; I've got to write a letter to Cousin Helen about somefing." (Elsie never could quite pronounce the *th*.)

"What?" asked Clover.

"Oh, somefing," answered Elsie, wagging her head mysteriously. "None of the rest of you must know, Cousin Helen said so; it's a secret she and me has got."

"I don't believe Cousin Helen said so at all," said Katy, crossly. "She wouldn't tell secrets to a silly little girl like you."

"Yes, she would too," retorted Elsie, angrily. "She said I was just as good to trust as if I were ever so big. And she said I was her pet. So there! Katy Carr! "

"Stop disputing," said Aunt Izzie. "Katy, your top drawer is all out of order. I never saw anything look so badly. Go upstairs at once and straighten it, before you do anything else. Children, you must keep in the shade this morning. It's too hot for you to be running about in the sun. Elsie, go into the kitchen and tell Debby I want to speak to her."

"Yes," said Elsie, in an important tone. "And afterwards I'm coming back to write my letter to Cousin Helen."

Katy went slowly upstairs, dragging one foot after the

other. It was a warm, languid day. Her head ached a little, and her eyes smarted and felt heavy from crying so much. Everything seemed dull and hateful. She said to herself that Aunt Izzie was very unkind to make her work in vacation, and she pulled the top drawer open with a disgusted groan.

It must be confessed that Miss Izzie was right. A bureau drawer could hardly look worse than this one did. It reminded one of the White Knight's recipe for a pudding, which began with blotting-paper and ended with sealing-wax and gunpowder. All sorts of things were mixed together, as if somebody had put in a long stick and stirred them well up. There were books and paint-boxes and bits of scribbled paper and lead-pencils and brushes. Stocking-legs had come unrolled, and twisted themselves about pocket-handkerchiefs, and ends of ribbons and linen collars. Ruffles, all crushed out of shape, stuck up from under the heavier things, and sundry little paper boxes lay empty on top, the treasures they once held having sifted down to the bottom of the drawer and disappeared beneath the general mass.

It took much time and patience to bring order out of this confusion. But Katy knew that Aunt Izzie would be up by-and-by, and she dared not stop till all was done. By the time it was finished she was very tired. Going downstairs she met Elsie coming up with a slate in her hand, which, as soon as she saw Katy, she put behind her.

"You mustn't look," she said; "it's my letter to Cousin Helen. Nobody but me knows the secret. It's all written, and I'm going to send it to the post-office. See—there's a stamp on it"—and she exhibited a corner of the slate. Sure enough, there was a stamp stuck on the frame.

"You little goose!" said Katy, impatiently; "you can't send *that* to the post-office. Here, give me the slate; I'll copy what you've written on paper, and Papa'll give you an envelope."

"No, no," cried Elsie, struggling, "you mustn't! You'll see what I've said, and Cousin Helen said I wasn't to tell.

It's a secret. Let go of my slate, I say! I'll tell Cousin Helen what a mean girl you are, and then she won't love you a bit."

"There, then, take your old slate! " said Katy, giving her a vindictive push. Elsie slipped, screamed, caught at the banisters, missed them, and, rolling over and over, fell with a thump on the hall floor.

It wasn't much of a fall, only half a dozen steps, but the bump was a hard one, and Elsie roared as if she had been half killed. Aunt Izzie and Mary came rushing to the spot.

"Katy—pushed—me," sobbed Elsie. "She wanted me to tell my secret, and I wouldn't. She's a bad naughty girl! "

"Well, Katy Carr, I *should* think you'd be ashamed of yourself," said Aunt Izzie, "wreaking your temper on your poor little sister! I think your Cousin Helen will be surprised when she hears this. There, there, Elsie! Don't cry any more, dear. Come upstairs with me. I'll put on some arnica, and Katy shan't hurt you again."

So they went upstairs. Katy, left below, felt very miserable: repentant, defiant, discontented, and sulky all at once. She knew in her heart that she had not meant to hurt Elsie, and was thoroughly ashamed of that push; but Aunt Izzie's hint about telling Cousin Helen had made her too angry to allow of her confessing this to herself or anybody else.

"I don't care! " she murmured, choking back her tears. "Elsie is a real cry-baby, anyway. And Aunt Izzie always takes her part. Just because I told the little silly not to go and send a great heavy slate to the post-office."

She went by the side-door into the yard. As she passed the shed the new swing caught her eye.

"How exactly like Aunt Izzie," she thought, "ordering the children not to swing till she gives them leave. I suppose she thinks it's too hot, or something. *I* shan't mind her, anyhow."

She seated herself in the swing. It was a first-rate one, with a broad comfortable seat and thick new ropes. The seat hung just the right distance from the floor. Alexander was a capital hand at putting up swings, and the wood-shed the nicest possible spot in which to have one.

It was a big place, with a very high roof. There was not much wood left in it just now, and the little there was, was piled neatly about the sides of the shed, so as to leave plenty of room. The place felt cool and dark, and the motion of the swing seemed to set the breeze blowing. It waved Katy's hair like a great fan, and made her dreamy and quiet. All sorts of sleepy ideas began to flit through her brain. Swinging to and fro like the pendulum of a great clock, she gradually rose higher and higher, driving herself along by the motion of her body, and striking the floor smartly with her foot at every sweep. Now she was at the top of the high-arched door. Then she could almost touch the cross-beam above it, and through the small square window could see pigeons sitting and pluming themselves on the eaves of the barn and white clouds blowing over the blue sky. She had never swung so high before. It was like flying she thought, as she bent and curved more strongly in the seat, trying to send herself yet higher and graze the roof with her toes.

Suddenly at the very highest point of the sweep there was a sharp noise of cracking. The swing gave a violent twist, spun half round and tossed Katy into the air. She clutched the rope—felt it dragged from her grasp—then down—down—she fell. All grew dark, and she knew no more.

When she opened her eyes she was lying on the sofa in the dining-room. Clover was kneeling beside her with a pale, scared face, and Aunt Izzie was dropping something cold and wet on her forehead.

"What's the matter?" said Katy, faintly.

"Oh, she's alive—she's alive!" and Clover put her arms round Katy's neck and sobbed.

"Hush, dear!" Aunt Izzie's voice sounded unusually gentle. "You've had a bad tumble, Katy. Don't you recollect?"

"A tumble? Oh, yes—out of the swing," said Katy, as it all came slowly back to her. "Did the rope break, Aunt Izzie? I can't remember about it."

"No, Katy, not the rope. The staple drew out of the roof. It was a cracked one, and not safe. Don't you recollect my telling you not to swing to-day? Did you forget?"

"No, Aunt Izzie—I didn't forget. I——" but here Katy broke down. She closed her eyes, and big tears rolled from under the lids.

"Don't cry," whispered Clover, crying herself; "please don't. Aunt Izzie isn't going to scold you." But Katy was too weak and shaken not to cry.

"I think I'd like to go upstairs and lie on the bed," she said. But when she tried to get off the sofa everything swam before her, and she fell back again on the pillow.

"Why, I can't stand up!" she gasped, looking very much frightened.

"I'm afraid you've given yourself a sprain somewhere," said Aunt Izzie, who looked rather frightened herself. "You'd better lie still a while, dear, before you try to move. Ah, here's the doctor! well, I *am* glad." And she went forward to meet him. It wasn't Papa, but Dr. Alsop, who lived quite near them.

"I am so relieved that you could come," Aunt Izzie said. "My brother has gone out of town, not to return till to-morrow, and one of the little girls has had a bad fall."

Dr. Alsop sat down beside the sofa and counted Katy's pulse. Then he began feeling all over her.

"Can you move this leg?" he asked.

Katy gave a feeble kick.

"And this?"

The kick was a good deal more feeble.

"Did that hurt you?" asked Dr. Alsop, seeing a look of pain on her face.

"Yes, a little," replied Katy, trying hard not to cry.

"In your back, eh? Was the pain high up or low down?" and the doctor punched Katy's spine for some minutes, making her squirm uneasily.

"I'm afraid she's done some mischief," he said, at last, "but it is impossible to tell yet exactly what. It may only be a twist or a slight sprain," he added, seeing the look of terror on Katy's face. "You'd better get her upstairs and undress her as soon as you can, Miss Carr. I'll leave a prescription to rub her with." And Dr. Alsop took out a bit of paper and began to write.

"Oh, must I go to bed?" said Katy. "How long will I have to stay there, doctor?"

"That depends on how fast you get well," replied the doctor; "not long, I hope. Perhaps only a few days."

"A few days!" repeated Katy in a despairing tone.

After the doctor was gone, Aunt Izzie and Debby lifted Katy and carried her slowly upstairs. It was not easy, for every motion hurt her, and the sense of being helpless hurt most of all. She couldn't help crying after she was undressed and put into bed. It all seemed so dreadful and strange. If only Papa was here, she thought. But Dr. Carr had gone into the country to see somebody who was very sick, and couldn't possibly be back till to-morrow.

Such a long, long afternoon as that was! Aunt Izzie sent up some dinner, but Katy couldn't eat. Her lips were parched and her head ached violently. The sun began to pour in; the room grew warm. Flies buzzed in the window and tormented her by lighting on her face. Little prickles of pain ran up and down her back. She lay with her eyes shut, because it hurt to keep them open, and all sorts of uneasy thoughts went rushing through her mind.

"Perhaps, if my back is really sprained, I shall have to lie here as much as a week," she said to herself. "Oh, dear, dear! I *can't*. The vacation is only eight weeks, and I was going to do such lovely things! How can people be so patient as Cousin Helen when they have to lie still? Won't she be sorry when she hears! Was it really yesterday that she went away? It seems a year. If only I hadn't got into that nasty old swing!" And then Katy began to imagine how it would have been if she *hadn't*, and how she and Clover had meant to go to Paradise that afternoon. They might have been there under the cool trees now. As these thoughts ran through her mind, her head grew hotter and her position in the bed more uncomfortable.

Suddenly she became conscious that the glaring light from the window was shaded, and that the wind seemed to be blowing freshly over her. She opened her heavy eyes. The blinds were shut, and there beside the bed sat little Elsie, fanning her with a palm-leaf fan.

"Did I wake you up, Katy?" she asked in a timid voice.

Katy looked at her with startled, amazed eyes.

"Don't be frightened," said Elsie, "I won't disturb you. Johnny and me are *so* sorry you're sick," and her little lips trembled. "But we mean to keep real quiet, and never bang the nursery door, or make noises on the stairs, till you're all well again. And I've brought you something real nice. Some of it's from John, and some from me. It's because you got tumbled out of the swing. See——" and Elsie pointed triumphantly to a chair, which she had pulled up close to the bed, and on which were solemnly set forth: 1st, A pewter tea-set; 2nd, A box with a glass lid, on which flowers were painted; 3rd, A jointed doll; 4th, A transparent slate; and lastly, two new lead pencils!

"They're all yours—yours to keep," said generous little Elsie. "You can have Pikery, too, if you want. Only he's pretty big, and I'm afraid he'd be lonely without me. Don't you like the fings, Katy? They're real pretty!"

It seemed to Katy as if the hottest sort of a coal of fire was burning into the top of her head as she looked at the treasures on the chair, and then at Elsie's face all lighted up with affectionate self-sacrifice. She tried to speak, but began to cry instead, which frightened Elsie very much.

"Does it hurt you so bad?" she asked, crying too from sympathy.

"Oh, no! it isn't *that*," sobbed Katy, "but I was so cross to you this morning Elsie, and pushed you. Oh, please forgive me, please do!"

96

"Why, it's got well," said Elsie, surprised. "Aunt Izzie put a fing out of a bottle on it, and the bump all went away. Shall I go and ask her to put some on you too?— I will." And she ran towards the door.

"Oh, no!" cried Katy, "don't go away, Elsie. Come here and kiss me, instead."

Elsie turned, as if doubtful whether this invitation could be meant for her. Katy held out her arms. Elsie ran right into them, and the big sister and the little exchanged an embrace which seemed to bring their hearts closer together than they had ever been before.

"You're the most *precious* little darling," murmured Katy, clasping Elsie tight. "I've been real horrid to you, Elsie. But I'll never be again. You shall play with me and Clover and Cecy just as much as you like, and write notes in all the post-offices, and everything else."

"Oh, goody, goody!" cried Elsie, executing little skips of transport. "How sweet you are, Katy! I mean to love you next best to Cousin Helen and Papa! And"—racking her brains for some way of repaying this wonderful kindness—"I'll tell you the secret, if you want me to so *very* much. I guess Cousin Helen would let me."

"No," said Katy; "never mind about the secret. I don't want you to tell it to me. Sit down by the bed and fan me some more instead."

"No!" persisted Elsie, who, now that she had made up her mind to part with the treasured secret, could not bear to be stopped. "Cousin Helen gave me a half-dollar, and told me to give it to Debby, and tell her she was much obliged to her making such nice things to eat. And I did. And Debby was real pleased. And I wrote Cousin Helen a letter, and told her that Debby liked the half-dollar. That's the secret! Isn't it a nice one? Only you mustn't tell anybody about it, ever—just as long as you live."

"No!" said Katy, smiling faintly, "I won't."

All the rest of the afternoon Elsie sat beside the bed with her palm-leaf fan, keeping off the flies and "shueing" away the other children when they peeped in at the door.

"Do you really like to have me here?" she asked more than once, and smiled, oh *so* triumphantly, when Katy said "Yes!" But though Katy said "Yes," I am afraid it was only half the truth, for the sight of the dear little forgiving girl whom she had treated unkindly gave her more pain than pleasure.

"I'll be *so* good to her when I get well," she thought to herself, tossing uneasily to and fro.

Aunt Izzie slept in her room that night. Katy was feverish. When morning came and Dr. Carr returned, he found her in a good deal of pain, hot and restless, with wide-open anxious eyes.

"Papa!" she cried the first thing, "must I lie here as much as a week?"

"My darling, I'm afraid you must," replied her father, who looked worried and very grave.

"Dear, dear!" sobbed Katy, "how can I bear it?"

CHAPTER NINE

Dismal Days

IF ANYBODY had told Katy that first afternoon that at the end of a week she would still be in bed and in pain, and with no time fixed for getting up, I think it would have almost killed her. She was so restless and eager, that to lie still seemed one of the hardest things in the world. But to lie still and have her back ache all the time was worse yet.

Day after day she asked Papa with quivering lip: "Mayn't I get up and go downstairs this morning?" And when he shook his head, the lip would quiver more and tears would come. But if she tried to get up it hurt her so much that, in spite of herself, she was glad to sink back again on the soft pillows and mattress, which felt so comfortable to her poor bones.

Then there came a time when Katy didn't even ask to be allowed to get up. A time when sharp, dreadful pain, such as she never imagined before, took hold of her. When days and nights got all confused and tangled up together, and Aunt Izzie never seemed to go to bed. A time when Papa was constantly in her room. When other doctors

99

came and stood over her, and punched and felt her back, and talked to each other in low whispers. It was all like a long, bad dream, from which she couldn't wake up, though she tried ever so hard. Now and then she would rouse a little, and catch the sound of voices, or be aware that Clover or Elsie stood at the door crying softly; or that Aunt Izzie, in creaking slippers, was going about the room on tiptoe. Then all these things would slip away again, and she would drop off into a dark place, where there was nothing but pain, and sleep, which made her forget pain, and so seemed the best thing in the world.

We will hurry over this time, for it is hard to think of our bright Katy in such a sad plight. By-and-by the pain grew less and the sleep quieter. Then, the pain became easier still, Katy woke up as it were; began to take notice of what was going on about her; to put questions.

"How long have I been sick?" she asked, one morning.

"It is four weeks, yesterday," replied Papa.

"Four weeks!" said Katy. "Why, I didn't know it was so long as that. Was I very sick, Papa?"

"Very, dear. But you are a great deal better now."

"How did I hurt myself when I tumbled out of the swing?" asked Katy, who was in an unusually wakeful mood.

"I don't believe I could make you understand, dear."

"But try, Papa!"

"Well did you know that you had a long bone down your back called a spine?"

"I thought that was a disease," said Katy; "Clover said that Cousin Helen had the spine."

"No—the spine is a bone. It is made up of a row of smaller bones—or knobs—and in the middle of it is a sort of rope of nerves called the spinal cord. Nerves, you know, are the things we feel with. Well, this spinal cord is rolled up for safe keeping in a soft wrapping called membrane. When you fell out of the swing you struck against one of these knobs and bruised the membrane inside, and the nerve inflamed and gave you a fever in the back. Do you see?"

"A little," said Katy, not quite understanding, but too tired to question further. After she had rested awhile, she said; "Is the fever well now, Papa? Can I get up again and go downstairs right away?"

"Not right away, I'm afraid," said Dr. Carr, trying to speak cheerfully.

Katy didn't ask any more questions then. Another week passed, and another. The pain was almost gone. It only came back now and then for a few minutes. She could sleep now, and eat, and be raised in bed without feeling giddy. But still the once active limbs hung heavy and lifeless, and she was not able to walk, or even stand alone.

"My legs feel so queer," she said, one morning; "they are just like the Prince's legs which were turned to black marble in the *Arabian Nights*. What do you suppose is the reason, Papa? Won't they feel natural soon?"

"Not soon," answered Dr. Carr. Then he said to himself: "Poor child! she had better know the truth." So he went on, aloud: "I am afraid, my darling, that you must make up your mind to stay in bed a long time."

"How long?" said Katy, looking frightened; "a month more?"

"I can't tell exactly how long," answered her father. "The doctors think, as I do, that the injury to your spine is one which you will outgrow by-and-by, because you are so young and strong. But it may take a good while to do it. It may be that you will have to lie here for months, or it may be more. The only cure for such a hurt is time and patience. It is hard, darling"—for Katy began to sob wildly —"but you have hope to help you along. Think of poor Cousin Helen, bearing all these years without hope!"

"Oh, Papa!" gasped Katy, between her sobs, "doesn't it seem dreadful that just getting into the swing for a few minutes should do so much harm? Such a little thing as that!"

101

"Yes, such a little thing!" repeated Dr. Carr, sadly. "And it was only a little thing too, forgetting Aunt Izzie's order about the swing. Just for the want of the small 'horse-shoe nail' of obedience, Katy."

Years afterwards Katy told somebody that the six longest weeks of her life were those which followed this conversation with Papa. Now that she knew there was no chance of getting well at once, the days dragged dreadfully.

Each seemed duller and dismaler than the day before. She lost heart about herself, and took no interest in anything. Aunt Izzie brought her books, but she didn't want to read, or to sew. Nothing amused her. Clover and Cecy would come to sit with her, but hearing them tell about their plays, and the things they had been doing, made her cry so miserably that Aunt Izzie wouldn't let them come often. They were very sorry for Katy, but the room was so gloomy and Katy so cross that they didn't mind much not being allowed to see her. In those days Katy made Aunt Izzie keep the blinds shut tight, and she lay in the dark, thinking how miserable she was, and how wretched all the rest of her life was going to be. Everybody was very kind and patient with her, but she was too selfishly miserable to notice it. Aunt Izzie ran up and downstairs, and was on her feet all day, trying to get something which would please her, but Katy hardly said, "Thank you," and never saw how tired Aunt Izzie looked. So long as she was forced to stay in bed Katy could not be grateful for anything that was done for her.

But doleful as the days were, they were not so bad as the nights, when, after Aunt Izzie was asleep, Katy would lie wide awake, and have long, hopeless fits of crying. At these times she would think of all the plans she had made for doing beautiful things when she was grown up. "And now I shall never do any of them," she would say to herself; "only just lie here. Papa says I might get well by-and-by, but I shan't, I know I shan't. And even if I

102

do, I shall have wasted all these years; and the others will grow up and get ahead of me, and I shan't be a comfort to them or to anybody else. Oh, dear! oh, dear! how dreadful it is! "

The first thing which broke in upon this sad state of affairs was a letter from Cousin Helen, which Papa brought one morning and handed to Aunt Izzie.

"Helen tells me she is going home this week," said Aunt Izzie from the window, where she had gone to read the letter. "Well, I'm sorry, but I think she is quite right not to stop. It's just as she says: one invalid at a time *is* enough in a house. I'm sure I have my hands full with Katy."

"Oh, Aunt Izzie!" cried Katy, "is Cousin Helen coming this way when she goes home? Oh! do make her stop. If it's just for one day, do ask her! I want to see her so much! I can't tell you how much! Won't you? Please! Please, dear Papa."

She was almost crying with eagerness.

"Why, yes, darling, if you wish it so much," said Dr. Carr. "It will cost Aunt Izzie some trouble, but she's so kind that I'm sure she'll manage it if it is to give you so much pleasure. Can't you, Izzie?" And he looked eagerly at his sister.

"Of course I will!" said Aunt Izzie, heartily. Katy was so glad, that, for the first time in her life, she threw her arms round Aunt Izzie's neck and kissed her.

"Thank you, dear Auntie!" she said.

Aunt Izzie looked as pleased as could be. She had a warm heart hidden under her fidgety ways—only Katy had never been sick before to find it out.

For the next week Katy was feverish with expectation. At last Cousin Helen came. This time Katy was not on the steps to welcome her, but after a little while Papa brought Cousin Helen in his arms, and sat her in a big chair beside the bed.

"How dark it is," she said, after they had kissed each other and talked for a minute or two; "I can't see your face at all. Would it hurt your eyes to have a little more light?"

"Oh, no," answered Katy. "It don't hurt my eyes, only I hate to have the sun come in. It makes me feel worse, somehow."

"Push the blind open a little bit then, Clover"; and Clover did so.

"Now I can see," said Cousin Helen.

It was a forlorn-looking child enough which she saw lying before her. Katy's face had grown thin, and her eyes had red circles about them from continual crying. Her hair had been brushed twice that morning by Aunt Izzie, but Katy had run her fingers impatiently through it, till it stood out above her head like a frowsy bush. She wore a calico dressing-gown, which, though clean, was particularly ugly in pattern; and the room, for all its tidiness, had a dismal look, with the chairs set up against the wall, and a row of medicine-bottles on the chimney-piece.

"Isn't it horrid?" sighed Katy, as Cousin Helen looked around. "Everything's horrid. But I don't mind so much now that you've come. Oh, Cousin Helen, I've had such a dreadful, *dreadful* time!"

"I know," said her cousin, pityingly. "I've heard all about it, Katy, and I'm very sorry for you! It is a hard trial, my poor darling."

"But how do *you* do it?" cried Katy. "How do you manage to be so sweet and beautiful and patient when you're feeling badly all the time, and can't do anything, or walk, or stand?"—her voice was lost in sobs.

Cousin Helen didn't say anything for a little while. She just sat and stroked Katy's hand.

"Katy," she said at last, "has Papa told you that he thinks you are going to get well by-and-by?"

104

"Yes," replied Katy, "he did say so. But perhaps it won't be for a long, long time. And I want to do so many things. And now I can't do anything at all!"

"What sort of things?"

"Study, and help people, and become famous. And I wanted to teach the children. Mamma said I must take care of them, and I meant to. And now I can't go to school or learn anything myself. And if ever I do get well, the children will be almost grown up and they won't need me."

"But why must you wait till you get well?" asked Cousin Helen, smiling.

"Why, Cousin Helen, what can I do lying here in bed?"

"A good deal. Shall I tell you Katy, what it seems to me that I should say to myself if I were in your place?"

"Yes, please," replied Katy, wonderingly.

"I should say this: 'Now, Katy Carr, you wanted to go to school, and learn to be wise and useful, and here's a chance for you. God is going to let you go to *His* school —where He teaches all sorts of beautiful things to people. Perhaps He will only keep you for one term, or perhaps it may be for three or four; but whichever it is, you must make the very most of the chance, because He gives it to you Himself.'"

"But what is the school?" asked Katy. "I don't know what you mean."

"It is called the School of Pain," replied Cousin Helen, with her sweetest smile. "And the place where the lessons are to be learned is this room of yours. The rules of the school are pretty hard, but the good scholars, who keep them best, find out after a while how right and kind they are. And the lessons aren't easy, either, but the more you study the more interesting they become."

"What are the lessons?" asked Katy, getting interested, and beginning to feel as if Cousin Helen were telling her a story.

"Well, there's the lesson of Patience. That's one of the hardest studies. You can't learn much of it at a time, but every bit you get by heart makes the next bit easier. And there's the lesson of Cheerfulness. And the lesson of Making the Best of Things."

"Sometimes there isn't anything to make the best of," remarked Katy, dolefully.

"Yes, there is, always! Everything in the world has two handles. Didn't you know that? One is a smooth handle. If you take hold of it the thing comes up lightly and easily, but if you seize the rough handle it hurts your hand and the thing is hard to lift. Some people always manage to get hold of the wrong handle."

"Is Aunt Izzie a 'thing'?" asked Katy. Cousin Helen was glad to hear her laugh.

"Yes- -Aunt Izzie is a *thing*—and she has a nice pleasant handle too, if you just try to find it. And the children are 'things' also, in one sense. All their handles are different. You know human beings aren't made just alike, like red flower-pots. We have to feel and guess before we can make out just how other people go, and how we ought to take hold of them. It is very interesting— I advise you to try it. And while you are trying you will learn all sorts of things which will help you to help others."

"If I only could!" sighed Katy. "Are there any other studies in the school, Cousin Helen?"

"Yes, there's the lesson of Hopefulness. That class has ever so many teachers. The Sun is one. He sits outside the window all day waiting for a chance to slip in and get at his pupil. He's a first-rate teacher too. I wouldn't shut him out, if I were you.

"Every morning, the first thing when I woke up, I would say to myself: 'I am going to get well, so Papa thinks. Perhaps it may be to-morrow. So, in case this *should* be the last day of my sickness, let me spend it *beautifully*, and make my sickroom so pleasant that everybody will like to remember it.

"Then, there is one more lesson, Katy—the lesson of

Neatness. Schoolrooms must be kept in order, you know. A sick person ought to be as fresh and dainty as a rose."

"But it is such a fuss," pleaded Katy. "I don't believe you've any idea what a bother it is to always be nice and in order. You never were careless like me, Cousin Helen; you were born neat."

"Oh, was I?" said her cousin. "Well, Katy, we won't dispute that point, but I'll tell you a story, if you like, about a girl I once knew, who *wasn't* born neat."

"Oh, do!" cried Katy, enchanted. Cousin Helen had done her good already. She looked brighter and less listless than for days.

"This girl was quite young," continued Cousin Helen; "she was strong and active, and liked to run and climb and ride, and do all sorts of jolly things. One day something happened—an accident—and they told her that all the rest of her life she had got to lie on her back and suffer pain, and never walk any more, or do any of the things she enjoyed most."

"Just like you and me!" whispered Katy, squeezing Cousin Helen's hand.

"Something like me; but not so much like you, because you know, we hope *you* are going to get well one of these days. The girl didn't mind it so much when they first told her, for she was so ill that she felt sure she should die. But when she got better, and began to think of the long life which lay before her, that was worse than ever the pain had been. She was so wretched that she didn't care what became of anything, or how anything looked. She had no Aunt Izzie to look after things, so her room soon got into a dreadful state. It was full of dust and confusion, and dirty spoons and phials of physic. She kept the blinds shut, and let her hair tangle every way, and altogether was a dismal spectacle.

"This girl had a dear old father," went on Cousin Helen, "who used to come every day and sit beside her bed. One morning he said to her:

107

" 'My daughter, I'm afraid you've got to live in this room for a long time. Now there's one thing I want you to do for my sake.'

" 'What is that?' she asked, surprised to hear there was anything left which she could *do* for anybody.

" 'I want you to turn out all these physic bottles, and make your room pleasant and pretty for *me* to come and sit in. You see, I shall spend a good deal of my time here. Now I don't like dust and darkness. I like to see flowers on the table and sun shine in at the window. Will you do this to please me?'

" 'Yes,' said the girl, but she gave a sigh, and I am afraid she felt as if it were going to be a dreadful trouble.

" 'Then, another thing,' continued her father, 'I want *you* to look pretty. Can't night-gowns and wrappers be trimmed and made becoming just as much as dresses? A sick woman who isn't neat is a disagreeable object. Do, to please me, send for something pretty, and let me see you looking nice again. I can't bear to have my Helen turn into a slattern.' "

"Helen! " exclaimed Katy, with wide-open eyes, "was it *you*?"

"Yes," said her cousin, smiling. "It was I, though I didn't mean to let the name slip out so soon. So, after my father was gone away, I sent for a looking-glass. Such a sight, Katy! My hair was a perfect mouse's nest, and I had frowned so much that my forehead was all criss-crossed with lines of pain, till it looked like an old woman's."

Katy stared at Cousin Helen's smooth brow and glossy hair.

"I can't believe it," she said; "your hair never could be rough."

"Yes it was—a great deal worse than yours looks now. But that peep in the glass did me good. I began to think how selfishly I was behaving, and to desire to do better. And after that, when the pain came on, I used to lie and

108

keep my forehead smooth with my fingers, and try not to let my face show what I was enduring. So by-and-by the wrinkles wore away, and, though I am a good deal older now, they have never come back.

"It was a great deal of trouble at first to have to think and plan to keep my room and myself looking nice. But after a while it grew to be a habit, and then it became easy. And the pleasure it gave my dear father repaid for all. He had been proud of his active, healthy girl, but I think she was never such a comfort to him as his sick one lying there in the bed. My room was his favourite sitting-place, and he spent so much time there that now the room and everything in it makes me think of him."

There were tears in Cousin Helen's eyes as she ceased speaking.

But Katy looked bright and eager. It seemed somehow to be a help, as well as a great surprise, that ever there should have been a time when Cousin Helen was less perfect than she was now.

"Do you really think I could do so too?" she asked.

"Do what? Comb your hair?" Cousin Helen was smiling now.

"Oh no! Be nice and sweet and patient, and a comfort to people. You know what I mean."

"I am sure you can, if you try."

"But what would you do first?" asked Katy; who, now that her mind had grasped a new idea, was eager to begin.

"Well—first I would open the blinds, and make the room look a little less dismal. Are you taking all those medicines in the bottles now?"

"No—only that big one with the blue label."

"Then you might ask Aunt Izzie to take away the others. And I'd get Clover to pick a bunch of fresh flowers every day for your table. By the day, I don't see the little white vase."

"No; it got broken the very day after you went away; the day I fell out of the swing," said Katy, sorrowfully.

"Never mind, pet, don't look so doleful. I know the tree those vases grow upon, and you shall have another. Then after the room is made pleasant, I would have all my lesson-books fetched up, if I were you, and I would study a couple of hours every morning."

"Oh!" cried Katy, making a wry face at the idea.

Cousin Helen smiled. "I know," said she, "it sounds like dull work, learning geography and doing sums up here all by yourself. But I think if you make the effort you'll be glad by-and-by. You won't lose so much ground, you see—won't slip back quite so far in your education. And then, studying will be like working at a garden where things don't grow easily. Every flower you raise will be a sort of triumph, and you will value it twice as much as a common flower which has cost no trouble."

"Well," said Katy, rather forlornly, "I'll try. But it won't be a bit nice studying without anybody to study with me. Is there anything else, Cousin Helen?"

Just then the door creaked, and Elsie timidly put her head into the room.

"Oh, Elsie, run away!" cried Katy. "Cousin Helen and I are talking. Don't come just now."

Katy didn't speak unkindly, but Elsie's face fell, and she looked disappointed. She said nothing, however, but shut the door and stole away.

Cousin Helen watched this little scene without speaking. For a few minutes after Elsie was gone she seemed to be thinking.

"Katy," she said, at last, "you were saying just now that one of the things you were sorry about was that while you were ill you could be of no use to the children. Do you know, I don't think you have that reason for being sorry."

"Why not?" said Katy, astonished.

"Because you *can* be of use. It seems to me that you have more of a chance with the children now than you ever could have had when you were well and flying about

110

as you used. You might do almost anything you liked with them."

"I can't think what you mean," said Katy, sadly. "Why, Cousin Helen, half the time I don't even know where they are or what they are doing. And I can't get up and go after them, you know."

"But you can make your room such a delightful place that they will want to come to you! Don't you see, a sick person has one splendid chance—she is always on hand. Everybody who wants her knows just where to go. If people love her she gets naturally to be the heart of the house. Once make the little ones feel that your room is the place of all the others to come to when they are tired, or happy, or grieved, or sorry about anything, and that the Katy who lives there is sure to give them a loving reception—and the battle is won. For you know we never do people good by lecturing; only by living their lives with them, and helping a little here and a little there to make them better. And when one's own life is laid aside for a while, as yours is now, that is the very time to take up other people's lives, as we can't do when we are scurrying and bustling over our own affairs. But I didn't mean to preach a sermon. I'm afraid you're tired."

"No, I'm not a bit," said Katy, holding Cousin Helen's hand tight in hers; "you can't think how much better I feel. Oh, Cousin Helen, I *will* try!"

"It won't be easy," replied her cousin. "There will be days when your head aches, and you feel cross and fretted, and don't want to think of any one but yourself. And there'll be other days when Clover and the rest will come in, as Elsie did just now, and you will be doing something else, and will feel as if their coming was a bother. But you must recollect that every time you forget and are impatient and selfish, you chill them and drive them farther away. They are loving little things, and are so sorry for you now that nothing you do makes them angry. But by-and-by they will get used to having you sick, and if you

111

haven't won them as friends they will grow away from you as they get older."

Just then Dr. Carr came in.

"Oh, papa! you haven't come to take Cousin Helen, have you?" cried Katy.

"Indeed I have," said her father. "I think the big invalid and the little invalid have talked quite long enough. Cousin Helen looks tired."

For a minute Katy felt just like crying. But she choked back the tears. "My first lesson in patience," she said to herself, and managed to give a faint, watery smile as Papa looked at her.

"That's right, dear," whispered Cousin Helen, as she bent forward to kiss her. "And one last word, Katy. In this school, to which you and I belong, there is one great comfort, and that is that the Teacher is always at hand. He never goes away. If things puzzle us, there He is close by, ready to explain and make all easy. Try to think of this, darling, and don't be afraid to ask Him for help if the lesson seems too hard."

Katy had a strange dream that night. She thought she was trying to study a lesson out of a book which wouldn't come quite open. She could just see a little bit of what was inside, but it was in a language which she did not understand. She tried in vain: not a word could she read; and yet for all that it looked so interesting that she longed to go on.

"Oh, if somebody would only help us!" she cried, impatiently.

Suddenly a hand came over her shoulder and took hold of the book.

It opened at once, and showed the whole page. And then the forefinger of the hand began to point to line after line, and as it moved the words became plain, and Katy could read them easily. She looked up. There, stooping over her, was a great beautiful Face. The eyes met hers. The lips smiled.

112

"Why didn't you ask Me before, little scholar?" said a voice.

"Why, it is *You*, just as Cousin Helen told me!" cried Katy.

She must have spoken in her sleep, for Aunt Izzie half woke up, and said:

"What is it? Do you want anything?"

The dream broke, and Katy roused, to find herself in bed, with the first sunbeams struggling in at the window, and Aunt Izzie raised on her elbow looking at her with a sort of sleepy wonder.

CHAPTER TEN

St. Nicholas and St. Valentine

"WHAT are the children all doing to-day?" said Katy, laying down *Norway and the Norwegians*, which she was reading for the fourth time; "I haven't seen them since breakfast."

Aunt Izzie, who was sewing on the other side of the room, looked up from her work.

"I don't know," she said; "they're over at Cecy's, or somewhere. They'll be back before long, I guess."

Her voice sounded a little odd and mysterious, but Katy didn't notice it.

"I thought of such a nice plan yesterday," she went on. "That was, that all of them should hang their stockings up here to-morrow night instead of the nursery. Then I could see them open their presents, you know. Mayn't they, Aunt Izzie? It would be real fun."

"I don't believe there will be any objection," replied her aunt. She looked as if she were trying not to laugh. Katy wondered what *was* the matter with her.

It was more than two months now since Cousin Helen went away, and winter had fairly come. Snow was falling out-doors. Katy could see the thick flakes go whirling past the window, but the sight did not chill her. It only made the room look warmer and more cosy. It was a pleasant room now. There was a bright fire in the grate. Everything was neat and orderly, the air was sweet with mignonette, from a little glass of flowers which stood on the table, and

114

the Katy who lay in bed was a very different-looking Katy from the forlorn girl of the last chapter.

Cousin Helen's visit, though it lasted only one day, did great good. Not that Katy grew perfect all at once. None of us do that, even in books. But it is everything to be started in the right path. Katy's feet were on it now; and though she often stumbled and slipped, and often sat down discouraged, she kept on pretty steadily, in spite of bad days, which made her say to herself that she was not getting forward at all.

These bad days, when everything seemed hard, and she herself was cross and fretful, and drove the children out of the room, cost Katy many bitter tears. But after them she would pick herself up, and try again, and harder. And I think that, in spite of drawbacks, the little scholar, on the whole, was learning her lesson pretty well.

Cousin Helen was a great comfort all this time. She never forgot Katy. Nearly every week some little thing came from her. Sometimes it was a pencil note written from her sofa. Sometimes it was an interesting book, or a new magazine, or some pretty little thing for the room. The crimson wrapper which Katy wore was one of her presents, so were the bright chromos of autumn leaves which hung on the walls, the little stand for the books—all sorts of things. Katy loved to look about her as she lay. All the room seemed full of Cousin Helen and her kindness.

"I wish I had something pretty to put into everybody's stocking," she went on, wistfully; "but I've only got the muffatees for Papa, and these reins for Phil." She took them from under her pillow as she spoke--gay worsted affairs, with bells sewed on here and there. She had knitted them herself, a very little bit at a time.

"There's my pink sash," she said, suddenly, "I might give that to Clover. I only wore it once, you know, and I don't *think* I got any spots on it. Would you please fetch it and let me see, Aunt Izzie? It's in the top drawer."

Aunt Izzie brought the sash. It proved to be quite fresh, and they both decided that it would do nicely for Clover.

"You know I shan't want sashes for ever so long," said Katy, in a rather sad tone. "And this is a beauty."

When she spoke next her voice was bright again.

"I wish I had something real nice for Elsie. Do you know, Aunt Izzie—I think that Elsie is the dearest little girl that ever was."

"I'm glad you've found it out," said Aunt Izzie, who had always been specially fond of Elsie.

"What she wants most of all is a writing-desk," continued Katy. "And Johnny wants a sled. But, oh, dear! Those are such big things. And I've only got two dollars and a quarter."

Aunt Izzie marched out of the room without saying anything. When she came back she had something folded up in her hand.

"I didn't know what to give you for Christmas, Katy," she said, "because Helen sends you such a lot of things that there don't seem to be anything you haven't already. So I thought I'd give you this and let you choose for yourself. But if you've set your heart on getting presents for the children perhaps you'd rather have it now." So saying, Aunt Izzie laid on the bed a crisp, new five-dollar bill!

"How good you are!" cried Katy, flushed with pleasure. And indeed Aunt Izzie *did* seem to have grown wonderfully good of late. Perhaps Katy had got hold of her smooth handle!

Being now in possession of seven dollars and a quarter, Katy could afford to be gorgeously generous. She gave Aunt Izzie an exact description of the desk she wanted.

"It's no matter about its being very big," said Katy; "but it must have a blue velvet lining, and an inkstand with a silver top. And please buy some little sheets of paper and envelopes and a pen-handle—the prettiest you can find. Oh! and there must be a lock and key. Don't forget that, Aunt Izzie."

"No, I won't. What else?"

"I'd like the sled to be green," went on Katy, "and to have a nice name. Sky-Scraper would be nice if there was one. Johnny saw a sled once called Sky-Scraper, and she said it was splendid. And if there's money enough left, Aunty, won't you buy me a real nice book for Dorry, and another for Cecy, and a silver thimble for Mary? Her old one is full of holes. Oh! and some candy. And something for Debby and Bridget—some little thing, you know. I think that's all!"

Was ever seven dollars and a quarter expected to do so much? Aunt Izzie must have been a witch indeed to make it hold out. But she did, and next day all the precious bundles came home. How Katy enjoyed untying the strings!

Everything was exactly right.

"There wasn't any Sky-Scraper," said Aunt Izzie, "so I got Snow-Skimmer instead."

"It's beautiful, and I like it just as well," said Katy, contentedly.

"Oh, hide them, hide them!" she cried, with sudden terror; "somebody's coming." But the somebody was only Papa, who put his head into the room as Aunt Izzie, laden with bundles, scuttled across the hall.

Katy was glad to catch him alone. She had a little private secret to talk over with him. It was about Aunt Izzie, for whom she, as yet, had no present.

"I thought perhaps you'd get me a book like that one of Cousin Helen's which Aunt Izzie liked so much," she said. "I don't recollect the name exactly. It was something about a shadow. But I've spent all my money."

"Never mind about that," said Dr. Carr. "We'll make that right. *The Shadow of the Cross*—was that it? I'll buy it this afternoon."

"Oh, thank you, Papa! And please get a brown cover, if you can, because Cousin Helen's was brown. And you won't let Aunt Izzie know, will you? Be careful, Papa!"

"I'll swallow the book first, brown cover and all," said Papa, making a funny face. He was pleased to see Katy so interested about anything again.

These delightful secrets took up so much of her thoughts that Katy scarcely found time to wonder at

117

the absence of the children, who generally haunted her room, but who for three days back had hardly been seen. However, after supper they all came up in a body, looking very merry, and as if they had been having a good time somewhere.

"You don't know what we've been doing," began Philly.

"Hush, Phil!" said Clover, in a warning voice. Then she divided the stockings which she held in her hand. And everybody proceeded to hang them up.

Dorry hung his on one side of the fireplace, and John hers exactly opposite. Clover and Phil suspended theirs side by side, on two handles of the bureau.

"I'm going to put mine here, close to Katy, so that she can see it the first thing in the morning," said Elsie, pinning hers to the bed-post.

Then they all sat down round the fire to write their wishes on bits of paper, and see whether they would burn, or fly up the chimney. If they did the latter, it was a sign that Santa Claus had them safe, and would bring the things wished for.

John wished for a sled and a doll's tea-set, and the continuation of the *Swiss Family Robinson*. Dorry's list ran thus:

> A plum cake,
> A new Bibel,
> *Harry and Lucy*,
> A kellidescope,
> Everything else Santa Claus likes.

When they had written these lists they threw them into the fire. The fire gave a flicker just then, and the papers vanished. Nobody saw exactly how. John thought they flew up the chimney, but Dorry said they didn't.

Phil dropped his piece in very solemnly. It flamed for a minute, then sank into ashes.

"There, you won't get it, whatever it was!" said Dorry. "What did you write, Phil?"

"Nofing," said Phil, "only just Philly Carr."

The children shouted.

"I wrote 'a writing-desk' on mine," remarked Elsie, sorrowfully, "but it all burned up."

Katy chuckled when she heard this.

And now Clover produced her list. She read aloud:

> *"Strive and Thrive,*
> A pair of kid gloves,
> A muff,
> A good temper! "

Then she dropped it into the fire. Behold, it flew straight up the chimney.

"How queer!" said Katy; "none of the rest of them did that."

The truth was, that Clover, who was a canny little mortal, had slipped across the room and opened the door just before putting her wishes in. This, of course, made a draught, and sent the paper right upward.

Pretty soon Aunt Izzie came in and swept them all off to bed.

"I know how it will be in the morning," she said, "you'll all be up and racing about as soon as it is light. So you must get your sleep now, if ever."

After they had gone, Katy recollected that nobody had offered to hang a stocking up for her. She felt a little hurt when she thought of it. "But I suppose they forgot," she said to herself.

A little later Papa and Aunt Izzie came in, and they filled the stockings. It was great fun. Each was brought to Katy as she lay in bed, that she might arrange it as she liked.

The toes were stuffed with candy and oranges. Then came the parcels, all shapes and sizes, tied in white paper with ribbons, and labelled.

"What's that?" asked Dr. Carr, as Aunt Izzie rammed a long, narrow package into Clover's stocking.

"A nail-brush," answered Aunt Izzie; "Clover needed a new one."

How Papa and Katy laughed! "I don't believe Santa Claus ever had such a thing before," said Dr. Carr.

"He's a very dirty old gentleman, then," observed Aunt Izzie grimly.

The desk and sled were too big to go into any stocking, so they were wrapped in paper and hung beneath the other things. It was ten o'clock before all was done, and Papa and Aunt Izzie went away. Katy lay a long time watching the queer shapes of the stocking-legs as they dangled in the fire-light. Then she fell asleep.

It seemed only a minute before something touched her and woke her up. Behold, it was day-time, and there was Philly in his night-gown climbing up on the bed to kiss her. The rest of the children, half dressed, were dancing about with their stockings in their hands.

"Merry Christmas! Merry Christmas!" they cried. "Oh Katy, such beautiful, *beautiful* things!"

"Oh!" shrieked Elsie, who at that moment spied her desk, "Santa Claus *did* bring it after all! Why, it's got 'from Katy' written on it! Oh, Katy, it's so sweet, and I'm *so* happy!" and Elsie hugged Katy, and sobbed for pleasure.

But what was that strange thing beside the bed? Katy stared and rubbed her eyes. It certainly had not been there when she went to sleep. How had it come?

It was a little evergreen tree planted in a red flower-pot. The pot had stripes of gilt paper stuck on it, and gilt stars and crosses, which made it look very gay. The boughs of the tree were hung with oranges and nuts and shiny red apples and pop-corn balls and strings of bright berries. There were also a number of little packages tied with blue and crimson ribbon, and altogether the tree looked so pretty that Katy gave a cry of delighted surprise.

"It's a Christmas-tree for you, because you're sick, you know!" said the children, all trying to hug her at once.

"We made it ourselves," said Dorry, hopping about on one foot. "I pasted the black stars on the pot."

"And I popped the corn," cried Philly.

"Do you like it?" asked Elsie, cuddling close to Katy. "That's my present—that one tied with a green ribbon. I wish it was nicer. Don't you want to open them right away?"

Of course Katy wanted to. All sorts of things came out of the little bundles. The children had arranged every parcel themselves. No grown person had been allowed to help in the least.

Elsie's present was a pen-wiper, with a grey flannel kitten on it. Johnnie's, a doll tea-tray of scarlet tin.

"Isn't it beau-ti-ful?" she said, admiringly.

Dorry's gift, I regret to say, was a huge red-and-yellow spider, which whirred wildly when waved at the end of it's string.

"They didn't want me to buy it," said he; "but I did. I thought it would amoose you. Does it amoose you, Katy?"

"Yes, indeed," said Katy, laughing and blinking as Dorry waved the spider to and fro before her eyes.

"You can play with it when we ain't here and you're all alone, you know," remarked Dorry, highly gratified.

"But you don't notice what the tree's standing upon," said Clover.

It was a chair, a very large and curious one, with a long cushioned back which ended in a footstool.

"That's Papa's present," said Clover; "see, it tips back so as to be just like a bed. And Papa says he thinks pretty soon you can lie on it in the window, where you can see us play."

"Does he really?" said Katy, doubtfully. It still hurt her very much to be touched or moved.

"And see what's tied to the arm of the chair," said Elsie. It was a little silver bell with "Katy" engraved on the handle.

"Cousin Helen sent it. It's for you to ring when you want anybody to come," explained Elsie.

121

More surprises. To the other arm of the chair was fastened a beautiful book. It was *The Wide, Wide World* —and there was Katy's name written on it, "from her affectionate Cecy." On it stood a great parcel of dried cherries from Mrs. Hall. Mrs. Hall had the most *delicious* dried cherries, the children thought.

"How perfectly lovely everybody is!" said Katy, with grateful tears in her eyes.

That was a pleasant Christmas. The children declared it to be the nicest they had ever had. And though Katy couldn't quite say that, she enjoyed it too, and was very happy.

It was several weeks before she was able to use the chair, but when once she became accustomed to it, it proved very comfortable. Aunt Izzie would dress her in the morning, tip the chair back till it was on a level with the bed, and then, very gently and gradually, draw her over on to it. Wheeling across the room was always painful, but sitting in the window and looking out at the clouds, the people going by, and the children playing in the snow was delightful. How delightful nobody knows, excepting those who, like Katy, have lain for six months in bed without a peep at the outside world. Every day she grew brighter and more cheerful.

"How jolly Santa Claus was this year!" she happened to say one day, when talking with Cecy. "I wish another Saint would come and pay us a visit. But I don't know any more except Cousin Helen, and she can't."

"There's St. Valentine," suggested Cecy.

"Sure enough. What a bright thought!" cried Katy clapping her hands. "Oh, Cecy, let's do something funny on Valentine's Day! Such a good idea just popped into my mind."

So the two girls put their heads together and held a long mysterious confabulation. What it was about we shall see farther on.

Valentine's Day was the next Friday. When the children came home from school on Thursday afternoon Aunt

Izzie met them, and, to their great surprise, told them that Cecy was to come to drink tea, and they must all go upstairs and be made nice.

"But Cecy comes most every day," remarked Dorry, who didn't see the connection between this fact and having his face washed.

"Yes—but to-night you are to take tea in Katy's room," said Aunt Izzie; "here are the invitations: one for each of you."

Sure enough, there was a neat little note for each, requesting the pleasure of their company at "Queen Katherine's Palace," that afternoon, at six o'clock.

This put quite a different aspect on the affair. The children scampered upstairs, and pretty soon, all nicely brushed and washed they were knocking formally at the door of the "Palace." How fine it sounded!

The room looked bright and inviting. Katy in her chair, sat close to the fire, Cecy was beside her, and there was a round table all set out with a white cloth and mugs of milk and biscuit, and strawberry jam and doughnuts. In the middle was a loaf of frosted cake. There was something on the icing which looked like pink letters, and Clover, leaning forward, read aloud, "St. Valentine."

"What's that for?" asked Dorry.

"Why you know this is St. Valentine's Eve," replied Katy. "Debby remembered it, I guess, so she put that on."

Nothing more was said about St. Valentine just then. But when the last pink letter of his name had been eaten, and the supper had been cleared away, suddenly, as the children sat by the fire, there was a loud rap at the door.

"Who can that be?" Katy said; "please see, Clover!"

So Clover opened the door. There stood Bridget, trying very hard not to laugh, and holding a letter in her hand.

"It's a note as has come for you, Miss Clover," she said.

"For me!" cried Clover, much amazed. Then she shut the door, and brought the note to the table.

"How very funny!" she exclaimed, as she looked at the envelope, which was a green and white one. There was something hard inside. Clover broke the seal. Out tumbled a small green velvet pincushion made in the shape of a clover-leaf, with a tiny stem of wire wound with green silk. Pinned to the cushion was a paper, with these verses:

> " Some people love roses well,
>   Tulips gaily dressed,
> Some love violets blue and sweet—
>   I love Clover best.

> " Though she has a modest air,
>   Though no grace she boast,
> Though no gardener call her fair,
>   I love Clover most.

> " Butterfly may pass her by,
>   He is but a rover,
> I'm a faithful, loving Bee—
>   And I stick to Clover."

This was the first valentine Clover had ever had. She was perfectly enchanted.

"Oh, who *do* you suppose sent it?" she cried.

But before anybody could answer there came another loud knock at the door, which made them all jump. Behold, Bridget again, with a second letter!

"It's for you, Miss Elsie, this time," she said, with a grin.

There was an instant rush from all the children, and the envelope was torn open in the twinkling of an eye. Inside was a little ivory seal with "Elsie" on it in old English letters, and these rhymes:

> " I know a little girl,
>   She is very dear to me,
>   She is just as sweet as honey
>   When she chooses so to be,
> And her name begins with E, and ends with E.

124

> " She has brown hair with curls,
>   And black eyes for to see
>   With teeth like tiny pearls,
>   And dimples, one, two, three,
> And her name begins with E, and ends with E.

> " Her little feet run faster
>   Than other feet can flee,
>   As she brushes quickly past, her
>   Voice hums like a bee,
> And her name begins with E, and ends with E.

> " Do you ask me why I love her?
>   Then I shall answer thee—
>   Because I can't help loving,
>   She is so sweet to me,
> This little girl whose name begins and ends with E."

"It's just like a fairy story," said Elsie, whose eyes had grown as big as saucers from surprise, while these verses were being read aloud by Cecy.

Another knock. This time there was a perfect handful of letters. Everybody had one. Katy, to her great surprise, had *two*.

"Why, what *can* this be?" she said. But when she peeped into the second one she saw Cousin Helen's handwriting, and she put it into her pocket till the valentines should be read.

Dorry's was opened first. It had the picture of a pie at the top—I ought to explain that Dorry had lately been paying a visit to the dentist.

> " Little Jack Horner
>   Sat in his corner
>   Eating his Christmas pie,
> When a sudden grimace
> Spread over his face,
>   And he began loudly to cry.

" His tender Mamma
    Heard the sound from afar,
        And hastened to comfort her child,
    ' What aileth my John? '
    She inquired in a tone
        Which belied her question mild.

" ' Oh, Mother,' he said,
    ' Every tooth in my head
        Jumps and aches and is loose, O my!
    And it hurts me to eat
    Anything that is sweet—
        So what *will* become of my pie?'

" It were vain to describe
    How he roared and he cried,
        And howled like a miniature tempest;
    Suffice it to say,
    That the very next day
        He had all his teeth pulled by a dentist!"

This valentine made the children laugh for a long time.
Johnnie's envelope held a paper doll named "Red
Riding-Hood." These were the verses:

" I send you my picture, dear Johnnie, to show
    That I'm just as alive as you,
And that you needn't cry over my fate
    Any more, as you used to do.

" The wolf didn't hurt me at all that day,
    For I kicked and fought and cried,
Till he dropped me out of his mouth, and ran
    Away in the woods to hide.

" And Grandma and I have lived ever since
    In the little brown house so small,
And churned fresh butter and made cream cheeses,
    Nor see the wolf at all.

" So cry no more for fear I am eaten,
   The naughty wolf is shot,
And if you will come to tea some evening
   You shall see for yourself I'm not."

Johnny was immensely pleased at this, for Red Riding-Hood was a great favourite of hers.

Philly had a bit of india-rubber in his letter, which was written with very black ink on a big sheet of foolscap:

" I was once a naughty man,
   And I hid beneath the bed,
To steal your india-rubbers,
   But I chewed them up instead.

" Then you called out, 'Who is there?'
   I was thrown most in a fit,
And I let the india-rubbers fall—
   All but this little bit.

" I'm sorry for my naughty ways,
   And now to make amends,
I send the chewed piece back again,
   And beg we may be friends.
                    "ROBBER."

"Just listen to mine," said Cecy, who had all along pretended to be as much surprised as anybody, and now behaved as if she could hardly wait till Philly's was finished. Then she read aloud:

" TO CECY "

"If I were a bird
And you were a bird,
   What would we do?
Why, you should be little and I would be big,
And, side by side on a cherry-tree twig,
We'd kiss with our yellow bills, and coo—
   That's what we'd do!

"If I were a fish
And you were a fish,
   What would we do?
We'd frolic, and whisk our little tails,
And play all sorts of tricks with the whales,
And call on the oysters, and order a 'stew'—
   That's what we'd do!

"If I were a bee
And you were a bee,
   What would we do?
We'd find a home in a breezy wood,
And store it with honey sweet and good.
You should feed me and I should feed you
   That's what we'd do!

"VALENTINE"

"I think that's the prettiest of all," said Clover.

"I don't," said Elsie. "I think mine is the prettiest. Cecy didn't have any seal in hers, either." And she folded the little seal, which all this time she had held in her hand.

"Katy, you ought to have read yours first, because you are the oldest," said Clover.

"Mine isn't much," replied Katy, and she read:

"The rose is red, the violet blue,
Sugar is sweet, and so are you."

"What a mean valentine!" cried Elsie, with flashing eyes. "It's a real shame, Katy! You ought to have had the best of all."

Katy could hardly keep from laughing. The fact was that the verses for the others had taken so long that no time had been left for writing a valentine to herself. So, thinking it would excite suspicion to have none, she had scribbled this old rhyme at the last moment.

"It isn't very nice," she said, trying to look as pensive as she could, "but never mind."

"It's a shame!" repeated Elsie, petting her very hard to make up for the injustice.

128

"Hasn't it been a funny evening?" said John; and Dorry replied, "Yes; we never had such good times before Katy was sick, did we?"

Katy heard this with a mingled feeling of pleasure and pain. "I think the children do love me a little more of late," she said to herself. "But, oh, why couldn't I be good to them when I was well and strong!"

She didn't open Cousin Helen's letter until the rest were all gone to bed. I think somebody must have written and told her about the valentine party, for instead of a note there were these verses in Cousin Helen's own clear, pretty hand. It wasn't a valentine, because it was too solemn, as Katy explained to Clover next day. "But," she added, "it is a great deal beautifuller than any valentine that ever was written." And Clover thought so too.

These were the verses:

"IN SCHOOL"

"I used to go to a bright school
    Where Youth and Frolic taught in turn;
But idle scholar that I was
    I liked to play, I would not learn;
So the Great Teacher did ordain
That I should try the School of Pain.

"One of the infant class I am
    With little easy lessons, set
In a great book; the higher class
    Have harder ones than I, and yet
I find mine hard, and can't restrain
My tears while studying thus with Pain.

"There are two teachers in the school,
    One has a gentle voice and low,
And smiles upon her scholars, as
    She softly passes to and fro.
Her name is Love; 'tis very plain
She shuns the sharper teacher, Pain.

"Or so I sometimes think; and then,
    At other times they meet and kiss,
And look so strangely like, that I
Am puzzled to tell how it is,
Or whence the change which makes it vain
To guess if it be—Love or Pain.

"They tell me if I study well,
    And learn my lessons, I shall be
Moved upward to that higher class
    Where dear Love teaches constantly;
And I work hard, in hopes to gain
Reward, and get away from Pain.

"Yet Pain is sometimes kind, and helps
    Me on when I am very dull;
I thank him often in my heart.
    But Love is far more beautiful;
Under her tender, gentle reign
I must learn faster than of Pain.

"So I will do my very best,
    Nor chide the clock, nor call it slow;
That when the teacher calls me up
    To see if I am fit to go,
I may to Love's high class attain,
And bid a sweet good-bye to Pain."

CHAPTER ELEVEN

A New Lesson to Learn

IT WAS a long time before the children ceased to talk and laugh over that jolly evening. Dorry declared he wished there could be a Valentine's Day every week.

"Don't you think St. Valentine would be tired of writing verses?" asked Katy. But she too had enjoyed the frolic, and the bright recollection helped her along through the rest of the long, cold winter.

Spring opened late that year, but the summer, when it came, was a warm one. Katy felt the heat very much. She could not change her seat and follow the breeze about from window to window as other people could. The long burning days left her weak and parched. She hung her head, and seemed to wilt like the flowers in the garden-beds. Indeed she was worse off than they, for every evening Alexander gave them a watering with the hose, while nobody was able to bring a watering-pot and pour out what she needed- -a shower of cold, fresh air.

It wasn't easy to be good-humoured under these circumstances, and one could hardly have blamed Katy if she had sometimes forgotten her resolutions and been cross and fretful. But she didn't—not very often. Now and then bad days came, when she was discouraged and forlorn. But Katy's long year of schooling had taught her self-control, and, as a general thing, her discomforts were borne patiently. She could not help growing pale and thin, however, and Papa saw with concern that as the summer went on she became too languid to read, or study, or sew, and just sat hour after hour, with folded hands, gazing wistfully out of the window.

He tried the experiment of taking her to drive. But the motion of the carriage, and the being lifted in and out, brought on so much pain that Katy begged that he would not ask her to go again. So there was nothing to be done but wait for cooler weather. The summer dragged on, and all who loved Katy rejoiced when it was over.

When September came, with cool mornings and nights, and fresh breezes, smelling of pine woods and hill-tops, all things seemed to revive, and Katy with them. She began to crochet and to read. After a while she collected her books again, and tried to study, as Cousin Helen had advised. But so many idle weeks made it seem harder work than ever. One day she asked Papa to let her take French lessons.

"You see, I'm forgetting all I knew," she said, "and Clover is going to begin this term, and I don't like that she should get so far ahead of me. Don't you think Mr. Berger would be willing to come here, Papa? He does go to houses sometimes."

"I think he would if we asked him," said Dr. Carr, pleased to see Katy waking up with something like life again.

So the arrangement was made. Mr. Berger came twice every week, and sat beside the big chair, correcting Katy's exercise and practising her in the verbs and pronunciation. He was a lively little old Frenchman, and knew how to make lesson-time pleasant.

"You take more pain than you used, Mademoiselle," he said, one day; "if you go on so, you shall be my best scholar. And if to hurt the back make you study, it would be well that some other of my young ladies shall do the same."

Katy laughed. But in spite of Mr. Berger and his lessons, and in spite of her endeavours to keep cheerful and busy, this second winter was harder than the first. It is often so with sick people. There is a sort of excitement in being ill which helps along just at the beginning.

But as months go on, and everything grows an old story, and one day follows another day, all just alike and all tiresome, courage is apt to flag and spirits to grow dull. Spring seemed a long, long way off whenever Katy thought about it.

"I wish something would happen," she often said to herself. And something was about to happen. But she little guessed what it was going to be.

"Katy!" said Clover, coming in one day in November, "do you know where the camphor is? Aunt Izzie has got *such* a headache."

"No," replied Katy, "I don't. Or—wait—Clover, it seems to me that Debby came for it the other day. Perhaps if you look in her room you'll find it."

"How very queer!" she soliloquised, when Clover was gone; "I never knew Aunt Izzie to have a headache before."

"How is Aunt Izzie?" she asked, when Papa came in at noon.

"Well, I don't know. She has some fever and a bad pain in her head. I have told her that she had better lie still, and not try to get up this evening."

"Old Mary will come in to undress you, Katy. You won't mind, will you, dear?"

"N-o!" said Katy, reluctantly. But she did mind. Aunt Izzie had grown used to her and her ways. Nobody else suited her so well.

"It seems so strange to have to explain just how every little thing is to be done," she remarked to Clover, rather petulantly.

It seemed stranger yet, when the next day, and the next, and the next after that passed, and still no Aunt Izzie came near her. Blessings brighten as they take their flight. Katy began to appreciate for the first time how much she had learned to rely on her aunt. She missed her dreadfully.

"When *is* Aunt Izzie going to get well?" she asked her father; "I want her so much."

"We all want her," said Dr. Carr, who looked disturbed and anxious.

"Is she very ill?" asked Katy, struck by the expression on his face.

"I'm afraid so," he replied. "I'm going to get a regular nurse to take care of her."

Aunt Izzie's attack proved to be a typhoid fever. The doctors said that the house must be kept quiet, so John and Dorry and Phil were sent over to Mrs. Hall's to stay. Elsie and Clover were to have gone too, but they begged so hard, and made so many promises of good behaviour, that finally Papa permitted them to remain. The dear little things stole about the house on tiptoe, as quietly as mice, whispering to each other, and waiting on Katy, who would have been lonely enough without them, for everybody else was absorbed in Aunt Izzie.

It was a confused, melancholy time. The three girls didn't know much about sickness, but Papa's grave face and the hushed house weighed upon their spirits, and they missed the children very much.

"Oh, dear!" sighed Elsie. "How I wish Aunt Izzie would hurry and get well."

"We'll be real good to her when she does, won't we?" said Clover. "I never mean to leave my over-shoes in the hat-stand any more, because she doesn't like to see them there. And I shall pick up the croquet-balls and put them in the box every night."

"Yes," added Elsie, "so will I, when she gets well."

It never occurred to either of them that perhaps Aunt Izzie might not get well. Little people are apt to feel as if grown folks are so strong and so big that nothing can possibly happen to them.

Katy was more anxious. Still she did not fairly realise the danger. So it came like a sudden and violent shock

134

to her, when, one morning on waking up, she found old Mary crying quietly beside the bed, with her apron at her eyes. Aunt Izzie had died in the night!

All their kind, penitent thoughts of her, their resolutions to please, their plans for obeying her wishes and saving her trouble, were too late! For the first time the three girls, sobbing in each other's arms, realised what a good friend Aunt Izzie had been to them. Her worrying ways were all forgotten now. They could only remember the many kind things she had done for them since they were little children. How they wished that they had never teased her, never said sharp words about her to each other. But it was no use to wish.

"What shall we do without Aunt Izzie?" thought Katy, as she cried herself to sleep that night. And the question came into her mind again and again, after the funeral was over, and the little ones had come back from Mrs. Hall's, and things began to go on in their usual manner.

For several days she saw almost nothing of her father. Clover reported that he looked very tired, and scarcely said a word.

"Did Papa eat any dinner?" asked Katy, one afternoon.

"Not much. He said he wasn't hungry. And Mrs. Jackson's boy came for him before we were through."

"Oh, dear! " sighed Katy, "I do hope *he* isn't going to be ill. How it rains! Clovy, I wish you'd run down and get out his slippers and put them by the fire to warm. Oh, and ask Debby to make some cream-toast for tea! Papa likes cream-toast."

After tea, Dr. Carr came upstairs to sit a while in Katy's room. He often did so, but this was the first time since Aunt Izzie's death.

Katy studied his face anxiously. It seemed to her that it had grown older of late, and there was a sad look upon it which made her heart ache. She longed to do something for him, but all she could do was to poke the fire bright, and then to possess herself of his hand, and stroke it gently with both hers. It wasn't much, to be sure, but I think Papa liked it.

"What have you been about all day?" he asked.

"Oh, nothing much," said Katy. "I studied my French lesson this morning. And after school Elsie and John brought in their patchwork and we had a 'Bee.' That's all."

"I've been thinking how we are to manage about the housekeeping," said Dr. Carr. "Of course we shall have to get somebody to come and take charge. But it isn't easy to find just the right person. Mrs. Hall knows of a woman who might do, but she is out West just now, and it will be a week or two before we can hear from her. Do you think you can get on as you are for a few days?"

"Oh, Papa!" cried Katy, in dismay, "must we have anybody?"

"Why, how did you suppose we are going to arrange it? Clover is much too young for housekeeper. And beside, she is at school all day."

"I don't know—I hadn't thought about it," said Katy, in a perplexed tone.

But she did think about it—all that evening, and the first thing when she awoke in the morning.

"Papa," she said, the next time she got him to herself, "I've been thinking over what you were saying last night, about getting somebody to keep the house, you know. And I wish you wouldn't. I wish you would let *me* try. Really and truly, I think I could manage."

"But how?" asked Dr. Carr, much surprised. "I really don't see. If you were well and strong, perhaps—but even then you would be pretty young for such a charge, Katy."

"I shall be fourteen in two weeks," said Katy, drawing herself up in her chair as straight as she could. "And if I *were* well, Papa, I should be going to school, you know, and then of course I couldn't. No, I'll tell you my plan. I've been thinking about it all day. Debby and Bridget have been with us so long that they know Aunt Izzie's ways, and they're such good women that all they want is just to be told a little now and then. Now why couldn't they come up

136

to me when anything is wanted—just as well as to have me go down to them? Clover and old Mary will keep watch, you know, and see if anything is wrong. And you wouldn't mind if things were a little crooked just at first, would you? because, you know, I should be learning all the time. Do let me try! It will be real nice to have something to think about as I sit up here alone; so much better than having a stranger in the house who doesn't know the children or anything. I'm sure it will make me happier. Please say 'Yes,' Papa, please do!"

"It's too much for you, a great deal too much," replied Dr. Carr. But it was not easy to resist Katy's "Please! Please!" and after a while it ended with—

"Well, darling, you may try, though I am doubtful as to the result of the experiment. I will tell Mrs. Hall to put off writing to Wisconsin for a month, and we will see."

"Poor child, anything to take her thoughts off herself!" he muttered, as he walked downstairs. "She'll be glad enough to give the thing up by the end of a month."

But Papa was mistaken. At the end of a month Katy was eager to go on. So he said, "Very well—she might try it till spring."

It was not such hard work as it sounds. Katy had plenty of quiet thinking-time for one thing. The children were at school all day, and few visitors came to interrupt her, so she could plan out her hours and keep to the plans. This is a great help to a housekeeper.

Then Aunt Izzie's regular, punctual ways were so well understood by the servants that the house seemed almost to keep itself. As Katy had said, all Debby and Bridget needed was a little "telling" now and then.

As soon as breakfast was over and the dishes were washed and put away, Debby would tie on a clean apron and come upstairs for orders. At first Katy thought this great fun. But after ordering dinner a good many times it began to grow tiresome. She never saw the dishes after they were cooked; and, being inexperienced, it seemed impossible to think of things enough to make a variety.

137

"Let me see—there is roast beef—leg of mutton—boiled chicken," she would say, counting on her fingers, "roast beef—leg of mutton—boiled chicken. Debby, you might roast the chickens. Dear!—I wish somebody would invent a new animal; Where all the things to eat are gone to I can't imagine!"

Then Katy would send for every recipe-book in the house, and pore over them by the hour, till her appetite was as completely gone as if she had swallowed twenty dinners. Poor Debby learned to dread these books. She would stand by the door with her pleasant red face drawn up into a pucker, while Katy read aloud some impossible-sounding rule.

"This looks as if it were delicious, Debby; I wish you'd try it; take a gallon of oysters, a pint of beef stock, sixteen soda crackers, the juice of two lemons, four cloves, a glass of white wine, a sprig of marjoram, a sprig of thyme, a sprig of bay, a sliced shallot——"

"Please, Miss Katy, what's them?"

"Oh, don't you know, Debby? It must be something quite common, for it's in almost all the recipes."

"No, Miss Katy, I never heard tell of it before. Miss Carr never gave me no shell-outs at all at all!"

"Dear me, how provoking!" Katy would cry, flapping over the leaves of her book; "then we must try something else."

Poor Debby! If she hadn't loved Katy so dearly, I think her patience must have given way. But she bore her trials meekly, except for an occasional grumble when alone with Bridget. Dr. Carr had to eat a great many queer things in those days. But he didn't mind, and as for the children, they enjoyed it. Dinner-time became quite exciting, when nobody could tell exactly what any dish on the table was made of. Dorry, who was a sort of Dr. Livingstone where strange articles of food were concerned, usually made the first experiment, and if he said that it was good, the rest followed suit.

After a while Katy grew wiser. She ceased teasing Debby

to try new things, and the Carr family went back to plain roast and boiled, much to the advantage of all concerned. But then another series of experiments began. Katy got hold of a book upon "The Stomach," and was seized with a rage for wholesome food. She entreated Clover and the other children to give up sugar and butter and gravy and pudding-sauce and buckwheat cakes and pies, and almost everything else that they particularly liked. Boiled rice seemed to her the most sensible dessert, and she kept the family on it until finally John and Dorry started a rebellion, and Dr. Carr was forced to interfere.

"My dear, you are overdoing it sadly," he said, as Katy opened her book and prepared to explain her views; "I am glad to have the children eat simple food—but really, boiled rice five times a week is too much."

Katy sighed, but submitted. Later, as the spring came on, she had a fit of over-anxiousness, and was always sending Clover down to ask Debby if her bread was not burning, or if she was sure that the pickles were not fermenting in the jars? She also fidgeted the children about wearing overshoes, and keeping on their coats, and behaved altogether as if the cares of the world were on her shoulders.

But all these were but the natural mistakes of a beginner. Katy was too much in earnest not to improve. Month by month she learned how to manage a little better, and a little better still. Matters went on more smoothly. Her cares ceased to fret her. Dr. Carr, watching the increasing brightness of her face and manner, felt that the experiment was a success. Nothing more was said about "somebody else," and Katy, sitting upstairs in her big chair, held the threads of the house firmly in her hands.

CHAPTER TWELVE

Two Years Afterward

IT WAS a pleasant morning in early June. A warm wind was rustling the trees, which were covered thickly with half-opened leaves, and looked like fountains of green spray thrown high into the air. Dr. Carr's front door stood wide open. Through the parlour window came the sound of piano practice, and in the steps, under the budding roses, sat a small figure busily sewing.

This was Clover, little Clover still, though more than two years had passed since we saw her last, and she was now over fourteen. Clover was never intended to be tall. Her eyes were as blue and sweet as ever, and her apple-blossom cheeks as pink. But the brown pig-tails were pinned up into a round knot, and the childish face had gained almost a womanly look. Old Mary declared that Miss Clover was getting quite young-ladyfied, and "Miss Clover" was quite aware of the fact, and mightily pleased with it. It delighted her to turn up her hair; and she was very particular about having her dresses made to come below the tops of her boots. She had also left off ruffles, and wore narrow collars instead, and little cuffs with sleeve-buttons to fasten them. These sleeve-buttons, which were a present from Cousin Helen, Clover liked best of all her things. Papa said that he was sure she took them to bed with her, but of course that was only a joke, though she certainly was never seen without them in the day-time. She glanced frequently at these beloved buttons as she sat sewing, and every now and then laid down her work to twist them into a better position, or give them an affection-ate pat with her forefinger.

Very soon the side-gate swung open, and Philly came round the corner of the house. He had grown into a big boy. All his pretty baby curls were cut off, and his frocks had given place to jacket and trousers. In his hand he held something. What, Clover could not see.

"What's that?" she said, as he reached the steps.

"I'm going upstairs to ask Katy if these are ripe," replied Phil, exhibiting some currants faintly streaked with red.

"Why, of course they're not ripe!" said Clover, putting one into her mouth. "Can't you tell by the taste? They're as green as can be."

"I don't care, if Katy says they're ripe I shall eat 'em," answered Phil, defiantly, marching into the house.

"What did Philly want?" asked Elsie, opening the parlour door as Phil went upstairs.

"Only to know if the currants are ripe enough to eat."

"How particular he always is about asking now!" said Elsie; "he's afraid of another dose of salts."

"I should think he would be," replied Clover, laughing. "Johnnie says she never was so scared in her life as when Papa called them, and they looked up, and saw him stand-ing there with the bottle in one hand and a spoon in the other!"

"Yes," went on Elsie, "and you know Dorry held his in his mouth for ever so long, and then went round the corner of the house and spat it out! Papa said he had a good mind to make him take another spoonful, but he re-membered that after all Dorry had the bad taste a great deal longer than the others, so he didn't. I think it was an *awful* punishment, don't you?"

"Yes, but it was a good one, for none of them have ever touched green gooseberries since. Have you got through practising? It doesn't seem like an hour yet."

"Oh, it isn't—it's only twenty-five minutes. But Katy told me not to sit more than half an hour at a time without getting up and running round to rest. I'm going to walk twice down to the gate, and twice back. I promised her I would." And Elsie set off, clapping her hands briskly before and behind her as she walked.

"Why—what is Bridget doing in Papa's room?" she asked, as she came back the second time. "She's flapping things out of the window. Are the girls up there? I thought they were cleaning the dining-room."

"They're doing both. Katy said it was such a good chance, having Papa away, that she would have both the carpets taken up at once. There isn't going to be any dinner to-day, only just bread and butter, and milk, and cold ham, up in Katy's room, because Debby is helping too, so as to get through and save Papa all the fuss. And see," exhibiting her sewing, "Katy's making a new cover for Papa's pincushion, and I'm hemming the ruffle to go round it."

"How nicely you hem!" said Elsie. "I wish I had something for Papa's room too. There's my washstand mats—but the one for the soap-dish isn't finished. Do you suppose, if Katy would excuse me from the rest of my practising, I could get it done? I've a great mind to go and ask her."

"There's her bell!" said Clover, as a little tinkle sounded upstairs; "I'll ask her if you like."

"No, let me go. I'll see what she wants." But Clover was already half-way across the hall, and the two girls ran up side by side.

There was often a little strife between them as to which should answer Katy's bell. Both liked to wait on her so much.

Katy came to meet them as they entered. Not on her feet: that, alas! was still only a far-off possibility; but in a

142

chair with large wheels, with which she was rolling herself across the room. This chair was a great comfort to her. Sitting in it she could get to her closet and to her bureau drawers, and help herself to what she wanted without troubling anybody. It was only lately that she had been able to use it. Dr. Carr considered her doing so as a hopeful sign, but he had never told Katy this. She had grown accustomed to her invalid life at last, and was cheerful in it, and he thought it unwise to make her restless by exciting hopes which might after all end in fresh disappointment.

She met the girls with a bright smile as they came in, and said:

"Oh, Clovy, it was you I rang for! I am troubled for fear Bridget will meddle with the things on Papa's table. You know he likes them to be left just so. Will you please go and remind her that she is not to touch them at all? After the carpet is put down, I want you to dust the table, so as to be sure that everything is put back in the same place. Will you?"

"Of course I will!" said Clover, who was a born housewife, and dearly loved to act as Katy's prime minister.

"Shan't I fetch you the pincushion too, while I'm there?"

"Oh, yes, please do! I want to measure."

"Katy," said Elsie, "those mats of mine are almost done, and I would like to finish them and put them on Papa's washstand before he comes back. Mayn't I stop practising now and bring my crochet up here instead?"

"Will there be plenty of time to learn the new exercise before Miss Phillips comes, if you do?"

"I think so, plenty. She doesn't come till Friday, you know."

"Well, then, it seems to me that you might as well as not. And Elsie, dear, run into Papa's room first and bring me the drawer out of his table. I want to put that in order myself."

Elsie went cheerfully. She laid the drawer across Katy's

lap, and Katy began to dust and arrange the contents. Pretty soon Clover joined them.

"Here's the cushion," she said. "Now we'll have a nice quiet time all by ourselves, won't we? I like this sort of day when nobody comes in to interrupt us."

Somebody tapped at the door as she spoke. Katy called out, "Come in!" and in marched a tall, broad-shouldered lad, with a solemn, sensible face, and a little clock carried carefully in both his hands.

This was Dorry. He has grown and improved very much since we saw him last, and is turning out clever in several ways. Among the rest, he has developed a strong turn for mechanics.

"Here's your clock, Katy," he said. "I've got it fixed so that it strikes all right, Only you must be careful not to hit the striker when you start the pendulum."

"Have you really?" said Katy. "Why, Dorry, you're a genius! I'm ever so much obliged."

"It's four minutes to eleven now," went on Dorry. "So it'll strike pretty soon. I guess I'd better stay and hear it, so as to be sure that it is right. That is," he added politely, "unless you're busy and would rather not."

"I'm never too busy to want you, old fellow," said Katy, stroking his arm. "Here, this drawer is arranged now. Don't you want to carry it into Papa's room and put it back into the table? Your hands are stronger than Elsie's." Dorry looked gratified. When he came back the clock was just beginning to strike.

"There!" he exclaimed; "that's splendid, isn't it?"

But alas! the clock did not stop at eleven. It went on—twelve, thirteen, fourteen, fifteen, sixteen!

"Dear me!" said Clover, "what does all this mean? It must be the day after to-morrow, at least."

Dorry stared with open mouth at the clock, which was still striking as though it would split its sides. Elsie, screaming with laughter, kept count.

"Thirty, thirty-one—Oh, Dorry! Thirty-two! thirty-three! thirty-four!"

"You've bewitched it, Dorry!" said Katy, as much entertained as the rest.

Then they all began counting. Dorry seized the clock—shook it, slapped it, turned it upside down. But still the sharp, vibrating sounds continued, as if the clock, having got its own way for once, meant to go on till it was tired out. At last, at the one-hundred-and-thirtieth stroke it suddenly ceased; and Dorry, with a red, amazed countenance, faced the laughing company.

"It's very queer," he said, "but I'm sure it's not because of anything I did. I can fix it, though, if you'll let me try again. May I, Katy? I'll promise not to hurt it."

For a moment Katy hesitated. Clover pulled her sleeve, and whispered "Don't!" Then seeing the mortification on Dorry's face she made up her mind.

"Yes! take it, Dorry. I'm sure you'll be careful. But if I were you, I'd carry it down to Wetherell's first of all, and talk it over with them. Together you could hit on just the right thing. Don't you think so?"

"Perhaps," said Dorry; "yes, I think I will." Then he departed with the clock under his arm, while Clover called after him teasingly. "Lunch at 132 o'clock; don't forget!"

"No I won't!" said Dorry. Two years before he would not have borne to be laughed at so good-naturedly.

"How come you let him take your clock again?" said Clover, as soon as the door was shut. "He'll spoil it. And you think so much of it."

"I thought he would feel mortified if I didn't let him try," replied Katy quietly; "I don't believe he'll hurt it. Wetherell's man likes Dorry, and he'll show him what to do."

"You were real good to do it," responded Clover; "but if it had been mine, I don't think I could."

Just then the door flew open, and Johnnie rushed in, two years taller, but otherwise looking exactly as she used to do.

"Oh, Katy!" she gasped, "won't you please tell Philly not to wash the chickens in the rain-water tub? He's put in every one of Speckle's, and is just beginning on Dame Durden's. I'm afraid one little yellow one is dead already ——"

"Why, he mustn't—of course he mustn't!" said Katy. "What made him think of such a thing?"

"He says they're dirty, because they've just come out of egg-shells! And he insists that the yellow on them is yolk of egg. I told him it wasn't, but he wouldn't listen to me." And Johnnie wrung her hands.

"Clover!" cried Katy, "won't you run down and ask Philly to come up to me? Speak pleasantly, you know!"

"I spoke pleasantly—real pleasantly, but it wasn't any use," said Johnnie, on whom the wrongs of the chicks had evidently made a deep impression.

"What a mischief Phil is getting to be!" said Elsie. "Papa says his name ought to be Pickle."

"Pickles turn out very nice sometimes, you know," replied Katy, laughing.

Pretty soon Philly came up, escorted by Clover. He looked a little defiant, but Katy understood how to manage him. She lifted him into her lap, which, big boy as he was, he liked extremely, and talked to him so affectionately about the poor little shivering chicks that his heart was quite melted.

"I didn't mean to hurt 'em, really and truly," he said, "but they were all dirty and yellow—with egg, you know, and I thought you'd like me to clean them up."

"But that wasn't egg, Philly—it was dear little clean feathers like a canary-bird's wings."

"Was it?"

"Yes, and now the chickies are as cold and forlorn as you would feel if you tumbled into a pond and nobody gave you any dry clothes. Don't you think you ought to go and warm them?"

"How?"

"Well—in your hands, very gently. And then I would let them run around in the sun."

"I will!" said Philly, getting down from her lap. "Only

146

kiss me first, because I didn't mean to, you know!"—
Philly was very fond of Katy. Miss Petingill said it was
wonderful to see how that child let himself be managed.
But I think the secret was that Katy didn't "manage," but
tried to be always kind and loving and considerate of
Phil's feelings.

Before the echo of Phil's boots had fairly died away on
the stairs, old Mary put her head into the door. There was
a distressed expression on her face.

"Miss Katy," she said, "I wish *you'd* speak to Alexander
about putting the wood-shed in order. I don't think you
know how bad it looks."

"I don't suppose I do," said Katy, smiling and then
sighing. She had never seen the wood-shed since the day
of her fall from the swing. "Never mind, Mary; I'll talk
to Alexander about it, and he shall make it nice."

Mary trotted downstairs satisfied. But in the course of
a few minutes she was up again.

"There's a man come with a box of soap, Miss Katy,
and here's the bill. He says it's receipted."

It took Katy a little time to find her purse, and then she
wanted her pencil and account-book, and Elsie had to
move from her seat at the table.

"Oh, dear!" she said, "I wish people wouldn't keep
coming and interrupting us. Who'll be next, I wonder?"

She was not left to wonder long. Almost as she spoke
there was another knock at the door.

"Come in!" said Katy, rather wearily. The door opened.

"Shall I?" said a voice. There was a rustle of skirts, a
clatter of boot-heels, and Imogen Clark swept into the
room. Katy could not think who it was at first. She had
not seen Imogen for almost two years.

"I found the front-door open," explained Imogen, in her
high-pitched voice, "and as nobody seemed to hear when
I rang the bell, I ventured to come right upstairs. I hope
I'm not interrupting anything private?"

"Not at all," said Katy, politely. "Elsie, dear, move up
that low chair, please. Do sit down, Imogen! I'm sorry no-

body answered your ring, but the servants are cleaning house to-day, and I suppose they didn't hear."

So Imogen sat down and began to rattle on in her usual manner, while Elsie, from behind Katy's chair, took a wide-awake survey of her dress. It was of cheap material, but very gorgeously made and trimmed, with flounces and puffs; and Imogen wore a jet necklace and long black earrings, which jingled and clicked when she waved her head about. She still had the little round curls stuck on to her cheeks, and Elsie wondered anew what kept them in their places.

By-and-by the object of Imogen's visit came out. She had called to say good-bye. The Clark family were all going back to Jacksonville to live.

"Did you ever see the Brigand again?" asked Clover, who had never forgotten that eventful tale told in the parlour.

"Yes," replied Imogen, "several times. And I get letters from him quite often. He writes *beau*tiful letters. I wish I had one with me, so that I could read you a little bit. You would enjoy it, I know. Let me see—perhaps I have." And she put her hand into her pocket. Sure enough there *was* a letter. Clover couldn't help suspecting that Imogen knew it all the time.

The Brigand seemed to write a bold, black hand, and his note-paper and envelope was just like anybody else's. But perhaps his band had surprised a pedlar with a box of stationery.

"Let me see," said Imogen, running her eye down the page. " 'Adored Imogen'—*that* wouldn't interest you— hm, hm, hm—ah, here's something! 'I took dinner at the Rock House on Christmas. It was lonesome without you. I had roast turkey, roast goose, roast beef, mince pie, plum pudding, and nuts and raisins. A pretty good dinner, was it not? But nothing tastes first-rate when friends are away.' "

Katy and Clover stared, as well they might. Such language from a Brigand!

"John Billings has bought a new horse," continued

148

Imogen; "hm, hm, hm—him. I don't think there is anything else you'd care about. Oh, yes! just here, at the end, is some poetry:

> " 'Come, little dove, with azure wing,
> And brood upon my breast.'

"That's sweet, ain't it?"

"Hasn't he reformed?" said Clover; "he writes as if he had."

"Reformed!" cried Imogen, with a toss of the jingling ear-rings. "He was always just as good as he could be!"

There was nothing to be said in reply to this. Katy felt her lips twitch, and for fear she would be rude, and laugh out, she began to talk as fast as she could about something else. All the time she found herself taking measure of Imogen, and thinking—"Did I ever really like her? How queer! Oh, what a wise man Papa is!"

Imogen stayed half an hour. Then she took her leave.

"She never asked how you were!" cried Elsie, indignantly; "I noticed, and she didn't—not once."

"Oh, well— I suppose she forgot. We were talking about her, not about me," replied Katy.

The little group settled down again to their work. This time half an hour went by without any more interruptions. Then the door-bell rang, and Bridget, with a disturbed face, came upstairs.

"Miss Katy," she said, "it's old Mrs. Worrett, and I reckon she's come to spend the day, for she's brought her bag. Whatever shall I tell her?"

Katy looked dismayed. "Oh, dear!" she said, "how unlucky. What can we do?"

Mrs. Worrett was an old friend of Aunt Izzie's who lived in the country, about six miles from Burnet, and was in the habit of coming to Dr. Carr's for lunch, on days when shopping or other business brought her into town. This did not occur often; and, as it happened, Katy had never had to entertain her before.

"Tell her ye're busy, and can't see her," suggested Bridget. "There's no dinner nor nothing, you know."

The Katy of two years ago would probably have jumped at this idea. But the Katy of to-day was more considerate.

"N-o," she said; "I don't like to do that. We must just make the best of it, Bridget. Run down, Clover, dear, that's a good girl! and tell Mrs. Worrett that the dining-room is all in confusion, but that we're going to have lunch here, and, after she's rested, I should be glad to have her come up. And, oh, Clovy! give her a fan the first thing. She'll be *so* hot. Bridget, you can bring up the luncheon just the same, only take out some canned peaches, by way of dessert, and make Mrs. Worrett a cup of tea. She drinks tea always, I believe.

"I can't bear to send the poor old lady away when she has come so far," she explained to Elsie, after the others were gone. "Pull the rocking-chair a little this way, Elsie. And oh! push all those little chairs back against the wall. Mrs. Worrett broke down in one the last time she was here —don't you recollect?"

It took some time to cool Mrs. Worrett off, so nearly twenty minutes passed before a heavy, creaking step on the stairs announced that the guest was on her way up. Elsie began to giggle. Mrs. Worrett always made her giggle. Katy had just time to give her a warning glance before the door opened.

Mrs. Worrett was the most enormously fat person ever seen. Nobody dared to guess how much she weighed, but she *looked* as if it might be a thousand pounds. Her face was extremely red. In the coldest weather she appeared hot, and on a mild day she seemed absolutely ready to melt. Her bonnet-strings were flying loose as she came in, and she fanned herself all the way across the room, which shook as she walked.

"Well, my dear," she said, as she plumped herself into the rocking-chair, "and how do you do?"

"Very well, thank you," replied Katy, thinking that she

150

never saw Mrs. Worrett look half so fat before, and wondering how she *was* to entertain her.

"And how's your Pa?" inquired Mrs. Worrett. Katy answered politely and then asked after Mrs. Worrett's own health.

"Well, I'm so's to be round," was the reply, which had the effect of sending Elsie into a fit of convulsive laughter behind Katy's chair.

"I had business at the bank," continued the visitor; "and I thought while I was about it, I'd step up to Miss Petingill's and see if I couldn't get her to come and let out my black silk. It was made a long while ago, and I seem to have grown stouter since then, for I can't make the hooks and eyes meet at all. But when I got there she was out, so I'd my walk for nothing. Do you know where she's sewing now?"

"No," said Katy, feeling her chair shake, and keeping her own countenance with difficulty, "she was here for three days last week to make Johnnie a school-dress. But I haven't heard anything about her since. Elsie, you might run downstairs and ask Bridget to bring a—a—a glass of iced water for Mrs. Worrett. She looks warm after her walk."

Elsie, dreadfully ashamed, made a bolt from the room, and hid herself in the hall closet to have her laugh out. She came back after a while, with a perfectly straight face. Luncheon was brought up. Mrs. Worrett made a good meal, and seemed to enjoy everything. She was so comfortable that she never stirred till four o'clock! Oh, how long that afternoon did seem to the poor girls, sitting there and trying to think of something to say to their vast visitor! At last Mrs. Worrett got out of her chair and prepared to depart.

"Well," she said, tying her bonnet-strings, "I've had a good rest, and feel all the better for it. Aren't some of you young folks coming out to see me one of these days? I'd like to have you first-rate if you will. 'Tain't every girl would know how to take care of a fat old woman, and

151

make her feel at home, as you have me, Katy. I wish your aunt could see you all as you are now. She'd be pleased; I know that."

Somehow this sentence rang pleasantly in Katy's ears.

"Ah! don't laugh at her," she said later in the evening, when the children, after their tea in the clean, fresh-smelling dining-room, were come up to sit with her, and Cecy, in her pretty pink lawn and white shawl, had dropped in to spend an hour or two; "she's a real kind old woman, and I don't like to have you laugh at her. It isn't her fault that she's fat. And Aunt Izzie was fond of her, you know. It is doing something for her, when we can show a little attention to one of her friends. I was sorry when she came; but now it's over, I'm glad."

"It feels so nice when it stops aching," said Elsie, mischievously, while Cecy whispered to Clover:

"Isn't Katy sweet?"

"Isn't she!" replied Clover. "I wish I was half as good. Sometimes I think that I shall be really sorry if she ever gets well. She's such a dear old darling to us all, sitting there in her chair, that it wouldn't seem so nice to have her anywhere else. But then, I know it's horrid of me. And I don't believe she'd be different, or grow rough and horrid, like some of the girls, even if she were well."

"Of course she wouldn't!" replied Cecy.

CHAPTER THIRTEEN

At Last

IT WAS about six weeks after this, that one day, Clover and Elsie were busy downstairs, they were startled by the sound of Katy's bell ringing in a sudden and agitated manner. Both ran up two steps at a time, to see what was wanted.

Katy sat in her chair, looking very much flushed and excited.

"Oh, girls! " she exclaimed, "what do you think? I stood up! "

"What?" cried Clover and Elsie.

"I really did! I stood up on my feet! by myself! "

The others were too much astonished to speak, so Katy went on explaining.

"It was all at once, you see. Suddenly, I had the feeling that if I tried I could, and almost before I thought, I *did* try, and there I was, up and out of the chair. Only I kept hold of the arm all the time! I don't know how I got back, I was so frightened. Oh, girls! "—and Katy buried her face in her hands.

"Do you think I shall ever be able to do it again?" she asked, looking up with wet eyes.

"Why, of course you will! " said Clover; while Elsie

danced about, crying out anxiously: "Be careful! Do be careful!"

Katy tried, but the spring was gone. She could not move out of the chair at all. She began to wonder if she had dreamed the whole thing.

But next day, when Clover happened to be in the room, she heard a sudden exclamation, and turning, there stood Katy absolutely on her feet.

"Papa! Papa!" shrieked Clover, rushing downstairs. "Dorry, John, Elsie—come! Come and see!"

Papa was out, but all the rest crowded up at once. This time Katy found no trouble in "doing it again." It seemed as if her will had been asleep; and now that it had waked up the limbs recognised its orders and obeyed them.

When Papa came in he was as much excited as any of the children. He walked round and round the chair, questioning Katy and making her stand up and sit down.

"Am I really going to get well?" she asked, almost in a whisper.

"Yes, my love, I think you are," said Dr. Carr, seizing Phil and giving him a toss into the air. None of the children had ever before seen Papa behave so like a boy. But pretty soon, noticing Katy's burning cheeks and excited eyes, he calmed himself, sent the others all away, and sat down to soothe and quiet her with gentle words.

"I think it is coming, my darling," he said; "but it will take time, and you must have a great deal of patience. After being such a good child all these years, I'm sure you won't fail now. Remember, any imprudence will put you back. You must be content to gain very little at a time. There is no royal road to walking any more than there is to learning. Every baby finds that out."

"Oh, Papa!" said Katy, "it's no matter if it takes a year —if only I get well at last."

How happy she was that night—too happy to sleep. Papa noticed the dark circles under her eyes in the morning and shook his head.

"You *must* be careful," he told her, "or you'll be laid up again. A course of fever would put you back for years."

Katy knew Papa was right, and she *was* careful, though it was by no means easy to be so with that new life tingling in every limb. Her progress was slow, as Dr. Carr had predicted. At first she only stood on her feet a few seconds, then a minute, then five minutes, holding tightly all the while by the chair. Next she ventured to let go the chair and stand alone. After that she began to walk a step at a time, pushing a chair before her as children do when they are learning the use of their feet. Clover and Elsie hovered about her as she moved, like anxious mammas. It was droll, and a little pitiful, to see tall Katy with her feeble, unsteady progress, and the active figures of the little sisters following her protectingly. But Katy did not consider it either droll or pitiful; to her it was simply delightful—the most delightful thing possible. No baby of a year old was ever prouder of his first steps than she.

Gradually she grew adventurous, and ventured on a bolder flight. Clover, running upstairs one day to her own room, stood transfixed at the sight of Katy sitting there, flushed, panting, but enjoying the surprise she caused.

"You see," she explained, in an apologising tone, "I was seized with a desire to explore. It is such a time since I saw any room but my own! But oh dear, how long that hall is! I had forgotten it could be so long. I shall have to take a good rest before I go back."

Katy did take a good rest, but she was very tired next day. The experiment, however, did no harm. In the course of two or three weeks she was able to walk all over the second storey.

This was a great enjoyment. It was like reading an interesting book to see all the new things and the little changes. She was for ever wondering over something.

"Why, Dorry," she would say, "what a pretty bookshelf! When did you get it?"

"That old thing! Why, I've had it two years. Didn't I ever tell you about it?"

"Perhaps you did," Katy would reply, "but you see I never *saw it* before, so it made no impression."

By the end of August she was grown so strong that she began to talk about going downstairs. But Papa said, "Wait."

"It will tire you much more than walking about on a level," he explained, "you had better put it off a little while—till you are quite sure of your feet."

"I think so too," said Clover; "and besides, I want to have the house all put in order and made nice before your sharp eyes see it, Mrs. Housekeeper. Oh, I'll tell you! Such a beautiful idea has come into my head! You shall fix a day to come down, Katy, and we'll be all ready for you, and have a 'celebration' among ourselves. That would be just lovely! How soon may she, Papa?"

"Well—in ten days, I should say, it might be safe."

"Ten days! that will bring it to the seventh of September, won't it?" said Katy. "Then, Papa, if I may, I'll come down for the first time on the eighth. It was Mamma's birthday, you know," she added in a lower voice.

So it was settled. "How delicious!" cried Clover, skipping about and clapping her hands; "I never, never, never *did* hear anything so perfectly lovely. Papa, when are you coming downstairs? I want to speak to you *dreadfully*."

"Right away—rather than have my coat-tails pulled off," answered Dr. Carr, laughing, and they went away together. Katy sat looking out of the window in a peaceful, happy mood.

"Oh!" she thought, "can it really be? Is school going to 'let out,' just as Cousin Helen's hymn said? Am I going to

'Bid a sweet good-bye to Pain?'

But there was Love in the Pain. I see it now. How good the dear Teacher has been to me!"

Clover seemed to be very busy all the rest of that week. She was "having windows washed," she said, but this explanation hardly accounted for her long absences, and the mysterious exultation on her face, not to mention certain sounds of hammering and sawing which came from downstairs. The other children had evidently been warned to say nothing; for once or twice Philly broke out with, "O Katy! " and then hushed himself up, saying, "I most forgot! "

Katy grew very curious. But she saw that the secret, whatever it was, gave immense satisfaction to everybody except herself; so, though she longed to know, she concluded not to spoil the fun by asking any questions.

At last it wanted but one day of the important occasion.

"See," said Katy, as Clover came into the room a little before tea-time. "Miss Petingill has brought home my new dress. I'm going to wear it for the first time to go downstairs in."

"How pretty! " said Clover, examining the dress, which was a soft, dove-coloured cashmere, trimmed with ribbon of the same shade. "But, Katy, I came up to shut your door. Bridget's going to sweep the hall, and I don't want the dust to fly in, because your room was brushed this morning, you know."

"What a queer time to sweep the hall! " said Katy, wondering. "Why don't you make her wait till morning?"

"Oh, she can't! There are—she has—I mean there will be other things for her to do to-morrow. It's a great deal more convenient that she should do it now. Don't worry, Katy, darling, but just keep your door shut. You will, won't you? Promise me! "

"Very well," said Katy, more and more amazed, but yielding to Clover's eagerness. "I'll keep it shut." Her curiosity was excited. She took a book and tried to read, but the letters danced up and down before her eyes, and she couldn't help listening. Bridget was making a most ostentatious noise with her broom but, through it all, Katy seemed to hear other sounds—feet on the stairs, doors opening and shutting—once, a stifled giggle. How queer it all was!

"Never mind," she said, resolutely stopping her ears, "I shall know all about it to-morrow."

To-morrow dawned fresh and fair—the very ideal of a September day.

"Katy!" said Clover, as she came in from the garden with her hands full of flowers, "that dress of yours is sweet. You never looked so nice before in your life!" And she stuck a beautiful carnation pink under Katy's breastpin, and fastened another in her hair.

"There," she said, "now you're adorned. Papa is coming up in a few minutes to take you down."

Just then Elsie and Johnnie came in. They had on their best frocks. So had Clover. It was evidently a festival day to all the house. Cecy followed, invited over for the special purpose of seeing Katy walk downstairs. She, too, had on a new frock.

"How fine we are!" said Clover, as she remarked this magnificence. "Turn round, Cecy—a pannier, I do declare—and a sash! You are getting awfully grown up, Miss Hall."

"None of us will ever be so 'grown up' as Katy," said Cecy, laughing.

And now Papa appeared. Very slowly they all went downstairs, Katy leaning on Papa, with Dorry on her other side, and the girls behind, while Philly clattered ahead. And there were Debby and Bridget and Alexander peeping out of the kitchen door to watch her, and dear old Mary with her apron at her eyes crying for joy.

"Oh, the front door is open!" said Katy, in a delighted tone. "How nice! And what a pretty oil-cloth. That's new since I was here."

"Don't stop to look at *that*!" cried Philly, who seemed in a great hurry about something. "It isn't new. It's been there ever and ever so long! Come into the parlour instead."

"Yes!" said Papa, "dinner isn't quite ready yet, you'll have time to rest a little after your walk downstairs. You have borne it admirably, Katy. Are you very tired?"

"Not a bit!" replied Katy, cheerfully. "I could do it alone, I think. Oh! the bookcase door has been mended! How nice it looks."

"Don't wait, oh, don't wait!" repeated Phil, in an agony of impatience.

So they moved on. Papa opened the parlour door. Katy took one step into the room—then stopped. The colour flashed over her face, and she held by the door-knob to support herself. What was it that she saw?

Not merely the room itself, with its fresh muslin curtains and vases of flowers. Nor even the wide, beautiful window which had been cut toward the sun, or the inviting little couch and table which stood there, evidently for her. No, there was something else! The sofa was pulled out, and there upon it, supported by pillows, her bright eyes turned to the door, lay—Cousin Helen! When she saw Katy she held out her arms.

Clover and Cecy agreed afterward that they never were so frightened in their lives at this moment; for Katy, forgetting her weakness, let go of Papa's arm, and absolutely *ran* toward the sofa. "Oh, Cousin Helen! dear, dear Cousin Helen!" she cried. Then she tumbled down by the sofa somehow, the two pairs of arms and the two faces met, and for a moment or two not a word more was heard from anybody.

"Isn't it a nice 'prise?" shouted Philly, turning a somersault by way of relieving his feelings, while John and Dorry executed a sort of war-dance round the sofa.

Phil's voice seemed to break the spell of silence, and a perfect hubbub of questions and exclamations began.

It appeared that this happy thought of getting Cousin Helen to the "celebration" was Clover's. She it was who had proposed to Papa, and made all the arrangements. And, artful puss! she had set Bridget to sweep the hall on purpose that Katy might not hear the noise of the arrival.

"Cousin Helen's going to stay three weeks this time—isn't that nice?" asked Elsie, while Clover anxiously questioned: "Are you sure that you didn't suspect? Not one bit? Not the least tiny, weeny mite?"

"No, indeed—not the least. How could I suspect anything so perfectly delightful?" and Katy gave Cousin Helen another rapturous kiss.

Such a short day as that seemed! There was so much to see, to ask about, to talk over, that the hours flew, and evening dropped upon them all like another great surprise.

Cousin Helen was perhaps the happiest of the party. Besides the pleasure of knowing Katy to be almost well again, she had the additional enjoyment of seeing for herself how many changes for the better had taken place during the four years among the little cousins she loved so much.

It was very interesting to watch them all. Elsie and Dorry seemed to her the most improved of the family. Elsie had quite lost her plaintive look and little injured tone, and was as bright and beaming a maiden of twelve as any one could wish to see. Dorry's moody face had grown open and sensible, and his manners were good-humoured and obliging. He was still a sober boy, and not specially quick in catching an idea, but he promised to turn out a valuable man. And to him, as to all the other children, Katy was evidently the centre and sun. They all revolved about her, and trusted her for everything. Cousin Helen looked on as Phil came in crying, after a hard tumble, and was consoled; as Johnnie whispered an important secret, and Elsie begged for help in her work. She saw Katy meet them all pleasantly and sweetly, without a bit of the dictatorial elder-sister in her manner, and with none of her old impetuous tone. And, best of all, she saw the change in Katy's own face; the gentle expression of her eyes, the womanly look, the pleasant voice, the politeness, the tact in advising the others without seeming to advise.

"Dear Katy," she said, a day or two after her arrival, "this visit is a great pleasure to me—you can't think how great. It is such a contrast to the last I made, when you were so sick, and everybody so sad. Do you remember?"

"Indeed I do! And how good you were, and how you helped me! I shall never forget that."

"I'm glad! But what I could do was very little. You have been learning by yourself all this time. And Katy, darling, I want to tell you how pleased I am to see how bravely you have worked your way up. I can perceive it in everything—in Papa, in the children, in yourself. You have won the place, which, you recollect, I once told you an invalid should try to gain, of being to everybody 'the Heart of the house.'"

"Oh, Cousin Helen, don't!" said Katy, her eyes filling with sudden tears. "I haven't been brave. You can't think how badly I sometimes have behaved—how cross and ungrateful I am, how stupid, and slow. Every day I see things which ought to be done, and I don't do them. It's too delightful to have you praise me—but you mustn't. I don't deserve it."

But although she said she didn't deserve it, I think that Katy did.

THE END

What Katy Did at School

What Katy Did at School was
first published in this edition in the U.K. in a single volume
in 1964 by William Collins Sons & Co. Ltd,
and in Armada in 1968

Contents

CHAPTER ONE

CONIC SECTION

IT WAS just after that happy visit mentioned at the end of *What Katy Did*, that Elsie and John made their famous excursion to Conic Section; an excursion which neither of them ever forgot, and about which the family teased them for a long time afterward.

The summer had been cool; but, as often happens after cool summers, the autumn proved unusually hot. It seemed as if the months had been playing a game, and had "changed places" all round; and as if September were determined to show that he knew how to make himself just as disagreeable as August, if only he chose to do so.

All the last half if Cousin Helen's stay, the weather was excessively sultry. She felt it very much, though the children did all they could to make her comfortable, with shaded rooms, and iced water, and fans. Every evening the boys would wheel her sofa out on the porch, in hopes of coolness; but it was of no use: the evenings were as warm as the days, and the yellow dust hanging in the air made the sunshine look thick and hot. A few bright leaves appeared on the trees, but they were wrinkled, and of an ugly colour. Clover said she thought they had been *boiled* red like lobsters. Altogether, the month was a trying one, and the coming of October made little or no difference; still the dust continued, and the heat; and the wind, when it blew, had no refreshment in it, but seemed to have passed over some great furnace, which had burned out of it all life and flavour.

In spite of this, however, it was wonderful to see how Katy gained and improved. Every day added to her powers. First she came down to dinner, then to breakfast.

She sat on the porch in the afternoons; she poured out the tea. It was like a miracle to the others, in the beginning, to watch her going about the house; but they got used to it surprisingly soon—one does to pleasant things. One person, however, never got used to it, never took it as a matter of course; and that was Katy herself. She could not run downstairs, or out into the garden; she could not open the kitchen door to give an order, without a sense of gladness and exultation which was beyond words. The wider and more active life stimulated her in every way. Her cheeks grew round and pink, her eyes bright. Cousin Helen and Papa watched this change with indescribable pleasure; and Mrs. Worrett, who dropped in to lunch one day, fairly screamed with surprise at the sight of it.

"To think of it!" she cried, "why, the last time I was here you looked as if you had taken root in that chair of yours for the rest of your days, and here you are stepping around as lively as I be! Well, well! Wonders will never cease. It does my eyes good to see you, Katherine. I wish your poor aunt were here today; that I do. How pleased she'd be!"

It is doubtful whether Aunt Izzie would have been so pleased, for the lived-in look of the best parlour would have horrified her extremely; but Katy did not recollect that just then. She was touched at the genuine kindness of Mrs. Worrett's voice, and took very willingly her offered kiss. Clover brought lemonade and grapes, and they all devoted themselves to making the old lady comfortable. Just before she went away, she said:

"How is it that I can't never get any of you to come out to Conic Section? I'm sure I've asked you often enough. There's Elsie, now, and John: they're just the age to enjoy being in the country. Why won't you send them out for a week? Johnnie can feed chickens, and chase 'em too, if she likes," she added, as Johnnie dashed then into view, pursuing one of Phil's bantams round the house. "Tell her so, won't you, Katherine? There is lots of chickens on the farm. She can chase 'em from morning to night, if she's a mind to."

Katy thanked her, but she didn't think the children would care to go. She gave Johnnie the message, and then the whole matter passed out of her mind. She was surprised, a few days later, by having it brought up again by Elsie. The family were in low spirits that morning because of Cousin Helen's having just gone away; and Elsie was lying on the sofa, fanning herself with a great palm-leaf fan.

"Oh, dear!" she sighed. "Do you suppose it's ever going to be cool again in this world? It does seem as if I couldn't bear it any longer."

"Aren't you well, darling?" inquired Katy, anxiously.

"Oh, yes! Well enough," replied Elsie. "It's only this horrid heat, and never going away to where it's cooler. I keep thinking about the country, and wishing I was there feeling the wind blow. I wonder if Papa wouldn't let John and me go to Conic Section, and see Mrs. Worrett. Do you think he would if you asked him?"

"But," said Katy, amazed, "Conic Section isn't exactly country, you know. It is just out of the city—only six miles from here. And Mrs. Worrett's house is close to the road, Papa said. Do you think you'd like it, dear? It *can't* be very much cooler than this."

"Oh, yes! it can," rejoined Elsie, in a tone which was a little fretful. "It's quite near woods; Mrs. Worrett told me so. Besides it's *always* cooler on a farm. There's more room for the wind, and—oh, everything's pleasanter! You can't think how tired I am of this hot house. Last night I hardly slept at all; and, when I did, I dreamed that I was a loaf of brown bread, and Debby was putting me into the oven to bake. It was a horrid dream. I was so glad to wake up. Won't you ask Papa if we may go, Katy?"

"Why, of course I will, if you wish it so much. Only"— Katy stopped and did not finish her sentence. A vision of fat Mrs. Worrett had risen before her, and she could not help doubting if Elsie would find the farm as pleasant as she expected. But sometimes the truest kindness is in giving people their own unwise way, and Elsie's eyes looked so wistful that Katy had no heart to argue or refuse.

169

Dr. Carr looked doubtful when the plan was proposed to him.

"It's too hot," he said. "I don't believe the girls will like it."

"Oh, yes; we will, Papa; indeed we will," pleaded Elsie and John, who had lingered near the door to learn the fate of their request.

Dr. Carr smiled at the imploring faces, but he looked a little quizzical. "Very well," he said, "you may go. Mr. Worrett is coming into town tomorrow, on some bank business. I'll send word by him; and in the afternoon, when it is cooler, Alexander can drive you out."

"Goody! goody!" cried John, jumping up and down, while Elsie put her arms round Papa's neck and gave him a hug.

"And Thurday I'll send for you," he continued.

"But, Papa," expostulated Elsie, "that's only two days. Mrs. Worrett said a week."

"Yes, she said a week," chimed in John; "and she's got ever so many chickens, and I'm to feed 'em, and chase 'em about as much as I like. Only it's too hot to run much," she added, reflectively.

"You won't really send for us on Thursday, will you, Papa?" urged Elsie, anxiously. "I like to stay ever and ever so long; but Mrs. Worrett said a week."

"I shall send on Thursday," repeated Dr. Carr in a decided tone. Then, seeing that Elsie's lip was trembling and her eyes were full of tears, he continued: "Don't look so woeful, Pussy. Alexander shall drive out for you; but if you want to stay longer, you may send him back with a note to say what day you would like to have him come again. Will that do?"

"Oh, yes;" said Elsie, wiping her eyes; "that will do beautifully, Papa. Only it seems such a pity that Alexander should have to go twice when it's so hot; for we're perfectly sure to want to stay a week."

Papa only laughed as he kissed her All being settled, the children began to get ready. It was quite an excitement packing the bags, and deciding what to take and what not to take. Elsie grew bright and gay with the bustle. Just to think of being in the country—the cool, green country—made her perfectly happy, she declared. The truth was, she was a little feverish and not quite well, and didn't know exactly how she felt or what she wanted.

The drive out was pleasant, except that Alexander upset John's gravity, and hurt Elsie's dignity very much, by inquiring, as they left the gate, "Do the little misses know where it is that they want to go?" Part of the way the road ran through woods. They were rather boggy woods: but the dense shade kept off the sun, and there was a spicy smell of evergreens and sweet fern. Elsie felt that the good time had fairly begun, and her spirits rose with every turn of the wheels.

By and by they left the woods, and came out again into the sunshine. The road was dusty, and so were the fields, and the ragged sheaves of corn-stalks which dotted them here and there looked dusty too. Piles of dusty-red apples lay on the grass, under the orchard trees. Some cows going down a lane toward their milking-shed in a dispirited and thirsty way, which made the children feel thirsty also.

"I want a drink of water very badly," said John. "Do you suppose it's much farther? How long will it be before we get to Mrs. Worrett's, Alexander?"

"'Most there, miss," replied Alexander, laconically.

Elsie put her head out of the carriage, and looked eagerly round. Where was the delightful farm? She saw a big, pumpkin-coloured house by the road-side, a little farther on; but surely that couldn't be it! Yes; Alexander drew up at the gate, and jumped down to lift them out. It really was! The surprise quite took away her breath.

She looked about. There was the woods, to be sure, but half a mile away across the fields. Near the house there were no trees at all; only some lilac bushes at one side; there was no green grass either. A gravel path took up the whole of the narrow front yard; and, what with the blazing colour of the paint and the wideawake look of the blindless windows, the house had somehow the air of standing on

171

tiptoe and staring hard at something—the dust in the road, perhaps, for there seemed nothing else to stare at.

Elsie's heart sank indescribably as she and John got very slowly out of the vehicle, and Alexander, putting his arm over the fence, rapped loudly at the front door. It was some minutes before the rap was answered. Then a heavy step was heard creaking through the hall, and somebody began fumbling at an obstinate bolt, which would not move. Next, a voice which they recognised as Mrs. Worrett's called, "Isaphiny! Isaphiny! Come and see if you can open this door."

"How funny!" whispered Johnny, beginning to giggle.

"Isaphiny" seemed to be upstairs, for presently they heard her running down, after which a fresh rattle began at the obstinate bolt. But still the door did not open, and at length Mrs. Worrett put her lips to the keyhole, and asked:

"Who is it?"

The voice sounded so hollow and ghostly, that Elsie jumped, as she answered: "It's I, Mrs. Worrett—Elsie Carr. And Johnnie's here too."

"Ts, ts, ts!" sounded from within, and then came a whispering, after which Mrs. Worrett put her mouth again to the keyhole, and called out:

"Go round to the back, children. I can't make this door open anyway. It's all swelled up with the damp."

"Damp!" whispered Johnnie, "why, it hasn't rained since the third week in August; Papa said so yesterday."

"That's nothing, Miss Johnnie," put in Alexander, overhearing her. "Folks hereaway don't open their front doors much—only for weddings, and funerals, and such like. Very likely this has stood shut these five years. I know the last time I drove Miss Carr out before she died, it was just so; and she had to go round to the back as you're a-doing now."

John's eyes grew wide with wonder, but there was no time to say anything, for they had turned the corner of the house, and there was Mrs. Worrett waiting at the kitchen door to receive them. She looked fatter than ever, Elsie thought; but she kissed them both, and said she was real glad to see a Carr in her house at last.

"It was too bad," she went on, "to keep you waiting so. But the fact is I got asleep, and when you knocked I waked up all in a daze, and for a minute it didn't come to me who it must be. Take the bags right upstairs, Isaphiny, and put them in the keeping-room chamber. How's your Pa, Elsie —and Katy? Not laid up again, I hope."

"Oh, no: she seems to get better all the time."

"That's right," responded Mrs. Worrett, heartily.

"I didn't know but, what with hot weather, and company in the house, and all—there's a chicken. Johnnie," she exclaimed, suddenly interrupting herself, as a long-legged hen ran past the door. "Want to chase it right away? You can if you like. Or would you rather go upstairs first?"

"Upstairs, please," replied John, while Elsie went to the door, and watched Alexander driving away down the dusty road. She felt as if their last friend had deserted them. Then she and Johnnie followed Isaphiny upstairs. Mrs. Worrett never "mounted" in hot weather, she told them.

The spare chamber was just under the roof. It was very hot, and smelled as if the windows had never been opened since the house was built. As soon as they were alone, Elsie ran across the room, and threw up the sash; but the moment she let go down it fell again, with a crash that shook the floor and made the pitcher dance and rattle in the washbowl. The children were dreadfully frightened, especially when they heard Mrs. Worrett at the foot of the stairs calling to ask what was the matter.

"It's only the window," explained Elsie, going into the hall. "I'm so sorry; but it won't stay open. Something's the matter with it."

"Did you stick the nail in?" inquired Mrs. Worrett.

"The nail? No, ma'am."

"Why, how on earth did you expect it to stay up, then? You young folks never see what's before your eyes. Look on the window-sill, and you'll find it. It's put there a purpose."

Elsie returned, much discomfited. She looked, and,

173

sure enough, there was a big nail, and there was a hole in the side of the window-frame in which to stick it. This time she got the window open without accident; but a long blue paper shade caused her much embarrassment. It hung down, and kept the air from coming in. She saw no way of fastening it.

"Roll it up and put in a pin," suggested John.

"I'm afraid of tearing the paper. Dear, what a horrid thing it is! " replied Elsie, in a disgusted tone.

However, she stuck in a couple of pins and fastened the shade out of the way. After that they looked about the room. It was plainly furnished, but very nice and neat. The bureau was covered with a white towel, on which stood a pincushion, with "Remember Ruth" stuck upon it in pins. John admired this very much, and felt that she could never make up her mind to spoil the pattern by taking out a pin, however great her need of one might be.

"What a high bed! " she exclaimed. "Elsie, you'll have to climb on a chair to get into it; and so shall I."

Elsie felt it. "Feathers! " she cried, in a tone of horror. "Oh, John! Why did we come? What shall we do?"

"I guess we shan't mind it much," replied John who was perfectly well, and considered these little variations on home habits rather as fun than otherwise. But Elsie gave a groan. Two nights on a feather bed! How should she bear it!

Tea was ready in the kitchen when they went downstairs. A little fire had been lighted to boil the water. It was almost out, but the room felt stiflingly warm, and the butter was so nearly melted that Mrs. Worrett had to help it with a teaspoon. Buzzing flies hovered above the table and gathered thick on the plate of cake. The bread was excellent, and so were the cottage cheeses and the stewed quince; but Elsie could eat nothing. She was in a fever of heat. Mrs. Worrett was distressed at this want of appetite, and so was Mr. Worrett, to whom the children had just been introduced. He was a kindly-looking old man, with a bald head, who came to supper in his shirt sleeves, and was as thin as his wife was fat.

174

"I'm afraid the little girl don't like her supper, Lucinda," he said. "You must see about getting her something different tomorrow."

"Oh! It isn't that. Everything is very nice, only I'm not hungry," pleaded Elsie, feeling as if she should like to cry. She did cry a little after tea, as they sat in the dusk; Mr. Worrett smoking his pipe and slapping mosquitoes outside the door, and Mrs. Worrett sleeping rather noisily in a big rocking-chair. But not even Johnnie found out that she was crying, for Elsie felt that she was the naughtiest child in the world to behave so badly when everybody was so kind to her. She repeated this to herself many times, but it didn't do much good. As often as the thought of home and Katy and Papa came, a wild longing to get back to them would rush over her, and her eyes would fill again with sudden tears.

The night was very uncomfortable. Not a breath of wind was stirring, or none found its way to the stifling bed where the little sisters lay. John slept pretty well, in spite of heat and mosquitoes, but Elsie hardly closed her eyes. Once she got up and went to the window, but the blue-paper shade had become unfastened, and rattled down upon her head with a sudden bump, which startled her very much. She could find no pins in the dark, so she left it hanging; whereupon it rustled and flapped through the rest of the night, and did its share towards keeping her awake. About three o'clock she fell into a doze; and it seemed only a minute after that before she waked up to find bright sunshine in the room, and half a dozen roosters crowing and calling under the windows. Her head ached violently. She longed to stay in bed, but feared Mrs. Worrett would think it impolite: so she dressed and went down with Johnnie; but she looked so pale, and ate so little breakfast, that Mrs. Worrett was quite troubled, and said she had better not try to go out, but just lie on the lounge in the best room, and amuse herself with a book.

The lounge in the best room was covered with slippery, purple chintz. It was a high lounge, and very narrow. There was nothing at the end to hold the pillow in its place;

so the pillow constantly tumbled off and jerked Elsie's head suddenly backward, which was not at all comfortable. Worse, Elsie having dropped into a doze, she herself tumbled to the floor, rolling from the glassy, smooth chintz as if it had been a slope of ice. This adventure made her so nervous that she dared not go to sleep again, though Johnnie fetched two chairs, and placed them beside the sofa to hold her on. So she followed Mrs. Worrett's advice, and "amused herself with a book." There were not many books in the best room. The one Elsie chose was a fat black volume called *The Complete Works Of Mrs. Hannah More*. Part of it was prose, and part was poetry. Elsie began with a chapter called "Hints On The Formation of the Character of a Youthful Princess." But there were a great many long words in it; so she turned to a story named *Coelebs in Search of a Wife*. It was about a young gentleman who wanted to get married, but who didn't feel sure that there were any young ladies nice enough for him; so he went about making visits, first to one and then to another; and, when he had stayed a few days at a house, he would always say, "No, she won't do," and then he would go away. At last, he found a young lady who seemed the very person, who visited the poor, and got up early in the morning, and always wore white, and never forgot to wind up her watch or do her duty; and Elsie almost thought that now the difficult young gentleman must be satisfied, and say, "This is the very thing." When, lo! her attention wandered a little, and the next thing she knew she was rolling off the lounge for the second time, in company with Mrs. Hannah More. They landed in the chairs, and Johnnie ran and picked them both up. Altogether, lying on the best parlour sofa was not very restful; and as the day went on, and the sun beating on the blindless windows made the room hotter, Elsie grew continually more and more feverish and homesick and disconsolate.

Meanwhile Johnnie was kept in occupation by Mrs. Worrett, who had got the idea firmly fixed in her mind, that the chief joy in a child's life was to chase chickens. Whenever a hen fluttered past the kitchen door, which was about once in three minutes she would cry, "Here, Johnnie, here's another chicken for you to chase"; and poor Johnnie would feel obliged to dash out into the sun. Being a very polite little girl, she did not like to say to Mrs. Worrett that running in the heat was disagreeable; so by dinner-time she was thoroughly tired out, and would have been cross if she had known how; but she didn't—Johnnie was never cross. After dinner it was even worse; for the sun was hotter, and the chickens, who didn't mind sun, seemed to be walking all the time. "Hurry, Johnnie, here's another," came so constantly, that at last Elsie grew desperate, got up, and went to the kitchen with a languid appeal. "Please, Mrs. Worrett, won't you let Johnnie stay by me, because my head aches so hard?" After that, Johnnie had rest; for Mrs. Worrett was the kindest of women, and had no idea that she was not amusing her little guest in the most delightful manner.

A little before six, Elsie's head felt better; and she and Johnnie put on their hats, and went for a walk in the garden. There was not much to see; beds of vegetables, a few currant bushes, that was all. Elsie was leaning against a paling, and trying to make out why the Worrett house had that queer tiptoe expression, when a sudden loud grunt startled her, and something touched the top of her head. She turned, and there was an enormous pig standing on his hind legs, on the other side of the paling. He was taller than Elsie as he stood thus, and it was his cold nose which had touched her head. Somehow, appearing in this unexpected way, he seemed to the children like some dreadful wild beast. They screamed with fright, and fled to the house, from which Elsie never ventured to stir again during their visit. John chased chickens at intervals, but it was a doubtful pleasure; and all the time she kept a wary eye on the distant pig.

That evening, while Mrs. Worrett slept and Mr. Worrett smoked outside the door, Elsie felt so very miserable that she broke down altogether. She put her head in Johnnie's lap, as they sat together in the darkest corner of the room, and sobbed and cried, making as little noise as she possibly

177

could. Johnnie comforted her with soft pats and strokings; but did not dare to say a word, for fear Mrs. Worrett should wake up and find them out.

When the morning came, Elsie's one thought was, would Alexander come for them in the afternoon? All day she watched the clock and the road with feverish anxiety. Oh! if Papa had changed his mind, had decided to let them stay for a week at Conic Section, what should she do? It was just possible to worry through and keep alive till afternoon, she thought; but if they were forced to spend another night in that feather-bed, with those mosquitoes, hearing the blue shade rattle and quiver hour after hour, she should die, she was sure she should die!

But Elsie was not called upon to die, or even to discover how easy it is to survive a little discomfort. About five, her anxious watch was rewarded by the appearance of a cloud of dust, out of which presently emerged old Whitey's ears and the top of the well-known carriage. They stopped at the gate. There was Alexander, brisk and smiling, very glad to see his "little misses again," and to find them so glad to go home. Mrs. Worrett, however, did not discover that they were glad; no, indeed! Elsie and John were much too polite for that. They thanked the old lady, and said goodbye so prettily that, after they were gone, she told Mr. Worrett that it hadn't been a bit of trouble having them there, and she hoped they would come again, they enjoyed everything so much; only it was a pity that Elsie looked so peaked. And that very moment Elsie was sitting on the floor of the vehicle with her head in John's lap, crying and sobbing for joy that the visit was over, and that she was on the way home. "If only I live to get there," she said, "I'll never, no never, go into the country again!'" which was silly enough; but we must forgive her, because she was half sick.

Ah, how charming home did look, with the family grouped in the shady porch, Katy in her white wrapper, Clover with rose-buds in her belt, and everybody ready to welcome and pet the little absentees! There was much hugging and kissing, and much to tell of what had happened in two days: how a letter had come from Cousin Helen; how Daisy White had four kittens as white as herself; how Dorry had finished his water-wheel—a wheel which turned in the bath-tub, and was "really ingenious," Papa said; and Phil had "swapped" one of his bantam chicks for one of Eugene Slack's Brahmapootras. It was not till they were all seated round the tea-table that anybody demanded an account of the visit. Elsie felt this a relief, and was just thinking how delicious everything was, from the sliced peaches to the clinking ice in the milk-pitcher, when Papa put the dreaded question:

"Well, Elsie, so you decided to come, after all. How was it? Why didn't you stay your week out? You look pale, it seems to me. Have you been enjoying yourself too much? Tell us all about it."

Elsie looked at Papa, and Papa looked at Elsie. Dr. Carr's eyes twinkled just a little, but otherwise he was perfectly grave. Elsie began to speak, then to laugh, then to cry, and the explanation, when it came, was given in a mingled burst of all three.

"Oh, Papa, it was horrid! That is, Mrs. Worrett was just as kind as could be, but so fat; and oh, such a pig! I never imagined such a pig. And the calico on that horrid sofa was so slippery that I rolled off five times, and once I hurt myself very badly. And we had a feather-bed; and I was so some-sick that I cried all the evening."

"That must have been gratifying to Mrs. Worrett," put in Dr. Carr.

"Oh! she didn't know it, Papa. She was asleep, and snoring so that nobody could hear. And the flies!—such flies, Katy!—and the mosquitoes, and our window wouldn't open till I put in a nail. I am so glad to get home! I never want to go into the country again, never, never! Oh, if Alexander hadn't come!—why, Clover, what are you laughing for? And Dorry, I think it's very unkind," and Elsie ran to Katy, hid her face, and began to cry.

"Never mind, darling, they didn't mean to be unkind. Papa, her hands are quite hot; you must give her something." Katy's voice shook a little; but she would not hurt Elsie's feelings by showing that she was amused. Papa gave Elsie "something" before she went to bed—a very mild dose, I fancy; for doctor's little girls, as a general rule, don't take medicine, and next day she was much better. As the adventures of the Conic Section visit leaked out bit by bit, the family laughed till it seemed as if they would never stop. Phil was for ever enacting the pig, standing on his triumphant hind legs, and patting Elsie's head with his nose; and many and many a time, "It will end like your visit to Mrs. Worrett," proved a useful check when Elsie was in a self-willed mood and bent on some scheme which for the moment struck her as delightful. For one of the good things about our childish mistakes is, that each one teaches us something; and so, blundering on, we grow wiser till, when the time comes, we are ready to take our places among the wonderful grown-up people who never make mistakes.

CHAPTER TWO

A NEW YEAR AND A NEW PLAN

WHEN summer lingers on into October, it often seems as if winter, anxious to catch a glimpse of her, hurries a little; and so people are cheated out of their autumn. It was so that year. Almost as soon as it ceased to be hot, it began to be cold. The leaves, instead of drifting away in soft, dying colours, like sunset clouds, turned yellow all at once; and were whirled off the trees in a single gusty night, leaving everything bare and desolate. Thanksgiving* came; and before the smell of the turkey was fairly out of the house, it was time to hang up stockings and dress the Christmas tree. They had a tree that year in honour of

*Thanksgiving Day. National holiday in the United States, commemorating the fine harvest reaped by the Pilgrim colony in 1623, after a winter of great suffering and privation.

Katy's being downstairs. Cecy, who had gone away to boarding-school, came home; and it was all delightful, except that the days flew too fast. Clover said it seemed to her very queer that there was so much less time than usual in the world. She couldn't imagine what had become of it; there used to be plenty. And she was certain that Dorry must have been tinkering all the clocks—they struck so often.

It was just after New Year that Dr. Carr walked in one day with a letter in his hand, and remarked, "Mr. and Mrs. Page are coming to stay with us."

"Mr. and Mrs. Page," repeated Katy, "who are they, Papa? Did I ever see them?"

"Once, when you were four years old, and Elsie a baby. Of course you don't remember it."

"But who are they, Papa?"

"Mrs. Page was your dear mother's second cousin; and at one time she lived in your grandfather's family, and was like a sister to Mamma and Uncle Charles. It is a good many years since I have seen her. Mr. Page is a railroad engineer. He is coming this way on business, and they will stop for a few days with us. Your Cousin Olivia writes that she is anxious to see all you children. Have everything as nice as you can, Katy."

"Of course I will. What day are they coming?"

"Thursday—no, Friday," replied Dr. Carr, consulting the letter, "Friday evening, at half past six. Order something substantial for tea that night, Katy. They'll be hungry after travelling."

Katy worked with a will for the next two days. Twenty times, at least, she went into the blue room to make sure that nothing was forgotten; repeating, as if it had been a lesson in geography, "Bath towels, face towels, matches, soap, candles, cologne, extra blanket, ink." A nice little fire was lighted in the bedroom on Friday afternoon, and a big, beautiful one in the parlour, which looked very pleasant with the lamp lit and Clover's geraniums and china roses in the window. The tea-table was set with the best linen and the pink and white china. Debby's muffins were very light.

The crab-apple jelly came out of its mould clear and whole, and the cold chicken looked appetising, with its green wreath of parsley. There was stewed potato, too, and, of course, oysters. Everybody in Burnet had oysters for tea when company was expected. They were counted a special treat; because they were rather dear, and could not always be procured. Burnet was a thousand miles from the sea, so the oysters were of the tin-can variety. The cans gave the oysters a curious taste—tinny, or was it more like solder? At all events, Burnet people liked it, and always insisted that it was a striking improvement on the flavour which oysters have on their native shores. Everything was as nice as could be, when Katy stood in the dining-room to take a last look at her arrangements; and she hoped Papa would be pleased, and that Mamma's cousin would think her a good housekeeper.

"I don't want to have on my other jacket," observed Phil, putting his head in at the door. "Need I? This is nice."

"Let me see," said Katy, gently turning him round. "Well, it goes pretty well; but I think I'd rather you should put on the other, if you don't mind much. We want everything as nice as possible, you know; because this is Papa's company, and he hardly ever has any."

"Just one little sticky place isn't much," said Phil, rather gloomily, wetting his finger and rubbing at a shiny place in his sleeve. "Do you really think I'd better? Well, then, I will."

"That's a dear"—kissing him. "Be quick, Philly, for it's almost time they were here. And please tell Dorry to make haste. It's ever so long since he went upstairs."

"Dorry's an awful dandy," remarked Phil, confidentially. "He looks in the glass, and makes faces if he can't get his parting straight. I wouldn't care so much about my clothes for a good deal. It's like a girl. Jim Slack says a boy who shines his hair up like that'll never get to be President, not if he lives a thousand years."

"Well," said Katy, laughing; "it's something to be clean, even if you cannot be a President."

She was not at all alarmed by Dorry's recent reaction in favour of personal adornment. He came down pretty soon, very spick and span in his best suit and asked her to fasten the blue ribbon under his collar, which she did most obligingly; though he was very particular as to the size of the bows and length of the ends, and made her tie and retie more than once. She had just arranged it to suit him when a carriage stopped.

"There they are," she cried. "Run and open the door, Dorry."

Dorry did so; and Katy, following, found Papa ushering in a tall gentleman, and a lady who was not tall, but whose Roman nose and long neck, and general air of style and fashion, made her look so. Katy bent quite over to be kissed; but for all that she felt small, and young, and unformed, as the eyes of Mamma's cousin looked her over and over, and through and through, and Mrs. Page said:

"Why, Philip, is it possible that this tall girl is one of yours? Dear me! How the time flies! I was thinking of the little creatures I saw when I was here last. And this other great creature can't be Elsie? That mite of a baby! Impossible! I cannot realise it. I really cannot realise it in the least."

"Won't you come to the fire, Mrs. Page?" said Katy, rather timidly.

"Don't call me Mrs. Page, my dear. Call me Cousin Olivia."

Then the newcomer rustled into the parlour, where Johnnie and Phil were waiting to be introduced; and again she remarked that she "couldn't realise it." I don't know why Mrs. Page's not realising it should have made Katy uncomfortable; but it did.

Supper went off well. The guests ate and praised; and Dr. Carr looked pleased, and said: "We think Katy an excellent housekeeper for her age." At which Katy blushed and was delighted, till she caught Mrs. Page's eyes fixed upon her, with a look of scrutiny and amusement, whereupon she felt awkward and ill at ease. It was so all the evening. Mamma's cousin was entertaining and bright, and told lively stories; but the children felt that she was watching them, and passing judgment on their ways. Children are very quick to suspect when older people hold within themselves these little private courts of inquiry, and they always resent it.

Next morning Mrs. Page sat by while Katy washed the breakfast things, fed the birds, and did various odd jobs about the room and house.

"My dear," she said at last, "what a solemn girl you are! I should think from your face that you were at least five-and-thirty. Don't you ever laugh or frolic, like other girls of your age? Why, my Lilly, who is four months older than you, is a perfect child still; impulsive as a baby, bubbling over with fun from morning till night."

"I've been shut up a good deal," said Katy, trying to defend herself; "but I didn't know I was solemn."

"My dear, that's the very thing I complain of; you don't know it! You are altogether ahead of your age. It's very bad for you, in my opinion. All this housekeeping and care, for young girls like you and Clover, is wrong and unnatural. I don't like it; indeed I don't."

"Oh! housekeeping doesn't hurt me a bit," protested Katy, trying to smile. "We have lovely times; indeed we do, Cousin Olivia."

Cousin Olivia only pursed up her mouth, and repeated, "It's wrong, my dear. It's unnatural It's not the thing for you. Depend upon it, it's not the thing."

This was unpleasant; but what was worse. had Katy known it, Mrs. Page attacked Dr. Carr upon the subject. He was quite troubled to learn that she considered Katy grave and careworn and unlike what girls of her age should be. Katy caught him looking at her with a puzzled expression.

"What is it, dear Papa? Do you want anything?"

"No, child, nothing. What are you doing there? Mending the parlour curtain, eh? Can't old Mary attend to that, and give you a chance to frisk about with the other girls?"

"Papa! As if I wanted to frisk! I declare you're as

184

bad as Cousin Olivia. She's always telling me that I ought to bubble over with mirth. I don't wish to bubble. I don't know how."

"I'm afraid you don't," said Dr. Carr, with an odd sigh, which set Katy to wondering. What should Papa sigh for? Had she done anything wrong? She began to rack her brains and memory as to whether it could be this or that; or, if not, what could it be? Such needless self-examination does no good. Katy looked "more solemn" than ever after it.

Altogether, Mrs. Page was not a favourite in the family. She had every intention of being kind to her cousin's children, "so dreadfully in want of a mother, poor things!" but she could not hide the fact that their ways puzzled and did not please her; and the children detected this, as children always will. She and Mr. Page were very polite. They praised the housekeeping, and the excellent order of everything, and said that there were never better children in the world than John, and Dorry, and Phil. But, through all, Katy perceived the hidden disapproval; and she couldn't help feeling glad when the visit ended, and they went away.

With their departure, matters went back to their old train, and Katy forgot her disagreeable feelings. Papa seemed a little grave and preoccupied; but doctors often are when they have bad cases to think of, and nobody noticed it particularly, or remarked that several letters came from Mrs. Page, and nothing was heard of their contents, except that "Cousin Olivia sent her love." So it was a shock when, one day Papa called Katy into the study to tell her of a new plan. She knew at once that it was something important when she heard his voice; it sounded so grave. Besides, he said, "My daughter," a phrase he never used except upon the most impressive occasions.

"My daughter," he began, "I want to talk to you about something which I have been thinking of. How would you and Clover like going away to school together?"

"To school? To Mrs. Knight's?"

"No, not to Mrs. Knight's. To a boarding-school at the

East, where Lilly Page has been for two years. Didn't you hear Cousin Olivia speak of it when she was here?"

"I believe I did. But, Papa, you won't really?"

"Yes, I think so," said Dr. Carr, gently. "Listen, Katy, and don't feel so badly, my dear child. I've thought the plan over carefully; and it seems to me a good one, though I hate to part from you. It is pretty much as your cousin says; these home cares, which I can't take from you while you are at home, are making you old before your time. Heaven knows, I don't want to turn you into a silly giggling miss; but I should like you to enjoy your youth while you have it, and not grow middle-aged before you are twenty."

"What is the name of the school?" asked Katy. Her voice sounded a good deal like a sob.

"The girls call it 'The Nunnery.' It is at Hillsover, on the Connecticut River. pretty far north. An th winters are pretty cold, I fancy; but the air is sure to be good and bracing. That is one thing which has inclined me to the plan. The climate is just what you need."

"Hillsover? Isn't there a college there too?"

"Yes; Arrowmouth College. I believe there is always a college where there is a boarding-school; though why, I can't for the life of me imagine. That's neither here nor there, however, I'm not afraid of your. getting into silly scrapes, as girls sometimes do."

"College scrapes? Why, how could I? We don't have anything to do with the .college, do we?" said Katy. opening her candid eyes with such a wondering stare. that Dr. Carr laughed, as he patted her cheek and replied. "No, my dear, not a thing."

"The term opens the third week in April," he went on. "You must begin to get ready at once. Mrs. Hall has just fitted out Cecy; so she can tell you what you will need. You'd better consult her, tomorrow."

"But, Papa," cried Katy beginning to realise it. "what are you gong to do? Elsie's a darling. but she's so very little. I don't see how you can possibly manage. I'm sure you'll miss us. and so will the children."

"I rather think we shall," said Dr. Carr with a smile,

186

which ended in a sigh; "but we shall do very well, Katy; never fear. Miss Finch will see to us."

"Miss Finch? Do you mean Mrs. Knight's sister-in-law?"

"Yes. Her mother died in the summer; so she has no particular home now, and is glad to come for a year and keep house for us. Mrs. Knight says she is a good manager; and I dare say she'll fill your place sufficiently well, as far as that goes. We can't expect her to be *you*, you know: that would be unreasonable." And Dr. Carr put his arm round Katy, and kissed her so fondly that she was quite overcome and clung to him, crying:

"O Papa! Don't make us go. I'll frisk, and be as young as I can, and not grow middle-aged or anything disagreeable, if only you'll let us stay. Never mind what Cousin Olivia says; she doesn't know. Cousin Helen wouldn't say so, I'm sure."

"On the contrary, Helen thinks well of the plan; only she wishes the school were nearer," said Dr. Carr. "No, Katy, don't coax. My mind is made up. It will do you and Clover both good; and once you are settled at Hillsover, you'll be very happy, I hope."

When Papa spoke in this decided tone, it was never any use to urge him. Katy knew this, and ceased her pleadings. She went to find Clover and tell her the news, and the two girls had a hearty cry together. A sort of "clearing-up shower" it turned out to be; for when once they had wiped their eyes, everything looked brighter, and they began to see a pleasant side to the plan.

"The travelling part of it will be very nice," pronounced Clover. "We never went so far away from home before."

Elsie, who was still looking very woeful, burst into tears afresh at this remark.

"Oh, don't, darling!" said Katy. "Think how pleasant it will be to send letters, and to get them from us. I shall write to you every Saturday. Run for the big atlas—there's a dear, and let us see where we are going."

Elsie brought the atlas; and the three heads bent eagerly over it, as Clover traced the route of the journey with her

187

forefinger. How exciting it looked! There was the railroad, twisting and curving over half a dozen States. The black dots which followed it were towns and villages, all of which they should see. By and by the road made a bend, and swept northward by the side of the Connecticut River and toward the hills. They had heard how beautiful the Connecticut valley is.

"Only think! we shall be close to it," remarked Clover; "and we shall see the hills. I suppose they are very high, a great deal higher than the hill at Bolton."

"I hope so," laughed Dr. Carr, who came into the room just then. The hill at Bolton was one of his favourite jokes. When Mamma first came to Burnet, she had paid a visit to some friends at Bolton; and one day, when they were all out walking, they asked her if she felt strong enough to go to the top of the hill. Mamma was used to hills, so she said yes, and walked on, very glad to find that there was a hill in the flat country, but wondering a little why they did not see it. At last she asked where it was, and, behold, they had just reached the top! The slope had been so gradual that she had never found out that they were going uphill at all. Dr. Carr had told this story to the children, but had never been able to make them see the joke very clearly. In fact, when Clover went to Bolton, she was quite struck with the hill: it was so much higher than the sand-bank which bordered the lake at Burnet.

There was a great deal to do to make the girls ready for school by the third week in April. Mrs. Hall was very kind, and her advice was sensible; though, except for Dr. Carr, the girls would hardly have had furs and flannels enough for so cold a place as Hillsover. Everything for winter as well as for summer had to be thought of; for it had been arranged that the girls should not come home for the autumn vacation, but should spend it with Mrs. Page. This was the hardest thing about the plan. Katy begged very hard for Christmas; but when she learned that it would take three days to come and three to go, and that the holidays lasted less than a week, she saw it was of no use, and gave up the idea, while Elsie tried to comfort herself by planning a Christmas-box. The preparations kept them so busy that there was no time for anything else. Mrs. Hall was always wanting them to go with her to shops, or Miss Petingill demanding that they should try on linings; and so the days flew by. At last all was ready. The nice half-dozens of pretty underclothes came home from the sewing-machine woman's, and were done up by Bridget, who dropped many a tear into the starch, at the thought of the young ladies going away. Mrs. Hall, who was a good packer, put the things into the new trunks. Everybody gave the girls presents, as if they had been brides starting on a wedding journey.

Papa's was a watch for each. They were not new, but the girls thought them beautiful. Katy's had belonged to her Mother. It was large and old-fashioned, with a finely-wrought case. Clover's, which had been her grandmother's, was larger still. It had a quaint ornament on the back—a sort of true-love knot, done in gold of different tints. The girls were excessively pleased with these watches. They wore them with guard chains of black watered ribbon, and every other minute they looked to see what the time was.

Elsie had been in Papa's confidence, so her presents were watch-cases, embroidered on perforated paper. Johnnie gave Katy a box of pencils, and Clover a pen-knife with a pearl handle. Dorry and Phil clubbed to buy a box of notepaper and envelopes, which the girls were requested to divide between them. Miss Petingill contributed a bottle of ginger balsam, and a box of opodeldoc salve, to be used in case of possible chilblains. Old Mary's offering was a couple of needle-books, full of bright, sharp needles.

"I wouldn't give you scissors," she said; "but you can't cut love—or, for the matter of that, anything else—with a needle."

Miss Finch, the new housekeeper, arrived a few days before they started: so Katy had time to take her over the house and explain all the different things she wanted done and not done to secure Papa's comfort and the children's. Miss Finch was meek and gentle. She seemed glad of a comfortable home. And Katy felt that she would be kind

*The little crew stood on the point fluttering their
handkerchiefs, radiant with smiles.*

to the boys, and not fret Debby, and drive her into marrying Alexander and going away—an event which Aunt Izzie had been used to predict. Now that all was settled, she and Clover found themselves looking forward to the change with pleasure. There was something new and interesting about it which excited their imaginations.

The last evening was a melancholy one. Elsie had been too much absorbed in the preparations to realise her loss; but, when it came to locking the trunks, her courage gave way altogether. She was in such a state of affliction that everybody else became afflicted too; and there is no knowing what would have happened, had not a parcel arrived by express and distracted their attention. The parcel was from Cousin Helen, whose things, like herself, had a knack of coming at the moment when most wanted. It contained two pretty silk umbrellas—one brown, and one dark green, with Katy's initials on one handle, and Clover's on the other. Opening these treasures, and exclaiming over them, helped the family through the evening wonderfully; and next morning there was such a bustle of getting off that nobody had time to cry.

After the last kisses had been given, and Philly, who had climbed on the horse-block, was clamouring for "one more —just one more," Dr. Carr, looking at the sober faces, was struck by a bright idea; and calling Alexander, told him to hurry old Whitey into the carryall, and drive the children down to Willett's Point, that they might wave their handkerchiefs to the boat as she went by. This suggestion worked like a charm on the spirits of the party. Phil began to caper, and Elsie and John ran in to get their hats. Half an hour later, when the boat rounded the point, there stood the little crew, radiant with smiles, fluttering their handkerchiefs and kissing their hands as cheerfully as possible. It was a pleasant last look to the two who stood beside Papa on the deck; and, as they waved back their greetings to the little ones, and then looked forward across the blue water to the unknown places they were going to see, Katy and Clover felt that the new life opened well, and promised to be very interesting indeed.

CHAPTER THREE

ON THE WAY

THE JOURNEY from Burnet to Hillsover was a very long one. It took the greater part of three days, and as Dr. Carr was in a hurry to get back to his patients, they travelled without stopping; spending the first night on the boat, and the second on a railroad train. Papa found this tiresome; but the girls, to whom everything was new, thought it delightful. They enjoyed their state room, with its narrow shelves of beds, as if it had been a baby-house, and they two children playing in it. To tuck themselves away for the night in the car-section seemed the greatest fun in the world. When older people fretted, they laughed. Everyhing was interesting, from the telegraph-poles by the wayside, to the faces of their fellow-passengers. It amused them to watch strange people, and make up stories about them—where they were going, and what relation they could be to each other. The strange people, in their turn, cast curious glances towards the bright, happy-faced sisters; but Katy and Clover did not mind that, or, in fact, notice it. They were too much absorbed to think of themselves, or the impression they were making on others.

It was early on the third morning that the train, puffing and shrieking, ran into the Springfield depot. Other trains stood waiting; and there was such a chorus of snorts and whistles, and such clouds of smoke, that Katy was half-frightened. Papa, who was half-asleep, jumped up, and told the girls to collect their bags and books; for they were to breakfast here, and to meet Lilly Page, who was going on to Hillsover with them.

"Do you suppose she is here already?" asked Katy, tucking the railway-guide into the shawl-strap, and closing her bag with a snap.

"Yes; we shall meet her at the Massasoit. She and her father were to pass the night there."

The Massasoit was close at hand, and in less than five minutes the girls and Papa were seated at a table in its pleasant dining-room. They were ordering their breakfast, when Mr. Page came in, accompanied by his daughter—a pretty girl, with light hair, delicate, rather sharp features, and her mother's stylish ease of manner. Her travelling dress was simple, but had the finish which a French dressmaker knows how to give a simple thing; and all its appointments—boots, hat, gloves, collar, neck-ribbon— were so perfect, each in its way, that Clover, glancing down at her own grey alpaca, and then at Katy's, felt suddenly countrified and shabby.

"Well, Lilly, here they are; here are your cousins," said Mr. Page, giving the girls a cordial greeting. Lilly only said, "How do you do?" Clover saw her glancing at the grey alpacas, and was conscious of a sudden flush. But perhaps Lilly looked at something beside the alpaca; for after a minute her manner changed, and became more friendly.

"Did you order waffles?" she asked.

"Waffles? No, I think not," replied Katy.

"Oh, Why not? Don't you know how celebrated they are for waffles at this hotel? I thought everybody knew *that*." Then she tinkled her fork against her glass, and, when the waiter came, said, "Waffles, please," with an air which impressed Clover extremely. Lilly seemed to her like a young lady in a story, so elegant and self-possessed. She wondered if all the girls at Hillsover were going to be like her?

The waffles came, crisp and hot, with delicious maple syrup to eat on them; and the party made a satisfactory breakfast. Lilly, in spite of all her elegance, displayed a wonderful appetite. "You see," she explained to Clover, "I don't expect to have another decent thing to eat till next September—not a thing, so I'm making the most of this." Accordingly she disposed of nine waffles, in quick succession, before she found time to utter anything further,

193

except, "Butter please." or "May I trouble you for the molasses?" As she swallowed the last morsel, Dr. Carr, looking at his watch, said that it was time to start for the train; and they set off. Mr. Page went with them. As they crossed the street, Katy was surprised to see that Lilly, who had seemed quite happy only a minute before, had begun to cry.

After they reached the car, her tears increased to sobs; she grew almost hysterical.

"Oh! don't make me go, Papa," she implored, clinging to her father's arm. "I shall be so home-sick! It will kill me, I know it will. Please let me stay. Please let me go home with you."

"Now, my darling," protested Mr. Page, "this is foolish; you know it is."

"I can't help it," blubbered Lilly. "I ca—n't help it. Oh! don't, don't make me go. Don't, Papa, dear, I ca—n't bear it."

Katy and Clover felt embarrassed during this scene. They had always been used to considering tears as things to be rather ashamed of—to be kept back, if possible; or, if not, shed in private corners, in dark closets, or behind the bed in the nursery. To see the stylish Lilly crying like a baby, in the midst of a railway carriage, with strangers looking on, quite shocked them. It did not last long, however. The whistle sounded, the conductor shouted, "All right!" and Mr. Page, giving Lilly a last kiss, disengaged her clinging arms, put her into the seat beside Clover, and hurried out of the car. Lilly sobbed loudly for a few seconds; then she dried her eyes, lifted her head, adjusted her veil and the wrists of her three-buttoned gloves and remarked:

"I always go on in this way. Ma says I am a real cry-baby; and I suppose I am. I don't see how people can be calm and composed when they're leaving home, do you? You'll be just as bad tomorrow, when you come to say goodbye to your Papa."

"Oh, I hope not," said Katy. "Because Papa would feel so badly."

Lilly stared. "I shall think you real cold-hearted if you don't," she said, in an offended tone.

Katy took no notice of the tone; and before long Lilly recovered from her pettishness, and began to talk about the school. Katy and Clover asked eager questions. They were eager to hear all that Lilly could tell.

"You'll adore Mrs. Florence," she said. "All the girls do. She's the most fascinating woman! She does just what she likes with everybody. Why, even the students think her perfectly splendid; and yet she's just as strict as she can be."

"Strict with the students?" asked Clover, looking puzzled.

"No; strict with us girls. She never lets any one call, unless it's a brother or first cousin; and then you must have a letter from your parents, asking permission. I wanted Ma to write and say that George Hickman might call on me. He isn't a first cousin exactly, but his father married Pa's sister-in-law's sister. So it's just as good. But Ma was real mean about it. She says I'm too young to have gentlemen coming to see me! I can't think why. Ever so many girls who are younger than I have 'em. Which row are you going to sleep in?" she went on.

"I don't know. Nobody told us that there were any rows."

"Oh, yes! Shaker Row, and Quaker Row, and Attic Row. Attic Row is the nicest, because it's highest up, and farthest away from Mrs. Florence. My room is in Attic Row. Annie Silsbie and I engaged it last term. You'll be in Quaker Row, I guess. Most of the new girls are."

"Is that a nice row?" asked Clover, greatly interested.

"Pretty nice. It isn't so good as Attic, but it's very much better than Shaker; because there you're close to Mrs. Florence, and can't have a bit of fun without her hearing you. I'd try to get the end room, if I were you. Mary Andrews and I had it once. There is a splendid view of Berry Searles's windows."

"Berry Searles?"

"Yes; President Searles, you know; his youngest son.

He's an elegant fellow. All the girls are cracked about him —perfectly cracked! The President's house is next door to the Nunnery, you know; and Berry rooms at the very end of the back building, just opposite Quaker Row. It used to be such fun! He'd sit at his window, and we'd sit at ours, in silent study hour, you know; and he'd pretend to read, and all the time keep looking over the top of his book at us, and trying to make us laugh. Once Mary did laugh right out; and Miss Jane heard her, and came in. But Berry is just as quick as a flash, and he ducked down under the window-sill; so she didn't see him. It was such fun! "

"Who's Miss Jane?" asked Katy.

"The horridest old thing. She's Mrs. Florence's niece, and engaged to a missionary. Mrs. Florence keeps her on purpose to spy on us girls, and report when we break the rules. Oh, those rules! Just wait till you come to read 'em over. They're nailed up on all the doors—thirty-two of them—and you can't help breaking 'em if you try ever so much."

"What are they? What sort of rules?" cried Katy and Clover in a breath.

"Oh! about being punctual to prayers, and turning your mattress, and smoothing over the under-sheet before you leave your room, and never speaking a word in the hall, or in private-study hour, and hanging your towel on your own nail in the wash-room and all that."

"Wash-room? What do you mean?" said Katy, aghast.

"At the head of Quaker's Row, you know. All the girls wash there, except on Saturdays, when they go to the bath-house. You have your own bowl, and soap-dish and a hook for your towel. Why, what's the matter? How big your eyes are! "

"I never heard anything so horrid! " cried Katy, when she had recovered her breath. "Do you really mean that the girls don't have wash-stands in their own rooms?"

"You'll get used to it. All the girls do," responded Lilly.

"I don't want to get used to it," said Katy, resolving to appeal to Papa; but Papa had gone into the smoking-car, and she had to wait. Meantime Lilly went on talking.

"If you have that end room in Quaker Row, you'll see all the fun that goes on at commencement time. Mrs. Searles always has a big party, and you can look right in, and watch the people and the supper-table, just as if you were there. Last summer Berry and Alpheus Seccomb got a lot of cakes and mottoes from the table and came out into the yard, and threw them up one by one to Rose Red and her room-mate. They didn't have the end room, though; but the one next to it."

"What a funny name!—Rose Red," said Clover.

"Oh, her real name is Rosamond Redding; but the girls call her Rose Red. She's the greatest witch in the school; not exactly pretty, you know, but sort of killing and fascinating. She's always getting into the most awful scrapes. Mrs. Florence would have expelled her long ago if she hadn't been such a favourite; and Mr. Redding's daughter, besides. He's a member of Congress, you know, and all that; and Mrs. Florence is quite proud of having Rose in her school.

"Berry Searles is so funny!" she continued. "His mother is a horrid old thing, and always interfering with him. Sometimes when he has a party of fellows in his room, and they're playing cards, we can see her coming with her candle through the house; and when she gets to his door, she tries it, and then she knocks, and calls out, 'Abernethy, my son!' And the fellows whip the cards into their pockets, and stick the bottles under the table, and get out their books and dictionaries in a minute; and when Berry unlocks the door, there they sit, studying away; and Mrs. Searles looks so disappointed! I thought I should die one night, me and Mary Andrews laughed so."

I verily believe that if Dr. Carr had been present at this conversation, he would have stopped at the next station, and taken the girls back to Burnet. But he did not return from the smoking-car till the anecdotes about Berry were finished, and Lilly had begun again on Mrs. Florence.

"She's a sort of queen, you know. Everybody minds her. She's tall, and always dresses beautifully. Her eyes are lovely; but, when she gets angry, they're perfectly awful.

Rose Red says she'd rather face a mad bull any day than Mrs. Florence in a fury; and Rose ought to know, for she's had more reprimands than any other girl in the school."

"How many girls are there?" inquired Dr. Carr.

"There were forty-eight last term. I don't know how many there'll be this, for they say Mrs. Florence is going to give up. It's she who makes the school so popular."

All this time the train was moving northward. With every mile the country grew prettier. Spring had not fairly opened; but the grass was green, and the buds on the trees gave a tender mist-like colour to the woods. The road followed the river, which here and there turned upon itself in long links and windings. Ranges of blue hills closed the distance. Now and then a nearer mountain rose, single and alone, from the plain. The air was cool, and full of a brilliant zest, which the Western girls had never before tasted.

Katy felt as if she were drinking champagne. She and Clover flew from window to window, exclaiming with such delight that Lilly was surprised.

"I can't see what there is to make such a fuss about," she remarked. "That's only Deerfield. It's quite a small place."

"But how pretty it looks, nestled in among the hills! Hills are lovely, Clover, aren't they?"

"These hills are nothing. You should see the White Mountains," said the experienced Lilly. "Ma and me spent three weeks at the Profile House, last vacation. It was perfectly elegant."

In the course of the afternoon Katy drew Papa away to a distant seat, and confided her distress about the wash-stands.

"Don't you think it is horrid, Papa? Aunt Izzie always said that it isn't lady-like not to take a sponge-bath every morning; but how can we, with forty-eight girls in the room? I don't see what we are going to do."

"I fancy we can arrange it; don't be distressed, my dear," replied Dr. Carr. And Katy was satisfied; for when

Papa undertook to arrange things, they were very apt to be done.

It was almost evening when they reached their final stopping-place.

"Now, two miles in the stage, and then we're at the horrid old Nunnery," said Lilly. "Ugh! Look at that snow. It never melts here till long after it's all gone at home. How I do hate this station! I'm going to be frightfully home-sick; I know I am."

But just then she caught sight of the stage-coach, which stood waiting, and her mood changed; for the stage was full of girls who had come by the other train.

"Hurrah! There's Mary Edwards and Mary Silver," she exclaimed; "and, I declare, Rose Red! Oh, you precious darling! How do you do?"

Scrambling up the steps, she plunged at a girl with waving hair, and a rosy, mischievous face; and began kissing her with effusion.

Rose Red did not seem equally enchanted. "Well, Lilly, how are you?" she said, and then went on talking to a girl who sat by her side, and whose hand she held; while Lilly rushed up and down the line, embracing and being embraced. She did not introduce Katy and Clover; and, as Papa was outside, on the driver's box, they felt a little lonely, and strange. All the rest were chattering merrily, and were evidently well acquainted: they were the only ones left out.

Clover watched Rose Red, to whose face she had taken a fancy. It made her think of a pink carnation, or of a twinkling wild rose, with saucy whiskers of brown calyx. Whatever she said or did seemed full of a flavour especially her own. Her eyes, which were blue, and not very large, sparkled with fun and mischief. Her cheeks were round and, soft like a baby's: when she laughed, two dimples broke their pink, and made you want to laugh too. A cunning white throat supported this pretty head, as a stem supports a flower; and, altogether, she was like a flower, except that flowers don't talk, and she talked all the time. What she said seemed very droll, for the girls about her

199

were in fits of laughter; but Clover only caught a word now and then, the stage made such a noise.

Suddenly Rose Red leaned forward, and touched Clover's hand.

"What's your name?" she said. "You've got eyes like my sister's. Are you coming to the Nunnery?"

"Yes," replied Clover, smiling back. "My name is Clover—Clover Carr."

"What a dear little name! It sounds just as you look!"

"So does your name, Rose Red," said Clover, shyly.

"It's a ridiculous name," protested Rose Red, trying to pout.

Just then the stage stopped.

"Why? Who's going to the hotel?" cried the schoolgirls in a chorus.

"I am," said Dr. Carr, putting his head in at the door, with a smile which captivated every girl there. "Come, Katy; come, Clover. I've decided that you shan't begin school till tomorrow."

"Oh, my! Don't I wish he was my Pa!" cried Rose Red. Then the stage moved on.

"Who are they? What's their names?" asked the girls. "They look nice."

"They're sort of cousins of mine, and they come from the West," replied Lilly, not unwilling to own the relationship, now that she perceived that Dr. Carr had made a favourable impression.

"Why on earth didn't you introduce them, then? I declare that was just like you, Lilly Page," put in Rose Red, indignantly. "They looked so lonesome that I wanted to pat and stroke both of 'em. That little one has the sweetest eyes!"

Meantime Katy and Clover entered the hotel, very glad of the reprieve, and of one more quiet evening alone with Papa. They needed to get their ideas straightened out and put to rights, after the confusions of the day and Lilly's extraordinary talk. It was very evident that the Nunnery was to be quite different from their expectations; but another thing was equally evident—it would not be dull!

200

Rose Red by herself and without any one to help her, would be enough to prevent that!

CHAPTER FOUR

THE NUNNERY

THE NIGHT seemed short; for the girls, tired by their journey, slept like dormice. About seven o'clock, Katy was roused by the click of a blind; and, opening her eyes, saw Clover standing in the window, and peeping out through the half-opened shutters. When she heard Katy move, she cried out:

"Oh, do come! It's so interesting! I can see the colleges and the church, and, I guess, the Nunnery; only I am not quite sure, because the houses are all so much alike."

Katy jumped up and hurried to the window. The hotel stood on one side of a green common, planted with trees. The common had a lead-coloured fence, and gravel-paths, which ran across it from corner to corner. Opposite the hotel was a long row of red buildings, broken by one or two brown ones, with cupolas. These were evidently the colleges, and a large grey building with a spire was as evidently the church; but which one of the many white, green-blinded houses which filled the other sides of the common, was the Nunnery, the girls could not tell. Clover thought it was one with a garden at the side, but Katy thought not, because Lilly had said nothing of a garden. They discussed the point so long, that the breakfast-bell took them by surprise; and they were forced to rush through their dressing as fast as possible, so as not to keep Papa waiting.

When breakfast was over, Dr. Carr told them to put on their hats, and get ready to walk with him to the school. Clover took one arm, and Katy the other; and the three passed between some lead-coloured posts, and took one of the diagonal paths which led across the common.

"That's the house," said Dr. Carr, pointing.

"It isn't the one you picked out, Clover," said Katy.

"No," replied Clover, a little disappointed. The house Papa indicated was by no means so pleasant as the one she had chosen.

It was a tall, narrow building, with dormer windows in the roof, and a square porch supported by whitewashed pillars. A pile of trunks stood in the porch. From above came sounds of voices. Girls heads were popped out of upper windows at the swinging of the gate; and, as the door opened, more heads appeared looking over the balusters from the hall above.

The parlour into which they were taken was full of heavy, old-fashioned furniture, stiffly arranged. The sofa and chairs were covered with black hair-cloth, and stood closely against the wall. Some books lay upon the table, arranged two by two; each upper book being exactly at a right angle with each lower book. A bunch of dried grasses stood in the fireplace. There were no pictures, except one portrait in oils, of a forbidding old gentleman in a wig and glasses, sitting with his middle finger majestically inserted in a half-open Bible. Altogether, it was not a cheerful room, nor one calculated to raise the spirits of newcomers; and Katy, whose long seclusion had made her sensitive on the subject of rooms, shrank instinctively nearer Papa as they went in.

Two ladies rose to receive them. One, a tall, dignified person, was Mrs. Florence. The other she introduced as "My assistant principal, Mrs. Nipson." Mrs. Nipson was not tall. She had a round face, pinched lips, and half-shut grey eyes.

"This lady is fully associated with me in the management of the school," explained Mrs. Florence. "When I go, she will assume the entire control."

"Is that likely to be soon?" inquired Dr. Carr, surprised, and not well pleased that the teacher of whom he had heard, and with whom he had proposed to leave his children, was planning to yield her place to a stranger.

"The time is not yet determined," replied Mrs. Florence. Then she changed the subject—gracefully, but so decidedly, that Dr. Carr had no chance for further question. She spoke of classes, and discussed what Katy and Clover were to study. Finally, she proposed to take them upstairs to see their room. Papa might come too, she said.

"I dare say that Lilly Page, who tells me that she is a cousin of yours, has described the arrangements of the house," she remarked to Katy. "The room I have assigned to you is in the back building. Quaker Row, the girls call it."

She smiled as she spoke; and Katy, meeting her eyes for the first time, felt that there was something in what Lilly had said. Mrs. Florence *was* a sort of a queen.

They went upstairs. Some girls, who were peeping over the baluster, hurried away at their approach. Mrs. Florence shook her head at them.

"The first day is always one of licence," she said, leading the way along an uncarpeted entry to a door at the end, from which, by a couple of steps, they went down into a square room—round three sides of which ran a shelf, on which stood rows of wash-bowls and pitchers. Above were hooks for towels. Katy perceived that this was the much-dreaded wash-room.

"Our lavatory," remarked Mrs. Florence, blandly.

Opening from the wash-room was a very long hall, lighted at each end by a window. The doors on either side were numbered "one, two, three," and so on. Some of them were half open; as they went by, Katy and Clover caught glimpses of girls and trunks, and beds strewed with things. At No. 6 Mrs. Florence paused.

"Here is the room which I propose to give you," she said.

Katy and clover looked eagerly about. It was a small room, but the sun shone in cheerfully at the window. There was a maple bedstead and table, a couple of chairs, and a row of hooks; that was all, except that in the wall was set a case of black-handled drawers, with cupboard-doors above them.

"These take the place of a bureau, and hold your clothes," explained Mrs. Florence, pulling out one of the drawers. "I hope, when once you are settled, you will find yourselves comfortable. The rooms are small; but young people do not require so much space as older ones. Though, indeed, your elder daughter, Dr. Carr, looks more advanced and grown up than I was prepared to find her. What did you say was her age?"

"She is past sixteen; but she has been so long confined to her room by the illness of which I wrote, that you may probably find her behind-hand in some respects, which reminds me," (this was very adroit of Papa!) "I am anxious that she should keep up the system to which she has been accustomed at home—among other things, sponge-baths of cold water every morning; and, as I see that the bedrooms are not furnished with wash-stands, I will ask your permission to provide one for the use of my little girls. Perhaps you will kindly tell me where I had better look for it?"

Mrs. Florence was not pleased, but she could not object, so she mentioned a shop. Katy's heart gave a bound of relief. She thought No. 6 with a wash-stand might be very comfortable. Its bareness and simplicity had the charm of novelty. Then there was something very interesting to her in the idea of a whole house full of girls.

They did not stay long after seeing the room, but went off on a shopping excursion. Shops were few and far between at Hillsover, but they found a neat little maple wash-stand and rocking-chair, and Papa also bought a comfortable low chair, with a slatted back and a cushion. This was for Katy.

"Never study till your back aches," he told her; "when you are tired, lie flat on the bed for half an hour, and tell Mrs. Florence that it was by my direction."

"Or Mrs. Nipson," said Katy, laughing rather ruefully. She had taken no liking to Mrs. Nipson, and did not enjoy the idea of a divided authority.

A hurried lunch at the hotel followed, and then it was time for Dr. Carr to go away. They all walked to the school together, and said goodbye on the steps. The girls would not cry, but they clung very tightly to Papa, and put as much feeling into their last kisses as would have furnished forth half a dozen fits of tears. Lilly might have thought them cold-hearted, but Papa did not; he knew better.

"That's my brave girls! " he said. Then he.kissed them once more and hurried away. Perhaps he did not wish them to see that his eyes too were a little misty.

As the door closed behind them, Katy and Clover realised that they were alone among strangers. The sensation was not pleasant, and they felt forlorn as they went upstairs, and down Quaker Row, toward No. 6.

"Aha! So you're going to be next door," said a gay voice, as they passed No. 5, and Rose Red popped her head into the hall. "Well, I'm glad," she went on, shaking hands cordially. "I was in hopes you would, and yet I didn't know; and there are some awful stiffies among the new girls. How do you both do?"

"Oh, are we next door to you?" cried Clover, brightening.

"Yes. It's rather good of me not to hate you, for I wanted the end room myself, and Mrs. Florence wouldn't give it to me. Come in, and let me introduce you to my room-mate. It's against the rules, but that's no matter, nobody pretends to keep rules the first day."

They went in. No. 5 was precisely like No. 6, in shape, size, and furniture; but Rose had unpacked her trunk, and decorated her room with odds and ends of all sorts. The table was covered with books and boxes; coloured lithographs were pinned on the walls; a huge blue rosette ornamented the head-board of the bed; the blinds were tied together with pink ribbon; over the top of the window was a festoon of hemlock boughs, fresh and spicy. The effect was fantastic, but cherry, and Katy and Clover exclaimed with one voice, "How pretty! "

The room-mate was a pale, shy girl, with a half-scared

look in her eyes, and small hands which twisted uneasily together when she moved and spoke. Her name was Mary Silver. She and Rose were so utterly unlike, that Katy thought it odd that they should have chosen to be together. Afterwards she understood it better. Rose liked to protect, and Mary to be protected; Rose to talk, and Mary to listen. Mary evidently considered Rose the most entertaining creature in the world; she giggled violently at all her jokes, and then stopped short and covered her mouth with her fingers, in a frightened way, as if giggling were wrong.

"Only think," began Rose, after introducing Katy and Clover, "these young ladies have got the end room. What do you suppose was the reason that Mrs. Florence did not give it to us? It's very peculiar."

Mary laughed her uneasy laugh. She looked as if she could tell the reason, but did not dare.

"Never mind," continued Rose. "Trials are good for one, they say. It's something to have nice people in that room, if we can't be there ourselves. You are nice, aren't you?" turning to Clover.

"Very," replied Clover, laughing.

"I thought so. I can almost always tell without asking; still, it is something to have it on the best authority. We'll be good neighbours, won't we? Look here," and she pulled one of the black-handled drawers completely out and laid it on the bed. "Do you see? your drawers are exactly behind ours. Any time in silent study hour, if I have something I want to say, I'll just rap and pop a note into your drawer, and you can do the same to me. Isn't it fun?"

Clover said, "Yes"; but Katy, though she laughed, shook her head.

"Don't entice us into mischief," she said.

"Oh, gracious!" exclaimed Rose. "Now, are you going to be good—you two? If you are, just break the news at once, and have it over. I can bear it." She fanned herself in such a comical way that no one could help laughing. Mary Silver joined, but stopped pretty soon in her sudden manner.

"There's Mary, now," went on Rose; "she's named Silver, but she's as good as gold. She's a paragon. It's

206

quite a trial to me, rooming with a paragon. But if any
more are coming in to the entry just give me fair notice,
and I pack and move up among the sinners in Attic Row.
Somehow, you don't look like paragons either—you
especially," nodding to Clover. "Your eyes are like violets;
but so are Sylvia's—that's my sister—and she's the greatest witch in Massachusetts. Eyes are dreadfully deceitful
things. As for you"—to Katy—"you're so tall that I can't
take you all in at once; but the piece I see doesn't look
dreadful a bit."

Rose was sitting in the window as she made these remarks, and, leaning forward suddenly, she gave a pretty
blushing nod to someone below. Katy glanced down, and
saw a handsome young man replacing the cap he had lifted
from his head.

"That's Berry Searles," said Rose. "He's the President's
son, you know. He always comes through the side yard
to get to his room. That's it—the one with the red curtain.
It's exactly opposite your window. Don't you see?"

"So it is!" exclaimed Katy, remembering what Lilly had
said. "Oh! was that the reason——" She stopped, afraid
of being rude.

"The reason we wanted the room?" inquired Rose,
coolly. "Well, I don't know. It hadn't occured to me to
look at it in that light. Mary," with sudden severity, "is
it possible that you had Berry Searles in your mind when
you were so pertinacious about that room?"

"Rose! How can you? You know I never thought of
such a thing," protested poor Mary.

"I hope not; otherwise I should feel it my duty to consult with Mrs. Florence on the subject," went on Rose,
with an air of dignified admonition. "I consider myself
responsible for you and your morals, Mary. Let us change
this painful subject." She looked gravely at the three girls
for a moment; then her lips began to twitch, the irresistible
dimples appeared in her cheeks, and, throwing herself back
in her chair, she burst into a fit of laughter.

"O Mary, you little goose! Some day or other you'll be
the death of me. Dear, dear! how I am behaving! It's

perfectly horrid of me. And I didn't mean it. I'm going to be real good this term; I promised mother. Please forget it, and don't take a dislike to me, and never come again," she added, coaxingly, as Katy and Clover rose to go.

Indeed, we won't, replied Katy. As for sensible Clover she was already desperately in love with Rose, on that very first day.

After a couple of hours of hard work, No. 6 was in order, and looked like a different place. Fringed towels were laid over the wash-stand and the table. Dr. Carr's photograph and some pretty chromos ornamented the walls; the rocking chair and the study chair stood by the window; the trunks were hidden by chintz covers, made for the purpose by old Mary. On the window-sill stood Cousin Helen's vase which Katy had brought carefully packed among her clothes. "Now," she said, tying the blinds together with a knot of ribbon in imitation of Rose Red's, "when we get a bunch of wild flowers for my vase, we shall be all right."

A tap at the door. Rose entered.

"Are you done?" she asked; "may I come in and see? Oh, this is pretty!" she exclaimed, looking about. "How you can tell in one minute what sort of girl one is, just by looking at her room! I should know you had been neat and dainty and housekeeperly all your days. And you would see in a minute that I am a Madge Wildfire, and that Ellen Grey is a saint, and Sally Satterlee a scatterbrain and Lilly Page an affected little hum—oh, I forgot! She is your cousin, isn't she? How dreadfully rude of me!" dimpling at Clover, who couldn't help dimpling back again.

"Oh, my!" she went on, "a wash-stand, I declare! Where did you get it?"

"Papa bought it," explained Katy; "he asked Mrs. Florence's permission."

"How nice of him! I shall just write to my father to ask for permission too." Which she did, and the result was that it set the fashion of wash-stands, and so many Papas wrote to "ask permission," that Mrs. Florence found it necessary to give up the lavatory system, and provide wash-stands for the whole house. Katy's request had been the opening wedge. I do not think this fact made her more popular with the principals.

"By the way, where is Lilly?" asked Katy. "I haven't seen her to-day."

"Do you want to know? I can tell you. She's sitting on the edge of one chair, with her feet on the rung of another chair, and her head on the shoulder of her room-mate (who is dying to get away and arrange her drawers); and she's crying——"

"How do you know? Have you been up to see her?"

"Oh! I haven't seen her. It isn't necessary. I saw her last term, and the term before. She always spends the first day at school in that way. I'll take you up, if you'd like to examine for yourselves."

Katy and Clover, much amused, followed as she led the way upstairs. Sure enough, Lily was sitting exactly as Rose predicted. Her face was swollen with crying. When she saw the girls, her sobs redoubled.

"Oh! isn't it dreadful!" she demanded. "I shall die, I know I shall. Oh! why did Pa make me come?"

"Now, Lilly, don't be an idiot," said the unsympathising Rose. Then she sat down and proceeded to make a series of the most grotesque faces, winking her eyes and twinkling her finger round the head of "Niobe," as she called Lilly, till the other girls were in fits of laughter, and Niobe, though she shrugged her shoulders pettishly and said, "Don't be so ridiculous, Rose Red," was forced to give way. First she smiled, then a laugh was heard; afterwards she announced that she felt better.

"That's right, Niobe," said Rose. "Wash your face now, and get ready for tea, for the bell is just going to ring. As for you, Annie, you might as well put your drawers in order," with a wicked wink. Annie hurried away with a laugh, which she tried in vain to hide.

"You heartless creature!" cried the exasperated Lilly. "I believe you're made of marble; you haven't one bit of feeling. Nor you either, Katy. You haven't cried a drop."

209

"Given this problem," said the provoking Rose: "when the nose without is as red as a lobster, what must be the temperature of the heart within, and *vice versa*!"

The tea-bell rang in time to avert a fresh flood of tears from Lilly. She brushed her hair in angry haste, and they all hurried down by a side staircase which, as Rose explained, the school-girls were expected to use. The dining-room was not large; only part of the girls could be seated at a time; so they took turns at dining at the first table, half one week and half the next.

Mrs. Nipson sat at the tea-tray, with Mrs. Florence beside her. At the other end of the long board sat a severe-looking person, whom Lilly announced in a whisper as "that horrid Miss Jane." The meal was very simple—tea, bread and butter, and dried beef—it was eaten in silence; the girls were not allowed to speak, except to ask for what they wanted. Rose Red indeed, who sat next to Mrs. Florence, talked to her, and even ventured once or twice on daring little jokes, which caused Clover to regard her with admiring astonishment. No one else said anything, except, "Butter, please," or "Pass the bread." As they filed upstairs after the cheerless meal, they were met by rows of hungry girls, who were waiting to go down, and who whispered, "How long you have been! What's for tea?"

The evening passed in making up classes and arranging for recitation-rooms and study-hours. Katy was glad when bedtime came. The day, with all its new impressions and strange faces, seemed to her like a confused dream. She and Clover undressed very quietly. Among the printed rules, which hung on the bedroom door, they read: "All communication between room-mates, after the retiring-bell has rung, is strictly prohibited." Just then it did not seem difficult to keep this rule. It was only after the candle was blown out, that Clover ventured to whisper—very low indeed, for who knew but Miss Jane was listening outside the door?—"Do you think you're going to like it?" and Katy, in the same cautious whisper responded, "I'm not quite sure." And so ended the first day at the Nunnery.

CHAPTER FIVE

ROSES AND THORNS

"OH! WHAT IS IT? What has happened?" cried Clover, starting up in bed, the next morning, as a clanging sound roused her suddenly from sleep. It was only the rising-bell, ringing at the end of Quaker Row.

Katy held her watch up to the dim light. She could just see the hands. Yes: they pointed to six. It was actually morning! She and Clover jumped up, and began to dress as fast as possible.

"We've only got half an hour," said Clover, unhooking the rules, and carrying them to the window—"half an hour; and this says we must turn the mattress, smooth the under-sheet over the bolster, and spend five minutes in silent devotion. We'll have to be quick to do that, besides dressing ourselves!"

It is never easy to be quick, when one is in a hurry. Everything sets itself against you. Fingers turn into thumbs; dresses won't button, nor pins keep their place. With all their haste, Katy and Clover were barely ready when the second bell sounded. As they hastened downstairs, Katy fastening her breast-pin, and Clover her cuffs, they met other girls, some looking half asleep, others half dressed; all yawning, rubbing their eyes, and complaining of the early hour.

"Isn't it horrid?" said Lilly Page, hurrying by with no collar on, and her hair hastily tucked into a net. "I never get up till nine o'clock when I'm at home. Ma saves my breakfast for me. She says I shall have my sleep out while I have the chance."

"You don't look quite awake now," remarked Clover.

"No, because I haven't washed my face. Half the time I don't, before breakfast. There's that old mattress has to

211

be turned; and when I sleep too long, I just do that first, and then scramble my clothes on the best way I can. Anything not to be marked!"

After prayers and breakfast were done, the girls had half an hour for putting their bedrooms to right, during which interval it is to be hoped that Lilly found time to wash her face. After that, lessons began, and lasted till one o'clock. Dinner followed, with an hour's "recreation"; then the bell rang for "silent study hour," when the girls sat with their books in their bedrooms, but were not allowed to speak to each other. Next came a walk.

"Who are you going to walk with?" asked Rose Red, meeting Clover in Quaker Row.

"I don't know. Katy, I guess."

"Are you, really? You and she like each other, don't you? Do you know, you're the first sisters I ever knew at school who did! Generally, they quarrel awfully. The Stearns girls, who were here last term, scarcely spoke to each other. They didn't even sleep together; and Sarah Stearns was always telling tales against Sue, and Sue against Sarah."

"How disgusting! I never heard of anything so mean," cried Clover, indignantly. "Why, I wouldn't tell tales about Katy if we quarrelled ever so much. We never do, though —Katy is so sweet."

"I suppose she is," said Rose, rather doubtfully; "but, do you know, I'm half afraid of her. It's because she's so tall. Tall people always scare me. And then she looks so grave and grown up! Don't tell her I said so though; for I want her to like me."

"Oh, she isn't a bit grave or grown up. She's the funniest girl in the world. Wait till you know her," replied loyal Clover.

"I'd give anythng if I could walk with you part of this term," went on Rose, putting her arm around Clover's waist. "But you see, unluckily, I'm engaged straight through. All of us old girls are. I walk with Mary Mather this week and next; then Esther Dearborn for a month; and then Lilly Page for two weeks; and all the rest of the

212

time with Mary. I can't think why I promised Lilly. I'm sure I don't want to go with her. I'd ask Mary to let me off, only I'm afraid she would not like it. I say, suppose we engage now to walk with each other for the first half of next term."

"Why, that's not till October!" said Clover.

"I know it; but it's nice to be beforehand. Will you?"

"Of course I will—provided that Katy has somebody pleasant to go with," replied Clover, immensely flattered at being asked by the popular Rose. Then they ran downstairs, and took their places in the long procession of girls, who were ranged two and two, ready to start. Miss Jane walked at the head; and Miss Marsh, another teacher, brought up the rear. Rose Red whispered that it was like a funeral and a caravan mixed—"as cheerful as hearses at both ends, and wild beasts in the middle."

The walk was along a wooded road—a mile out and a mile back. The procession was not permitted to stop, or straggle, or take any of the liberties which make walking pleasant. Still, Katy and Clover enjoyed it. There was a spring smell in the air, and the woods were beginning to be pretty. They even found a little trailing arbutus blossoming in a sunny hollow. Lilly was just in front of them, and amused them with histories of different girls, whom she pointed out in the long line. That was Esther Dearborn—Rose Red's friend. Handsome, wasn't she? but terribly sarcastic. The two next were Amy Alsop and Ellen Gray. They always walked together, because they were so intimate. Yes; they were nice enough, only so distressingly good. Amy did not get one single mark last term! That child with pig-tails was Bella Arkwright. Why on earth did Katy want to know about her? She was a nasty little thing.

"She's just about Elsie's height," replied Katy. "Who's that pretty girl with pink velvet on her hat?"

"Dear me! Do you think she's pretty? I don't. Her name is Louisa Agnew. She lives at Ashburn—quite near us; but we don't know them. Her family are not at all in good society."

"What a pity! She looks so sweet and ladylike."

Lilly tossed her head. "They're quite common people," she said. "They live in a little mite of a house and her father paints portraits."

"But I should think that would be nice. Doesn't she ever take you to see his pictures?"

"Take me!" cried Lilly, indignantly. "I should think not. I tell you we don't visit. I just speak when we're here, but I never see her when I'm at home."

"Move on, young ladies. What are you stopping for?" cried Miss Jane.

"Yes; move on," muttered Rose Red from behind. "Don't you hear Policeman X?"

From walking-hour till tea-time was "recreation" again. Lilly improved this opportunity to call at No. 6. She had waited to see how the girls were likely to take in the school before committing herself to intimacy; but, now that Rose Red had declared in their favour, she was ready to begin to be friendly.

"How lovely!" she said, looking about. "You got the end room, after all, didn't you? What splendid times you'll have! Oh, how plainly you can see Berry Searles's window! Has he spoken to you yet?"

"Spoken to us? Of course not! Why should he?" replied Katy. "He doesn't know us, and we don't know him."

"That's nothing. Half the girls in the school bow, and speak, and carry on with young men they don't know. You won't have a bit of fun if you're so particular."

"I don't want that kind of fun," replied Katy with energy in her voice; "neither does Clover. And I can't imagine how the girls can behave so. It isn't lady-like at all."

Katy was very fond of this word, "lady-like." She always laid great stress upon it. It seemed in some way to be connected with Cousin Helen, and to mean everything that was good, and graceful, and sweet.

"Dear me! I'd no idea you were so dreadfully proper," said Lilly, pouting. "Mother said you were as prim and precise as your grandmother; but I didn't suppose——"

"How unkind!" broke in Clover, taking fire, as usual, at any affront to Katy. "Katy prim and precise! She isn't a bit! She's twice as much fun as the rest of you girls; but it's nice fun—not this horrid stuff about students. I wish your mother wouldn't say such things."

"I didn't—she didn't—I don't mean exactly that," stammered Lilly, frightened by Clover's indignant eyes. "All I meant was, that Katy is dreadfully dignified for her age, and we bad girls will have to look out. You needn't be so mad, Clover; I'm sure it's very nice to be proper and good, and set an example."

"I don't want to preach to anybody," said Katy, colouring, "and I wasn't thinking about examples. But really and truly, Lilly, wouldn't your mother, and all the girls' mothers, be shocked if they knew about these performances here?"

"Gracious! I should think so; Ma would kill me. I wouldn't have her know of my goings on for all the world."

Just then Rose pulled out a drawer, and called through to ask if Clover would please come in and help her a minute. Lilly took advantage of her absence to say:

"I came on purpose to ask you to walk with me for four weeks. Will you?"

"Thank you; but I'm engaged to Clover."

"To Clover! But she's your sister; you can get off."

"I don't want to get off. Clover and I like dearly to go together."

Lilly stared. "Well, I never hear of such a thing," she said; "you're really romantic. The girls will call you 'The Inseparables'."

"I wouldn't mind being inseparable from Clover," said Katy, laughing.

Next day was Saturday. It was nominally a holiday; but so many tasks were set for it, that it hardly seemed like one. The girls had to practise in the gymnasium, to do their mending and have all their drawers in apple-pie order, before afternoon, when Miss Jane went through the rooms on a tour of inspection. Saturday, also, was the day for writing home letters; so, altogether, it was about the busiest of the week.

Early in the morning Miss Jane appeared in Quaker Row with some slips of paper in her hand, one of which she left at each door. They told the hours at which the girls were to go to the bath-house.

"You will carry, each a bath towel, a sponge, and soap," she announced to Katy, "and will be in the entry, at the foot of the stairs, at twenty-five minutes after nine precisely. Failures in punctuality will be punished by a mark." Miss Jane always delivered her words like a machine, and closed her mouth with a snap at the end of the sentence.

"Horrid thing! Don't I wish her missionary would come and carry her off. Not that I blame him for staying away," remarked Rose Red, from the door; making a face at Miss Jane as she walked down the entry.

"I don't understand about the bath-house," said Katy. "Does it belong to us? And where it it?"

"No, it doesn't belong to us. It belongs to Mr. Perrit, and anybody can use it; only on Saturday it is reserved for us nuns. Haven't you ever noticed it when we have been out walking? It's in that street by the bakery, which we pass to take the Lebanon Road. We go across the green, and down by Professor Seccomb's, and we are in plain sight from the college all the way; and, of course, those abominable boys sit there with spy-glasses, and stare as hard as ever they can. It's perfectly horrid. 'A bath towel, a sponge, and soap,' indeed! I wish I could make Miss Jane eat the pieces of soap which she has forced me to carry across this village."

"Oh, Rose," remonstrated Mary Silver.

"Well, I do. And the bath towel afterwards, by way of a dessert," replied the incorrigible Rose. "Never mind! Just wait! A bright idea strikes me."

"Oh! what?" cried the other three; but Rose only pursed up her mouth, arched her eyebrows and vanished into her own room, locking the door behind her. Mary Silver, finding herself shut out, sat down meekly in the hall till such time as it should please Rose to open the door. This was not till the bath hour. As Katy and Clover went by, Rose put her head out, and called that she would be down in a minute.

The bathing party consisted of eight girls, with Miss Jane for escort. They were half-way across the common before Miss Jane noticed that everybody was shaking with stifled laughter, except Rose, who walked along demurely, apparently unconscious that there was anything to laugh at.

Miss Jane looked sharply from one to another for a moment, then stopped short and exclaimed, "Rosamond Redding! how dare you?"

"What is it, ma'am?" asked Rose, with a face of a lamb.

"Your bath towel! your sponge!" gasped Miss Jane.

"Yes, ma'am, I have them all," replied the audacious Rose, putting her hand to her hat. There, to be sure, was the long towel, hanging down behind like a veil, while the sponge was fastened on one side like a great cockade; and in front appeared a cake of pink soap, neatly pinned into the middle of a black velvet bow.

Miss Jane seized Rose and removed these ornaments in a twinkling. "We shall see what Mrs. Florence thinks of this conduct," she grimly remarked. Then, dropping the soap and sponge in her own pocket, she made Rose walk beside her, as if she were a criminal in custody.

The bath-house was a neat place, with eight small rooms, well supplied with hot and cold water. Katy would have found her bath very nice, had it not been for the thought of the walk home. They must look so absurd, she reflected, with their sponges and damp towels

Miss Jane was as good as her word. After dinner, Rose was sent for by Mrs. Florence, and had an interview of two hours with her: she came out with red eyes, and shut herself into her room with a disconsolate bang. Before long, however, she revived sufficiently to tap on the drawers and push through a note with the following words:

My heart is broken! —R.R.

Clover hastened in to comfort her. Rose was sitting on the floor, with a very clean pocket-handkerchief in her hand. She wept, and put her head against Clover's knee.

"I suppose I'm the nastiest girl in the world," she said. "Mrs. Florence thinks so. She said I was an evil influence in the school. Wasn't that unkind?" with a little sob.

"I meant to be so good this term," she went on; "but what's the use? A codfish might as well try to play the piano! It was always so, even when I was a baby. Sylvia says I have got a little fiend inside of me. Do you believe I have? Is it that makes me so horrid?"

Clover purred over her. She could not bear to have Rose feel unhappy. "Wasn't Miss Jane funny?" went on Rose, with a sudden twinkle; "and did you see Berry, and Alfred Seccomb?"

"No; where were they?"

"Close to us, standing by the fence. All the time Miss Jane was unpinning the towel, they were splitting their sides, and Berry made such a face at me that I nearly laughed out. That boy has a perfect genius for faces. He used to frighten Sylvia and me into fits, when we were little tots, up here on visits."

"Then you knew him before you came to school?"

"Oh, dear, yes! I know all the Hillsover boys. We used to make mud pies together. They're grown up now, most of them, and in college; and when we meet, we're very dignified, and say, 'Miss Redding,' and 'Mr. Seccomb,' and 'Mr. Searles'; but we're just as good friends as ever. When I go to take tea with Mrs. Seccomb, Alfred always invites Berry to drop in, and we have the greatest fun. Mrs. Florence won't let me go this term, though, I guess, she's so mad about the towel."

Katy was quite relieved when Clover reported this conversaton. Rose, for all her wickedness, seemed to be a little lady. Katy did not like to class her among the girls who flirted with students whom they did not know.

It was wonderful how soon they all settled down. and became accustomed to their new life. Before six weeks were over, Katy and Clover felt as if they had lived at

Hillsover for years. This was partly because there was so much to do. Nothing makes time fly like having every moment filled, and every hour set apart for a distinct employment.

They made several friends, chief among whom were Ellen Gray and Louisa Agnew; this last intimacy Lilly resented highly, and seemed to consider as an affront to herself. With no one, however, was Katy so intimate as Clover was with Rose Red. This cost Katy some jealous pangs at first. She was so used to considering Clover her own exclusive property that it was not easy to share her with another; and she had occasional fits of feeling resentful, and injured, and left out. These were but momentary, however. Katy was too good of heart to let unkind feelings grow, and by and by she grew fond of Rose and Rose of her, so that in the end the sisters shared their friend as they did other nice things, and neither of them was jealous of the other.

But, charming as she was, a certain price had to be paid for the pleasure of intimacy with Rose. Her overflowing spirits, and "the little fiend inside her," were always provoking scrapes, in which her friends were apt to be more or less involved. She was very penitent and afflicted after these scrapes, but it didn't make a bit of difference; the next time she was just as naughty as ever.

"What are you doing?" said Katy one day, meeting her in the hall with a heap of black shawls and aprons on her arm.

"Hush!" whispered Rose, mysteriously; "don't say a word. Senator Brown is dead—our senator, you know. I'm going to put my window into mourning for him, that's all. It's a proper token of respect."

Two hours later, Mrs. Nipson, walking sedately across the common, noticed quite a group of students in the President's side yard, looking up at the Nunnery. She drew nearer. They were admiring Rose's window, hung with black, and decorated with a photograph of the deceased senator, suspended in the middle of a wreath of weeping-willow. Of course she hurried upstairs, and tore down the

But at that moment the door opened and there stood Miss Janel

shawls and aprons; and, equally, of course, Rose had a lecture and a mark. But, dear me! What good did it do? The next day but one, as Katy and Clover sat together in silent-study hour, their lower drawer was pushed open very noiselessly and gently, till it came out entirely, and lay on the floor, and in the aperture thus formed appeared Rose's saucy face, flushed with mischief. She was crawling through from her own room.

"Such fun!" she whispered; "I never thought of this before! We can have parties in study hours, and all sorts of things."

"Oh, go back, Rosy!" whispered Clover, in agonised entreaty, though laughing all the time.

"Go back? Not at all! I'm coming in," answered Rose, pulling herself through a little farther. But at that moment the door opened: there stood Miss Jane! She had caught the buzz of voices as she passed in the hall, and had entered to see what was going on.

Rose, dreadfully frightened, made a rapid movement to withdraw. But the space was narrow, and she had wedged herself, and could move neither backward nor forward. She had to submit to being helped through by Miss Jane, in a series of pulls, while Katy and Clover sat by, not daring to laugh or offer assistance. When Rose was on her feet, Miss Jane released her with a final shake, which she seemed unable to refrain from giving.

"Go to your room," she said. "I shall report all of you young ladies for this flagrant act of disobedience."

Rose went, and in two minutes the drawer, which Miss Jane had replaced, opened again, and there was this note:

If I am never heard of more, give my love to my family, and mention how I died. I forgive my enemies, and leave Clover my band bracelet.

My blessings on you both.

With the deepest regard,

Your afflicted friend, R.R.

Mrs. Florence was very angry on this occasion, and

would listen to no explanations, but gave Katy and Clover a "disobedience mark" also. This was very unfair, and Rose felt dreadfully about it. She begged and entreated, but Mrs. Florence only replied, "There is blame on both sides, I have no doubt."

"She's entirely changed from what she used to be," declared Rose. "I don't know what's the matter; I don't like her half so much as I did."

The truth was, that Mrs. Florence had secretly determined to give up her connection with the school at midsummer; and, regarding it now rather as Mrs. Nipson's school than her own, she took no pains to study character or mete out justice carefully among scholars with whom she was not likely to have much to do.

CHAPTER SIX

THE S.S.U.C.

It was Saturday afternoon, and Clover, having finished her practising, dusting, and mending, had settled herself in No. 6 for a couple of hours of quiet enjoyment. Everything was in beautiful order to meet Miss Jane's inspecting eye; and Clover, as she sat in the rocking-chair, writing-case in lap, looked extremely cosy and comfortable.

A half-finished letter to Elsie lay in the writing-case; but Clover felt lazy, and instead of writing was looking out of the window, in a dreamy way, to where Berry Searles and some other young men were playing ball in the yard below. She was not thinking of them or of anything else in particular. A vague sense of pleasant idleness possessed her, and it was like the breaking of a dream when the door opened and Katy came in, not quietly, after her wont, but with a certain haste and indignant rustle, as if vexed by something. When she saw Clover at the window, she cried out hastily, "Oh, Clover, don't!"

"Don't what?" asked Clover, without turning her head.

"Don't sit there looking at those boys."

"Why? Why not? They can't see me. The blinds are shut."

"No matter for that. It's just as bad as if they could see you. Don't do it. I would much rather that you did not."

"Well, I won't then," said Clover, good humouredly, facing round with her back to the window. "I wasn't looking at them either—not exactly. I was thinking about Elsie and John, and wondering—But what's the matter, Katy? What makes you fire up so about it? You've watched the ball-playing yourself, plenty of times."

"I know I have, and I didn't mean to be cross, Clovy. The truth is, I am very much put out. These girls, with their incessant talk about the students, make me absolutely sick. It is so unladylike and so bad, especially for the little ones. Fancy that mite of a Carrie Steele informing me that she is 'in love' with Harry Crosby. In love! A baby like that! She has no business to know that there is such a thing."

"Yes," said Clover, laughing; "she wrote his name on a wintergreen lozenge, and bored a hole and hung it round her neck on a blue ribbon. But it melted and stuck to her frock, and she had to take it off."

"Whereupon she ate it," added Rose, who came in at that moment.

The girls shouted, but Katy soon grew grave.

"One can't help laughing," she said; "but isn't it a shame to have such things going on? Just fancy our Elsie behaving so, Clover! Why, Papa would have a fit. I declare I've a great mind to get up a society to put down flirting."

"Do," said Rose. "What fun it would be! Call it 'The Society for the Suppression of Young Men.' I'll join."

"You, indeed!" replied Katy, shaking her head. "Didn't I see Berry Searles throw a bunch of syringa into your window only this morning?"

"Dear me! Did he? I shall have to speak to Mary again. It's quite shocking to have her go on so. But really and truly do let us have a Society. It would be so jolly. We could meet on Saturday afternoons, and write pieces and have signals and a secret, as Sylvia's Society did when she was at school. Get one up, Katy—that's a dear."

"But," said Katy, taken aback by having her random idea so suddenly adopted, "if I did get one up, it would be in real earnest, and it would be a society against flirting. And you know you can't help it, Rosy."

"Yes, I can. You are doing me great injustice. I don't behave like those girls in Attic Row. I never did. I just bow to Berry and the rest whom I really know—never to anybody else. And you must see, Katherine, darling, that it would be the height of ingratitude if I didn't bow to boys who made mud pies for me when I was little, and lent me their marbles, and did all sorts of kind things. Now wouldn't it?"—coaxingly.

"Per—haps," admitted Katy, with a smile. "But you're such a witch!"

"I'm not—indeed I'm not. I'll be a pillar of society if only you'll provide a society for me to be a pillar of. Now, Katy, do—ah, do, do!"

When Rose was in a coaxing mood, few people could resist her. Katy yielded, and between jest and earnest the matter was settled. Katy was to head the plan and invite the members.

"Only a few at first," suggested Rose. "When it is proved to be a success ,and everybody wants to join, we can let in two or three more as a great favour. What shall the name be? We'll keep it a secret, whatever it is. There's no fun in a society without a secret."

What should the name be? Rose invented half a dozen, each more absurd than the last. "The Anti-Jane Society" would sound well, she insisted. Or, no!—the "Put-him-down Club" was better yet! Finally they settled upon "The Society for the Suppression of Unladylike Conduct."

"Only we'll never use the whole name," said Rose; "we'll say, 'The S.S.U.C.' That sounds brisk and snappy and will drive the whole school wild with curiosity. What larks! ! How I long to begin!"

The next Saturday was fixed upon for the first meeting. During the week Katy proposed the plan to the elect few, all of whom accepted enthusiastically.

Lilly Page was the only person who declined. She said it would be stupid; that for her part she didn't set up to be good or better than she was, and that in any case she shouldn't wish to be mixed up in a Society of which "Miss Agnew" was a member. The girls did not break their hearts over this refusal. They had felt obliged to ask her for relationship's sake, but everybody was a little relieved that she did not wish to join.

No. 6 looked very full indeed that Saturday afternoon when the S.S.U.C. came together for the first time. Ten members were present. Mary Silver and Louisa were two; and Rose's crony, Esther Dearborn, another. The remaining four were Sally Alsop and Amy Erskine; Alice Gibbons, one of the new scholars, whom they all liked, but did not know very well; and Ellen Gray, a pale, quiet girl, with droll blue eyes, a comical twist to her mouth, and a trick of saying things in such a demure way that half the people who listened never found out that they were funny. All of Rose's chairs had been borrowed for the occasion. Three girls sat on the bed, and three on the floor. With a little squeezing there was plenty of room for everybody.

Katy was chosen President, and requested to take the rocking-chair as a sign of office. This she did with much dignity, and proceeded to read the Constitution and Bye-Laws of the Society, which had been drawn up by Rose Red. and copied on an immense sheet of blue paper.

They ran thus:

CONSTITUTION OF THE SOCIETY FOR THE SUPPRESSION OF UNLADYLIKE CONDUCT, KNOWN TO THE UNINITIATED AS THE S.S.U.C.

ARTICLE I.

The object of this Society is twofold: it combines having a good time with the pursuit of VIRTUE.

Article II.

The good time is to take place once a week in No. 6, Quaker Row, between the hours of four and six p.m.

Article III.

The nature of the good time is to be decided upon by a Committee to be appointed each Saturday by the members of the Society.

Article IV.

VIRTUE is to be pursued at all times and in all seasons, by the members of the Society setting their faces against—"The window-panes," put in Rose Red. "No, the practice of bowing and speaking to College students who are not acquaintances," read on Katy, shaking her head at naughty Rose—"waving handkerchiefs, signals from windows, and every species of unladylike conduct."

Article V.

The members of the Society pledge themselves to use their influence against these practices, both by precept and example.

In witness whereof we sign,

KATHERINE CARR, *President.*
ROSAMOND REDDING, *Secretary.*
CLOVER E. CARR.
MARY L. SILVER.
ESTHER DEARBORN.
SALLY P. ALSOP.
AMY W. ERSKINE.
ALICE GIBBONS.
ELLEN WHITWORTH GRAY.

Next followed the Bye-laws. Katy had been able to see the necessity of having any Bye-Laws, but Rose had insisted. She had never heard of a Society without them, she said, and she didn't think it would be "legal" to leave them out. It had cost her some trouble to invent them, but at last they stood thus:

Bye-Law No. 1.

The members of the S.S.U.C. will observe the following signals:

1st. *The Grip.*—This is given by inserting the first and middle finger of the right hand between the thumb and fourth finger of the respondent's left, and describing a rotatory motion in the air with the little finger. N.B.—Much practice is necessary to enable members to exchange this signal in such a manner as not to attract attention.

2nd. *The Signal of Danger.*—This signal is for use when Miss Jane, or any other foe-woman, heaves in sight. It consists in rubbing the nose violently, and at the same time giving three stamps on the floor with the left foot. It must be done with an air of unconsciousness.

3rd. *The Signal of Consultation.*—This signal is for use when immediate communication is requisite between members of the Society. It consists of a pinch on the back of the right hand, accompanied by the word "Holofernes" pronounced in a low voice.

Bye-Law No. 2.

The members of the S.S.U.C. pledge themselves to inviolable secrecy about all Society proceedings.

Bye-Law No. 3.

The members of the S.S.U.C. will bring their Saturday corn-balls to swell the common entertainment.

Bye-Law No. 4.

Members having boxes from home are at liberty to contribute such part of the contents as they please to the aforementioned common entertainment.

Here the Bye-Laws ended. There was much laughter over them, especially over the last.

"Why did you put that in, Rosy?" asked Ellen Gray; "it strikes me as hardly necessary."

"Oh," replied Rose, "I put that in to encourage Silvery Mary there. She's expecting a box soon, and I knew that she would pine to give the Society a share, but would be too timid to propose it; so I thought I would just pave the way."

"How truly kind!" laughed Clover.

"Now," said the President, "the entertainment of the meeting will begin by the reading of 'Trailing Arbutus,' a poem by C.E.C."

Clover had been very unwilling to read the first piece, and had only yielded after much coaxing from Rose, who had bestowed upon her in consequence the name of Quintia Curtia. She felt very shy as she stood up with her paper in her hand, and her voice trembled perceptibly; but after a minute she grew used to the sound of it, and read steadily:

TRAILING ARBUTUS

"I always think, when looking
    At its mingled rose and white,
Of the pink lips of children
    Put up to say goodnight.

Cuddled its green leaves under,
    Like babies in their beds,
Its blossoms shy and sunny
    Conceal their pretty heads.

And when I lift the blanket up,
    And peep inside of it,
They seem to give me smile for smile,
    Nor be afraid a bit.

Dear little flower, the earliest
    Of all the flowers that are;
Twinkling upon the bare, brown earth,
    As on the clouds a star.

How can we fail to love it well,
  Or prize it more and more!
It is the first small signal
  That winter time is o'er;

That Spring has not forgotten us,
  Though late and slow she be,
But is upon her flying way,
  And we her face shall see."

This production caused quite a sensation among the
girls. They had never heard any of Clover's verses before,
and thought these wonderful.

"Why," cried Sally Alsop, "it is almost as good as
Tupper!"

Sally meant this for a great compliment, for she was
devoted to the "Proverbial Philosophy."

"A Poem by E.D." was the next thing on the list. Esther
Dearborn rose with great pomp and dignity, cleared her
throat, put on a pair of eyeglasses, and began:

MISS JANE

"Who ran to catch me on the spot
If I the slightest rule forgot,
Believing and excusing not?
    Miss Jane.

Who lurked outside my door all day,
In hopes that I would disobey,
And some low whispered word would say?
    Miss Jane.

Who sternly bade me come and go,
Do this, do that, or else forgo
The other thing I longed for so?
    Miss Jane.

Who caught our Rose-bud half way through
The wall which parted her from two
Friends, and that small prank made her rue?
        Miss Jane.

Who is our bane, our foe, our fear?
Who's always certain to appear
Just when we do not think her near?
        Miss Jane."

"Who down the hall is creeping now
With stealthy step, but knowing not how
Exactly to discover——"

broke in Rose, improvising rapidly. Next moment came a knock at the door. It was Miss Jane.

"Your drawers, Miss Carr—your cupboard," she said, going across the room, and examining each in turn. There was no fault to be found with either, so she withdrew, giving the laughing girls a suspicious glance, and remarking that it was a bad habit to sit on beds—it always injured them.

"Do you suppose she heard?" whispered Mary Silver.

"No, I don't think she did," replied Rose. "Of course she suspected us of being in some mischief or other—she always does that. Now, Mary, it's your turn to give us an intellectual treat. Begin."

Poor Mary shrank back, blushing and protesting.

"You know I can't," she said. "I'm too stupid."

"Rubbish!" cried Rose. "You're the dearest girl that ever was." She gave Mary's shoulder a reassuring pat.

"Mary is excused this time," put in Katy. "It is the first meeting, so I shall be indulgent. But, after this, every member will be expected to contribute something for each meeting. I mean to be very strict."

"Oh, I never, never can!" cried Mary.

Rose was down on her at once.

"Nonsense! Hush!" she said. "Of course you can. You shall, if I have to write it for you myself."

"Order!" said the President, rapping on the table with a pencil. "Rose has something to read to us."

Rose stood up with great gravity. "I would ask for a moment's delay, that the Society may get out its pocket-handkerchiefs," she said. "My piece is an affecting one. I didn't mean it, but it came so. We cannot always be cheerful." Here she heaved a sigh, which set the S.S.U.C. to laughing, and began:

A SCOTCH POEM

"Wee, crimson-tipped Willie Wink,
    Wae's me, drear, dree, and dra,
A waefu' thought, a fearsome flea,
    A wuthering wind, and a'.

Sair, sair thy mither sabs her lane,
    Her een, her mou' are wat;
Her cauld kail hae the corbies ta'en,
    And greviously she grat.

Ah, me, the suthering of the wind!
    Ah, me, the waesome mither!
Ah, me, the bairnies left ahind,
    The shither, hither, blither!"

"What *does* it mean?" cried the girls, as Rose folded up the paper and sat down.

"Mean?" said Rose; "I'm sure I don't know. It's Scotch, I tell you. It's the kind of thing that people read, and then they say, 'One of the loveliest gems that Burns ever wrote!' I thought I'd see if I couldn't do one too. Anybody can, I find: it's not at all difficult."

All the poems having been read, Katy now proposed that they should play "Word and Question." She and Clover were accustomed to the game at home, but to some of the others it was quite new.

Each girl was furnished with a slip of paper and a pencil.

231

and was told to write a word at the top of the paper, fold it over, and pass it to her next left-hand neighbour.

"Dear me! I don't know what to write," said Mary Silver.

"Oh, write anything," said Clover.

So Mary obediently wrote "Anything," and folded it over.

"What next?" asked Alice Gibbons.

"Now a question," said Katy. "Write it under the word and fold it over again. No, Amy, not on the fold. Don't you see, if you do, the writing will be on the wrong side of the paper when we come to read?"

The questions were more troublesome than the words, and the girls sat frowning and biting their pencil-tops for some minutes before all were done. As the slips were handed in, Katy dropped them into the lid of her work-basket, and thoroughly mixed and stirred them up.

"Now," she said, passing it about, "each draw one, read, and write a rhyme in which the word is introduced and the question answered. It needn't be more than two lines unless you like. Here, Rose, it's your turn first."

"Oh, what a hard game!" cried some of the girls; but pretty soon they grew interested, and began to work over their verses.

"I should uncommonly like to know who wrote this abominable word," said Rose, in a tone of despair. "Clover, you witch, I believe it was you."

Clover peeped over her shoulder, nodded, and laughed.

"Very well, then!" snatching up Clover's slip, and putting her own in its place, "you can just write on it yourself—I shan't! I never heard of such a word in my life! You made it up for the occasion. you know you did!"

"I didn't! It's in the Bible," replied Clover, setting to work composedly on the fresh paper.

But when Rose opened Clover's slip, she groaned again.

"It's just as bad as the other," she cried. "Do change back again, Clovy, that's a dear."

"No indeed!" said Clover, guarding her paper, "you've changed once, and now you must keep what you have."

Rose made a face, chewed her pencil awhile, and then began to write rapidly. For some minutes not a word was spoken.

"I've done," said Esther Dearborn at last, flinging her paper into the basket-lid.

"So have I," said Katy.

One by one the papers were collected and jumbled into a heap. Then Katy, giving all a final shake, drew out one, opened it, and read:

"Word.—Radishes.
Question.—How do you like your clergymen done?

How do I like them done? Well, that depends,
    I like them *done* on sleepy, drowsy Sundays;
I like them under-done on other days;
    Perhaps a little *over*-done on Mondays.
But always! I prefer them old as pa,
And not like radishes, all red and raw."

"Oh, *what* a rhyme!" cried Clover.

"Well, what is one to do?" said Ellen Gray. Then she stopped and bit her lip, remembering that no one was supposed to know who wrote the separate papers.

"Aha! It's yours, is it, Ellen?" said Rose. "You're an awfully clever girl, and an ornament to the S.S.U.C. Go on, Katy."

Katy opened the second slip.

"Word—Anything.
Question.—Would you rather be a greater fool than you seem, or seem a greater fool than you are?

I wouldn't seem a fool for anything, my dear.
If I could help it; but I can't, I fear."

"Not bad," said Rose, nodding her head at Sally Alsop, who blushed crimson.

The third paper ran:

233

"*Word*.—Maharshalalhashbaz.
Question.—Does your mother know you're out?"

Rose and Clover exchanged looks.

> "Why, of course my mother knows it,
>   For she sent me out herself, and
> She told me to run quickly, for
>   It wasn't but a mile;
> But I found it was much farther,
>   And my feet grew tired and weary,
> And I couldn't hurry greatly,
>   So it took a long, long while.
> Beside, I stopped to read your word.
> A stranger one I never heard!
> I've met with *Pa*-pistical,
>   That's pat;
> But *Ma*-harshalalhashbaz,
>   What's that?"

"Oh, Clovy, you bright little thing!" cried Rose, in fits of laughter.

But Mary Silver looked quite pale.

"I never heard of anything so awful!" she said. "If that word had come to me. I should have fainted away on the spot—I know I should!"

Next came:

"*Word*.—Buttons.
Question.—What is the best way to make home happy?

> To me 'tis quite clear I can answer this right:
>   Sew on the buttons, and sew them on tight."

"I suspect that is Amy's," said Esther; "she's such a model for mending and keeping things in order."

"It's not fair, guessing aloud in this way," said Sally Alsop. Sally always spoke for Amy, and Amy for Sally. "Voice and Echo," Rose called them; only, as she remarked, nobody could tell which was Echo and which Voice.

The next word was "Mrs. Nipson," and the question, "Do you like flowers?"

> "Do I like flowers? I will not write a sonnet,
>   Singing their beauty as a poet might do:
> I just detest those on Aunt Nipson's bonnet,
>   Because they're just like her—all grey and blue,
>   Dusty and pinched, and fastened on askew!
> And as for heaven's own buttercups and daisies,
> I am not good enough to sing their praisies."

Nobody knew who wrote this verse. Katy suspected Louisa, and Rose suspected Katy.

The sixth slip was a very brief one.

"Word.—When?
Question.—Are you willing?

> If I wasn't willing, I would tell you;
>   But when——Oh, dear, I *can't.*"

"What an extraordinary rhyme!" began Clover; but Rose spied poor Mary blushing and looking distressed, and hastily interposed:

"It's very good; I'm sure. I wish I'd written it. Go on, Katy."

So Katy went on:

"Word.—Unfeeling.
Question.—Which would you rather do, or go fishing?

> I don't feel up to fishing, or such;
>   And so, if you please, I'd rather do—which?"

"I don't seem to see the word in that poem," said Rose. "The distinguished author will please write another."

"The distinguished author," made no reply to this

235

suggestion; but, after a minute or two, Esther Dearborn, "quite disinterestedly," as she stated, remarked that, after all, to "don't feel" was pretty much the same as unfeeling. There was a little chorus of groans at this, and Katy said she should certainly impose a fine if such dodges and evasions were practised again. This was the first meeting, however, and she would be merciful. After this speech she unfolded another paper. It ran:

> *"Word*.—Flea.
> *Question*.—What would you do, love?
>
> What would I do, love? Well, I do not know
> How can I tell till you are more explicit?
> If 'twere a rose you held me, I would smell it;
> If 'twere a mouth you held me, I would kiss it;
> If 'twere a frog, I'd scream than furies louder;
> If 'twere a flea, I'd fetch the Lyon's Powder."

Only two slips remained. One was Katy's own. She knew it by the way in which it was folded, and had almost instinctively avoided and left it for the last. Now, however, she took courage and opened it. The word was "Measles," and the question, "Who was the grandmother of Invention?" These were the lines:

> "The night it was horribly dark,
> The measles broke out in the Ark:
> Little Japhet, and Shem, and all the young Hams,
> Were screaming at once for potatoes and clams.
> And 'What shall I do,' said poor Mrs. Noah,
> 'All alone by myself in this terrible shower?
> I know what I'll do: I'll step down in the hold,
> And wake up a lioness grim and old,
> And tie her close to the children's door,
> And give her a ginger-cake to roar
> At the top of her voice for an hour or more;
> And I'll tell the children to cease their din,
> Or I'll let that grim old party in,

236

To stop their squeazles and likewise their measles.'—
She practised this with greatest success.
She was every one's grandmother, I guess."

"That's much the best of all!" pronounced Alice
Gibbons, "I wonder who wrote it?"

"Dear me! Did you like it so much?" said Rose
simpering, and doing her best to blush.

"Did you really write it?" said Mary: but Louisa
laughed, and exclaimed, "No use, Rosy! You can't take us
in—we know better!"

"Now for the last," said Katy. "The word is
'Buckwheat,' and the question, 'What is the origin of
dreams?'"

"When the nuns are sweetly sleeping,
Mrs. Nipson comes a-creeping,
Creeping like a kitty-cat from door to door:
And she listens to their Slumbers,
And most carefully she numbers,
Counting for every nun a nunlet snore!
And the nuns in sweet forgetfulness who lie,
Dreaming of buckwheat cakes, parental love, and—pie,
    Moan softly, twist and turn, and see
    Black cats and fiends, who frolic in their glee:
    And nightmares prancing wildly do abound
    While Mrs. Nipson makes her nightly round."

"Who did write that?" exclaimed Rose. Nobody
answered. The girls looked at each other, and Rose
scrutinised them all with sharp glances.

"Well! I never saw such creatures for keeping their
countenances." she said. "Somebody is as bold as brass.
Didn't you see how I blushed when my piece was read?"

"You monkey!" whispered Clover, who at that moment
caught sight of the handwriting on the paper. Rose gave
her a warning pinch, and they both subsided with an
unseen giggle.

"What! the tea-bell!" cried everybody. "We wanted to play another game."

"It's a complete success!" whispered Rose, ecstatically, as they went down the hall. "The girls all say they never had such fun in their lives. I'm so glad I didn't die with the measles when I was little!"

"Well," demanded Lilly, "so the high and mighty Society has had a meeting! How did it go off?"

"*Delicious!*" replied Rose, smacking her lips as at the recollection of something very nice. "But you mustn't ask any questions, Lilly. Outsiders have nothing to do with the S.S.U.C. Our proceedings are strictly private." She ran downstairs with Katy.

"I think you're real mean!" called Lilly after them. Then she said to herself, "They're just trying to tease. I know it was stupid."

CHAPTER SEVEN

INJUSTICE

SUMMER was always slow in getting to Hillsover, but at last she arrived, and woods and hills suddenly put on new colours and became beautiful. The sober village shared in the glorifying process. Vines budded on piazzas. Wisteria purpled whitewashed walls. The brown elm boughs which hung above the Common turned into trailing garlands of fresh green. Each walk revealed some change, or ended in some delightful discovery, trilliums, dog-teeth violets, apple-trees in blossom, or wild strawberries turning red. The wood flowers and mosses, even the birds and bird-songs, were new to our Western girls. Hillsover in summer, was a great deal prettier than Burnet, and Katy and Clover began to enjoy school very much indeed.

Towards the end of June, however, something took place which gave them quite a different feeling—something so disagreeable that I hate to tell about it; but, as it really happened, I must.

It was on a Saturday morning. They had just come back from the bath-house, and were going upstairs, laughing, and feeling very merry; for Clover had written a droll piece for the S.S.U.C. meeting, and was telling Katy about it, when, just at the head of the stairs, they met Rose Red. She was evidently in trouble, for she looked flushed and excited, and was under the escort of Miss Barnes, who marched before her with the air of a policeman. As she passed the girls, Rose opened her eyes very wide, and made a face expressive of dismay.

"What's the matter?" whispered Clover. Rose only made another grimace, clawed with her fingers at Miss Barnes's back, and vanished down the entry which led to Mrs. Florence's room. They stood looking after her.

"Oh dear!" sighed Clover, "I'm so afraid Rose is in a scrape."

They walked on toward Quaker Row. In the wash-room was a knot of girls, with their heads close together, whispering. When they saw Katy and Clover, they became silent, and gazed at them curiously.

"What has Rose Red gone to Mrs. Florence about?" asked Clover, too anxious to notice the strange manner of the girls. But at that moment she caught sight of something which so amazed her that she forgot her question. It was nothing less than her own trunk, with "C.E.C." at the end, being carried along the entry by two men Miss Jane followed close behind, with her arms full of clothes and books. Katy's well-known scarlet pin-cushion topped the pile; in Miss Jane's hand were Clover's comb and brush.

"Why, what does this mean?" gasped Clover, as she and Katy darted after Miss Jane, who had turned into one of the rooms. It was No. 1, at the head of the row—a room which no one had wanted, on account of its smallness and lack of light. The window looked out on a brick wall not ten feet away; there was never a ray of sun to make it cheerful; and Mrs. Nipson had converted it into a store-room for empty trunks. The trunks were taken away now,

"Why, what does this mean?" gasped Clover as she and
Kate darted after Miss Jane.

and the bed was strewn with Katy's and Clover's possessions.

"Miss Jane, what is the matter? What are you moving our things for?" exclaimed the girls in great excitement.

Miss Jane laid down her load of dresses, and looked at them sternly.

"You know the reason as well as I do," she said. icily.

"No, I don't. I haven't the least idea what you mean!" cried Katy. "Oh, please, be careful!" as Miss Jane flung a pair of boots on top of Cousin Helen's vase, "you'll break it! Dear, dear! Clover, there's your Cologne bottle tipped over, and all the Cologne spilt! What does it mean? Is our room going to be painted, or what!"

"Your room," responded Miss Jane, "is for the future to be this—No. 1. Miss Benson and Miss James will take No. 6; and, it is hoped, will conduct themselves more properly than you have done."

"Than we have done!" cried Katy, hardly believing her ears.

"Do not repeat my words in that rude way!" said Miss Jane, tartly. "Yes, than you have done!"

"But what have we done? There is some dreadful mistake! Do tell us what you mean, Miss Jane! We have done nothing wrong, so far as I know."

"Indeed!" replied Miss Jane, sarcastically. "Your ideas of right and wrong must be peculiar! I advise you to say no more on the subject. but be thankful that Mrs. Florence keeps you in the school at all, instead of dismissing you. Nothng but the fact that your home is at such a distance prevents her from doing so."

Katy felt as if all the blood in her body were turned to fire as she heard these words, and met Miss Jane's eyes. Her old hasty temper, which had seemed to die out during years of pain and patience. flashed into sudden life, as a smouldering coal flashes. when you least expect it, into flame. She drew herself up to her full height, gave Miss Jane a look of scorching indignation. and, with a rapid impulse, darted out of the room and along the hall towards Mrs. Florence's door. The girls she met scattered from her path right and left. She looked so tall, and moved so impetuously that she absolutely frightened them.

"Come in," said Mrs. Florence, in answer to her sharp, quivering knock. Katy entered. Rose was not there, and Mrs. Florence and Mrs. Nipson sat together, side by side, in close consultation.

"Mrs. Florence," said Katy, too much excited to feel in the least afraid, "will you please tell me why our things are being changed to No. 1?"

Mrs. Florence flushed with anger. She looked Katy all over for a minute before she answered; then she said, in a severe voice. "It is done by my orders, and for good and sufficient reasons. What those reasons are, you know as well as I."

"No, I do not!" replied Katy, as angry as Mrs. Florence. "I have not the least idea what they are, and I insist on knowing!"

"I cannot answer questions put in such an improper manner," said Mrs. Florence, with a wave of the hand, which meant that Katy was to go, but Katy did not stir.

"I am sorry if my manner was improper," she said, trying to speak quietly, "but I think I have a right to ask what this means. If we are accused of doing wrong, it is only fair to tell us what it is."

Mrs. Florence only waved her hand again; but Mrs. Nipson, who had been twisting uneasily in her chair, said, "Excuse me, Mrs. Florence, but perhaps it would be better —would satisfy Miss Carr better—if you were to be explicit."

"It does not seem to me that Miss Carr can be in need of any explanation," replied Mrs. Florence. "When a young lady writes underhand notes to young gentlemen, and throws them from her window, and they are discovered, she must naturally expect that persons of correct ideas will be shocked and disgusted. Your note to Mr. Abernethy Searles, Miss Carr, was found by his mother while mending his pocket, and was handed by her to me. After this statement, you will hardly be surprised that I do not consider it best to permit you to room longer on that side of the house. I did not suppose I had a girl in my school capable of such conduct."

For a moment Katy was too much stunned to speak. She took hold of a chair to steady herself, and her colour changed so quickly from red to pale and back again to red, that Mrs. Florence and Mrs. Nipson, who sat watching her, might be pardoned for thinking that she looked guilty. As soon as she recovered her voice, she stammered out, "But I didn't! I never did! I haven't written any note! I wouldn't for the world! Oh, Mrs. Florence, please believe me!"

"I prefer to believe the evidence of my eyes," replied Mrs. Florence, as she drew a paper from her pocket "Here is the note. I suppose you will hardly deny your own signature."

Katy seized the note. It was written in a round, unformed hand, and ran thus:

DEAR BERRY,

I saw you last night on the Green. I think you are splendid. All the nuns think so. I look at you very often out of my window. If I let down a string, would you tie a cake to it, like that kind you threw to Mary Andrews last term? Tie two cakes please; one for me, and one for my room-mate. The string will be at the end of the Row.

MISS CARR.

In spite of her agitation, Katy could hardly keep back a smile as she read this absurd production. Mrs. Florence saw the smile, and her tone was more severe than ever, as she said:

"Give that back to me, if you please. It will be my justification with your father if he objects to your change of room."

"But, Mrs. Florence," cried Katy, "I never wrote that note. It isn't my handwriting; it isn't my—Oh, surely, you can't think so! It's too ridiculous."

"Go to your room at once," said Mr. Florence, "and be thankful that your punishment is such a mild one. If your nome were not so distant, I should write to ask your father to remove you from the school; instead of which, I merely put you on the other side of the entry, out of reach of further correspondence of this sort."

"But *I* shall write him, and he will take us away immediately," cried Katy, stung to the quick by this obstinate injustice. "I will not stay, neither shall Clover, where our word is disbelieved, and we are treated like this. Papa knows! Papa will never doubt us a moment when we tell him that this is not true."

With these passionate words she left the room. I do not think that either Mrs. Florence or Mrs. Nipson felt very comfortable after she was gone.

That was a dreadful afternoon. The girls had no heart to arrange No. 1, or do anything towards making it comfortable, but lay on the bed in the midst of their belongings, crying and receiving visits of condolence from their friends. The S.S.U.C. meeting was put off. Katy was in no humour to act as president, or Clover to read her funny poem. Rose and Mary Silver sat by, kissing them at intervals, and declaring that it was a shame, while the other members dropped in one by one to re-echo the same sentiments.

"If it had been anybody else!" said Alice Gibbons; "but Katy—Katy of all persons! It is too much!"

"So I told Mrs. Florence," sobbed Rose Red. "Oh, why was I born so bad? If I'd always been good, and a model to the rest of you, perhaps she'd have believed me, instead of scolding harder than ever."

The idea of Rose as a "model" made Clover smile in the midst of her dolefulness.

"It's an outrageous thing," said Ellen Gray, "if Mrs. Florence only knew it, you two have done more to keep the rest of us steady than any girls in school."

"So they have," blubbered Rose, whose pretty face was quite swollen with crying. "I've been getting better and better every day since they came." She put her arms round Clover as she spoke, and sobbed harder than ever.

It was in the midst of this excitement that Miss Jane saw

fit to come in and "inspect the room." When she saw the crying girls and the general confusion of everything, she was very angry.

"I shall mark you both for disorder," she said. "Get off the bed, Miss Carr. Hang your dresses up at once, Clover, and put your shoes away. I never saw anything so disgraceful. All these things must be in order when I return fifteen minutes. from now, or I shall report you to Mrs. Florence."

"It's of no consequence what you do. We are not going to stay," muttered Katy. But soon she was ashamed of having said this. Her anger was melting, and grief taking its place. "Oh, Papa, Papa! Elsie! Elsie! " she whispered to herself, as she slowly hung up the dresses; and, unseen by the girls, she hid her face in the folds of Clover's grey alpaca, and shed some hot tears. Till then she had been too angry to cry.

This softer mood followed her all through the evening. Clover and Rose sat by, talking over the affair, and keeping their wrath warm with discussion. Katy said hardly a word. She felt too weary and depressed to speak.

"Who could have written the note?" asked Clover again and again. It was impossible to guess. It seemed absurd to suspect any of the older girls; but, then, as Rose suggested. the absurdity as well as the signature might have been imitated to avoid detection.

"I know one thing," remarked Rose, "and that is, that I should like to kill Mrs. Searles. Horrid old thing! — peeping and prying into pockets. She has no business to be alive at all."

Rose's ferocious speeches always sounded specially comical when taken in connection wth her pink cheeks and her dimples.

"Shall you write to Papa tonight, Katy?" asked Clover.

Katy shook her head. She was too heavy-hearted to talk. Big tears rolled down unseen and fell upon the pillow. After Rose was gone, and the candle out, she cried herself to sleep.

Waking early in the dim dawn, she lay and thought it
245

over, Clover slumbering soundly beside her meanwhile.
"Morning brings counsel," says the old proverb. In this
case it seemed true. Katy, to her surprise, found a train of
fresh thoughts filling her mind, which were not there when
she fell asleep. She recalled her passionate words and
feelings of the day before. Now that the mood had passed,
they seemed to her worse than the injury which provoked
them. Quick-tempered and generous people often
experience this. It was easier for Katy to forgive Mrs.
Florence, because it was needful also that she should
forgive herself.

"I said I would write to Papa to take us away," she
thought. "Why did I say that? What good would it do? It
wouldn't make anybody disbelieve this horrid story.
They'd only think I wanted to get away because I was
found out. And Papa would be so worried and
disappointed. It has cost him a great deal to get us ready
and send us here, and he wants us to stay a year. If we
went home now, all the money would be wasted. And yet
how horrid it is going to be after this! I don't feel as if I
could ever bear to see Mrs. Florence again. I must write."

"But then," her thoughts flowed on, "home wouldn't
seem like home if we went away from school in disgrace,
and knew that everybody here was believing such things.
Suppose, instead, I were to write to Papa to come on and
make things straight. He'd find out the truth, and force
Mrs. Florence to see it. It would be very expensive,
though; and I know he oughtn't to leave home again so
soon. Oh, dear! How hard it is to know what to do!"

"What would Cousin Helen say?" she continued, going
in imagination to the sofa-side of the dear friend who was
to her like a second conscience. She shut her eyes and
invented a long talk—her questions, Cousin Helen's replies.
But as everybody knows, it is impossible to play croquet by
yourself and be strictly impartial to all the four balls. Katy
found that she was making Cousin Helen play (that is,
answer) as she herself wished, and not, as something
whispered, she would answer were she really there.

"It is just the 'Little Scholar' over again," she said, half-aloud, "I can't see. I don't know how to act." She remembered the dream she once had, of a great beautiful face and a helping hand. "And it was real," she murmured, "and just as near, now as then."

The result of this long meditation was that, when Clover woke up, she found Katy leaning over, ready to kiss her for good morning, and looking bright and determined.

"Clovy," she said, "I've been thinking; and I'm not going to write to Papa about this affair at all!"

"Are you not? Why not?" asked Clover, puzzled.

"Because it would worry him, and be of no use. He would come on and take us right away, I'm sure; but Mrs. Florence and all the teachers, and a great many of the girls, would always believe that this horrid, ridiculous story is true. I can't bear to have them. Let's stay, instead, and convince them that it isn't. I think we can."

I would a great deal rather go home," said Clover. "It won't ever be nice here again. We shall have this nasty room, and Miss Jane will be more horrid than ever, and the girls will think you wrote that note, and Lilly Page will say hateful things!" She buttoned her boots with a vindictive air.

"Never mind," said Katy, trying to feel brave. "I don't suppose it will be pleasant, but I'm pretty sure it's right. And Rosy and all the girls we really care for know how it is."

"I can't bear it," sighed Clover, with tears in her eyes. "It is so cruel that they should say such things about you."

"I mean that they shall say something quite different before we go away," replied Katy, stroking her hair. "Cousin Helen would tell us to stay, I'm pretty sure. I was thinking about her just now, and I seemed to hear her voice in the air, saying over and over, 'Live it down! Live it down! Live it down!'" She half-sang this, and took two or three dancing steps across the room.

"What a girl you are!" said Clover, consoled by seeing Katy look so bright.

Mrs. Florence was surprised that morning, as she sat in

247

her room, by the appearance of Katy. She looked pale, but perfectly quiet and gentle.

"Mrs. Florence," she said, "I've come to say that I shall not write to my father to take us away, as I told you I should."

Mrs. Florence bowed stiffly, by way of answer.

"Not," went on Katy, with a little flash in her eyes, "that he would hesitate, or doubt my word one moment, if I did. But he wished us to stay here a year, and I don't wish to disappoint him. I'd rather stay. And, Mrs. Florence, I'm sorry I spoke as I did yesterday. It was not right; but I was angry, and felt that you were unjust."

"And today you own that I was not?"

"Oh, no!" replied Katy, "I can't do that. You were unjust, because neither Clover nor I wrote that note. We would not do such a horrid thing for the world, and I hope some day you will believe us. But I ought not to have spoken so."

Katy's face and voice were so truthful as she said this, that Mrs. Florence was almost shaken in her opinion.

"We will say no more about the matter," she remarked, in a kinder tone. "If your conduct is perfectly correct in future, it will go far to make this forgotten."

Few things are more aggravating than to be forgiven when one has done no wrong. Katy felt this as she walked away from Mrs. Florence's room. But she would not let herself grow angry again. "Live it down!" she whispered, as she went into the schoolroom.

She and Clover had a good deal to endure for the next two or three weeks. They missed their old room with its sunny window and pleasant outlook. They missed Rose, who, down at the far end of Quaker Row, could not drop in half so often as had been her custom. Miss Jane was specially grim and sharp; and some of the upstairs girls, who resented Katy's plain speaking, and the formation of a society against flirting, improved the chance to be provoking. Lilly Page was one of these. She didn't really believe Katy guilty, but she liked to tease her by pretending to believe it.

248

"Only to think of the President of the Saintly Stuck-up Society being caught like this!" she remarked, maliciously. "What are our great reformers coming to? Now, if it had been a sinner like me, no one would be surprised!"

All this naturally was vexatious. Even sunny Clover shed many tears in private over her mortifications. But the girls bore their trouble bravely, and never said one syllable about the matter in the letters home. There were consolations, too, mixed with the annoyances. Rose Red clung to her two friends closely, and loyally fought their battles. The S.S.U.C. to a girl rallied round its chief. After that sad Saturday the meetings were resumed with as much spirit as ever. Katy's steadiness and uniform politeness and sweet temper impressed even those who would have been glad to believe a tale against her, and in a short time the affair ceased to be a subject for discussion—was almost forgotten; in fact, except for a sore spot in Katy's heart and one page in Rose Red's album, upon which, under the date of that fatal day, were written these words, headed by an appalling skull and cross-bones in pen-and-ink:

N.B.—Pay Miss Jane off.

CHAPTER EIGHT

CHANGES

"Clover, where's Clover?" cried Rose Red, popping her head into the schoolroom, where Katy sat writing her composition. "Oh, Katy, there you are. I want you too. Come down to my room right away. I've such a thing to tell you."

"What is it? Tell me too!" said Bella Arkwright. Bella was a veritable "little pitcher," of the kind mentioned in the Proverb, and had an insatiable curiosity to know everything that other people knew.

"Tell you, miss? I should really like to know why!" replied Rose, who was not at all fond of Bella.

"You're real mean, and real unkind," whined Bella. "You think you're a great grown-up lady, and can have secrets. But you ain't! You're a little girl too—most as little as me. So there!"

Rose made a face at her, and a sort of growling rush, which had the effect of sending Bella screaming down the hall. Then, returning to the schoolroom:

"Do come, Katy," she said; "find Clover, and hurry! Really and truly I want you. I feel as if I should burst if I don't tell somebody right away what I've found out."

"Now," said Rose, locking the door, and pushing forward a chair for Katy and another for Clover, "swear that you won't tell, for this is a real secret—the greatest secret that ever was, and Mrs. Florence would flay me alive if she knew that I knew!" She paused to enjoy the effect of her words, and suddenly began to snuff the air in a peculiar manner.

"Girls," she said, solemnly, "that little wretch of a Bella is in this room, I am sure of it."

"What makes you think so?" cried the others, surprised.

"I smell that dreadful pomatum that she puts on her hair! Don't you notice it? She's hidden somewhere." Rose looked sharply about for a minute, then made a pounce, and from under the bed dragged a small kicking heap. It was the guilty Bella.

"What were you doing there, you bad child?" demanded Rose, seizing the kicking feet and holding them fast.

"I don't care," blubbered Bella, "you wouldn't tell me your secret. You're a real horrid girl, Rose Red. I don't love you a bit."

"Your affection is not a thing which I particularly pine for," retorted Rose, seating herself, and holding the culprit before her by the ends of her short pig-tails. "I don't want little girls who peep and hide to love me. I'd rather they wouldn't. Now listen. Do you know what I shall do if you ever come again into my room without leave? First, I shall cut off your hair, pomatum and all, with my pen-knife"—

Bella screamed—"and then I'll turn myself into a bear—a great brown bear—and eat you up!" Rose pronounced this threat with tremendous energy, and accompanied it with a snarl which showed all her teeth. Bella roared with fright, twitched away her pig-tails, unlocked the door and fled, Rose not pursuing her, but sitting comfortably in her chair and growling at intervals, till her victim was out of hearing. Then she rose and bolted the door again.

"How lucky that the imp is so fond of that smelly pomatum!" she remarked; "one always knows where to look for her. It's as good as a bell round her neck! Now for the secret. You promise not to tell? Well, then, Mrs. Florence is going away week after next, and, what's more—she's going to be married!"

"Not really!" cried the others.

"Really and truly. She's going to be married to a clergyman."

"How did you find out?"

"Why, it's the most curious thing. You know my blue lawn, which Miss James is making. This morning I went to try it on. Miss Barnes with me, of course, and while Miss James was fitting the waist Mrs. Seccomb came in and sat down on the sofa by Miss Barnes. They began to talk, and pretty soon Mrs. Seccomb said, 'What day does Mrs. Florence go?'

"'Thursday week,' said Miss Barnes. She sort of mumbled it, and looked to see if I were listening. I wasn't: but of course after that I did—as hard as I could.

"'And where does the important event take place?' asked Mrs. Seccomb. She's so funny with her little bit of a mouth and her long words. She always looks as if each of them was a big pill, and she wanted to swallow it and couldn't.

"'In Lewisberg, at her sister's house,' said Miss Barnes. She mumbled more than ever, but I heard.

"'What a deplorable loss she will be to our limited circle!' said Mrs. Seccomb. I couldn't imagine what they meant. But don't you think, when I got home there was this letter from Sylvia, and she says, 'Your adored Mrs.

Florence is going to be married. I'm afraid you'll all break your hearts about it. Mother met the gentleman at a party the other night. She says he looks clever, but isn't at all handsome, which is a pity, for Mrs. Florence is a raving beauty in my opinion. He's an excellent preacher, we hear; and won't she manage the parish to perfection? How shall you like being left to the tender mercies of Mrs. Nipson?' Now did you ever hear anything so droll in your life?" went on Rose, folding up her letter. "Just think of those two things coming together the same day! It's like a sum in arithmetic, with an answer which 'proves' the sum, isn't it?"

Rose had counted on producing an effect, and she certainly was not disappointed. The girls could think and talk of nothing else for the remainder of that afternoon.

It was a singular fact that before two days were over, every scholar in the school knew that Mrs. Florence was going to be married! How the secret got out nobody could guess. Rose protested that it wasn't her fault—she had been a miracle of discretion, a perfect sphinx; but there was a guilty laugh in her eyes, and Katy suspected that the sphinx had unbent a little. Nothing so exciting had ever happened at the Nunnery before. Some of the older scholars were quite inconsolable. They bemoaned themselves, and got together in corners to enjoy the luxury of woe. Nothing comforted them but the project of getting up a "testimonial" for Mrs. Florence.

What this testimonial should be caused great discussion in the school. Everybody had a different idea, and everybody was sure that her idea was better than anybody else's. All the school contributed. The money collected amounted to nearly forty dollars, and the question was, what should be bought?

Every sort of thing was proposed. Lilly Page insisted that nothing could possibly be so appropriate as a bouquet of wax flowers and a glass shade to put over it. There was a strong party in favour of spoons. Annie Silsbie suggested "a statue"; somebody else a clock. Rose Red was for a cabinet piano, and Katy had some trouble in convincing her

252

that forty dollars would not buy one. Bella demanded that they should get "an organ."

"You can go along with it as monkey," said Rose, which remark made Bella caper with indignation.

At last, after long discussion and some quarrelling, a cake-basket was fixed upon. Sylvia Redding happened to be making a visit to Boston, and Rose was commissioned to write and ask her to select the gift and send it up by express.

The girls could hardly wait till it came.

"I do hope it will be pretty, don't you?" they said over and over again.

When the box arrived, they all gathered to see it opened. Esther Dearborn took out the nails, half a dozen hands lifted the lid, and Rose unwrapped the tissue-paper and displayed the basket up to general view.

"Oh, what a beauty!" cried everybody.

It was woven of twisted silver wire. Two figures of children with wings and garlands supported the handle on either side. In the middle of the handle were a pair of silver doves, billing and cooing in the most affectionate way, over a tiny shield, on which were engraved Mrs. Florence's initials.

"I never saw one like it!" "Doesn't it look heavy?" "Rose Red, your sister is splendid!" cried a chorus of voices, as Rose, highly gratified, held up the basket.

"Who shall present it?" asked Louise Agnew.

"Rose Red," said some of the girls.

"No, indeed, I'm not tall enough," protested Rose, "it must be somebody who'd kind of sweep into the room and be impressive. I vote for Katy."

"Oh, no!" said Katy, shrinking back. "I shouldn't do it well at all. Suppose we put it to the vote?"

Ellen Gray cut some slips of paper, and each girl wrote a name and dropped it into a box. When the votes were counted Katy's name appeared on all but three.

"I propose that we make this vote unanimous," said Rose, highly delighted.

253

The girls agreed; and Rose, jumping on a chair, exclaimed:

"Three cheers for Katy Carr! Keep time, girls—one, two, hip, hip, hurrah!"

The hurrahs were given with enthusiasm for Katy, almost without knowing it, had become popular. She was too much touched and pleased to speak at first. When she did, it was to protest against her election.

"Esther would do it beautifully," she said, "and I think Mrs. Florence would like the basket better if she gave it. You know ever since——" she stopped. Even now she could not refer with composure to the affair of the note.

"Oh," cried Louisa, "she's thinking of that ridiculous note Mrs. Florence made such a fuss about. As if anybody supposed you wrote it, Katy! I don't believe even Miss Jane is such a goose as that. Anyway, if she is, that's one reason more why you should present the basket, to show that we don't think so."

She gave Katy a kiss by way of period.

"Yes, indeed, you're chosen, and you must give it," cried the others.

"Very well," said Katy, extremely gratified, "what am I to say?"

"We'll compose a speech for you," said Rose. "Sugar your voice, Katy, and whatever you do, stand up straight. Don't crook over, as if you thought you were tall. It's a bad trick you have, child, and I'm always sorry to see it," concluded Rose, with the air of a wise mamma giving a lecture.

It is droll how much can go on in a school unseen and unsuspected by its teachers. Mrs. Florence never dreamed that the girls had guessed her secret. Her plan was to go away as if for a visit, and leave Mrs. Nipson to explain at her leisure.

She was therefore quite unprepared for the appearance of Katy holding the beautiful basket, which was full of fresh roses, crimson, white, and pink. I am afraid the rules of the S.S.U.C. had been slightly relaxed to allow of Rose

254

Red's getting these flowers; certainly they grew nowhere in Hillsover except in Professor Seccomb's garden!

"The girls wanted me to give you this, with a great deal of love from us all," said Katy, feeling strangely embarrassed, and hardly venturing to raise her eyes. She set the basket on the table. "We hope so much that you will be happy," she added, in a low voice, and moved towards the door.

Mrs. Florence had been too much surprised to speak, but now she called, "Wait!! Come back a moment."

Katy came back. Mrs. Florence's cheeks were flushed. She looked very handsome. Katy almost thought there were tears in her eyes.

"Tell the girls that I thank them very much. Their present is beautiful. I shall always value it!!"

She blushed as she spoke, and Katy blushed too. It made her shy to see the usually composed Mrs. Florence so confused.

"What did she say? What did she say?" demanded the others, who were collected in groups round the schoolroom door to hear a report of the interview.

Katy repeated the message. Some of the girls were disappointed. "Is that all?" they said. "We thought she would stand up and make a speech."

"Or a short poem," put in Rose Red—"a few stanzas thrown off on the spur of the moment; like this, for instance:

> Thank you, kindly, for your basket,
> Which I didn't mean to ask it;
> But I'll very gladly take it,
> And when 'tis full of cake, it
> Will frequently remind me
> Of the girls I left behind me!"

There was a universal giggle, which brought Miss Jane out of the schoolroom.

"Order!" she said, ringing the bell. "Young ladies, what are you about? Study hour has begun."

"We're so sorry Mrs. Florence is going away," said some of the girls.

"How did you know that she is going?" demanded Miss Jane, sharply.

Nobody answered.

Next day Mrs. Florence left. Katy saw her go with a secret regret.

"If only she would have said that she didn't believe I wrote that note!" she told Clover.

"I don't care what she believes! She's a stupid, unjust woman!" replied independent little Clover.

Mrs. Nipson was now in sole charge of the establishment. She had never tried school-keeping before, and had various pet plans and theories of her own, which she had only been waiting Mrs. Florence's departure to put into practice.

One of these was that the school was to dine three times a week on pudding and bread and butter. Mrs. Nipson had a theory—very convenient and economical for herself, but highly distasteful to her scholars—that it was injurious for young people to eat meat every day in hot weather.

The puddings were made of batter, with a sprinkling of blackberries or raisins. Now, rising at six, and studying four hours and a half on a light breakfast, has a wonderful effect on the appetite, as all who have tried it will testify. The poor girls would go down to dinner as hungry as wolves, and eye the large, pale slices on their plates with a wrath and dismay which I cannot pretend to describe. Very thick the slices were, and there was plenty of thin, sugared sauce to eat with them, and plenty of bread and butter; but somehow, the whole was unsatisfying, and the hungry girls would go upstairs almost as ravenous as when they came down. The second-table-ites were always hanging over the balusters to receive them, and when to the demand, "What did you have for dinner?" "Pudding!" was answered, a low groan would run from one to another, and a general gloom seemed to drop down and envelop the party.

It may have been in consequence of this experience of starvation that the orders for Fourth of July were that year so unusually large. It was an old custom in the school that the girls should celebrate the National Independence by buying as many goodies as they liked. There was no candy-shop in Hillsover, so Mrs. Nipson took the orders, and sent to Boston for the things, which were charged on the bills with other extras. Under these blissful circumstances, the girls felt that they could afford to be extravagant, and made out their lists regardless of expense. Rose Red's, for this Fourth, ran thus:

> "Two pounds of Chocolate Caramels.
> Two pounds of Sugar Almonds.
> Two pounds of Lemon Drops.
> Two pounds of Mixed Candy.
> Two pounds of Macaroons.
> A dozen Oranges.
> A dozen Lemons.
> A drum of Figs.
> A box of French Plums.
> A loaf of Almond Cake."

The result of this liberal order was that, after the great wash-baskets of parcels had been distributed, and the school had rioted for twenty-four hours upon these unaccustomed luxuries, Rose was found lying on her bed, ghastly and pallid.

"Never speak to me of anything sweet again so long as I live!" she gasped. "Talk of vinegar, or pickles, or sour apples; but don't allude to sugar in any form, if you love me! Oh, why, why did I send for those fatal things?"

In time all the candy was eaten up, and the school went back to its normal condition. Three weeks later came College Commencement.

"Are you and Clover Craters or Symposiums?" demanded Lilly Page, meeting Katy in the hall, a few days before this important event.

"What do you mean?"

"Why, has nobody told you about them? They are two great College Societies. All the girls belong to one or the other, and make the wreaths to dress their halls We work up in the Gymnasium; the Crater girls take the east side, and the Symposium girls the west, and when the wreaths grow too long we hang them out of the windows. It's the greatest fun in the world! Be a Symposium, do! I'm one!"

"I shall have to think about it before deciding," said Katy, privately resolving to join Rose Red's Society, whichever it was. The Crater it proved to be, so Katy and Clover enrolled themselves with the Craters. Three days before Commencement wreath-making began. The afternoons were wholly given up to the work, and, instead of walking, or piano practice, the girls sat plaiting oak-leaves into garlands many yards long. Baskets of fresh leaves were constantly brought in, and there was a strife between the rival Societies as to which should accomplish most.

It was great fun, as Lilly had said, to sit there amid the green boughs, and pleasant leafy smells, a buzz of gay voices in the air, and a general sense of holiday. The Gymnasium would have furnished many a pretty picture for an artist during those three afternoons, only, unfortunately, no artist was let in to see it.

One day, Rose Red, emptying a basket, lighted upon a white parcel, hidden beneath the leaves.

"Lemon drops!" she exclaimed, applying a finger and thumb with all the dexterity of Jack Horner. "Here, Crater girls, here's something for you? Don't you pity the Symposiums?"

But next day a big package of peppermints appeared in the Symposium basket, so neither Society could boast advantage over the other. They were pretty nearly equal, too, in the quantity of wreath made—the Craters measuring nine hundred yards and the Symposiums nine hundred and two. As for the Halls, which they were taken over to see the evening before Commencement, it was impossible to say which was most beautiful, trmimed. Each faction preferred its own, and President Searles said that both did the young ladies credit.

They all sat in the gallery of the church on

Commencement Day, and heard the speeches. It was very hot, and the speeches were not exactly interesting, being on such subjects as "The Influence of a Republic on Men of Letters," and "The Abstract Law of Justice, as applied to Human Affairs"; but the music, and the crowd, and the spectacle of six hundred ladies all fanning themselves at once, were entertaining, and the girls would not have missed them for the world. Later in the day another diversion was afforded them by the throngs of pink and blue ladies and white-gloved gentlemen who passed the house, on their way to the President's Levee; but they were not allowed to enjoy this amusement long, for Miss Jane, suspecting what was going on, went from room to room, and ordered everybody off to bed.

With the close of Commencement Day, a deep sleep seemed to settle over Hillsover. Most of the Professors' families went off to enjoy themselves at the mountains or at the sea-side, leaving their houses shut up. This gave the village a drowsy and deserted air. There were no boys playing balls on the Common, or swinging on the College fence; no look of life in the streets. The weather continued warm, the routine of study and exercise grew dull, and teachers and scholars alike were glad when the middle of September arrived, and with it the opening of the autumn vacation.

CHAPTER NINE

THE AUTUMN VACATION

THE LAST DAY of the term was one of confusion. Every part of the house was given over to trunks and packing. Mrs. Nipson sat at her desk, making out bills, and listening to requests about rooms and room-mates Miss Jane counted books and atlases, taking note of each ink-spot and dog-eared page. The girls ran about, searching for missing articles, deciding what to take home and what to leave, engaging each other for the winter walks. All rules were laid aside. The sober Nunnery seemed turned into a hive of buzzing bees. Bella slid twice down the baluster of the front stairs without being reproved; and Rose Red threw her arm round Katy's waist, and waltzed the whole length of Quaker Row.

"I'm so happy that I should like to scream!" she announced, as their last whirl brought them up against the wall. "Isn't vacation just lovely? Katy, you don't look half glad."

"We're not going home, you know," replied Katy, in rather a doleful tone. She and Clover were not so enraptured at the coming of vacation as the rest of the girls. Spending a month with Mrs. Page and Lilly was by no means the same thing as spending it with Papa and the children.

Next morning, however, when the big stage drove up, and the girls crowded in; when Mrs. Nipson stood in the doorway, blandly waving farewell, and the maids flourished their dusters out of the upper windows, they found themselves sharing the general excitement, and joining heartily in the cheer which arose as the stage moved away. The girls felt so happy and good-natured, that some of them even kissed their hands to Miss Jane.

Such a wild company is not often met with on a railroad train. They all went together as far as the Junction; and Mr. Gray, Ellen's father, who had been put in charge of the party by Mrs. Nipson had his hands full to keep them in any sort of order. He was a timid old gentleman, and, as Rose suggested, his expression resembled that of a sedate hen who suddenly finds herself responsible for the conduct of a brood of ducklings.

"My dear, my dear," he feebly remonstrated, "would you buy any more candy? Do you not think so many pea-nuts may be bad for you?"

"Oh, no sir!" replied Rose; "they never hurt me a bit, I can eat thousands!" Then, as a stout lady entered the car, and made a motion toward the vacant seat beside her, she

"Fits?" cried the stout lady and backed away from Rose in horror . . .

rolled her eyes wildly, and said, "Excuse me, but perhaps I had better take the end seat, so as to get out easily in case I have a fit."

"Fits!" cried the stout lady, and walked away with the utmost dispatch. Rose gave a wicked chuckle; the girls tittered; and Mr. Gray visibly trembled.

"Is she really afflicted in this way?" he whispered.

"Oh, no, Papa!! It's only Rose's nonsense!" apologised Ellen, who was laughing as hard as the rest. But Mr. Gray did not feel comfortable, and he was very glad when they reached the Junction, and half of his troublesome charge departed on the branch road.

At six o'clock they arrived in Springfield. Half a dozen papas were waiting for their daughters; trains stood ready; there was a clamour of goodbyes. Mr. Page was absorbed by Lilly, who kissed him incessantly, and chattered so fast that he had no eyes for any one else. Louisa was borne away by an uncle, with whom she was to pass the night; and Katy and Clover found themselves left alone. They did not like to interrupt Lilly, so they retreated to a bench, and sat down feeling rather left out and home-sick; and, though they did not say so, I am sure that each was thinking about papa.

It was only for a moment. Mr. Page spied them, and came forward with such a kind greeting, that the forlorn feeling fled at once. They were to pass the night at the Massasoit, it seemed; and he collected their bags, and led the way across the street to the hotel, where rooms were already engaged for them.

"Now for waffles," whispered Lilly, as they went upstairs; and when, after a few minutes of washing and brushing, they came down again into the dining-room, she called for so many things, and announced herself "starved" in such a tragical tone, that two amused waiters at once flew to the rescue, and devoted themselves to supply her wants. Waffle after waffle—each hotter and crisper than the last—did those long-suffering men produce, till even Lilly's appetite gave out, and she was forced to own that she could not swallow another morsel. This climax reached, they went into the parlour; and the girls sat down in the window to watch the people in the street—which, after quiet Hillsover, looked as brilliant and crowded as Broadway.

There were not many persons in the parlour. A grave-looking couple sat at a table at some distance, and a pretty little boy in a velvet jacket was playing around the room. He seemed about five years old; and Katy, who was fond of children, put out her hand as he went by, caught him, and lifted him into her lap. He did not seem shy, but looked her in the face composedly, like a grown person.

"What is your name, dear?" she asked.

"Daniel D'Aubigny Sparks," answered the little boy. His voice was prim and distinct.

"Do you live at this hotel?"

"Yes, ma'am. I reside here with my father and mother."

"And what do you do all day? Are there some other little boys for you to play with?"

"I do not wish to play with any little boys," replied Daniel D'Aubigny, in a dignified tone. "I prefer to be with my parents. Today we have taken a walk. We went to see a beautiful conservatory outside the city. There is a Victoria Regia there. I had often heard of this wonderful lily; and in the last number of the London *Musée* there is a picture of it, represented with a small negro child standing upon its leaves. My father said that he did not think this possible; but, when we saw the plant, we perceived that the print was not an exaggeration. Such is the size of the leaf, that a small negro child might very easily be supported upon it."

"Oh, my!" cried Katy, feeling as if she had accidentally picked up an elderly gentleman, or a college professor. "Pray, how old are you?"

"Nearly nine, ma'am," replied the little fellow, with a bow.

Katy, too much appalled for further speech, let him slide off her lap. But Mr. Page, who was much diverted, continued the conversation; and Daniel, mounting a chair, crossed his short legs, and discoursed with all the gravity of an old man. The talk was principally about himself—his tastes, his adventures, his ideas about art and science. Now and then he alluded to his papa and mamma and, once to his grandfather.

"My maternal grandfather," he said, "was a remarkable man. In his youth he spent a great deal of time in France. He was there at the time of the French Revolution, and, as it happened, was present at the execution of the unfortunate Queen Marie Antoinette. This of course was not intentional. It chanced thus. My grandfather was in a barber's shop, having his hair cut. He saw a great crowd going by, and went out to ask what was the cause. The crowd was so immense that he could not extricate himself; he was carried along against his will, and not only so, but was forced to the front and compelled to witness every part of the dreadful scene. He has often told my mother that, after the execution, the executioner held up the Queen's head to the people; the eyes were open, and there was in them an expression, not of pain, not of fear, but of great astonishment and surprise."

This anecdote carried "great astonishment and surprise" into the company who listened to it. Mr. Page gave a sort of chuckle, and saying, "By George!" got up and left the room. The girls put their heads out of the window that they might laugh unseen. Daniel gazed at their shaking shoulders with an air of wonder, while the grave couple at the end of the room, who for some moments had been looking disturbed, drew near and informed the youthful prodigy that it was time for him to go to bed.

"Goodnight, young ladies," said the small condescending voice. Katy alone had "presence of countenance" enough to return this salutation. It was a relief to find that Daniel went to bed at all.

Next morning at breakfast they saw him seated between his parents, eating bread and milk. He bowed to them over the edge of the bowl.

"Dreadful little prig! They should bottle him in spirits of wine as a specimen. It's the only thing he'll ever be fit for," remarked Mr. Page, who rarely said so sharp a thing about anybody.

Louisa joined them at the station. She was to travel under Mr. Page's care, and Katy was much annoyed at Lilly's manner to her. It grew colder and less polite with every mile. By the time they reached Ashburn it was absolutely rude.

"Come and see me very soon, girls," said Louisa, as they parted in the station. "I long to have you know Mother and little Daisy. Oh, there's Papa!" and she rushed up to a tall, pleasant-looking man, who kissed her fondly, shook hands with Mr. Page, and touched his hat to Lilly who scarcely bowed in return.

"Boarding-school is so horrid," she remarked, "you get all mixed up with people you don't want to know—people not in society at all."

"How can you talk such nonsense?" said her father; "the Agnews are thoroughly respectable, and Mr. Agnew is one of the cleverest men I know."

Katy was pleased when Mr. Page said this, but Lilly shrugged her shoulders and looked cross.

"Papa is so democratic," she whispered to Clover, "he don't care a bit who people are, so long as they are respectable and clever."

"Well, why should he?" replied Clover. Lilly was more disgusted than ever.

Ashburn was a large and prosperous town. It was built on the slopes of a picturesque hill, and shaded with fine elms. As they drove through the streets, Katy and Clover caught glimpses of conservatories and shrubberies, and beautiful houses with bay windows and piazzas.

"That's ours," said Lilly, as the carriage turned in at a gate. It stopped, and Mr. Page jumped out.

"Here we are," he said. "Gently, Lilly, you'll hurt yourself. Well, my dear, we're very glad to see you in our home at last."

This was kind and comfortable, and the girls were glad of it, for the size and splendour of the house quite dazzled and made them shy. They had never seen anything like it before. The hall had a marble floor, and busts and statues. Large rooms opened on either side; and Mrs. Page, who came forward to receive them, wore a heavy silk with train and laces, and looked altogether as if she were dressed for a party.

"This is the drawing-room," said Lilly, delighted to see the girls looked so impressed. "Isn't it splendid?" And she led the way into a stiff, chilly, magnificent apartment, where all the blinds were closed, and all the shades pulled down, and all the furniture shrouded in linen covers. Even the picture-frames and mirrors were sewn up in muslin, to keep off flies; and the bronzes and alabaster ornaments on the chimney-piece and *étagère* gleamed through the dim light in a ghostly way. Katy thought it very dismal. She couldn't imagine anybody sitting down there to read or sew, or do anything pleasant, and probably it was not intended that any one should do so: for Mrs. Page soon showed them out, and led the way into a smaller room at the back of the hall.

"Well, Katy," she said, "how do you like Hillsover?"

"Very well, ma'am," replied Katy; but she did not speak enthusiastically.

"Ah!" said Mrs. Page, shaking her head, "it takes time to shake off home habits, and to learn to get along with young people after living with older ones and catching their ways. You'll like it better as you go on."

Katy privately doubted whether this was true, but she did not say so. Pretty soon Lilly offered to show them upstairs to their room. She took them first into three large and elegant chambers, which she explained were kept for grand company, and then into a much smaller one in the wing.

"Mother always puts my friends in here," she remarked; "she says it's plenty good enough for schoolgirls to thrash about in!"

"What does she mean?" cried Clover, indignantly, as Lilly closed the door. "We don't thrash!"

"I can't imagine," answered Katy, who was vexed too. But pretty soon she began to laugh.

266

"People are so funny," she said. "Never mind, Clovy, this room is good enough, I'm sure."

"Must we unpack, or will it do to go down in our alpacas?" asked Clover.

"I don't know," replied Katy, in a doubtful tone. "Perhaps we had better change our gowns. Cousin Olivia always dresses so much! Here's your blue muslin right on top of the trunk. You might put on that, and I'll wear my purple."

The girls were glad they had done this, for it was evidently expected, and Lilly had dressed her hair and donned a fresh white piqué. Mrs. Page examined their dresses, and said that Clover's was a lovely blue, but that ruffles were quite gone out, and everything must be made with basques. She supposed they needed quantities of things, and she had already engaged a dressmaker to work for them.

"Thank you," said Katy, "but I don't think we need anything. We had our winter dresses made before we left home."

"Winter dresses! Last spring! My dear, what were you thinking of? They must be completely out of fashion."

"You can't think how little Hillsover people know about fashions," replied Katy, laughing.

"But, my dear, for your own sake!" exclaimed Mrs. Page, distressed by these lax remarks. "I'll look over your things tomorrow and see what you need."

Katy did not dare to say "No," but she felt rebellious. When they were half through tea, the door opened and a boy came in.

"You are late, Clarence," said Mr. Page, while Mrs. Page frowned, and observed, "Clarence makes a point of being late. He really deserves to be made to go without his supper. Shut the door, Clarence. O mercy! Don't bang it in that way. I wish you would learn to shut a door properly. Here are your cousins, Katy and Clover Carr. Now let me see if you can shake hands with them like a gentleman, and not like a ploughboy."

Clarence, a square, freckled boy of thirteen, with reddish

hair, and a sort of red sparkle in his eyes, looked very angry at this address. He did not offer to shake hands at all, but elevating his shoulders said, "How d'you do?" in a sulky voice, and sitting down at the table buried his nose without delay in a glass of milk. His mother gave a disgusted sigh.

"What a boy you are!" she said. "Your cousins will think that you have never been taught anything, which is not the case; for I'm sure I've taken twice the pains with you that I have with Lilly. Pray excuse him, Katy. It's no use trying to make boys polite!"

"Isn't it?" said Katy, thinking of Phil and Dorry, and wondering what Mrs. Page could mean.

"Hullo, Lilly!" broke in Clarence, spying his sister as it seemed for the first time.

"How d'you do?" said Lilly, carelessly. "I was wondering how long it would be before you would condescend to notice my existence."

"I didn't see you."

"I know you didn't. I never knew such a boy! You might as well have no eyes at all."

Clarence scowled and went on with his supper. His mother seemed unable to let him alone. "Clarence, don't take such large mouthfuls! Clarence, pray use your napkin! Clarence, your elbows are on the table, sir! Now, Clarence, don't try to speak until you have swallowed all that bread!"—came every other moment. Katy felt very sorry for Clarence. His manners were certainly bad, but it seemed quite dreadful that public attention should be thus constantly called to them.

The evening was rather dull. There was a sort of put-in-order-for-company air about the parlour, which made everybody stiff. Mrs. Page did not sew or read, but sat in a low chair, looking like a lady in a fashion-plate, and asked questions about Hillsover, some of which were not easy to answer, as, for example, "Have you any other intimate friends among the schoolgirls besides Lilly?" About eight o'clock a couple of young, very young, gentlemen came in, at the sight of whom Lilly, who was half asleep, brightened and became lively and talkative. One of them was the Mr. Hickman, whose father married Mr. Page's sister-in-law's sister, thus making him in some mysterious way a "first cousin" of Lilly's. He was an Arrowmouth student, and seemed to have so many jokes to laugh over with Lilly that before long they withdrew to a distant sofa where they conversed in whispers. The other youth, introduced as Mr. Eels, was left to entertain the other three ladies, which duty he performed by sucking the head of his cane in silence while they talked to him. He too was an Arrowmouth Sophomore.

In the midst of the conversation, the door, which stood ajar, opened a little wider, and a dog's head appeared, followed by a tail, which waggled so beseechingly for leave to come farther, that Clover, who liked dogs, put out her hand and said, "Come here, poor fellow!" The dog ran up to her at once. He was not pretty, being of a pepper-and-salt colour, with a blunt nose and no particular sort of a tail, but he looked good-natured; and Clover fondled him cordially, while Mr. Eels took his cane out of his mouth to ask, "What kind of a dog is that, Mrs. Page?"

"I'm sure I don't know," she replied; while Lilly, from the distance, added affectedly, "Oh, he's the most dreadful dog, Mr. Eels. My brother picked him up in the street, and none of us know the least thing about him, except that he's the commonest kind of dog—a sort of cur, I believe."

"That's not true!" broke in a stern voice from the hall, which made everybody jump; and Katy, looking that way, was aware of a vengeful eye glaring at Lilly through the crack of the door. "He's a very valuable dog, indeed—half mastiff and half terrier, with a touch of the bull-dog—so there, Miss!"

The effect of this remark was startling. Lilly gave a scream; Mrs. Page rose, and hurried to the door; while the dog, hearing his master's voice, rushed that way also, got before her, and almost threw her down. Katy and Clover could not help laughing, and Mr. Eels meeting their amused eyes, removed the cane from his mouth and grew conversible.

"That Clarence is a droll little chap!" he remarked confidentially. "Bright too! He'd be a nice fellow if he wasn't picked at so much. It never does a fellow any good to be picked at—now does it, Miss Carr?"

"No; I don't think it does."

"I say," continued Mr. Eels, "I've seen you young ladies up at Hillsover, haven't I? Aren't you both at the Nunnery?"

"Yes. It's vacation now, you know."

"I was sure I'd seen you. You had a room on the side next the President's, didn't you? I thought so. We fellows didn't know your names, so we called you 'The Real Nuns'."

"Real Nuns?"

"Yes, because you never looked out of the window at us. Real nuns and sham nuns—don't you see? Almost all the young ladies are sham nuns, except you, and two pretty little ones in the story above, fifth window from the end."

"Oh, I know!" said Clover, much amused. "Sally Alsop, you know, Katy, and Amy Erskine. They are such nice girls."

"Are they?" replied Mr. Eels, with the air of one who notes down names for future reference. "Well, I thought so. Not so much fun in them as some of the others, I guess; but a fellow likes other things as well as fun. I know if my sister was there I'd rather have her take the dull line than the other."

Katy treasured up this remark for the benefit of the S.S.U.C. Mrs. Page came back just then, and Mr. Eels resumed his cane. Nothing more was heard of Clarence that night.

Next morning Cousin Olivia fulfilled her threat of inspecting the girls' wardrobe. She shook her head over the simple, untrimmed merinos and thick cloth coats.

"There's no help for it," she said; "but it's a great pity. You would much better have waited and had things fresh. Perhaps it may be possible to match the merino, and have some sort of basque arrangement added on. I will talk to Madame Chonfleur about it. Meantime I shall get one

270

handsome thick dress for each of you, and have it stylishly made. That, at least you really need."

Katy was too glad to be so easily let off to raise objections. So that afternoon she and Clover were taken out "to choose their material," Mrs. Page said, but really to sit by while she chose it for them. At the dressmaker's it was the same; they stood passive while the orders were given, and everything decided upon.

"Isn't it funny?" whispered Clover; "but I don't like it a bit, do you? It's just like Elsie saying how she'll have her doll's things made."

"Oh, this dress isn't mine, it's Cousin Olivia's!" replied Katy. "She's welcome to have it trimmed just as she likes."

But when the suits came home she was forced to be pleased. There was no over-trimming, no look of finery; everything fitted perfectly and had the air of finish which they had noticed and admired in Lilly's clothes. Katy almost forgot that she had objected to the dresses as unnecessary.

"After all, it is nice to look nice," she confessed to Clover.

Excepting to go to the dressmaker's, there was not much to amuse them during the first half of vacation.

Mrs. Page took them to drive now and then, and Katy found some pleasant books in the library, and read a good deal. Clover meantime made friends with Clarence. I think his heart was won that first evening by her attentions to Guest the dog, that mysterious animal, "half mastiff and half terrier, with a touch of the bull-dog." Clarence loved Guest dearly, and was gratified that Clover liked him; for the poor animal had few friends in the household. In a little while Clarence became quite sociable with her, and tolerably so with Katy. They found him, as Mr. Eels had said, "a bright fellow," and pleasant and good-humoured when taken in the right way Lilly always seemed to take him wrong, and his treatment of her was most disagreeable, snappish, and quarrelsome to the last degree.

"Much you don't like oranges!" he said, one day at dinner, in answer to an innocent remark of hers. "Much!

I've seen her eat two at a time, without stopping. Pa, Lilly says she don't like oranges! I've seen her eat two at a time, without stopping! Much she doesn't! I've seen her eat two at a time without stopping." He kept this up for five minutes, looking from one person to another, and repeating, "Much she don't! Much!" till Lilly was almost crying from vexation, and even Clover longed to box his ears. Nobody was sorry when Mr. Page ordered him to leave the room, which he did with a last vindictive "Much," addressed to Lilly.

"How can Clarence behave so?" said Katy, when she and Clover were alone.

"I don't know," replied Clover. "He's such a nice boy sometimes; but when he isn't nice, he's the horridest boy I ever saw. I wish you'd talk to him, Katy, and tell him how dreadfully it sounds when he says such things."

"No, indeed. He'd take it much better from you. You're nearer his age, and could do it nicely and pleasantly, and not make him feel as if he were being scolded. Poor fellow, he gets plenty of that!"

Clover said no more about the subject, but she meditated. She had a good deal of tact for so young a girl, and took care to get Clarence into a specially amicable mood before she began her lecture. "Look here, you bad boy, how could you tease poor Lilly so, yesterday? Guest, speak up, sir, and tell your massa how naughty it was!"

"Oh, dear! Now you're going to nag!" growled Clarence, in an injured voice.

"No, I'm not—not the least in the world. I'll promise not to. But just tell me"—and Clover put her hand on the rough, red-brown hair, and stroked it—"just tell me why you 'go for to do' such things? They're not a bit nice."

"Lilly's so hateful!" grumbled Clarence.

"Well—she is sometimes, I know," admitted Clover, candidly. "But because she is hateful is no reason why you should be unmanly."

"Unmanly!" cried Clarence, flushing.

"Yes, I call it unmanly to tease and quarrel, and contradict like that. It's like girls. They do it sometimes,

272

but I didn't think a boy would. I thought he'd be ashamed."

"Doesn't Dorry ever quarrel or tease?" asked Clarence, who liked to hear about Clover's brothers and sisters.

"Not now, and never in that way. He used to sometimes when he was little, but now he's real nice. He wouldn't speak to a girl as you speak to Lilly for anything in the world. He'd think it wasn't being a gentleman."

"Stuff about gentlemen, and all that!" retorted Clarence. "Mother dings the word into my ears till I hate it."

"Well, it is rather teasing to be reminded all the time, I admit; but you can't wonder that your mother wants you to be a gentleman, Clarence. It's the best thing in the world, I think. I hope Phil and Dorry will grow up just like Papa, for everybody says he's the most perfect gentleman and it makes me so proud to hear them."

"But what does it mean anyway? Mother says it's how you hold your fork, and how you chew, and how you put on your hat. If that's all, I don't think it amounts to much."

"Oh, that isn't all. It's being gentle, don't you see? Gentle and nice to everybody, and just as polite to poor people as to rich ones," said Clover, talking fast, in her eagerness to explain her meaning—"and never being selfish, or noisy, or pushing people out of their place. Forks, and hats, and all that are only little ways of making oneself more agreeable to other people. A gentleman is a gentleman inside—all through. Oh, I wish I could make you see what I mean!"

"Oh, that's it, is it?" said Clarence.

Whether he understood or not, Clover could not tell; or whether she had done any good or not; but she had the discretion to say no more; and certainly Clarence was not offended, for after that day he grew fonder of her than ever. Lilly became absolutely jealous. She had never cared particularly for Clarence's affection, but she did not like to have any one preferred above herself.

"It's pretty hard, I think," she told Clover. "Clare does everything you tell him, and he treats me awfully. It isn't a bit fair! I'm his sister, and you're only a second cousin."

All this time the girls had seen almost nothing of Louisa Agnew. She called once but Lilly received the call with them, and was so cool and stiff that Louisa grew stiff also, and made but a short stay; and when the girls returned the visit she was out. A few days before the close of the vacation, however, a note came from her:

DEAR KATY,

I am so sorry not to have seen more of you and Clover. Won't you come and spend Wednesday with us? Mamma sends her love, and hopes you will come early, so as to have a long day, for she wants to know you. I long to show you the baby and everything. Do come. Papa will see you home in the evening. Remember me to Lilly. She has so many friends to see during vacation that I am sure she will forgive me for stealing you for one day.

Yours affectionately,
LOUISA.

Katy thought this message very politely expressed; but, Lilly, when she heard it, tossed her head, and said she "really thought Miss Agnew might let her name alone when she wrote notes." Mrs. Page seemed to pity the girls for having to go. They must, she supposed, as it was a schoolmate; but she feared it would be stupid for them. The Agnews were queer sort of people, not in society at all. Mr. Agnew was clever, people said; but, really, she knew very little about the family. Perhaps it would not do to decline.

Katy and Clover had no idea of declining. They sent a warm little note of acceptance, and on the appointed day set off bright and early with a good deal of pleasant anticipation. The vacation had been rather dull at Cousin Olivia's. Lilly was a good deal with her own friends, and Mrs. Page with hers; and there never seemed any special place where they might sit, or anything in particular for them to do.

Louisa's home was at some distant from Mr. Page's, and in a less fashionable street. It looked pleasant and cosy as the girls opened the gate. There was a small garden in front with gay flower-beds; and on the piazza, which was shaded with vines, sat Mrs. Agnew, with a little work-table by her side. She was a pretty and youthful-looking woman, and her voice and smile made them feel at home immediately.

"There is no need of anybody to introduce you," she said. "Lulu has described you so often that I know perfectly well which is Katy and which Clover. I am so glad you could come! Won't you go right in my bedroom by that long window and take off your things? Lulu has explained to you that I am lame and never walk, so you won't think it strange that I do not show you the way. She will be here in a moment. She ran upstairs to fetch the baby."

The girls went into the bedroom. It was a pretty and unusual-looking apartment. The furniture was simple as could be, but bed and toilet and windows were curtained and frilled with white, and the walls were covered thick with pictures, photographs, and pen-and-ink sketches, and water-colour drawings, unframed, most of them, and just pinned up without regularity, so as to give each the best possible light. It was an odd way of arranging pictures; but Katy liked it, and would gladly have lingered to look at each one, only that she feared Mrs. Agnew would expect them and would think it strange that they did not come back.

Just as they went out again to the piazza, Louisa came running downstairs with her little sister in her arms.

"I was curling her hair," she explained, "and did not hear you come in. Daisy, give Katy a kiss. Now another for Clover. Isn't she a darling?" embracing the child rapturously herself, "now isn't she a little beauty?"

"Perfectly lovely," cried the others, and soon all three were seated on the floor of the piazza, with Daisy in the midst, passing her from hand to hand as if she had been something good to eat. She was used to it, and submitted with perfect good nature to being kissed, trotted, carried up and down, and generally made love to. Mrs. Agnew sat by and laughed at the spectacle. When Baby was taken off for her noonday nap, Louisa took the girls into the parlour, another odd and pretty room full of prints and sketches, and pictures of all sorts, some with frames, others with a knot of autumn leaves, or a twist of ivy around them by way of a finish. There was a bowl of beautiful autumn roses on the table; and, though the price of one of Mrs. Page's damask curtains would probably have bought the whole furniture of the room, everything was so bright, and home-like, and pleasant-looking that Katy's heart warmed at the sight. They were examining a portrait of Louisa with Daisy in her lap, painted by her father, when Mr. Agnew came in. The girls liked his face at once. It was fine and frank; and nothing could be prettier than to see him pick up his sweet invalid wife as if she had been a child, and carry her into the dining-room to her place at the head of the table.

Katy and Clover agreed afterward that it was the merriest dinner they had had since they left home. Mr. Agnew told stories about painters and painting, and was delightful. No less so was the nice gossip upstairs in Louisa's room which followed dinner, or the afternoon frolic with Daisy, or the long evening spent in looking over books and photographs. Altogether the day seemed only too short. As they went out of the gate at ten o'clock, Mr. Agnew followed, lo! a dark figure emerged from behind a tree and joined Clover. It was Clarence!

"I thought I'd just walk this way," he explained, "the house has been dreadfully dull all day without you."

Clover was immensely flattered, but Mrs. Page's astonishment next day knew no bounds.

"Really," she said, "I have hopes of Clarence at last. I never knew him volunteer to escort anybody anywhere before in his life."

"I say," remarked Clarence, the evening before the girls went back to school—"I say, suppose you write to a fellow sometimes, Clover?"

"Do you mean yourself by 'a fellow'?" laughed Clover.

276

"You don't suppose I meant George Hickman, or that donkey of an Eels, did you?" retorted Clarence.

"No, I didn't. Well, I've no objection to writing to a fellow, if that fellow is you, provided the fellow answers my letters. Will you?"

"Yes," gruffly, "but you mustn't show 'em to any girls or laugh at my writing, or I'll stop. Lilly says my writing is like beetle-tracks. Little she knows about it, though! I don't write to her. Promise, Clover!"

"Yes, I promise," said Clover, pleased at the notion of Clare's proposing a correspondence of his own accord.

Next morning they all left for Hillsover. Clarence's friendship, and the remembrance of their day with the Agnews, were the pleasantest things that the girls carried away with them from their autumn vacation.

CHAPTER TEN

A BUDGET OF LETTERS

Hillsover, October 21st.

DEAREST ELSIE,—I didn't write you last Saturday, because that was the day we came back to school, and there hasn't been one minute when I could. We thought, perhaps, Miss Jane would let us off from the abstracts on Sunday, because it was the first day, and school was hardly begun; and, if she had, I was going to write to you instead, but she didn't. She said the only way to keep girls out of mischief was to keep them busy. Rose Red is sure that something has gone wrong with Miss Jane's missionary during the vacation—she's so dreadfully cross. Oh dear, how I do hate to come back and be scolded by her again!

I forget if I told you about the abstracts. They are of the sermons on Sunday, you know; and we have to give the texts, and the heads, and as much as we can remember of the rest. Sometimes Dr. Prince begins, 'I shall divide my subject into three parts,' and tells what they are going to be. When he does that, most of the girls take out their pencils and put them down, and then they don't listen any more. Katy and I don't, for she says it isn't right to act in that way. Miss Jane pretends that she reads all the abstracts through, but she doesn't; for once, Rose Red, just to try her, wrote in the middle of hers, 'I am sitting by my window at this moment, and a red cow is going down the street. I wonder if she is any relation to Mrs. Seccomb's cow?' and Miss Jane never noticed it, but marked her 'perfect' all the same. Wasn't it funny?

But I must tell you about our journey back. Mr. Page came all the way with us, and was ever so nice. Clarence rode down in the carriage to the depot. He gave me a real india-rubber and a gold pencil for a goodbye present. I think you and Dorry could like Clarence, only just at first you might say he was rather rude and cross. I did; but now I like him ever so much. Cousin Olivia gave Katy a worked collar and sleeves, and me an embroidered pocket-handkerchief with clover-leaves in the corner. Wasn't it kind? I'm sorry I said in my last letter that we didn't enjoy our vacation. We didn't much; but it wasn't exactly Cousin Olivia's fault. She meant we should, but she didn't know how. Some people don't, you know. And don't tell any one I said so, will you?

Rose Red got into the train before we did. She was so glad when we came that she cried. It was because she was home-sick waiting four hours at the Nunnery without us, she said. Rose is such a darling! She had a splendid vacation, and went to three parties and a picnic. Isn't it queer?—her winter bonnet is black velvet trimmed with pink, and so is mine. I wanted blue at first, but Cousin Olivia said pink was more stylish; and now I am glad, because I like to be like Rose.

Katy and I have got No. 2 this term. It's a great deal pleasanter than our old room, and the entry stove is just outside the door, so we shall keep warm. There is sun, too, only Mrs. Nipson has nailed thick cotton over all the

278

window except a little place at top. Every window in the house is just so. You can't think how mad the girls are about it. The first night we had an indignation meeting and passed resolutions, and some of the girls said they wouldn't stay—they should write to their fathers to come and take them home. None of them did, though. It's perfectly forlorn, not being able to look out. Oh, dear, how I wish it were spring!

We've got a new dining-room. It's a great deal bigger than the old one, so now we all eat together, and don't have any first and second tables. It's ever so much nicer, for I used to get so dreadfully hungry waiting, that I didn't know what to do. One thing is horrid, though; and that is, that every girl has to make a remark in French every day at dinner. The remarks are about a subject. Mrs. Nipson gives out the subjects. Today the subject was 'Les oiseaux,' and Rose Red said, 'J'aime beaucoup les oiseaux, especialment ceux qui sont rôtis,' which made us all laugh. That ridiculous little Bella Arkwright said, 'J'aime beaucoup les oiseaux qui sing.' She thought 'sing' was French! Every girl in school began, 'J'aime beaucoup les oiseaux!' Tomorrow the subject is 'Jules César,' I'm sure I don't know what to say. There isn't a word in Ollendorf about him.

There are not so many new scholars this term as there were last. The girls think it is because Mrs. Nipson isn't so popular as Mrs. Florence used to be. Two or three of the new ones look pleasant, but I don't know them yet. Louisa Agnew is the nicest girl here next to Rose. Lilly Page says she is vulgar, because her father paints portraits, and they don't know the same people that Cousin Olivia knows; but she isn't a bit. We went to spend the day there just before we left Ashburn, and her father and mother are splendid. Their house is just full of all sorts of queer, interesting things, and pictures; and Mr. Agnew told us ever so many stories about painters, and what they did. One was about a boy who used to make figures of lions in butter, afterwards he became famous. I forget his name. We had a lovely time. I wish you could see Lou's little sister Daisy. She's only two, and a perfect little beauty. She has got ten teeth, and hardly ever cries.

Please-ask Papa——

Just as Clover had got to this point, she was interrupted by Katy, who walked in with her hat on, and a whole handful of letters.

"See here!" she cried. "Isn't this delightful? Miss Marsh took me with her to the Post Office, and we found these. Three for you, and two for me, and one for Rose. Wait a moment till I give Rose hers, and we'll read them together."

In another moment the two were cosily seated, with their heads close together, opening their budget. First came one from Papa:

My Dear Daughters——

"It's for you too, you see," said Katy.

Last week came your letter of the 31st, and we were glad to hear that you were well, and ready to go back to school. By the time this reaches you, you will be in Hillsover, and your winter term begun. Make the most of it, for we all feel as if we could never let you go from home again. Johnny says she shall rub Spalding's Prepared Glue all over your dresses when you come back, so that you cannot stir. I am a little of the same way of thinking myself. Cecy has returned from boarding-school, and set up as a young lady. Elsie is much excited over the party dresses which Mrs. Hall is having made for her, and goes over every day to see if anything new has come. I am glad on this account, that you are away just now; for it would not be easy to keep steady heads and continue your studies, with so much going on next door. I have sent Cousin Olivia a cheque to pay for the things she bought for you, and am much obliged to her for seeing that you were properly fitted out. Katy was very right to consider expense, but I wish you to have all things needful. I enclose two ten-dollar bills, one for each

of you, for pocket-money; and, with much love from the
children, am,

Yours affectionately,

P. CARR.

P.S.—Cousin Helen has had a sharp attack, but is better.

"I wish Papa would write longer letters," said Katy. "He
always sends us money, but he don't send half enough
words with it." She folded the letter and fondled it
affectionately.

"He's always so busy," replied Clover. "Don't you
remember how he used to sit down at his desk, and scribble
off his letters: and how somebody always was sure to ring
the bell before he got through? I'm very glad to have some
money, for now I can pay the sixty-two cents I owe you.
It's my turn to read. This is from Elsie, and a real long
one. Put away the bills first, Katy, or they'll be lost. That's
right; now we'll begin together."

DEAR CLOVER,— You don't know how glad I am when
my turn comes to get a letter all to myself. Of course I read
Papa's, and all the rest you write to the family; but it never
seems as if you were talking to me unless you begin, 'Dear
Elsie.' I wish some time you'd put in a little note marked
'private,' just for me, which nobody else need see. It would
be such fun! Please do. I should think you would have
hated staying at Cousin Olivia's. When I read what she
said about your travelling-dresses looking as if they had
come out of the ark, I was just as mad as fire. But I
shouldn't think you'd want much to go back to school
either, though sometimes it must be splendid. John has
named her old stockinet doll, which she used to call
'Scratch-face,' 'Nippy,' after Mrs. Nipson; and I made a
muslin cap, and Dorry drew a pair of black spectacles
round her eyes. She is a perfect fright, and John prays all
the time that dreadful things happen to her. She pricks her
with pins, and pretends she has the earache, and lets her

tumble down and hurt herself, till sometimes I nearly feel sorry, though it's all make-believe. When you wrote us about only having pudding for dinner, I didn't a bit. John put her into the rag-closet that very day, and has been starving her to death ever since; and Phil says it serves her right. You can't think how awfully lonely I sometimes get without you. If it wasn't for Helen Gibbs, that new girl I told you about, I shouldn't know what to do. She is the prettiest girl in Miss McCrane's school. Her hair curls just like mine, only it is four times as long, and a million times as thick; and her waist is really and truly not much bigger round than a bed-post. We're the greatest friends. She says she loves me just exactly as much as if I was her sister, but she never had any real sisters. She was quite mad the other day because I said I couldn't love her quite so well as you and Katy; and all recess-time she wouldn't speak to me, but now we've made up. Dorry is so awfully in love with her, that I never can get him to come into the room when she is here, and he blushes when we tease him about her. But this is a great secret. Dorry and I play chess every evening. He almost always beats, unless Papa comes behind and helps me. Phil has learned too, because he always wants to do everything that we do. Dorry gives him a castle, and a bishop, and a knight, and four pawns, and then beats him in six moves. Phil gets so mad that we can't help laughing. Last night he buttoned his king up inside his jacket, and said, 'There! You can't checkmate me now, anyway!'

Cecy has come home. She is a young lady now. She does her hair up quite different, and wears long dresses. This winter she is going to parties, and Mrs. Hall is going to have a party for her on Thursday, with real, grown-up young ladies and gentlemen at it. Cecy has got some beautiful new dresses—a white muslin, a blue tarlatan, and a pink silk. The pink silk is the prettiest, I think. Cecy is real kind, and lets me see all her things. She has got a lovely breast-pin, too, and a new fan with ivory sticks, and all sorts of things. I wish I was grown-up. It must be so nice. I want to tell you something, only you mustn't tell anybody except Katy. Don't you remember how Cecy used to say that she never was going out to drive with young gentlemen, but was going to stay at home and read the Bible to poor people? Well, she didn't tell the truth; for she has been out three times already with Sylvester Slack in his buggy. When I told her she ought not to do so, because it was breaking a promise, she only laughed, and said I was a silly little girl. Isn't it queer?

I want to tell you what an awful thing I did the other night. Maria Avery invited me to tea, and Papa said I might go. I didn't want to much, but I didn't know what to tell Maria, so I went. You know how poor they are, and how Aunt Lizzie used to say that they were 'touchy,' so I thought I would take great care not to hurry home right after tea, for fear they would think I was not enjoying myself. So I waited, and waited, and waited, and got so sleepy that I had to pinch my fingers to keep awake. At last I was sure that it might be almost nine, so I asked Mr. Avery if he'd please take me home; and don't you believe, when we got there, it was a quarter past ten, and Papa was just coming for me! Dorry said he guessed I must be enjoying myself to stay late. I didn't tell anybody about it for three days, because I knew they'd laugh at me, and they did. Wasn't it funny? And old Mrs. Avery looked as sleepy as I felt, and kept yawning behind her hand. I told Papa if I had a watch of my own I shouldn't make such mistakes, and he laughed and said, 'We'll see.' Oh, do you suppose that means that he's going to give me one?

We are so proud of Dorry's having taken two prizes at the examination yesterday. He took the second Latin prize and the first mathematics. Dr. Pullman says he thinks Dorry is one of the most thorough boys he ever saw. Isn't that nice? The prizes were books: one was the life of Benjamin Franklin, and the other the life of General Butler. Papa says he doesn't think much of the Life of Butler; but Dorry has begun it, and says it is splendid. Phil says when he takes a prize he wants candy and a new knife; but he'll have to wait a good while unless he studies harder than he does now. He has just come in to tease me to go up into

283

the garret and help him to get down his sledge, because he thinks it is going to snow; but there isn't a sign of it, and the weather is quite warm. I asked him what I should say for him to you, and he said, 'Oh, tell her to come home, and anything you please.' I said, 'Shall I give her your love, and say that you are very well?' and he says, 'Oh, yes, Miss Elsie, I guess you'd think yourself mighty well if your head ached as much as mine does every day,' don't be frightened, however, for he's just as fat and rosy as can be; but almost every day he says he feels sick about school-time. When Papa was at Moorfield, Miss Finch believed him, and let him stay at home two mornings. I don't wonder at it, for you can think what a face he makes up; but he got well so fast that she pays no attention to him now. The other day, about eleven o'clock, Papa met him coming along the road, shying stones at the birds, and making lots of noise. He told Papa he felt so sick that his teacher had let him go home, but Papa noticed that his mouth looked sticky, so he opened his dinner-basket, and found that the little scamp had eaten up all his dinner on the road, corned beef, bread and butter, a great piece of mince pie, and six pears. Papa couldn't help laughing, but he made him turn round and go right back to school again.

I told you in my last about Johnnie's going to school with me now. She is very proud of it, and is always talking about 'Elsie's and my school.' She is twice as smart as the other little girls of her age. Miss McCrane has put her into the composition class, where they write compositions, on their slates. The first subject was, 'A Kitten'; and John's began, 'She's a dear, little, soft, scratching thing, only you'd better not pull her by the tail, but she's real cunning.' All the girls laughed, and Johnnie called out, 'Well, it's true, anyhow.'

I can't write any more, for I must study my Latin. Besides, this is the longest letter that ever was. I have been four days writing it. Please send me one just as long. Old Mary and the children send lots of love, and Papa says, 'Tell Katy if a pudding diet sets her to growing again, she must come home at once, for he couldn't afford it.' Oh,

dear, how I wish I could see you! Please give my love to
Rose Red She must be perfectly splendid.

Your affectionate,

ELSIE.

"Oh, the dear little duck! Isn't that just like her?" said
Clover. "I think Elsie has a real genius for writing, don't
you? She tells all the little things, and is so droll and
cunning. Nobody writes such nice letters. Who's that from,
Katy?"

"Cousin Helen, and it's been such a long time coming.
Just look at this date!! September 22—a whole month
ago!" Then she began to read.

"DEAR KATY,

It seems a long time since we have had a talk, but I
have been less well lately, so that it has been difficult to
write. Yesterday I sat up for the first time in several weeks;
and today I am dressed and beginning to feel like myself. I
wish you could see my room this morning—I often wish
this—but it is so particularly pretty, for little Helen has
been in with a great basket full of leaves and flowers, and
together we have dressed it to perfection. There are four
vases of roses, a bowl full of chrysanthemums, and red
leaves round all my pictures. The leaves are Virginia
creeper. It doesn't last long, but is lovely while it lasts.
Helen also brought a bird's nest which the gardener found
in a hawthorn-tree on the lawn. It hangs on a branch, and
she has tied it to one side of my book-shelves. On the
opposite side is another nest quite different—a great, grey
hornets' nest, as big as a bandbox. which came from the
mountains a year ago. I wondered if any such grow in the
woods about Hillsover. In spite of the red leaves the day
is warm as summer, and the windows stand wide open. I
suppose it is cooler with you, but I know it is delicious
cold. Now that I think of it, you must be in Ashburn by
this time. I hope you will enjoy every moment of your
vacation.

Oct. 19th. I did not finish my letter the day it was

begun, dear Katy, and next morning it proved that I was not so strong as I fancied, and I had to go to bed again. I am still there, and, as you see, writing with a pencil; but do not be worried about me, for the doctor says I am mending, and soon I hope to be up and in my chair The red leaves are gone, but the roses are lovely as ever, for little Helen keeps bringing me fresh ones. She has just been in to read me her composition. The subject was 'Stars,' and you can't think how much she found to say about them. She is a bright little creature, and it is a great pleasure to teach her. I am hardly ever so sick that she cannot come for her lessons, and she gets on fast. We have made an arrangement that when she knows more than I do, she is to give me lessons, and I am not sure that the time is so very far off.

I must tell you about my Ben. He is a new canary which was given me in the summer, and lately he has grown so delightfully tame that I feel as if it were not a bird at all, but a fairy prince come to live with me and amuse me. The cage door is left open always now, and he flies in and out as he likes. He is a restless, inquisitive fellow, and visits any part of the room, trying each fresh thing with his bill to see if it is good to eat, and then perching on it to see if it is good to sit upon. He mistakes his own reflection in the looking-glass for another canary, and sits on the pincushion twittering and making love to himself for half an hour at a time. To watch him is one of my greatest amusements, especially just now when I am in bed so much. Sometimes he hides and keeps so still that I have not the least idea where he is. But the moment I call, 'Ben, Ben,' and hold out my finger, wings begin to rustle, and out he flies and perches on my finger. He isn't the least bit in the world afraid, but sits on my head or shoulder, eats out of my mouth, and kisses me with his beak. He is on the pillow at this moment making runs at my pencil, of which he is mortally jealous. It is just so with my combs and brushes, if I attempt to do my hair; he cannot bear to have me do anything but play with him. I do wish I could show him to you and Clover.

Little Helen, my other pet, has just come in with a sponge cake which she frosted herself. She sends her love, and says when you come to see me next summer she will frost you each one just like it. Goodbye, my Kate, I had nothing to write about, and have written it, but I never like to keep silent too long, or let you feel as if you were forgotten by your loving cousin,

HELEN."

"P.S.—Be sure to wear plenty of warm wraps for your winter walks. And Katy, dear, you must eat meat every day. Mrs. Nipson will probably give up her favourite puddings now that the cold weather has begun; but, if not, write to Papa."

"Isn't that letter Cousin Helen all over?" said Katy. "So little about her illness, and so bright and merry, and yet she has really been sick. Papa says 'a sharp attack.' Isn't she the dearest person in the world, next to Papa, I mean?"

"Yes, indeed. There's nobody like her. I do hope we can go to see her next summer. Now it's my turn. I can't think who this letter is from. Oh, Clarence! Katy, I can't let you see this. I promised Clare that I wouldn't show his letters to anybody, not even you."

"Oh, very well. But you've got another. Dorry, isn't it? Read that first, and I'll go away and leave you in peace."

So Clover read:

"DEAR CLOVER,— Elsie says she is going to write to you today; but I won't stop, because next Saturday I'm going out fishing with the Slacks. There are a great many trout now in Blue Brook. Eugene caught six the other day—no, five, one was a minnow. Papa has given me a splendid rod; it lets out as tall as a house. I hope I shall catch with it. Alexander says the trout will admire it so much that they can't help biting; but he was only funning. Elsie and I play chess most every night. She plays a real good game for a girl. Sometimes Pa helps, and then she beats. Miss Finch is well. She don't keep house quite like Katy did, and I don't like her so well as I do you; but she's pretty nice.

The other day we had a nutting picnic, and she gave me and Phil a loaf of Election cake and six quince turnovers to carry. The boys gave three cheers for her when they saw them. Did Elsie tell you that I have invented a new machine? It is called 'The Intellectual Peach Parer.' There is a place to hold a book while you pare the peaches. It is very convenient. I don't think of anything else to tell you. Cecy has got home, and is going to have a party next week. She's grown up now, she says, and she wears her hair quite different. It's a great deal thicker than it used to be. Elsie says it's because there are rats in it; but I don't believe her. Elsie has got a new friend. Her name is Ellen Gibbs. She's quite pretty.

Your affectionate brother,
DORRY."

"P.S.—John wants to put in a note."

John's note was written in a round hand, as easy to read as print.

"DEAR CLOVER.— I am well, and hope you are the same, I wish you would write me a letter of my own. I go to school with Elsie now. We write compossizions. They are hard to write. We don't go up into the loft half so much as we used to when you ware at home. Mrs. Worrett came to dinner last week. She says she ways two hundred and atey pounds. I should think it would be dredful to way that. I only way 76. My head comes up to the mark on the door where you ware mesured when you ware twelve. Isn't that tal? Goodbye. I send a kiss to Katy.

Your loving
JOHN."

After they had finished this note, Katy went away, leaving Clover to open Clarence's letter by herself. It was not so well written or spelt as Dorry's, by any means.

"DEAR CLOVER,— Don't forget what you promised. I mene about not showing this. And don't tell Lilly I rote. If you do, she'll be as mad as hops. I haven't been doing much since you went away. School begun yesterday, and I am glad; for it's awfully dull now that you girls have gone. Mother says Guest has got flees on him, so she won't let him come into the house any more. I stay out in the barn with him insted. He is well, and sends you a wag of his tail. Jim and me are making him a colar. It is black, with G.P. on it, for Guest Page, you know. A lot of the boys had a camping out last week. I went. It was real jolly; but ma wouldn't let me stay all night, so I lost the best part. They roasted scullpins for supper, and had a bonfire. The camp was on Harstnet Hill. Next time you come I'll take you out there. Pa has gone to mane on bizness. He said I must take care of the house, so I've borrowed Jim's gun, and if any robers come I mean to shoot them. I always go to sleep with a broom agenst the door, so as to wake up when they open it. This morning I thought they had come, for the broom was gone, and the gun too; but it was only Briget. She opened the door and it fell down; but I didn't wake up, so she took it away, and put the gun in the closet. I was mad, I can tell you.

This is only a short letter, but I hope you will answer it soon. Give my love to Katy, and tell Dorry that if he likes I'll send him my compass for his machenery, because I've got two.

Your affectionate Cousin,
CLARENCE PAGE.

This was the last of the budget. As Clover folded it up, she was dismayed by the tinkle of the tea-bell.

"Oh, dear!" she cried, "there's tea, and I have not finished my letter to Elsie. Where has the afternoon gone? How splendid it has been! I wish I could have four letters every day as long as I live."

CHAPTER ELEVEN

CHRISTMAS BOXES

OCTOBER was a delightful month, clear and sparkling; but early in November the weather changed, and became very cold. Thick frosts fell, every leaf vanished from the woods, in the gardens only blackened stalks remained to show where once the summer flowers had been. In spite of the stove outside the door, No. 2 began to be chilly. More than once Katy found her tooth-brush stiff with ice in the morning. It was a foretaste of what winter was to be, and the girls shivered at the prospect.

Towards the end of November Miss Jane caught a heavy cold. Unsparing of herself as of others, she went on hearing her classes as usual; and nobody paid much attention to her hoarseness and flushed cheeks, until she grew so much worse that she was forced to go to bed. There she stayed for nearly four weeks. It made a great change in the school, and the girls found it such a relief to have her sharp voice and eyes taken away that I am afraid they were rather glad of her illness than otherwise.

Katy shared in this feeling of relief. She did not like Miss Jane; it was pleasant not to have to see or hear of her. But as day after day passed, and still she continued ill, Katy's conscience began to prick. One night she lay awake a long time, and heard Miss Jane coughing violently. Katy feared she was very sick, and wondered who took care of her all night and all day. None of the girls went near her. The servants were always busy. And Mrs. Nipson, who did not love Miss Jane, was busy too.

In the morning, while studying and practising, Katy caught herself thinking over this question. At last she asked Miss Marsh:

"How is Miss Jane today?"

"About the same. She is not dangerously ill, the doctor says; but she coughs a great deal, and has some fever."

"Is anybody sitting with her?"

"Oh, no! There is no need of any one. Susan answers the bell, and she has her medicine on the table within reach."

It sounded forlorn enough. Katy had lived in a sick-room so long herself that she knew just how dreary it is for an invalid to be left alone with "medicine within reach," and someone to answer a bell. She began to feel sorry for Miss Jane, and almost without intending it, went down to the entry, and tapped at her door. The "Come in!" sounded very faint; and Miss Jane as she lay in bed looked weak and dismal, and quite unlike the sharp, terrible person whom the girls feared so much. She was amazed at the sight of Katy, and made a feeble attempt to hold up her head and speak as usual.

"What is it, Miss Carr?"

"I only came to see how you are," said Katy, abashed at her own daring, "you coughed so much last night that I was afraid you were worse. Isn't there something I could do for you?"

"Thank you," said Miss Jane, "you are very kind."

Think of Miss Jane's thanking anybody, and calling anybody kind.

"I should be very glad Isn't there anything?" repeated Katy, encouraged.

"Well, I don't know; you might put another stick of wood on the fire," said Miss Jane, in an ungracious tone.

Katy did so; and seeing that the iron cup on top of the stove was empty, she poured some water into it. Then she took a look about the room. Books and papers were scattered over the table; clean clothes from the wash lay on the chairs; nothing was in its place; and Katy, who knew how particular Miss Jane was on the subject of order, guessed at the discomfort which this untidy state of affairs must have caused her.

291

"Wouldn't you like to have me put these away?" she asked, touching the pile of clothes.

Miss Jane sighed impatiently, but she did not say no; so Katy, taking silence for consent, opened the drawers, and laid the clothes inside, guessing at the right places with a sort of instinct, and making as little noise and bustle as possible. Next she moved quietly to the table, where she sorted and arranged the papers, piled up the books, and put the pens and pencils in a small tray which stood there for the purpose. Lastly, she began to dust the table with her pocket-handkerchief, which proceeding roused Miss Jane at once.

"Don't," she said, "there's a duster in the cupboard."

Katy could not help smiling; but she found the duster, and proceeded to put the rest of the room into nice order, laying a fresh towel over the bedside table, and arranging watch, medicine, and spoon within reach. Miss Jane lay and watched her. I think she was as much surprised at herself for permitting all this, as Katy was at being permitted to do it. Sick people often consent because they feel too weak to object. After all, it was comfortable to have someone come in and straighten the things which for ten days past had vexed her neat eyes with their untidyness.

Lastly, smoothing the quilt, Katy asked if Miss Jane wouldn't like to have her pillow shaken up?

"I don't care," was the answer.

It sounded discouraging; but Katy boldly seized the pillow, beat, smoothed, and put it again in place. Then she went out of the room as noiselessly as she could, Miss Jane never saying, "Thank you," or seeming to observe whether she went or stayed.

Rose Red and Clover could hardly believe their ears when told where she had been. They stared at her as people stare at Van Amburgh when he comes safely out of the lion's den.

"My stars!" exclaimed Rose, drawing a long breath. "You didn't really? And she hasn't bitten your head off!"

"Not a bit," said Katy, laughing. "What's more, I'm going again."

She was as good as her word. After that she went to see Miss Jane very often. Almost always there was some little thing which she could do, the fire needed mending, or the pitcher to be filled with ice-water, or Miss Jane wanted the blinds opened or shut. Gradually she grew used to seeing Katy about the room. One morning she actually allowed her to brush her hair; and Katy's touch was so light and pleasant that afterwards Miss Jane begged her to do it every day.

"What makes you such a good nurse?" she asked one afternoon, rather abruptly.

"Being sick myself," replied Katy, gently.

Then, in answer to further questioning, she told of her four years' illness, and her life upstairs, keeping house and studying lessons all alone by herself. Miss Jane did not say anything when she got through; but Katy fancied that she looked at her in a new and kinder way.

So time went on till Christmas. It fell on a Friday that year, which shortened the holidays by a day, and disappointed many of the girls. Only a few went home, the rest were left to pass the time as best they might till Monday, when lessons were to begin again.

"It isn't much like merry Christmas," sighed Clover to herself, as she looked up at the uncottoned space at the top of the window, and saw great snow-flakes wildly whirling by. No. 2 felt cold and dreary, and she was glad to exchange it for the schoolroom, round whose warm stove a cluster of girls was huddling. Everybody was in bad spirits; there was a tendency to talk about home, and the nice time which people were having there, and the very bad time they themselves were having at the Nunnery.

"Isn't it mis-e-ra-ble? I shall cry all night, I know I shall, I am so homesick," gulped Lilly, who had taken possession of her room-mate's shoulder and was weeping ostentatiously.

"I declare, you're just Mrs. Gummidge in *David Copperfield* over again," said Rose. "You recollect her, girls, don't you? When the porridge was burnt, you know —'All of us felt the disappointment, but Mrs. Gummidge

293

felt it the most.' Isn't Lilly a real Mrs. Gummidge, girls?"

This observation changed Lilly's tears into anger. "You're as hateful and as horrid as you can be, Rose Red," she exclaimed angrily. Then she flew out of the room, and shut the door behind her with a bang.

"There! She's gone upstairs cross," said Louisa Agnew.

"I don't care if she has," replied Rose, who was in a perverse mood.

"I wish you hadn't said that, Rosy," whispered Clover. "Lilly felt really badly."

"Well, what if she did? So do I feel badly, and you, and the rest of us. Lilly hasn't taken out a patent for bad feelings, which nobody must infringe. What business has she to make us feel badder by setting up to be so much worse off than the rest of the world?"

Clover said nothing, but went on with a book she was reading. In less than ten minutes, Rose, whose sun seldom stayed long behind a cloud, was at her elbow, dimpling and coaxing.

"I forgive you," she whispered, giving Clover's arm a little pinch.

"What for?"

"For being in the right. About Lilly, I mean. I was rather hateful to her, I confess. Never mind. When she comes downstairs, I'll make up for it. She's a crocodile, if ever there was one; but, as she's your cousin, I'll be good to her. Kiss me quick to prove that you're not vexed."

"Vexed indeed!" said Clover, kissing the middle of the pink cheek. "I wonder if anybody ever stayed vexed with you for ten minutes together, you Rosy-Posy you?"

"Bless you, yes! Miss Jane, for example. She hates me like poison, and all the time. Well, what of it? I know she's sick, but I 'can't tell a lie, Pa,' on that account. Where's Katy?"

"Gone in to see her, I believe."

"One of these days," prophesied Rose, solemnly, "she'll go into that room, and she'll never come out again! Miss Jane is getting back into biting condition. I advise Katy to be careful. What's that noise? Sleigh-bells, I declare!

Girls"—mounting a desk, and peeping out of the window—"somebody's got a big box—a big one! Here's old Joyce at the door, with his sledge. Now whose do you suppose it is?"

"It's for me. I'm sure it's for me," cried half a dozen voices.

"Bella, my love, peep over the balusters, and see if you can't see the name," cried Louisa; and Bella, nothing loath, departed at once on this congenial errand.

"No, I can't," she reported, coming back from the hall. "The name's tipped up against the wall. There's two boxes! One is big, and one is little!"

"Oh, who can they be for?" clamoured the girls. Half the school expected boxes, and had been watching the storm all day, with a dreadful fear that it would block the roads, and delay the expected treasures.

At this moment Mrs. Nipson came in.

"There will be the usual study-hour this evening," she announced. "All of you will prepare lessons for Monday morning. Miss Carr, come here for a moment, if you please."

Clover, wondering, followed her into the entry.

"A parcel has arrived for you, and a box," said Mrs. Nipson. "I presume that they contain articles for Christmas. I will have the nails removed, and both of them placed in your room this evening, but I expect you to refrain from examining them until tomorrow. The vacation does not open until after study-hour tonight, and it will then be too late for you to begin."

"Very well, ma'am," said Clover, demurely. But the minute Mrs. Nipson's back was turned she gave a jump, and rushed into the schoolroom.

"O girls," she cried, "what do you think? Both the boxes are for Katy and me!"

"Both!" cried a disappointed chorus.

"Yes, both. Mrs. Nipson said so. I'm so sorry for you. But isn't it nice for us? We never had a box from home before, you know; and I didn't think we should, it's so far off. It's too lovely! But I do hope yours will come tonight."

Clover's voice was so sympathising, for all its glee, that nobody could help being glad with her.

"You little darling!" said Louisa, giving her a hug. "I'm rejoiced that the box is yours. The rest of us are always getting them, and you and Katy never had a thing before. I hope it's a nice one!"

"Oh, it's sure to be nice! It's from home, you know," responded Clover, with a happy smile.

Then she left the room to find Katy, and tell the wonderful news.

Study-hour seemed unusually long that night. The minute it was over, the sisters ran to No. 2. There stood the boxes, a big wooden one, with all the nails taken out of the lid, and a small paper one, carefully tied up and sealed. It was almost more than the girls could do to obey orders and not peep.

"I feel something hard," announced Clover, inserting a finger-tip under the lid.

"Oh, do you?" cried Katy. Then, making an heroic effort, she jumped into bed.

"It's the only way," she said, "you'd better come too, Clovy. Blow the candle out, and let's get to sleep as fast as we can, so as to make morning come quicker."

Katy dreamed of home that night. Perhaps it was that which made her wake so early. It was not five o'clock, and the room was perfectly dark She did not like to disturb Clover, so she lay perfectly still, for hours as it seemed, till a faint grey dawn crept in, and revealed the outlines of the big box standing by the window. Then she could wait no longer, but crept out of bed, crossed the floor on tiptoe, and raising the lid a little, put in her hand, something crumby and sugary met it and when she drew it out, there, fitting on her finger like a ring, was a round cake with a hole in the middle of it.

"Oh, it's one of Debby's jumbles!" she exclaimed.

"Where? What are you doing? Give me one too!" cried Clover, starting up. Katy rummaged till she found

"Come in," cried the sisters, *"and help us open our box!"*

another, then, half frozen, she ran back to bed; and the two lay nibbling the jumbles, and talking about home, till dawn deepened into daylight, and morning was fairly come.

Breakfast was half an hour later than usual, which was comfortable. As soon as it was over, the girls proceeded to unpack their box. The day was so cold that they wrapped themselves in shawls, and Clover put on a hood and thick gloves.

Rose Red, passing the door, burst out laughing, and recommended that she should add india-rubber boots and an umbrella.

"Oh, come in," cried the sisters, "come in, and help us open our box."

"Oh, by the way, you have a box, haven't you?" said Rose, who was perfectly aware of the important fact, and had presented herself with the hope of being asked to look on. "Thank you, but perhaps I would better come some other time. I shall be in the way."

"You imposter!" said Clover, while Katy seized Rose and pulled her into the room . "There, sit on the bed, you ridiculous goose and put on my grey cloak. How can you be so absurd as to say you won't? You know we want you, and you know you came on purpose!"

"Did I? Well, perhaps I did," laughed Rose. Then Katy lifted off the lid and set it against the door. It was an exciting moment.

"Just look here!" cried Katy.

The top of the box was mostly taken up with four square paper boxes, round which parcels of all shapes and sizes were wedged and fitted. The whole was a miracle of packing. It had taken Miss Finch three mornings, with assistance from old Mary, and much advice from Elsie, to do it so beautifully.

Each box held a different kind of cake. One was full of jumbles, another of ginger-snaps, a third of crullers, and the fourth contained a big square loaf of frosted plum-cake, with a circle of sugar almonds set in the frosting. How the trio exclaimed at this! !

"I never imagined anything so nice," declared Rose, with

her mouth full of jumble. "As for those snaps, they're simply perfect. What can be in all those fascinating bundles? Do hurry and open one, Katy."

Dear little Elsie! The first bundles opened were hers, a white hood for Katy, and a blue one for Clover, both of her own knitting, and so nicely done. The girls were enchanted.

"How she has improved!" said Katy. "She knits better than either of us, Clover."

"There never was such a clever little darling!" responded Clover; and they patted the hoods, tried them on before the glass, and spent so much time in admiring them that Rose grew impatient.

"I declare," she cried, "it isn't any of my funeral, I know; but if you don't open another parcel soon, I shall certainly fall to myself. It seems as if, what with cold and curiosity, I couldn't wait."

"Very well," said Katy, laying aside her hood, with one final glance. "Take out a bundle, Clover. It's your turn."

Clover's bundle was for herself, "Evangeline" in blue and gold; and pretty soon the "Golden Legend," in the same binding, appeared for Katy. Both these were from Dorry. Next came a couple of round packages of exactly the same size. These proved to be inkstands, covered with russia leather: one marked, "Katy, from Johnnie," and the other, "Clover, from Phil." It was evident that the children had done their shopping together, for presently two long narrow parcels revealed carved pen-handles, precisely alike; and these were labelled, "Katy, from Phil," and "Clover, from Johnnie."

What fun it was opening those bundles! The girls made a long business of it, taking out but one at a time, explaining, admiring, and exhibiting to Rose, before they began upon another. They laughed, they joked, but I do not think it would have taken much to make either of them cry. It was almost too tender a pleasure, these proofs of loving remembrance from the little ones; and each separate article seemed full of the very look and feel of home.

"What can this be?" said Katy, as she unrolled a paper and disclosed a pretty round box. She opened. Nothing was visible but pink cotton wool. Katy peeped beneath, and gave a cry.

"Oh, Clovy! Such a lovely thing! It's from Papa—of course it's from Papa! How could he? It's a great deal too pretty."

The "lovely thing" was a long slender chain for Katy's watch, worked in fine yellow gold. Clover admired it extremely; and her joy knew no bounds when further search revealed another box with a precisely similar chain for herself. It was too much. The girls fairly cried with pleasure.

"There never was such a papa in the world," they said.

"Yes there is; mine is just as good," reclared Rose, twinkling away a little tear-drop from her own eyes. "Now don't cry, honeys. Your papa's an angel, there's no doubt about it. I never saw such pretty chains in my life--never. As for the children, they're little ducks. You certainly are a wonderful family. Katy, I'm dying to know what is in that blue parcel."

The blue parcel was from Cecy, and contained a pretty blue ribbon for Clover. There was a pink one also, with a pink ribbon for Katy. Everybody had thought of the girls. Old Mary sent them each a yard measure; Miss Finch, a threadcase, stocked with different coloured cottons. Alexander had cracked a bag full of hickory nuts.

"Did you ever?" said Rose, when this last was produced. "What a thing it is to be popular! Mrs. Hall! Who's Mrs. Hall?" as Clover unwrapped a tiny carved easel.

"She's Cecy's mother," explained Clover. "Wasn't she kind to send me this, Katy? And here's Cecy's photograph in a little frame for you."

Never was such a wonderful box. It appeared to have no bottom whatever. Under the presents were parcels of figs, prunes, almonds, raisins, candy; under those, apples and pears. There seemed no end to the surprises.

At last all were out.

"Now," said Katy, "let's throw back the apples and pears, and then I want you to help me divide the other things, and make up some packages for the girls. They are all so disappointed not to have their boxes. I should like to have them share ours. Wouldn't you, Clover?"

"Yes, indeed; I was just going to propose it."

So Clover cut twenty-nine squares of white paper, Rose and Katy sorted and divided, and pretty soon ginger-snaps and almonds and sugar-plums were walking down all the enteries, and a gladsome crunching showed that the girls had found pleasant enjoyment. None of the snowed-up boxes got through till Monday, so except for Katy and Clover the school would have had no Christmas treat at all.

They carried Mrs. Nipson a large slice of cake, and a basket full of the beautiful red apples. All the teachers were remembered, and the servants. The S.S.U.C. was convened and feasted; and as for Rose, Louisa and other special cronies, dainties were heaped upon them with such unsparing hand that they finally remonstrated.

"You're giving everything away. You'll have none left for yourselves."

"Yes, we shall—plenty," said Clover. "Oh, Rosy! Here's such a splendid pear! You must have this."

"No, no!" protested Rose; but Clover forced it into her pocket.

"The Carr's Box" was always quoted in the Nunnery afterward, as an example of what papas and mammas could accomplish, when they were of the right sort, and really wanted to make schoolgirls happy. Distributing their treasures kept Katy and Clover so busy that it was not until after dinner that they found time to open the smaller box. When they did so, they were sorry for the delay. The box was full of flowers—roses, geranium-leaves, heliotrope, beautiful red and white carnations, all so bedded in cotton that the frost had not touched them. But they looked chilled, and Katy hastened to put them in warm water, which she had been told was the best way to revive drooping flowers.

Cousin Helen had sent them; and underneath, sewed to the box, that they might not shake about and do mischief, were two flat parcels, wrapped in tissue paper, and tied with white ribbons, in Cousin Helen's dainty way. They were glove-cases, of quilted silk, delicately scented, one white, and one lilac; and to each was pinned a loving note, wishing the girls a Merry Christmas.

"How awfully good people are!" said Clover. "I do think we ought to be the best girls in the world."

Last of all, Katy made a choice little selection from her stores, a splendid apple, a couple of fine pears, a handful of raisins and figs, and, with a few of the freshest flowers in a wine-glass, she went down the Row and tapped at Miss Jane's door.

Miss Jane was sitting up for the first time. wrapped in a shawl, and looking very thin and pale. Katy, who had almost ceased to be afraid of her, went in cheerily.

"We've had a splendid box from home, Miss Jane, full of all sorts of things. It has been such fun unpacking it. I've brought an apple, and some pears, and this little bunch of flowers. Wasn't it a nice Christmas for us?"

"Yes," said Miss Jane, "very nice indeed. I heard someone say in the entry that you had a box. Thank you," as Katy set the basket and glass on the table. "Those flowers are very sweet. I wish you a merry Christmas, I'm sure."

This was much from Miss Jane. who could not help speaking shortly, even when she was pleased. Katy withdrew in high glee.

But that night, just before bed-time, something happened so surprising that Katy, telling Clover about it afterward, said she half fancied that she must have dreamed it all. It was about eight o'clock in the evening: she was passing down Quaker Row, and Miss Jane called and asked her to come in. Miss Jane's cheeks were flushed, and she spoke fast, as if she had resolved to say something, and thought the sooner it was over the better.

"Miss Carr," she began, "I wish to tell you that I made up my mind some time since that we did you an injustice last term. It is not your attentions to me during my illness which have changed my opinion—that was done before I fell ill. It is your general conduct, and the good influence which I have seen you exert. over other girls, which convinced me that we must have been wrong about you. That is all, I thought you might like to hear me say this, and I shall say the same to Mrs. Nipson."

"Thank you," said Katy, "you don't know how glad I am!" She half thought she would kiss Miss Jane, but somehow it didn't seem possible; so she shook hands very heartily instead, and flew to her room, feeling as if her feet were wings.

"It seems too good to be true. I want to cry, I am so happy," she told Clover. "What a lovely day this has been!"

And of all that she had received, I think Katy considered this explanation with Miss Jane as her very best Christmas box.

CHAPTER TWELVE

WAITING FOR SPRING

SCHOOL was a much happier place after this. Mrs. Nipson never alluded to the matter, but her manner altered. Katy felt that she was no longer watched or distrusted, and her heart grew light.

In another week Miss Jane was so much better as to be hearing her classes again. Illness had not changed her materially. It is only in novels that rheumatic fever sweetens tempers and makes disagreeable people over into agreeable ones. Most of the girls disliked her as much as ever. Her tongue was just as sharp, and her manner as grim. But for Katy, from that time forward, there was a difference. Miss Jane was not affectionate to her—it was not in her nature to be that—but she was civil and considerate, and, in a dry way, friendly; and gradually Katy grew to have an odd sort of liking for her

Do any of you know how incredibly long winter seems in climates where for weeks together the thermometer stands at zero? There is something hopeless in such cold. You think of summer as of a thing read about somewhere in a book, but which has no actual existence. Winter seems the only reality in the world.

Katy and Clover felt this hopelessness growing upon them as the days went on, and the weather grew more and more severe. Ten, twenty, even thirty degrees below zero, was no unusual register for the Hillsover thermometers. Such cold half frightened them, but nobody else was frightened or surprised. It was dry, brilliant cold. The December snows lay unmelted on the ground in March, and the paths cut then were crisp and hard still, only the white walls on either side had risen higher and higher, till only a moving line of hoods and tippets was visible above them, when the school went out for its daily walk. Morning after morning the girls woke to find thick crusts of frost on their window-panes, and every drop of water in wash-bowl or pitcher turned to solid ice. Night after night, Clover, who was a chilly little creature, lay shivering and unable to sleep, notwithstanding the hot bricks at her feet, and the many wraps which Katy piled upon her. To Katy herself the cold was more bracing than depressing. There was something in her blood which responded to the sharp tingle of frost, and she gained in strength in a remarkable way during this winter. But the long storms told upon her spirits. She pined for spring and home more than she liked to tell, and felt the need of variety in their monotonous life, where the creeping days appeared like weeks, and the weeks stretched themselves out, and seemed as long as months do in other places.

The girls resorted to all sorts of devices to keep themselves alive during this dreary season. They had little epidemics of occupation. At one time it was "spattering," when all faces and fingers had a tendency to smudges of India ink; and there was hardly a fine comb or toothbrush fit for use in the establishment. Then a rage for tatting set in, followed by a fever of fancy-work, every one falling in love with the same pattern at the same time, and copying and re-copying, till nobody could bear the sight of it. At one time Clover counted eighteen girls all at work on the same bead and canvas pincushion. Later there was a short period of *decalcomanie;* and then came the grand album craze, when thirty-three girls out of the thirty-nine sent for blank books bound in red morocco, and began to collect signatures and sentiments. Here, also, there was a tendency toward repetition.

Sally Austin added to her autograph these lines of her own composition:

> When on this page your beauteous eyes you bend,
> Let it remind you of your absent friend.
>
> SALLIE J. AUSTIN,
> Galveston, Texas.

The girls found this sentiment charming, at least a dozen borrowed it, and in half the albums in the school you might read:

> When on this page your beauteous eyes, etc.

Esther Dearborn wrote in Clover's book: "The better part of Valour is Discretion." Why she wrote it nobody knew, or why it was more applicable to Clover than to any one; but the sentiment proved popular, and was repeated over and over again, above various neatly-written signatures.

There was a strife as to whom should display the largest collection. Some of the girls sent home for autographs of distinguished persons, which they pasted in their books. Rose Red, however, outdid them all.

"Did I ever show you mine?" she asked one day, when most of the girls were together in the schoolroom.

"No, never!" cried a number of voices. "Have you got one? Oh, do let us see it."

"Certainly, I'll get it right away, if you like," said Rose, obligingly.

She went to her room, and returned with a shabby old blank book in her hand.

"The cover of mine isn't very nice," explained Rose. "I'm going to have it re-bound one of these days. You see it's not a new album at all, nor a school album; but it's very valuable to me." Here she heaved a sentimental sigh. "All my friends have written in it," she said.

The girls were quite impressed by the manner in which Rose said this. But, when they turned over the pages of the album, they were even more impressed. Rose had evidently been on intimate terms with a circle of most distinguished persons. Half the autographs in the book were from gentlemen, and they were dated all over the world.

"Just listen to this!" cried Louisa, and she read:

"Thou may'st forget me, but never, never shall I forget thee!

ALPHONSO OF CASTILE.
THE ESCURIAL, APRIL 1st."

"Who's he?" asked a circle of awe-struck girls.

"Didn't you ever hear of him? Youngest brother of the King of Spain," replied Rose, carelessly.

"Oh, my! And just hear this," exclaimed Annie Silsbie:

"If you ever deign to cast a thought in my direction, Miss Rose, remember me always as

Thy devoted servitor,
POTEMKIN MONTMORENCY.
ST. PETERSBURG, July 10th."

"And this!" shrieked Alice White.

"They say love is a thorn, I say it is a dart,
And yet I cannot tear thee from my heart.
ANTONIO, Count of Valambrosa."

"Do you really and truly know a count?" asked Bella, backing away from Rose, with eyes as big as saucers.

"Know Antonio de Valambrosa? I should think I did,"

306

replied Rose. "Nobody in this country knows him so well, I fancy."

"And he wrote that for you?"

"How else could it get into my book, goosey?"

This was unanswerable, and Rose was installed from that time forward in the minds of Bella and the rest as a heroine of the first water. Katy, however, knew better, and the first time she caught Rose alone she attacked her on the subject. "Now, Rosy-Posy, confess. Who wrote all those absurd autographs in your book?"

"Absurd autographs! What do you mean?"

"All those counts and things. No, it's no use; you shan't wriggle away till you tell me."

"Oh, Antonio and dear Potemkin, do you mean them?"

"Yes, of course I do."

"And you really want to know?"

"Yes."

"And will swear not to tell?"

"Yes."

"Well, then," bursting into a laugh, "I wrote every one of them myself."

"Did you really? When?"

"Day before yesterday. I thought Lilly needed taking down, she was so set up with her autographs of Wendell Phillips and Mr. Seward, so I just sat down and wrote a book full. It only took me half an hour. I meant to write some more; in fact, I had one all ready:

> "I am dead, or pretty near:
> David's done for me I fear.
>
> GOLIATH OF GATH"

but I was afraid even Bella wouldn't swallow that, so I tore out the page. I'm sorry I did now, for I really think the geese would have believed it. Written in his last moments, you know, to oblige an ancestor of my own," added Rose, in a tone of explanation.

"You monkey!" cried Katy, highly diverted. But she

kept Rose's counsel, and I dare say some of the Hillsover girls believe in that wonderful album to this day.

It was not long after that a sad piece of news came for Bella. Her father was dead. Their home was in Sorra, too far to allow of her returning for the funeral; so the poor little girl stayed at school, to bear her trouble as best she might. Katy, who was always kind to children, and had somewhat affected Bella from the first on account of her resemblance to Elsie in height and figure, was specially tender to her now, which Bella repaid with the gift of her whole queer little heart. Her affectionate demonstrations were rather of the monkey order, and not unfrequently troublesome; but Katy was never otherwise than patient and gentle with her, though Rose, and even Clover, remonstrated on what they called this "singular intimacy."

"Poor little soul! It's so hard for her, and she's only eleven years old," she told them.

"She has such a funny way of looking at you sometimes," said Rose, who was very observant. "It is just the air of a squirrel who has hidden a nut, and doesn't want you to find out where, and yet can hardly help indicating it with his paw. She's got something on her mind, I'm sure."

"Half a dozen things, very likely," added Clover; "she's such a mischief."

But none of them guessed what this "something" was.

Early in January Mrs. Nipson announced that in four weeks she proposed to give a "soirée," to which all young ladies whose records were entirely free from marks during the intervening period would be allowed to come. This announcement created great excitement, and the school set itself to be good; but marks were easy to get, and gradually one girl after another lost her chance, till by the appointed day only a limited party descended to join the festivities, and nearly half the school was left upstairs to sigh over past sins. Katy and Rose were among the unlucky ones. Rose had incurred a mark by writing a note in study-hour, and Katy by being five minutes late to dinner.

They consoled themselves by dressing Clover's hair, and making her look as pretty as possible, and then stationed themselves in the upper hall at the head of the stairs to watch her career, and get as much fun out of the occasion as they could.

Pretty soon they saw Clover below on Professor Seccomb's arm. He was a kindly, pleasant man, with a bald head, and it was a fashion among the girls to admire him.

"Doesn't she look pretty?" said Rose. "Just look at Mrs. Searles, Katy She's grinning at Clover like the Cheshire cat. What a wonderful cap that is of hers!! She had it when Sylvia was here at school, eight years ago."

"Hush! She'll hear you."

"No, she won't! There's Ellen beginning her piece. I know she's frightened by the way she plays. Hark how she hurries the time!"

"There, they're going to have refreshments after all!" cried Esther Dearborn, as trays of lemonade and cake-baskets appeared below on the way to the parlour. "Isn't it a shame to have to stay up here?"

"Professor Seccomb! Professor" called Rose, in a daring whisper. "Take pity on us. We are starving for a piece of cake."

The Professor gave a jump, then retreated, and looked upward. When he saw the circle of hungry faces peering down, he doubled up with laughter. "Wait a moment," he whispered back, and vanished into the parlour. Pretty soon the girls saw him making his way through the crowd with an immense slice of pound-cake in each hand.

"Here, Miss Rose," he said, "catch it." But Rose ran half-way downstairs, received the cake, dimpled her thanks, and retreated to the darkness above, whence sounds proceeded which sent the amused Professor into the parlour convulsed with suppressed laughter. Pretty soon Clover stole up the back stairs to report.

"Are you having a nice time? Is the lemonade good? Who have you been talking with?" inquired a chorus of voices.

"Pretty nice. Everybody is very old. I haven't been talking to anybody in particular, and the lemonade is only cream-of-tartar water. I think it's jollier up here with you," replied Clover. "I must go now; my turn to play comes next." Down she ran.

"Except for the glory of the thing, I think we're having more fun than she," answered Rose.

Next week came St. Valentine's Day. Several of the girls received valentines from home, and they wrote them to each other. Katy and Clover both had one from Phil, exactly alike, with the same purple bird in the middle of the page, and "I love you" printed underneath; and they joined in fabricating a gorgeous one for Rose, which was supposed to come from Potemkin de Montmorency, the hero of the album. But the most surprising valentine was received by Miss Jane. It came with the others, while all the household were at dinner. The girls saw her redden and look angry, but she put the letter in her pocket, and said nothing.

In the afternoon it came out through Bella that "Miss Jane's letter was in poetry, and that she was just as cross as possible about it." Just before tea, Louisa came running down the Row, to No. 5, where Katy was sitting with Rose.

"Girls, what do you think? That letter which Miss Jane got this morning was a valentine, the most dreadful thing, but so funny! " she stopped to laugh.

"How do you know?" cried the other two.

"Miss Marsh told Alice Gibbons. She's a sort of cousin, you know; and Miss Marsh often tells her things. She says Miss Jane and Mrs. Nipson are furious, and are determined to find out who sent it. It was from Mr. Hardhack, Miss Jane's missionary—or no, not from Mr. Hardhack, but from a cannibal who had just eaten Mr. Hardhack up; and he sent Miss Jane a lock of his hair, and the recipe the tribe cooked him by. They found him 'very nice,' he said, and 'He turned out quite tender.' That was one of the lines in the poem. Did you ever hear anything like it? Who do you suppose could have sent it?"

"Who could it have been?" cried the others. Katy had one moment's awful misgiving; but a glance at Rose's face, calm and innocent as a baby's reassured her. It was impossible that she could have done this mischievous thing. Katy, you see, was not privy to that entry in Rose's journal, "Pay Miss Jane off," nor aware that Rose had just written underneath, "Did it. Feb. 14, 1869."

Nobody ever found out the author of this audacious valentine. Rose kept her own counsel, and Miss Jane probably concluded that "the better part of valour was discretion," for the threatened inquiries were never made.

And now it lacked but six weeks to the end of the term. The girls counted the days, and practised various devices to make them pass more quickly. Esther Dearborn, who had a turn for arithmetic, set herself to a careful calculation of how many hours, minutes, and seconds must pass before the happy time should come. Annie Silsbie strung forty-two tiny squares of cardboard on a thread, and each night slipped one off and burned it up in the candle. Others made diagrams of the time, with a division for each day, and every night scored off one with a sense of triumph. None of these devices made the time hasten. It never moved more slowly than now, when life seemed to consist of a universal waiting.

But though Katy's heart bounded at the thought of home till she could hardly bear the gladness, she owned to Clover, "Do you know. much as I long to get away, I am half sorry to go! It is parting with something which we shall never have any more. Home is lovely, and I would rather be there than anywhere else; but if you and I live to be a hundred, we shall never be girls at a boarding-school again."

CHAPTER THIRTEEN

PARADISE REGAINED

"ONLY seven days more to cross off," said Clover, drawing her pencil through one of the squares on the diagram pinned beside her looking-glass. "Seven more, and then—oh, joy!—Papa will be there, and we shall start for home."

She was interrupted by the entrance of Katy, holding a letter, and looking pale and aggrieved.

"Oh, Clover," she cried, "just listen to this!! Papa can't come for us. Isn't it too bad?" And she read:

Burnet, March 20.

"MY DEAR GIRLS,

"I find that it will not be possible for me to come for you next week, as I intended. Several people are severely ill, and old Mrs. Barlow struck down suddenly with paralysis, so I cannot leave. I am sorry, and so will you be; but there is no help for it. Fortunately, Mrs. Hall has just heard that some friends of hers are coming westward with their family, and she has written to ask them to take charge of you. The drawback to this plan is, that you will have to travel alone as far as Albany, where Mr. Peters (Mrs. Hall's friend) will meet you. I have written to ask Mr. Page to see you in the train, and under the care of the guard, on Tuesday morning. I hope you will get through without embarrassment. Mr. Peters will be at the station in Albany to receive you; or, if anything should hinder him, you are to drive at once to the Delavan House, where they are staying. I enclose a cheque for your journey. If Dorry were five years older, I should send him after you.

"The children are most impatient to have you back. Miss Finch has been suddenly called away by the illness of her sister-in-law, so Elsie is keeping house till you return.

"God bless you, my dear daughters, and send you safe.

"Yours affectionately,

"P. CARR."

"Oh, dear!" said Clover, with her lip trembling, "now Papa won't see Rosy."

"No," said Katy, "and Rosy and Louisa, and the rest won't see him. That is the worst of all. I wanted them to so much. And just think how dismal it will be to travel with people we don't know. It's too—too bad, I declare."

"I do think old Mrs. Barlow might have put off being ill just one week longer," grumbled Clover. "It takes away half the pleasure of going home."

The girls might be excused for being cross, for this was a great disappointment. There was no help for it, however, as Papa said. They could only sigh and submit. But the journey, to which they had looked forward so much, was no longer thought of as a pleasure, only a disagreeable necessity, something which must be endured in order that they might reach home.

Five, four, three days—the last little square was crossed off, the last dinner was eaten, the last breakfast. There was much mourning over Katy and Clover among the girls who were to return for another year. Louisa and Ellen Gray were inconsolable; and Bella, with a very small pocket-handkerchief held tightly in her hand, clung to Katy every moment, crying and declaring that she would not let her go.

The last evening she followed her into No. 2 (where she was dreadfully in the way of the packing), and after various odd contortions and mysterious, half-spoken sentences, she said:

"Say, won't you tell if I tell you something?"

"What is it?" asked Katy, absently, as she folded and smoothed her best gown.

"Something," repeated Bella, wagging her head mysteriously, and looking more like a thievish squirrel than ever.

"Well, what is it? Tell me."

To Katy's surprise, Bella burst into a violent fit of crying.

"I'm very sorry I did it," she sobbed—"very sorry! And now you'll never love me any more."

"Yes, I will. What is it? Do stop crying, Bella, dear, and tell me," said Katy, alarmed at the violence of the sobs.

"It was for fun, really and truly it was. But I wanted some cake too," protested Bella, sniffing hard.

"What!"

"And I didn't think anybody would know. Berry Searles doesn't care a bit for us little girls, only for big ones. And I knew if I said 'Bella' he'd never give me the cake. So I said 'Miss Carr' instead."

"Bella, did you write that note?" inquired Katy, almost too surprised to speak.

"Yes. And I tied a string to your blind, because I knew I could go in and draw it up when you were practising. But I didn't mean to do any harm; and when Mrs. Florence was so cross, and changed your room, I was very sorry," moaned Bella, digging her knuckles into her eyes.

"Won't you ever love me any more?" she demanded. Katy lifted her into her lap, and talked so tenderly and seriously that her contrition, which was only half genuine, became real; and she cried in good earnest when Katy kissed her in token of forgiveness.

"Of course you'll go at once to Mrs. Nipson," said Clover and Rose, to whom Katy imparted this surprising discovery.

"No, I think not. Why should I? It would only get poor little Bella into a dreadful scrape, and she's coming back again, you know. Mrs. Nipson does not believe that story now—nobody does. We have 'lived it down,' just as I hoped we should. That is much better than having it contradicted."

"I don't think so; and I should enjoy seeing that little wretch of a Bella well whipped," persisted Rose.

But Katy was not to be shaken.

"To please me, promise that not a word shall be said about it," she urged; and to please her the girls consented.

314

I think Katy was right in saying that Mrs. Nipson no longer believed her guilty in the affair of the note. She had been very friendly to both the sisters of late; and when Clover carried in her album and asked for an autograph. she waxed quite sentimental and wrote. "I would not exchange the modest Clover for the most brilliant flower in our beautiful parterre, so bring it back I pray thee, to your affectionate teacher, Marianne Nipson"; which effusion quite overwhelmed "the modest Clover," and called out the remark from Rose—"Don't she wish she may get you!" Miss Jane said twice, "I shall miss you, Katy," a speech which, to quote Rose again, made Katy look as "surprised as Balaam." Rose herself was not coming back to school. She and the girls were half broken-hearted at parting. They lavished tears, kisses, promises of letters, and vows of eternal friendship. Neither of them. it was agreed. was ever to love anybody else so well. The final moment would have been almost too tragical, had it not been for the last bit of mischief on the part of Rose. It was after the stage was actually at the door and she had her foot upon the step, that, struck by a happy thought, she rushed upstairs again, collected the girls, and, each taking a window, they tore down the cotton, flung open sashes, and startled Mrs. Nipson, who stood below, by the simultaneous waving therefrom of many white flags. Katy, who was already in the stage, had the full benefit of this performance. Always after that, when she thought of the Nunnery, her memory recalled this scene—Mrs. Nipson in the doorway, Bella blubbering behind, and overhead the windows crowded with saucy girls, laughing and triumphantly flapping the long cotton strip which had for so many months obscured the daylight from them all.

At Springfield next morning she and Clover said goodbye to Mr. Page and Lilly. The ride to Albany was easy and safe. With every mile their spirits rose. At last they were actually on the way home.

At Albany they looked anxiously about the crowded depot for "Mr. Peters." Nobody appeared at first, and they had time to grow nervous before they saw a gentle.

carewom little man coming toward them in company with the conductor.

"I believe you are the young ladies I have come to meet," he said. "You must excuse my being late, I was detained by business. There is a great deal to do to move a family out West"; he wiped his forehead in a dispirited way. Then he put the girls into a carriage, and gave the driver a direction.

"We'd better leave your baggage at the office as we pass," he said, "because we have to get off so early in the morning."

"How early?"

"The boat goes at six, but we ought to be on board by half-past five, so as to be well settled before she starts."

"The boat?" said Katy, opening her eyes

"Yes. Erie Canal, you know. Our furniture goes that way, so we judged it best to do the same, and keep an eye on it ourselves. Never be separated from your property, if you can help it, that's my maxim. It's the *Prairie Belle*—one of the finest boats on the Canal."

"When do we get to Buffalo?" asked Katy, with an uneasy recollection of having heard that canal boats travel slowly.

"Buffalo? Let me see. This is Tuesday—Wednesday, Thursday—well, if we're lucky we ought to be there Friday evening; so, if we're not too late to catch the night boat on the lake, you reach home Saturday afternoon. Yes; I think we may pretty safely say Saturday afternoon."

Four days! The girls looked at each other with dismay too deep for words. Elsie was expecting them by Thursday at latest. What should they do?

"Telegraph," was the only answer that suggested itself. So Katy scribbled a despatch, "Coming by canal. Don't expect us till Saturday," which she begged Mr. Peters to send; and she and Clover agreed in whispers that it was dreadful, but they must bear it as patiently as they could.

Oh, the patience which is needed on a canal! The motion which is not so much motion as standing still! The crazy impulse to jump out and help the crawling boat along by pushing it from behind! How one grows to hate the slow, monotonous glide, the dull banks, and to envy every swift-moving thing in sight, each man on horseback, each bird flying through the air.

Mrs. Peters was a thin, anxious woman, who spent her life anticipating disasters of all sorts. She had her children with her, three little boys, and a teething baby; and such a load of bundles, and baskets, and brown-paper parcels, that Katy and Clover privately wondered how she could possibly have got through the journey without their help. Willy, the eldest boy, was always begging leave to go ashore and ride the towing horses; Sammy, the second, could only be kept quiet by means of crooked pins and fish-lines of blue yarn; while Paul, the youngest, was possessed with a curiosity as to the under side of the boat, which resulted in his dropping his new hat overboard five times in three days, Mr. Peters and the cabin-boy rowing back in a small boat each time to recover it. Mrs. Peters sat on deck with her baby in her lap, and was in perpetual agony lest the locks should work wrongly, or the boys be drowned, or someone fail to notice the warning cry, 'Bridge!" and have their heads carried off from their shoulders. Nobody did; but the poor lady suffered the anguish of ten accidents in dreading the one which never took place. The berths at night were small and cramped, restless children woke and cried, the cabins were close. the decks cold and windy. There was nothing to see, and nothing to do. Katy and Clover agreed that they never wanted to see a canal boat again.

They were very helpful to Mrs. Peters, amused the boys and kept them out of mischief; and she told her husband that she really thought she shouldn't have lived through the journey if it hadn't been for the Miss Carrs, they were such kind girls, and so fond of children. But the three days were terribly long. At last they ended. Buffalo was reached in time for the lake boat; and once established on board, feeling the rapid motion, and knowing that each stroke of the paddles took them nearer home, the girls were rewarded for their long trial of patience.

At four o'clock the next afternoon Burnet was in sight. Long before they touched the wharf Clover discovered old Whitey and the carriage, and Alexander, waiting for them among the crowd of carriages. Standing on the edge of the dock appeared a well-known figure.

"Papa! Papa!" she shrieked. It seemed as if the girls could not wait for the boat to stop, and the plank to be lowered. How delightful it was to feel Papa again! Such a sense of home and comfort and shelter as came with his touch!

"I'll never go away from you again, never, never!!" repeated Clover, keeping tight hold of his hand as they drove up the hill. Dr. Carr, as he gazed at his girls, was equally happy—they were so bright, so affectionate and loving. No, he could never spare them again, for boarding-school or anything else, he thought.

"You must be very tired," he said.

"Not a bit. I'm hardly ever tired now," replied Katy.

"Oh, dear! I forgot to thank Mr. Peters for taking care of us," said Clover.

"Never mind. I did it for you," answered her father.

"Oh, that baby!" she continued; "how glad I am that it has gone to Toledo, and I needn't hear it cry any more! Katy! Katy! There's home! We are at the gate!"

The girls looked eagerly out, but no children were visible. They hurried up the gravel path, under the locust boughs just beginning to bud. There, over the front door, was an arch of evergreens, with "Katy" and "Clover" upon it in scarlet letters; and as they reached the porch, the door flew open, and out poured the children in a tumultuous little crowd. They had been on the roof, looking through a spy-glass after the boat.

"We never knew you had come till we heard the gate," explained John and Dorry; while Elsie hugged Clover, and Phil, locked his arms round Katy's neck, took his feet off the floor, and swung them in an ecstasy of affection, until she begged for mercy.

"How you are grown! Dorry, you're as tall as I am! Elsie, darling, how well you look. Oh, isn't it delicious,

delicious, delicious, to be at home again!" There was such a hubbub of endearments and explanations, that Dr. Carr could hardly make himself heard.

"Clover your waist has grown as small as a pin. You look just like the beautiful princess in Elsie's story," said Johnny.

"Take the girls into the parlour." repeated Dr. Carr; "it is cold out here, with the door open."

"Take 'em upstairs! You don't know what is upstairs!" shouted Phil, whereupon Elsie frowned and shook her head at him.

The parlour was gay with daffodils and hyacinths and vases of blue violets, which smelt delightfully. Cecy had helped to arrange them, Elsie said. And just at that moment Cecy herself came in. Her hair was arranged in a sort of pincushion of puffs, with a row of curls on top, where no curls used to grow, and her appearance generally was very fine and fashionable; but she was the same affectionate Cecy as ever, and hugged the girls, and danced round them as she used to do at twelve. She had waited until they had had time to kiss once all round, she said, and then she really couldn't wait any longer.

"Now come upstairs," suggested Elsie, when Clover had warmed her feet, and the flowers had been admired, and everybody had said ten times over how nice it was to have the girls back, and the girls had replied that it was just as nice to come back.

So they all went upstairs, Elsie leading the way.

"Where are you going?" cried Katy: "that's the Blue Room." But Elsie did not pause.

"You see," she explained, with the door-knob in her hand, "Papa and I thought you ought to have a bigger room now, because you are grown-up young ladies! So we have fixed this for you. and your old one is going to be the spare room instead." Then she threw the door open, and led the girls in.

"See, Katy," she said. "this is your bureau, and this is Clover's. And see what nice drawers Papa has had put in the closet—two for you, and two for her. Aren't they

319

convenient? Don't you like it? And isn't it a great deal pleasanter than the old room?"

"Oh, a great deal," cried the girls. "It is delightful, everything about it." All Katy's old treasures had been transferred from her old quarters to this. There was her cushioned chair, her table, her book-shelf, the pictures from the walls. There were some new things too—a blue carpet, fresh paper on the walls, window curtains, of fresh chintz: and Elsie had made a tasteful pincushion for each bureau, and Johnnie crocheted mats for the washstand. Altogether, it was as pretty a bower as two sisters just grown into young ladies could desire.

"What are those lovely things hanging on either side of the bed?" asked Clover.

They were two illuminated texts, sent as a "welcome home," by Cousin Helen. One was a morning text and the other an evening text, Elsie exclaimed. The evening text, which bore the words, "I will lay me down to sleep, and take my rest, for it is thou, Lord, only who makest me dwell in safety," was painted in soft purples and greys, and among the poppies and silver lilies which wreathed it appeared a cunning little downy bird, fast asleep, with his head under his wing. The morning text, "When I awake, I am still with Thee," was in bright colours, scarlet and blue and gold, and had a frame of rose garlands and wideawake-looking butterflies and humming-birds. The girls thought they had never seen anything so pretty.

Such a gay supper as they had that night!! Katy would not take her old place at the tea-tray. She wanted to know how Elsie looked as housekeeper, she said. So she sat on one side of Papa, and Clover on the other, and Elsie poured out the tea, with a mixture of delight and dignity which was worth seeing.

"I'll begin tomorrow," said Katy.

And with that tomorrow, when she came out of her pretty room and took her place once more as manager of the household, her grown-up life may be said to have begun. So it is time that I should cease to write about her. Grown-up lives may be very interesting, but they have no rightful place in a child's book. If little girls will forget to be little, and take it upon them to become young ladies, they must bear the consequences, one of which is, that we can follow their fortunes no longer.

I wrote these last words sitting in the same green meadow where the first words of *What Katy Did* were written. A year had passed, but a cardinal-flower which seemed the same stood looking at itself in the brook, and from the bulrush-bed sounded tiny voices. My little goggle-eyed friends were discussing Katy and her conduct, as they did then, but with less spirit; for one voice came seldom and faintly, while the other, bold and defiant as ever, repeated over and over again, "Katy didn't! Katy didn't! She didn't, didn't didn't."

"Katy did!" sounded faintly from the farther rush.

"She didn't, she didn't," chirped the undaunted partisan. Silence followed. His opponent was either convinced or tired of the discussion.

"Katy didn't." The words repeated themselves in my mind, as I walked homeward. How much room for "Didn'ts" is in the world, I thought. What an important part they play. And how glad I am that, with all her own and other people's doing, so many of these very "Didn'ts" were included among the things which my Katy did at School!

What Katy Did Next

Contents

CHAPTER I

THE UNEXPECTED GUEST

THE September sun was glinting cheerfully into a pretty bedroom furnished with blue. It danced on the glossy hair and bright eyes of two girls, who sat together hemming ruffles for a white muslin dress. The half-finished skirt of the dress lay on the bed; and as each crisp ruffle was completed, the girls added it to the snowy heap, which looked like a drift of transparent clouds or a pile of foamy white-of-egg beaten stiff enough to stand alone.

These girls were Clover and Elsie Carr; and it was Clover's first evening dress for which they were hemming ruffles. It was more than three years since Clover and Katy had returned home from the boarding-school at Hillsover.

Clover was now eighteen. She was a very small Clover still, but it would have been hard to find anywhere a prettier little maiden than she had grown to be. Her skin was so exquisitely fair that her arms and wrists and shoulders seemed cut out of daisies or white rose leaves. Her thick, brown hair waved and coiled gracefully about her head. Her smile was peculiarly sweet; and the eyes, always Clover's chief beauty, had still that pathetic look which made them irresistible to tender-hearted people.

Elsie, who adored Clover, considered her as beautiful as girls in books, and was proud to be permitted to hem ruffles for the dress in which she was to burst upon the world. Though, as for that, not much "bursting" was possible in Burnet, where tea-parties of a middle-aged description, and now and then a mild little dance, represented "gaiety" and "society." Girls "came out" by slow degrees and gradual approaches, with no particular one moment

325

which could be fixed upon as having been the crisis of the joyful event.

"There," said Elsie, adding another ruffle to the pile on the bed—"there's the fifth done. It's going to be ever so pretty, I think. I'm glad you had it all white; it's a great deal nicer."

"Cecy tried to persuade me to get a long spray of pink roses for the skirt," said Clover.

"I'm so glad you didn't! Cecy was always crazy about pink roses. I only wonder she didn't wear them when she was married!"

Yes; the excellent Cecy, who at thirteen had announced her intention to devote her whole life to teaching Sunday School, visiting the poor, and setting a good example to her more worldly contemporaries, had actually forgotten these fine resolutions, and before she was twenty had become the wife of Sylvester Slack, a young lawyer in a neighbouring town! Cecy's wedding had been the great excitement of the preceding year in Burnet; and a fresh excitement had come since in the shape of Cecy's baby, now about two months old, and named "Katherine Clover," after her two friends. Johnnie, at the time we write of, was making her a week's visit.

"She *was* rather wedded to them," went on Clover, pursuing the subject of the pink roses. "She was almost vexed when I wouldn't buy the spray. But it cost lots; and I didn't want it in the least, so I stood firm. Besides, I always said that my first party dress should be plain white. Girls in novels always wear white to their first balls; and fresh flowers are a great deal prettier, anyway, than artificial. Katy says she'll give me some violets to wear."

"Oh, will she? That will be lovely!" cried the adoring Elsie. "Violets look just like you, somehow."

Just then the noise of someone running upstairs quickly made the sisters look up from their work.

Another moment, the door opened, and Katy dashed in calling out, "Papa!—Elsie, Clover, where's papa?"

"He went over the river to see that son of Mr. White's who broke his leg. Why, what's the matter?" asked Clover.

"Is someone hurt?" inquired Elsie, startled at Katy's agitated looks.

"No, not hurt; but poor Mrs. Ashe is in such trouble!"

Mrs. Ashe, it should be explained, was a widow who had come to Burnet some months previously, and had taken a pleasant house not far from the Carr's. She was a pretty, ladylike woman with a particularly graceful, appealing manner, and very fond of her one child, a little girl. Katy and papa both took a fancy to her at once; and the families had grown neighbourly and intimate in a short time.

"I'll tell you all about it in a minute," went on Katy. "But first I must find Alexander, and send him off to meet papa and beg him to hurry home." She went to the head of the stairs as she spoke, and called "Debby!" Katy gave her direction, and then came back again to the room where the other two were sitting. "I must explain as fast as I can, for I have got to go back. You know that Mrs. Ashe's little nephew is here for a visit, don't you?"

"Yes, he came on Saturday."

"Well, he was ailing all day yesterday, and to-day he is worse, and she is afraid it is scarlet fever. Luckily, Amy was spending the day with the Uphams yesterday, so she scarcely saw the boy at all; and as soon as her mother became alarmed, she sent her out into the garden to play, and hasn't let her come indoors since, so she can't have been exposed to any particular danger yet. I went by the house on my way down the street, and there sat the poor little thing all alone in the garden, with her dolly in her lap, looking so disconsolate. I spoke to her over the fence, and Mrs. Ashe heard my voice, and opened the window and called to me. She said Amy had never had the fever, and that the very idea of her having it frightened her to death. She is such a delicate child, you know."

"Oh, poor Mrs. Ashe!" cried Clover; "I am so sorry for her! Well, Katy, what did you do?"

"I hope I didn't do wrong, but I offered to bring Amy here. Papa won't object, I am almost sure."

"Why, of course he won't. Well?"

"I am going back now to fetch Amy. Mrs. Ashe is to let Ellen, who hasn't been in the room with the little boy, pack a bagful of clothes and put it out on the steps, and I shall send Alexander for it by and by. You can't think how troubled poor Mrs. Ashe was. She couldn't help crying when she said that Amy was all she had left in the world. She was so relieved when I said that we would take Amy. You know she has a great deal of confidence in papa."

"Yes, and in you too. Where will you put Amy to sleep, Katy?"

"What do you think would be best? In Dorry's room?"

"I think she'd better come in here with you, and I'll go into Dorry's room. She is used to sleeping with her mother, you know, and she would be lonely if she were left to herself."

"Perhaps that will be better, only it is a great bother to you, Clovy dear."

"I don't mind," responded Clover cheerfully. "I rather like to change about and try a new room once in a while. It's as good as going on a journey—almost."

She pushed aside the half-finished dress as she spoke, opened a drawer, took out its contents, and began to carry them across the entry to Dorry's room, doing everything with the orderly deliberation that was characteristic of whatever Clover did. Her preparations were almost complete before Katy returned, bringing with her little Amy Ashe.

Amy was a tall child of eight, with a frank, happy face, and long light hair hanging down her back. She looked like the pictures of *Alice in Wonderland*; but just at that moment it was a very woeful little Alice indeed that she resembled, for her cheeks were stained with tears and her eyes swollen with recent crying.

"Why, what is the matter?" said Clover. "Aren't you glad that you are coming to us? We are."

"Mamma didn't kiss me for good-bye," sobbed the little girl. "She didn't come downstairs at all. She just put her head out of the window and said: 'Good-bye, Amy! Be very good, and don't make Miss Carr any trouble,' and then she went away. I never went anywhere before without kissing mamma for good-bye."

"Mamma was afraid to kiss you for fear she might give you the fever," explained Katy, taking her turn as a comforter. "It wasn't because she forgot. She felt worse about it than you did, I imagine. You know the thing she cares most for is that you shall not be ill as your cousin Walter is. She would rather do anything than have that happen. As soon as he gets well she will kiss you dozens of times, see if she doesn't. Meanwhile, she says in this note that you must write her a little letter every day, and she will hang a basket by a string out of the window, and you and I will go and drop the letters into the basket, and stand by the gate and see her pull it up. That will be funny, won't it?"

"Shall I sleep with you?" demanded Amy.

"Yes, in that bed over there."

"It's a pretty bed," pronounced Amy after examining it gravely for a moment. "Will you tell me a story every morning?"

"If you don't wake up too early. My stories are always sleepy till seven o'clock. Let us see what Ellen has packed and then I'll give you some drawers of your own, and we will put the things away."

The bag was full of neat little frocks and underclothes stuffed hastily in all together. Katy took them out, smoothing the folds with her fingers. As she lifted the last skirt, Amy, with a cry of joy, pounced on something that lay beneath it.

"It's Maria Matilda," she said; "I'm glad of that. I thought Ellen would forget her, and the poor child wouldn't know what to do."

"What a pretty face she has!" said Katy, taking the doll out of Amy's hands.

"Yes, but not so pretty as Mabel. Miss Upham says that Mabel is the prettiest child she ever saw. Look, Miss Clover," lifting the other doll from the table where she had laid it, "hasn't she got *sweet* eyes? She's older than Maria Matilda, and she knows a great deal more. She's begun on French verbs!"

"Not really! Which ones?"

"Oh, only 'J'aime, tu aimes, il aime,' you know—the same one that our class is learning at school. She hasn't tried any but that. Sometimes she says it quite nicely, but sometimes she's very stupid, and I have to scold her." Amy had quite recovered her spirits by this time.

"Are these the only dolls you have?"

"Oh, please don't call them that!" urged Amy. "It hurts their feelings dreadfully. I never let them know that they are dolls. They think that they are real children, only sometimes, when they are very bad, I use the word for a punishment. I've got several other children. There's old Ragazza. My uncle named her, and she's made of rag, but she has such bad rheumatism that I don't play with her any longer; I just give her medicine. Then there's Effie Deans, she's only got one leg; and Mopsa the Fairy, she's a tiny one made out of china; and Peg of Linkinvaddy—but she don't count, for she's come all to pieces."

"What very queer names your children have!" said Elsie, who had come in during the enumeration.

"Yes; Uncle Ned named them. He's a very funny uncle, but he's nice. He's always so much interested in my children."

"There's papa now!" cried Katy; and she ran down-stairs to meet him.

"Did I do right?" she asked anxiously, after she had told her story.

"Yes, my dear, perfectly right," replied Dr. Carr. "I only hope Amy was taken away in time. I will go round at once to see Mrs. Ashe and the boy; and, Katy, keep away from me when I come back and keep the others away, till I have changed my coat."

It seemed to the Carrs after a few days as if they had always had Amy in the house with them. Papa's daily visit to the sickroom, their avoidance of him till after he had "changed his coat," Amy's lessons and games, her dressing and undressing, the walks, and the dropping of notes into the little basket, seemed part of the system of things which had been going on for a long time, and which everybody would miss should they suddenly stop.

But they by no means suddenly stopped. Little Walter Ashe's case proved to be a rather severe one; and after he had begun to mend, he caught cold somehow and was taken worse again. There were some serious symptoms, and for a few days Dr. Carr did not feel sure how things would turn. He did not speak of his anxiety at home, but kept silence and a cheerful face, as doctors know how to do. Only Katy, who was more intimate with her father than the rest, guessed that things were going gravely at the other house, and she was too well trained to ask questions. The threatening symptoms passed off, however, and little Walter slowly got better; but it was a long convalescence, and Mrs. Ashe grew thin and pale, before he began to look rosy. There was no one on whom she could devolve the charge of the child. His mother was dead; his father, an overworked business man, had barely time to run up once a week to see about him: there was no one at his home but a housekeeper, in whom Mrs. Ashe had not full confidence. So the good aunt denied herself the sight of her own child, and devoted her strength and time to Walter, and nearly two months passed, and still little Amy remained at Dr. Carr's.

She was entirely happy there. She had grown very fond of Katy, and was perfectly at home with the others. Phil and Johnnie, who had returned from her visit to Cecy, were by no means too old or too proud to be play-fellows to a child of eight; and with all the older members of the family Amy was a chosen pet. Debby baked turnovers, and twisted cinnamon cakes into all sorts of fantastic shapes to please her; Alexander would let her drive if she happened to sit on the front seat of the carry-all; Dr. Carr was seldom so tired that he could not tell her a story; Elsie invented all manner of charming games for the hour before bedtime; Clover made wonderful capes and bonnets for Mabel and Maria Matilda; and Katy—Katy did all sorts of things.

Katy had a peculiar gift with children which is not easy to define. Some people possess it, and some do not; it cannot be learned, it comes by nature. She was bright and firm and equable all at once. She both amused and influenced them. There was something about her which excited the childish imagination, and always they felt her sympathy. Amy was a tractable child, and intelligent beyond her age, but she was never quite so good with anyone as with Katy. She followed her about like a little lover; she lavished upon her certain special words and caresses which she gave to no one else; and would kneel on her lap, patting Katy's shoulders with her soft hand, and cooing up into her face like a happy dove, for a half-hour together. Katy laughed at these demonstrations, but they pleased her very much.

At last, the long convalescence ended, Walter was carried away by his father, and an army of work-people was turned into Mrs. Ashe's house. Plaster was scraped and painted, wall-papers torn down, mattresses made over, and clothing burned. At last Dr. Carr pronounced the premises in a sanitary condition, and Mrs. Ashe sent for her little girl to come home.

Amy was overjoyed at the prospect of seeing her mother; but at the last moment she clung to Katy and cried as if her heart would break.

"I want you too," she said. "Oh, if Dr. Carr would only let you come and live with me and mamma, I should be so happy! I shall be so lone-ly!"

"Nonsense!" cried Clover. "Lonely with mamma, and those poor children of yours who have been wondering all these weeks what has become of you! They'll want a great deal of attention at first, I am sure; medicine and new clothes and whippings—all manner of things. You remember I promised to make a dress for Effie Deans out of that blue-and-brown plaid like Johnnie's balmoral. I mean to begin it to-morrow."

"Oh, will you?"—forgetting her grief—"Lovely. She will be so pleased, for she's never had a new dress." Consoled by the prospect of Effie's satisfaction, Amy departed quite cheerfully, and Mrs. Ashe was spared the pain of seeing her only child in tears on the first evening of their reunion. But Amy talked so constantly of Katy, and seemed to love her so much, that it put a plan into her mother's head which led to important results.

CHAPTER II

AN INVITATION

IT IS a curious fact that generally speaking, none of us have any expectation that things are going to happen till the very moment when they do happen. We wake up some morning with no idea that a great happiness is at hand and before night it has come, and all the world is changed for us; or we wake bright and cheerful, with never a guess that clouds of sorrow are lowering in our sky, and before noon all is dark. Nothing whispers of either the joy or the grief.

Nothing whispered to Katy Car, as she sat at the window mending a long rent in Johnnie's school coat, and saw Mrs. Ashe come in at the side gate and ring the office bell, that the visit had any special significance for her Mrs. Ashe often did come to the office to consult Dr. Carr. Amy might not be quite well, Katy thought, or there might be a letter with something about Walter in it, or perhaps matters had gone wrong at the house, where paperers and painters were still at work. So she went calmly on with her darning, drawing the "ravelling," with which her needle was threaded, carefully in and out and taking nice even stitches without one prophetic thrill or tremor, while, if only she could have heard what Mrs. Ashe was saying, the school coat would have been thrown to the winds, and for all her tall stature and propriety she would have been skipping with delight and astonishment. For Mrs. Ashe was asking papa to let her do the very thing of all others that she most longed to do; she was asking him to let Katy go with her to Europe!

"I am not very well," she told the Doctor. "I got tired and run down while Walter was ill, and I don't seem to throw it off as I hoped I should. I feel as if a change would do me good. Don't you think so yourself?"

"Yes, I do," Dr. Carr admitted.

"This idea of Europe is not altogether a new one," continued Mrs. Ashe. "I have always meant to go sometime, and have put it off, partly because I dreaded going alone, and didn't know anybody whom I wanted to take with me. But if you will let me have Katy, Dr. Carr, it will settle all my difficulties. Amy loves her dearly, and so do I; she is just the companion I need; if I have her with me, I shan't be afraid of anything."

"How long do you mean to be away?" asked Dr. Carr, divided between pleasure at these compliments to Katy and dismay at the idea of losing her.

"About a year, I think. My plans are rather vague as yet; but my idea was to spend a few weeks in Scotland and England first—I have some cousins in London who will be good to us; and an old friend of mine married a gentleman who lives on the Isle of Wight; perhaps we might go there. Then we could cross over to France, and visit Paris; and before it gets cold, go down to Nice, and from there to Italy.

"There is one reason why I thought Italy would be particularly pleasant this winter for me," went on Mrs. Ashe; "and that is, because my brother will be there. He is a lieutenant in the navy, you know, and his ship the *Natchitoches,* is one of the Mediterranean squadron. They will be in Naples by and by, and if we were there at the same time we should have Ned to go about with; and he would take us to the receptions on the frigate, and all that, which would be a nice chance for Katy. Then towards spring I should like to go to Florence and Venice, and visit the Italian lakes and Switzerland in the early summer. But all this depends on your letting Katy go. If you decide against it, I shall give the whole thing up. But you won't decide against it"—coaxingly—"you will be kinder than that. I will take the best possible care of her, and do all I can to make her happy, if only you will consent to lend her to me; and I shall consider it *such* a favour. And it is to cost you nothing. You understand, Doctor, she is to be my

334

guest all through. I want to make that clear in the outset; for she goes for my sake, and I cannot take her on any other conditions. Now, Dr. Carr, please! I am sure you won't deny me, when I have so set my heart upon having her."

Mrs. Ashe was very pretty and persuasive, but still Dr. Carr hesitated. To send Katy for a year's pleasuring in Europe was a thing that had never occurred to his mind as possible. The cost alone would have prevented, for country doctors with six children are not apt to be rich men. It seemed equally impossible to let her go at Mrs. Ashe's expense; at the same time, the chance was such a good one, and Mrs. Ashe so much in earnest and so urgent, that it was difficult to refuse point-blank. He finally consented to take time for consideration before making his decision.

"I will talk it over with Katy," he said. "The child ought to have a say in the matter; and whatever we decide, you must let me thank you in her name as well as my own for your great kindness in proposing it."

"Doctor, I'm not kind at all, and I don't want to be thanked. My desire to take Katy with me to Europe is purely selfish. I am a lonely person," she went on; "I have no mother or sister, and my brother's profession keeps him at sea; I scarcely ever see him. I have no one but a couple of old aunts, too feeble in health to travel with me or to be counted on in case of any emergency. You see, I am a real case for pity."

Mrs. Ashe spoke gaily, but her brown eyes were dim with tears as she ended her little appeal. Dr. Carr, who was softhearted where women were concerned, was touched. Perhaps his face showed it, for Mrs. Ashe added in a more helpful tone:

"But I won't tease any more. I know you will not refuse me unless you think it right and necessary; and," she continued mischievously, "I have great faith in Katy as an ally. I am pretty sure that she will say that she wants to go."

And indeed Katy's cry of delight when the plan was proposed to her said that sufficiently, without need of further explanation. To go to Europe for a year with Mrs.

Ashe and Amy seemed simply too delightful to be true. All the things she had heard about and read about came rushing into her mind. Dr. Carr's objections, his reluctance to part with her, melted before the radiance of her satisfaction. He had no idea that Katy would care so much about it. After all, it was a great chance—perhaps the only one of the sort that she would ever have. Mrs. Ashe could well afford to give Katy this treat, he knew, and it was quite true what she said, that it was a favour to her as well as to Katy. This train of reasoning led to its natural results. Dr. Carr began to waver in his mind.

But, the first excitement over, Katy's second thoughts were more sober ones. How could papa manage without her for a whole year, she asked herself. He would miss her, she knew; and might not the charge of the house be too much for Clover? A host of housewifely cares began to troop through Katy's mind, a little pucker came into her forehead, and a worried look across the face which had been so bright a few minutes before.

Strange to say, it was that little pucker and the look of worry which decided Dr. Carr.

"She is only twenty-one," he reflected; "hardly out of childhood. I don't want her to settle into an anxious drudging state, and lose her youth with caring for us all. She shall go; though how we are to manage without her I don't see. Little Clover will have to come to the fore, and show what sort of stuff there is in her."

Little Clover came gallantly "to the fore" when the first shock of surprise was over, and she had relieved her mind with one long private cry over having to do without Katy for a year. Then she wiped her eyes, and began to revel unselfishly in the idea of her sister's having so great a treat. Anything and everything seemed possible to secure it for her; and she made light of all Katy's many anxieties and apprehensions.

"My dear child, I know a flannel undershirt when I see one, just as well as you do," she declared. "Tucks in Johnnie's dress, forsooth! Ripping out a tuck doesn't require any super-human ingenuity! Quince marmalade? Debby can make that. Hers is about as good as yours; and if it

336

Mrs. Ashe, Katy and Amy setting off on their journey

wasn't what should we care, as long as you are ascending
Mont Blanc, and hob-nobbing with Michael Angelo and
the crowned heads of Europe? I'll make the spiced
peaches! I'll order the kindling! And if there ever comes a
time when I feel lost and can't manage without advice, I'll
go across to Mrs. Hall. Don't worry about us. We shall get
on happily and easily; in fact, I shouldn't be surprised if I
develop such a turn for housekeeping, that when you
come back the family refused to change, and you had just
to sit for the rest of your life and twirl your thumbs!
Wouldn't that be fine?" and Clover laughed merrily. "So,
Katy darling, cast that shadow from your brow, and look
as a girl ought to look who's going to Europe. Why, if it
were I who were going, I should simply stand on my head
every moment of the time!"

"Not a very convenient position for packing," said
Katy, smiling.

"Yes, it is if you turn your trunk upside down! When I
think of all the delightful things you are going to do I can
hardly sit still. I *love* Mrs. Ashe for inviting you."

"So do I," said Katy soberly. "It was the kindest thing.
I can't think why she did it."

"Well, I can," replied Clover, always ready to defend
Katy even against herself. "She did it because she wanted
you, and she wanted you because you are the dearest old
thing in the world, and the nicest to have about. You
needn't say you're not, for you are! Now, Katy, don't
waste another thought on such miserable things as pickles
and undershirts. We shall get along perfectly well, I do
assure you. Just fix your mind instead on the dome of St.
Peter's, or try to fancy how you'll feel the first time you
step into a gondola or see the Mediterranean. There will
be a moment! What fun it will be to get your letters! We
shall fetch out the Encyclopædia and the big Atlas and the
History of Modern Europe, and read all about everything
you see and all the places you go to; and it will be as
good as a lesson in geography and history and political
economy all combined, only a great deal more interesting!
We shall stick out all over with knowledge before you
come back; and this makes it a plain duty to go, if it were

only for our sakes." With these zealous promises, Katy was forced to be content. Indeed, contentment was not difficult with such a prospect of delight before her. When once her little anxieties had been laid aside, the idea of the coming journey grew in pleasantness every moment.

Katy learned a great deal while talking over what she was to see and do. She read every scrap she could lay her hand on which related to Rome or Florence or Venice or London. The driest details had a charm for her now that she was likely to see the real places. She went about with scraps of paper in her pocket, on which were written such things as these: "Forum. When built? By whom built? More than one?" "What does *Cenacola* mean?" "Cecilia Metella. Who was she?" "Find out about Saint Catherine of Siena." "Who was Beatrice Cenci?" How she wished that she had studied harder and more carefully before this wonderful chance came to her!

All Burnet took an interest in Katy's plans, and almost everybody had some sort of advice or help, or some little gift to offer. Old Mrs. Worrett, who, though fatter than ever, still retained the power of locomotion, drove in from Conic Section in her roomy carry-all with the present of a rather obsolete copy of *Murray's Guide*, in faded red covers, which her father had used in his youth, also a bottle of Brown's Jamaica Ginger, in case of sea-sickness. Debby's sister-in-law brought a bundle of dried camomile for the same purpose. Someone had told her it was the "handiest thing in the world to take along with you on them steamboats." Cecy sent a wonderful old-gold and scarlet contrivance to hang on the wall of the state-room. There were pockets for watches, and pockets for medicines, and pockets for handkerchiefs and hairpins—in short, there were pockets for everything; besides a pin-cushion with "Bon Voyage" in rows of shining pins, a bottle of eau-de-Cologne, a cake of soap, and a hammer and tacks to nail the whole up with. Mrs. Hall's gift was a warm and very pretty woollen wrapper of dark blue flannel, with a pair of soft-knitted slippers to match. Old Mr. Worrett sent a note of advice, recommending Katy to take a quinine pill every day that she was away, never to stay out late, because the dews "over there" were said to be unwholesome, and on no account to drink a drop of water which had not been boiled.

From Cousin Helen came a delightful travelling-bag, light and strong at once, and fitted up with all manner of nice little conveniences. Miss Inches sent a *History of Europe* in five fat volumes, which was so heavy that it had to be left at home. In fact, a good many of Katy's presents had to be left at home, for both Mrs. Ashe and Cousin Helen had warned her of the inconvenient consequences of weight in baggage: and by their advice she had limited herself to a single trunk of moderate size, besides a little flat valise for use in her state-room.

Clover's gift was a set of blank books for notes, journals, etc. In one of these Katy made out a list of "Things I must see," "Things I must do," "Things I would like to see," "Things I would like to do." Another she devoted to various good shopping addresses which had been given her; for though she did not expect to do any shopping herself, she thought Mrs. Ashe might find them useful. Katy's ideas were still so simple and unworldly, and her experience of life so small, that it had not occurred to her how very tantalising it might be to stand in front of shop windows full of delightful things and not be able to buy any of them. She was accordingly overpowered with surprise, gratitude, and the sense of sudden wealth, when, about a week before the start, her father gave her three little thin strips of paper, which he told her were circular notes, and worth a hundred dollars apiece. He also gave her five English sovereigns.

"Those are for immediate use," he said. "Put the notes away carefully, and don't lose them. You had better have them cashed one at a time as you require them. Mrs. Ashe will explain how. You will need a gown or so before you come back, and you'll want to buy some photographs and so on, and there will be fees——"

"But, Papa," protested Katy, opening wide her candid eyes, "I didn't expect you to give me any money, and I'm afraid you are giving me too much. Do you think you can afford it? Really and truly, I don't want to buy things. I shall see everything, you know, and that's enough."

Her father only laughed.

"You'll be wiser and greedier before the year is out, my dear," he replied. "Three hundred dollars won't go far, as you'll find. But it's all I can spare, and I trust you to keep within it, and not come home with any long bills for me to pay."

"Papa! I should think not!" cried Katy, with unsophisticated horror.

One very interesting thing was to happen before they sailed, the thought of which helped both Katy and Clover through the last hard days, when the preparations were nearly complete, and the family had leisure to feel dull and out of spirits. Katy was to make Rose Red a visit.

Rose had by no means been idle during the three years and a half which had elapsed since they all parted at Hillsover, and during which the girls had not seen her. In fact, she had made more out of the time than any of the rest of them, for she had been engaged for eighteen months, had been married, and was now keeping house near Boston with a little Rose of her own, who, she wrote to Clover, was a perfect angel, and more delicious than words could say! Mrs. Ashe had taken passage in the *Spartacus*, sailing from Boston; and it was arranged that Katy should spend the last two days before sailing with Rose, while Mrs. Ashe and Amy visited an old aunt in Hingham. To see Rose in her own home, and Rose's husband, and Rose's baby, was only next in interest to seeing Europe. None of the changes in her lot seemed to have changed her particularly, to judge by the letter sent in reply to Katy's announcing her plans, which letter ran as follows:

Longwood,
September 20th

"MY DEAREST CHILD,

"Your note made me dance with delight. I stood on my head, waving my heels wildly to the breeze, till Deniston thought I must be taken suddenly mad; but when I explained he did the same. It is too enchanting, the whole of it. I put it at the head of all the nice things that ever happened, except my baby. Write the moment you get this by what train you expect to reach Boston, and when you roll into the station you will behold two forms, one tall and stalwart, the other short and fatsome, waiting for you. They will be those of Deniston and myself. Deniston is not beautiful, but he is good, and he is prepared to *adore* you. The baby is both good and beautiful, and you will adore her. I am neither; but you know all about me, and I always did adore you and always shall. I am going out this moment to the butcher's to order a calf fatted for your special behoof; and he shall be slain and made into cutlets the moment I hear from you. My funny little house, which is quite a dear little house too, assumes a new interest in my eyes from the fact that you so soon are to see it. It is somewhat queer, as you might know my house would be; but I think you will like it.

"I saw Silvery Mary the other day and told her you were coming. She is the same mouse as ever. I shall ask her and some of the other girls to come out to lunch on one of your days. Good-bye, with a hundred and fifty kisses to Clovy and the rest.

"Your loving
"Rose Red."

"She never signs herself Browne, I observe," said Clover, as she finished the letter.

"Oh, Rose Red Browne would sound too funny! Rose Red she must stay till the end of the chapter; no other name could suit her half so well, and I can't imagine her being called anything else. What fun it will be to see her and little Rose!"

"And Deniston Browne," put in Clover.

"Somehow I find it rather hard to take in the fact that there is a Deniston Browne," observed Katy.

"It will be easier after you have seen him, perhaps."

The last day came, as last days will. Katy's trunk, most carefully and exactly packed by the united efforts of the family, stood in the hall, locked and strapped, not to be opened again till the party reached London. The little valise was also ready; and Dorry, the neat-handed, had painted a red star on both ends of both it and the trunk, that they might be easily picked from among a heap of luggage. He now proceeded to prepare and paste on two square cards, labelled respectively, "Hold" and "Stateroom." Mrs. Hall had told them that this was the correct thing to do.

Mrs. Ashe had been full of business likewise in putting her house to rights for a family who had rented it for the time of her absence, and Katy and Clover had taken a good many hours from their own preparations to help her. All was done at last; and one bright morning in October, Katy stood on the wharf with her family about her, and a lump in her throat which made it difficult to speak. She stood so very still, and said so very little, that a bystander not acquainted with the circumstances might have dubbed her "unfeeling"; while the fact was that she was feeling too much!

The first bell rang. Katy kissed everybody quietly and went on board with her father. Her parting from him, hardest of all, took place in the midst of a crowd of people; then he had to leave her, and as the wheels began to revolve she went out on the side deck to have a last glimpse of the home faces. There they were: Elsie crying tumultuously, with her head on papa's coat-sleeve; John laughing, or trying to laugh, with big tears running down her cheeks the while; and brave little Clover waving her handkerchief encouragingly, but with a very sober look on her face. Katy's heart went out to the little group with a sudden passion of regret and yearning. Why had she said she would go? What was all Europe in comparison with what she was leaving? Life was so short, how could she take a whole year out of it to spend away from the people she loved best? If it had been left to her to choose, I think she would have flown back to the shore then and there, and given up the journey. I also think she would have been heartily sorry a little later, had she done so.

But it was not left for her to choose. Already the throb of the engines was growing more regular and the distance widening between the great boat and the wharf. Gradually the dear faces faded into distance; and Katy went to the

cabin with a heavy heart. But there were Mrs. Ashe and
Amy, inclined to be homesick also, and in need of cheering, and Katy, as she tried to brighten them, gradually
grew bright herself, and recovered her hopeful spirits.
Burnet pulled less strongly as it got farther away, and
Europe beckoned more brilliantly now that they were
fairly embarked on their journey. The sun shone, the lake
was a beautiful, dazzling blue, and Katy said to herself:
"After all, a year is not very long, and how happy I am
going to be!"

ROSE AND ROSEBUD

THIRTY-SIX hours later the Albany train brought the travellers to Boston.

Katy looked eagerly from the window for her first
glimpse of the city of which she had heard so much. After
flat Burnet, with its one bank down to the edge of the lake,
it looked large, imposing, and very picturesque. She studied
the towers, steeples, and red roofs crowding each other up
the slopes of the Tri-Mountain, and the big State House
dome crowning all, and made up her mind that she liked
the looks of it better than any other city she had ever seen.

The train slackened its speed, ran for a few moments between rows of tall, shabby brick walls, and with a long,
final screech of its whistle came to a halt in the station-
house. Everyone made a simultaneous rush for the door;
and Katy and Mrs. Ashe waiting to collect their books
and bags, found themselves wedged into their seats and
unable to get out.

But the discomfort brightened into a sense of relief as,
looking out of the window, Katy caught sight of a face
exactly opposite, which had evidently caught sight of her—

a fresh, pretty face, with light, waving hair, pink cheeks all a-dimple, and eyes which shone with laughter and welcome. It was Rose herself, not a bit changed during the years since they parted. A tall young man stood beside her, who must, of course, be her husband, Deniston Browne.

"There is Rose Red," cried Katy to Mrs. Ashe. "Oh, doesn't she look dear and natural? Do wait and let me introduce you. I want you to know her."

But the train had come in a little behind time, and Mrs. Ashe was afraid of missing the Hingham boat; so she only took a hasty peep from the window at Rose, pronounced her to be charming-looking, kissed Katy hurriedly, reminded her that they must be on the steamer at twelve o'clock the following Saturday, and was gone, so that Katy, following last of all the slow-moving line of passengers, stepped all alone down from the platform into the arms of Rose Red.

"You darling!" was Rose's first greeting. "I began to think you meant to spend the night in the car, you were so long getting out. Well, how lovely this is! Deniston, here is Katy; Katy, this is my husband."

Rose looked about fifteen as she spoke, and so absurdly young to have a husband, that Katy could not help laughing as she shook hands with Deniston, and his own eyes twinkled with fun and evident recognition of the same joke. He was a tall young man, with a pleasant, "steady" face, and seemed to be amused, in a quiet way, with everything which his wife said and did.

"Let us make haste and get out of this hole," went on Rose. "I can scarcely see for the smoke. Deniston, dear, please find a cab, and have Katy's luggage put on it. I am wild to get her home, and exhibit baby before she chews up her new sash or does something else that is dreadful, to spoil her looks. I left her sitting in state, Katy, with all her best clothes on, waiting to be made known to you."

"My large trunk is to go straight to the steamer," explained Katy, as she gave her checks to Mr. Browne. "I only want the little one taken out to Longwood, please."

"Now, this is cosy," remarked Rose, when they were

345

seated in the cab with Katy's bag at their feet. "Deniston, my love, I wish you were going out with us. There's a nice little bench here all ready and vacant, which is just suited to a man of your inches. You won't? Well, come in the early train, then. Don't forget. Now, isn't he just as nice as I told you he was?" she demanded, the moment the cab began to move.

"He looks very nice indeed, as far as I can judge in three minutes and a quarter."

"My dear, it ought not to take anybody of ordinary discernment a minute and a quarter to perceive that he is simply the dearest fellow that ever lived," said Rose. "I discovered it three seconds after I first beheld him, and was desperately in love with him before he had fairly finished his first bow after introduction."

"And was he equally prompt?" asked Katy.

"He says so," replied Rose, with a pretty blush. "But then he could hardly say less after such a frank confession on my part. It is no more than decent of him to make me believe, even if it is not true. Now, Katy, look at Boston, and see if you don't *love* it!"

Rose was quite satisfied with her raptures as they drove through Charles Street, between the Common and the Public Garden, all ablaze with autumn flowers, and down the length of Beacon Street with the blue bay shining between the handsome houses on the water-side. Every vestibule and bay-window was gay with potted plants and flower-boxes; and a concourse of happy-looking people, on foot, on horseback, and in carriages, was surging to and fro like an equal, prosperous tide, while the sunlight glorified all.

" 'Boston shows a soft Venetian side'," quoted Katy, after a while. "I know now what Mr. Lowell meant when he wrote that. I don't believe there is a more beautiful place in the world."

"Why of course there isn't," retorted Rose, who was a most devoted little Bostonian, in spite of the fact that she had lived in Washington nearly all her life. "I've not seen much beside, to be sure, but that is no matter; I know it is true. It is the dream of my life to come into the city to live. I don't care what part I live in, so long as it is Boston!"

"But don't you like Longwood?" asked Katy, looking out admiringly at the pretty places set amid vines and shrubberies which they were now passing. "It looks so very pretty and pleasant."

"Yes, it's well enough for anyone who has a taste for natural beauties," replied Rose. "I haven't; I never had. There is nothing I hate so much as Nature! I'm a born cockney. I'd rather live in one room over Jordan and Marsh's, and see the world wag past, than be the owner of the most romantic villa that ever was built."

The cab now turned in at a gate and followed a curving drive bordered with trees to a pretty stone house with a porch embowered with Virginia creepers, before which it stopped.

"Here we are!" cried Rose, springing out. "Now, Katy, you mustn't even take time to sit down before I show you the dearest baby that ever was sent to this sinful earth. Here, let me take your bag; come straight upstairs, and I will exhibit her to you."

They ran up accordingly, and Rose took Katy into a large sunny nursery, where, tied with pink ribbons into a little basket-chair and watched over by a pretty young nurse, sat a dear, fat, fair baby, so exactly like Rose that no one could possibly have mistaken the relationship. The baby began to laugh and coo as soon as it caught sight of its gay little mother and exhibited just such another dimple as hers in the middle of a pink cheek. Katy was enchanted.

"Oh, you darling!" she said. "Would she come to me, do you think, Rose?"

"Why, of course she shall!" replied Rose, picking up the baby as if she had been a pillow and stuffing her into Katy's arms head first. "Now, just look at her, and tell me if ever you saw anything so enchanting in the whole course of your life before? Isn't she big? Isn't she beautiful? Isn't she good? Just see her little hands and her hair! She never cries except when it is clearly her duty to cry. See her turn her head to look at me! Oh, you angel!" And, seizing the long-suffering baby, she smothered it with kisses. "I never, never, never did see anything so sweet."

Little Rose was indeed a delicious baby, all dimples and good-humour and violet powder, with a skin as soft as a lily's leaf, and a happy capacity for allowing herself to be petted and cuddled without remonstrance. She was so soft and sunny and equable that it was no more trouble to care for and amuse her than if she had been a bird or a kitten; and, as Rose remarked, it was "ten times better fun."

"I was never allowed as many dolls as I wanted in my

Katy and Rose Red with her baby

infancy," she said. "I suppose I tore them to pieces too soon; and they couldn't give me tin ones to play with, as they did wash-bowls, when I broke the china ones."

"Were you such a very bad child?" asked Katy.

"Oh, utterly depraved, I believe! You wouldn't think so now, would you? I recollect some dreadful occasions at school. Once I had my head pinned up in my apron because I *would* make faces at the other scholars and they laughed; but I promptly bit a bay-window through the apron, and ran my tongue out of it till they laughed worse than ever. The teacher used to send me home with notes fastened to my pinafore with things like this written in them: 'Little Frisk has been more troublesome than usual to-day. She has pinched all the younger children, and bent the bonnets of all the older ones. We hope to see an amendment soon, or we do not know what we shall do'."

"Why did they call you Little Frisk?" inquired Katy, after she had recovered from the laugh which Rose's reminiscences called forth.

"It was a term of endearment, I suppose; but somehow my family never seemed to enjoy it as they ought. I cannot understand," she went on reflectively, "why I had not sense enough to suppress those awful little notes. It would have been so easy to lose them on the way home, but somehow it never occurred to me. Little Rose will be wiser than that; won't you, my angel? She will tear up the horrid notes—mammy will show her how!"

All the time that Katy was washing her face and brushing the dust of the railway from her dress, Rose sat by with the little Rose in her lap, entertaining her thus. When she was ready, the droll little mamma tucked her baby under her arm and led the way downstairs to a large square parlour with a bay-window, through which the westering sun was shining. It was a pretty room, and had a flavour about it "just like Rose," Katy declared. No one else would have hung the pictures or hooked back the curtains in exactly that way, or have hit upon the happy device of filling the grate with a great bunch of marigolds, pale brown, golden, and orange, to simulate the fire. She had chosen a "greenery, yallery" paper for her walls, against which hung various articles which looked a great deal queerer then than they would to-day. There was a mandolin, picked up at some Eastern sale, a warming-pan in shining brass from her mother's attic, two old samplers worked in faded silks, and a quantity of gaily-tinted Japanese fans and embroideries. She had also begged from an old aunt at Beverly Farms a couple of droll little armchairs in white painted wood, with covers of antique needlework. One had Chit embroidered on the middle of its cushion; the other, Chat.

"Now, Katy," said Rose, seating herself in Chit, "pull up Chat, and let us begin."

So they did begin, and went on, interrupted only by Baby Rose's coos and splutters till the dusk fell, till appetising smells floated through the rear of the house, and the click of a latch-key announced Mr. Browne, come home just in time for dinner.

The two days' visit went only too quickly. There is nothing more fascinating to a girl than the *ménage* of a young couple of her own age. It is a sort of playing at real life without the cares and the sense of responsibility that real life is sure to bring. Rose was an adventurous housekeeper. She was still new to the position, she found it very entertaining, and she delighted in experiments of all sorts. If they turned out well, it was good fun; if not, that was funnier still! Her husband, for all his serious manner, had a real boy's love of a lark, and he aided and abetted her in all sorts of whimsical devices. They owned a dog who was only less dear than the baby, a cat only less dear than the dog, a parrot whose education required constant supervision, and a hutch of ring-doves whose melancholy little "whuddering" coos were the delight of Rose. The house seemed astir with young life all over. The only elderly thing in it was the cook, who had the reputation of a dreadful temper; only, unfortunately, Rose made her laugh so much that she never found time to be cross.

Katy felt quite an old, experienced person amid all this movement and liveliness and cheer. It seemed to her that nobody in the world could possibly be having such a good time as Rose; but Rose did not take the same view of the situation.

"It's all very well now," she said, "while the warm weather lasts; but in winter Longwood is simply gruesome. The wind never stops blowing day or night. It howls and it roars and it screams, till I feel as if every nerve in my body were on the point of snapping in two. And the snow, ugh! And the wind, ugh! And burglars! Every night of our lives they come—or I think they come—and I lie awake and hear them sharpening their tools and forcing the locks and murdering the cook and kidnapping Baby.

till I long to die and have done with them forever! Oh, Nature is the most unpleasant thing!"

"Burglars are not Nature," objected Katy.

"What are they, then? Art? High Art? Well, whatever they are, I do not like them. Oh, if ever the happy day comes when Deniston consents to move into town, I never wish to set my eyes on the country again as long as I live, unless—well, yes, I should like to come out just once more in the horse-cars and *kick* that elm-tree by the fence! The number of times that I have lain awake at night listening to its creaking!"

"You might kick it without waiting to have a house in town."

"Oh, I shouldn't dare as long as we are living here! You never know what Nature may do. She has ways of her own of getting even with people," remarked her friend, solemnly.

No time must be lost in showing Boston to Katy, Rose said. So, the morning after her arrival she was taken in bright and early to see the sights. Then the girls did a little shopping; and by that time they were quite tired enough to make the idea of luncheon agreeable, so they took the path across the Common to the Joy Street Mall.

Katy was charmed by all she had seen. The delightful nearness of so many interesting things surprised her. She perceived what is one of Boston's chief charms—that the Common and its surrounding streets make a natural centre and rally-point for the whole city. The stately old houses on Beacon Street, with their rounded fronts, deep window-casements, and here and there a mauve or a lilac pane set in the sashes, took her fancy greatly; and so did the State House, whose situation made it sufficiently imposing, even before the gilding of the dome.

Up the steep steps of the Joy Street Mall they went, to the house on Mt. Vernon Street which the Reddings had taken on their return from Washington nearly three years before. Rose had previously shown Katy the site of the old family house on Summer Street, where she was born, now given over wholly to warehouses and shops. Their present residence was one of those wide, old-fashioned brick houses on the crest of the hill, whose upper windows command the view across to the Boston Highlands; in the rear was a spacious yard, almost large enough to be called a garden, walled in with ivies and grape-vines, under which were long beds full of roses and chrysanthemums and marigolds and mignonette.

Rose carried a latch-key in her pocket, which she said had been one of her wedding-gifts; with this she unlocked the front door and let Katy into a roomy white-painted hall.

"We will go straight through to the back steps," she said. "Mamma is sure to be sitting there; she always sits there till the first frost; she says it makes her think of the country."

There, to be sure, Mrs. Redding was found sitting in a wicker-work chair under the shade of the grape-vines, with a big basket of mending at her side. It looked so homely and country-like to find a person thus occupied in the middle of a busy city that Katy's heart warmed to her at once.

Mrs. Redding was a fair little woman, scarcely taller than Rose and very much like her. She gave Katy a kind welcome.

"You do not seem like a stranger," she said. "Rose has told us so much about you and your sister. Sylvia will be very disappointed not to see you. She went off to make some visits when we broke up in the country, and is not to be home for three weeks yet."

Katy was disappointed too, for she had heard a great deal about Sylvia and had wished very much to meet her. She was shown her picture, from which she gathered that she did not look in the least like Rose; for, though equally fair, her fairness was of the tall aquiline type, quite different from Rose's dimpled prettiness. In fact, Rose resembled her mother, and Sylvia her father; they were only alike in little peculiarities of voice and manner, of which a portrait did not enable Katy to judge.

The two girls had a cosy little luncheon with Mrs. Redding, after which Rose carried Katy off to see the house and everything in it which was in any way connected with her own personal history—the room where she used to sleep, the high-chair in which she sat as a baby and which was presently to be made over to little Rose, the sofa where Deniston offered himself, and the exact spot on the carpet on which she had stood while they were being married! Last of all——

"Now you shall see the best and dearest thing in the whole house," she said, opening the door of a room in the second story—"Grandmamma, here is my friend Katy Carr, whom you have so often heard me tell about."

It was a large, pleasant room, with a little wood-fire blazing in the grate, by which, in an arm-chair full of cushions, with a solitaire-board on a little table beside her, sat a sweet old lady. This was Rose's father's mother. She was nearly eighty; but she was beautiful still, and her manner had a gracious old-fashioned courtesy which was full of charm. She had been thrown from a carriage the year before, and had never since been able to come downstairs or to mingle in the family life.

"They come to me instead," she told Katy. "There is no lack of pleasant company," she added; "everyone is very good to me. I have a reader for two hours a day, and I read to myself a little, and play Patience and Solitaire, and never lack entertainment."

There was something restful in the sight of such a lovely specimen of old age. Katy realised, as she looked at her, what a loss it had been to her own life that she had never known either of her grandparents. She sat and gazed at old Mrs. Redding with a mixture of regret and fascination. She longed to hold her hand, and kiss her, and play with her beautiful silvery hair, as Rose did. Rose was evidently the old lady's darling. They were on the most intimate terms; and Rose talked nonsense as freely as to a person of her own age. It was a delightful relation.

"Grandmamma has taken a fancy to you, I can see," she told Katy, as they drove back to Longwood. "She always wants to know my friends; and she has her own opinions about them, I can tell you."

"Do you really think she liked me?" said Katy warmly. "I am so glad if she did, for I *loved* her. I never saw a really beautiful old person before."

"Oh, there's nobody like her!" rejoined Rose. "I can't imagine what it would be not to have her." Her merry little face was quite sad and serious as she spoke. "I wish she were not so old," she added, with a sigh. "If we could only put her back twenty years! Then, perhaps, she would live as long as I do."

The second day of Katy's visit was devoted to the luncheon-party of which Rose had written in her letter, and which was meant to be a reunion or "side chapter" of the S.S.U.C. Rose had asked every old Hillsover girl who was within reach. There was Mary Silver, of course, and Esther Dearborn, both of whom lived in Boston; and by good luck Alice Gibbons happened to be making Esther a visit, and Ellen Gray came in from Waltham, where her father had recently been settled over a parish, so that altogether they made six of the original nine of the society.

The girls all seemed wonderfully unchanged to Katy, but they professed to find her very grown-up and dignified.

"I wonder if I am," she said. "Clover never told me so. But perhaps she has grown dignified too."

"Nonsense!" cried Rose; "Clover could no more be dignified than my baby could. Mary Silver, give me that child this moment! I never saw such a greedy thing as you are; you have kept her to yourself at least a quarter of an hour, and it isn't fair."

"Oh, I beg your pardon!" said Mary, laughing and covering her mouth with her hand exactly in her old, shy, half-frightened way.

"We only need Mrs. Nipson to make our little party complete," went on Rose, "or dear Miss Jane! What has become of Miss Jane, by the way? Do any of you know?"

"Oh, she is still teaching at Hillsover and waiting for her missionary! He has never come back."

"What a shame!" said Katy, though she could not help laughing. "Miss Jane was really quite nice—no, not *nice* exactly, but she had good things about her."

"Had she?" remarked Rose satirically. "I never observed them. It requires eyes like yours, real 'double million magnifying-glasses of h'extra power,' to find them out. She was all teeth and talons as far as I was concerned; but I think she really did have a softish spot in her old heart for you, Katy, and it's the only good thing I ever knew about her."

"What has become of Lilly Page?" asked Ellen.

"She's in Europe with her mother. I dare say you'll meet, Katy, and what a pleasure that will be! And have you heard about Bella? She's teaching school in the Indian Territory. Just fancy that scrap teaching school!"

It was a merry luncheon indeed, as little Rose seemed to think, for she laughed and cooed incessantly. The girls were enchanted with her, and voted her by acclamation an honorary member of the S.S.U.C. Her health was drunk in Apollinaris water with all the honours and Rose returned thanks in a droll speech. The friends told each other their histories for the past three years; but it was curious how little, on the whole, most of them had to tell. Though, perhaps, that was because they did not tell all; for Alice Gibbons confided to Katy in a whisper that she strongly suspected Esther of being engaged and at the same moment Ellen Gray was convulsing Rose by the intelligence that a theological student from Andover was "very attentive" to Mary Silver.

"My dear, I don't believe it," Rose said; "not even a theological student would dare! And if he did, I am quite sure Mary would consider it most improper. You must be mistaken, Ellen."

"No, I'm not mistaken; for the theological student is my second cousin. They are not engaged exactly, but she hasn't said no; so he hopes she will say yes."

"Oh, she'll never say no; but then she will never say yes, either! He would better take silence as consent! Well, I never did think I should live to see Silvery Mary married. She's a dear old thing, though, and as good as gold; and I shall consider your second cousin a lucky man if he persuades her."

"I wonder where we shall all be when you return, Katy," said Esther Dearborn, as they parted. "A year is a long time; all sorts of things may happen in a year."

These words rang in Katy's ears as she fell asleep that night. All sorts of things may happen in a year, she thought, and they may not be all happy things, either Almost she wished that the journey to Europe had never been thought of!

Next morning she and Rose went early into town, for old Mrs. Redding had made Katy promise to come to say good-bye. They found her sitting by the fire as usual, though her windows were open to admit the sun-warmed air. A little basket of grapes stood on the table beside her, with a nosegay of tea-roses on top. These were from Rose's mother, for Katy to take on board the steamer; and there was something else, a small parcel twisted up in thin white paper.

"It is my good-bye gift," said the dear old lady. "Don't open it now. Keep it till you are well out at sea, and get some little thing with it as a keepsake from me."

Grateful and wondering, Katy put the little parcel in her pocket. With kisses and good wishes she parted from these new-made friends, and she and Rose drove to the steamer, stopping for Mr. Browne by the way. They were a little late, so there was not much time for farewells.

The bell rang, and the great steam-vessel slowly backed into the stream. Then her head was turned to sea, and down the bay she went, leaving Rose and her husband still waving their handkerchiefs on the pier. Katy watched them to the last, and when she could no longer distinguish them, felt that the final link with home was broken.

It was not till she had settled her things in the little cabin which was to be her home for the next ten days, that she found time to examine the mysterious parcel.

Behold, it was a large, beautiful gold-piece twenty dollars!

"What a darling old lady!" said Katy; and she gave the gold-piece a kiss. "How did she come to think of such a thing? I wonder if there is anything in Europe good enough to buy with it?"

CHAPTER IV

ON THE "SPARTACUS"

A FEW hours out a head-wind lay waiting in the offing, and the *Spartacus* began to pitch and toss in a manner which made all her unseasoned passengers glad to betake themselves to their berths. Mrs. Ashe and Amy were among the earliest victims of sea-sickness; and Katy, after helping them to settle in their state-rooms, found herself too dizzy and ill to sit up a moment longer, and thankfully resorted to her own.

As the night came on, the wind grew stronger and the motion worse. The *Spartacus* had the reputation of being a dreadful "roller," and seemed bound to justify it on this particular voyage. The night seemed endless, for she was too frightened to sleep except in broken snatches; and when day dawned, and she looked through the little round pane of glass in the port-hole, only grey sky and grey weltering waves and flying spray and rain met her view.

"Oh, dear, why do people ever go to sea, unless they must?" she thought feebly to herself. She wanted to get up and see how Mrs. Ashe had lived through the night, but the attempt to move made her so miserably ill that she was glad to sink again on her pillows.

The stewardess looked in with offers of tea and toast, the very idea of which was simply dreadful, and pronounced the other lady " 'orribly ill, worse than you are, Miss," and the little girl "takin' on dreadful in the h'upper berth." Of this fact Katy soon had audible proof; for as her dizzy senses rallied a little, she could hear Amy in the opposite state-room crying and sobbing pitifully. She seemed to be angry as well as sick, for she was scolding her poor mother in the most vehement fashion.

"I hate being at sea," Katy heard her say. "I won't stay in this nasty old ship. Mamma! Mamma! Do you hear

me? I won't stay in this ship! It wasn't a bit kind of you
to bring me to such a horrid place. It was very un-kind; it
was cru-el. I want to go back, Mamma. Tell the captain to
take me back to the land. Mamma, why don't you speak to
me? Oh, I am so sick and so very un-happy! Don't you
wish you were dead? I do!"

And then came another storm of sobs, but never a sound
from Mrs. Ashe, who, Katy suspected, was too ill to speak.
She felt very sorry for poor little Amy, raging there in her
high berth like some imprisoned creature, but she was
powerless to help her. She could only resign herself to her
own discomforts, and try to believe that somehow, sometime, this state of things must mend—either they should all
get to land or all go to the bottom and be drowned, and at
that moment she didn't care very much which it turned
out to be.

The gale increased as the day wore on, and the vessel
pitched dreadfully. Twice Katy was thrown out of her
berth on the floor; then the stewardess came and fixed a
sort of movable side to the berth, which held her in, but
made her feel like a child fastened into a railed crib. At
intervals she could still hear Amy crying and scolding her
mother, and conjectured that they were having a dreadful
time of it in the other state-room. It was all like a bad
dream. And they call this travelling for pleasure, thought
poor Katy.

During the night the gale abated, the sea became
smoother, and she dropped asleep. When she woke the sun
was struggling through the clouds, and she felt better.

The stewardess opened the port-hole to freshen the air,
and helped her to wash her face and smooth her tangled
hair; then she produced a little basin of gruel and a tri-
angular piece of toast, and Katy found that her appetite
was come again and she could eat.

She managed to struggle into her dressing-gown and
slippers and across the entry to Mrs. Ashe's state-room.
Amy had fallen asleep at last and must not be waked up,
so their interview was conducted in whispers. Mrs. Ashe
had by no means got to the tea-and-toast stage yet, and
was feeling miserable enough.

"I have had the most dreadful time with Amy," she said. "All day yesterday, when she wasn't sick, she was raging at me from the upper berth, and I too ill to say a word in reply. I never knew her so naughty! And it seemed very neglectful not to come to see you, poor dear child! But really I couldn't raise my head."

"Neither could I, and I felt just as guilty not to be taking care of you," said Katy. "Well, the worst is over with all of us, I hope. The vessel doesn't pitch half so much now, and the stewardess says we shall feel a great deal better as soon as we get on deck. She is coming presently to help me up; and when Amy wakes, won't you let her be dressed, and I will take care of her while Mrs. Barrett attends to you?"

"I don't think I can be dressed," sighed poor Mrs. Ashe. "I feel as if I should just lie here till we get to Liverpool."

"Oh no, h'indeed, mum—no, you won't," put in Mrs. Barrett, who at that moment appeared, gruel-cup in hand. "I don't never let my ladies lie in their berths a moment longer than there is need of. I h'always gets them on deck as soon as possible to get the h'air. It's the best medicine you can 'ave, ma'am, the fresh h'air; h'indeed it h'is."

Stewardesses are all-powerful on board ship, and Mrs. Barrett was so persuasive as well as positive that it was not possible to resist her. She got Katy into her dress and wraps, and seated her on deck in a chair with a great rug wrapped about her feet. Then she dived down the companion-way again, and in the course of an hour appeared escorting a big, burly steward, who carried poor little pale Amy in his arms as easily as though she had been a kitten. Amy gave a scream of joy at the sight of Katy, and cuddled down in her lap under the warm rug with a sigh of relief and satisfaction.

"I thought I was never going to see you again," she said, with a little squeeze. "Oh, Miss Katy, it has been so horrid! I never thought that going to Europe meant such dreadful things as this!"

"This is only the beginning; we shall get across the sea in a few days, and then we shall find out what going to Europe really means. But what made you behave so, Amy, and cry and scold poor mamma when she was sick? I could hear you all the way across the entry."

"Could you? Then, why didn't you come to me?"

"I wanted to; but I was sick too, so sick that I couldn't move. But why were you so naughty?—you didn't tell me."

"I didn't mean to be naughty, but I couldn't help crying. You would have cried too, and so would Johnnie, if you had been cooped up in a dreadful old berth at the top of the wall that you couldn't get out of, and hadn't had anything to eat, and nobody to bring you any water when you wanted some. And mamma wouldn't answer when I called to her."

"She couldn't answer; she was too ill," explained Katy. "Well, my pet, it *was* pretty hard for you. I hope we shan't have any more such days. The sea is a great deal smoother now."

A good many passengers had come up by this time; and Robert, the deck steward, was going about, tray in hand, taking orders for lunch. Amy and Katy both felt suddenly ravenous; and when Mrs. Ashe a while later was helped up the stairs, she was amazed to find them eating cold beef and roasted potatoes, with the finest appetites in the world. They had served out their apprenticeships, the kindly old captain told them, and were made free of the nautical guild from that time on. So it proved, for after these two days none of the party were sick again during the voyage.

Amy had a clamorous appetite for stories as well as for cold beef; and to appease this craving, Katy started a sort of ocean serial, called "The History of Violet and Emma," which she meant to make last till they got to Liverpool, but which in reality lasted much longer. It might with equal propriety have been called "The Adventures of two little Girls who didn't have any Adventures," for nothing in particular happened to either Violet or Emma during the whole course of their long drawn-out history. Amy, however, found them perfectly enchanting, and was never weary of hearing how they went to school and came home again, how they got into scrapes and got out of them, how they made good resolutions and broke them, about their Christmas presents and birthday treats, and what they said and how they felt. The first instalment of this unexciting romance was given that first afternoon on deck; and after that, Amy claimed a new chapter daily, and it was a chief ingredient of her pleasure during the voyage.

On the third morning Katy woke and dressed so early that she gained the deck before the sailors had finished their scrubbing and holy-stoning. She took refuge within the companion-way, and sat down on the top step of the ladder, to wait till the deck was dry enough to venture upon it. There the Captain found her and drew near for a talk.

Captain Bryce was exactly the kind of sea-captain that is found in story-books, but not always in real life. He was stout, and grizzled, and brown, and kind. He had a bluff, weather-beaten face, lit up with a pair of shrewd blue eyes which twinkled when he was pleased; and his manner, though it was full of the habit of command, was quiet and pleasant. He was a martinet on board his ship. Not a sailor under him would have dared dispute his orders for a moment; but he was very popular with them, notwithstanding; they liked him as much as they feared him, for they knew him to be their best friend if it came to sickness or trouble with any of them.

Katy and he grew quite intimate during their long morning talk. The Captain liked girls. He had one of his own, about Katy's age, and was fond of talking about her. Lucy was his mainstay at home, he told Katy. Her mother had been "weakly" now this long time back, and Bess and Nanny were but children yet, so Lucy had to take command and keep things ship-shape when he was away.

"She'll be on the look-out when the steamer comes in," said the Captain. "There's a signal we've arranged which means 'All's well,' and when we get up the river a little way I always look to see if it's flying. It's a bit of towel hung from a particular window; and when I see it I say to myself, 'Thank God! another voyage safely done and no harm come of it.' It's a sad kind of work for a man to go off for a twenty-four days' cruise leaving a sick wife on shore behind him. If it wasn't that I have Lucy to look

361

after things, I should have thrown up my command long ago."

"Indeed, I am glad you have Lucy; she must be a great comfort to you," said Katy, sympathetically; for the Captain's hearty voice trembled a little as he spoke. She made him tell her the colour of Lucy's hair and eyes, and exactly how tall she was, and what she had studied, and what sort of books she liked. She seemed such a very nice girl, and Katy thought she should like to know her.

Later in the morning, Katy, going down to her stateroom for something, came across a pallid, exhausted-looking lady, who lay stretched on one of the long sofas in the cabin, with a baby in her arms and a little girl sitting at her feet, quite still, with a pair of small hands folded in her lap. The little girl did not seem to be more than four years old. She had two pig-tails of thick flaxen hair hanging over her shoulders, and at Katy's approach raised a pair of solemn blue eyes, which had so much appeal in them, that Katy stopped at once.

"Can I do anything for you?" she asked. "I am afraid you have been very ill."

At the sound of her voice the lady on the sofa opened her eyes. She tried to speak, but to Katy's dismay began to cry instead; and when the words came they were strangled with sobs.

"You are so kin-d to ask," she said. "If you would give my little girl something to eat! She has had nothing since yesterday, and I have been so ill; and nobody has c-ome near us!"

"Oh!" cried Katy, with horror, "nothing to eat since yesterday! How did it happen?"

"Everybody has been sick on our side of the ship," explained the poor lady, "and I suppose the stewardess thought, as I had a maid with me, that I needed her less than the others. But my maid has been sick too; and oh, so selfish! She wouldn't even take the baby into the berth with her; and I have had all I could do to manage with him, when I couldn't lift up my head. Little Gretchen has had to go without anything; and she has been so good and patient!"

Katy lost no time, but ran for Mrs. Barrett, whose indignation knew no bounds when she heard how the helpless party had been neglected.

"It's a new person that stewardess h'is, ma'am," she explained, "and most h'inefficient! I told the Captain when she came aboard that I didn't 'ave much opinion of her, and now he'll see how it h'is. I'm h'ashamed that such a thing should 'appen on the *Spartacus*, ma'am—I h'am, h'indeed. H'it never would 'ave been so h'under h'Eliza, ma'am—she's the one that went h'off and got herself married the trip before last, when this person came to take her place."

All the time that she talked Mrs. Barrett was busy in making Mrs. Ware—for that, it seemed, was the sick lady's name—more comfortable; and Katy was feeding Gretchen out of a big bowl full of bread-and-milk which one of the stewards had brought. The little uncomplaining thing was evidently half-starved, but with the mouthfuls the pink began to steal back into her cheeks and lips, and the dark circles lessened under the blue eyes. By the time the bottom of the bowl was reached she could smile, but still she said not a word except a whispered *danke schön*. Her mother explained that she had been born in Germany, and always had till now been cared for by a German nurse, so that she knew the language better than English.

Gretchen was a great amusement to Katy and Amy during the rest of the voyage. They kept her on deck with them a great deal, and she was perfectly content with them and very good, though always solemn and quiet. Pleasant people turned up among the passengers, as always happens on an ocean steamship, and others not so pleasant, perhaps, who were rather curious and interesting to watch.

On the whole, there was no one on the *Spartacus* whom Katy liked so well as sedate little Gretchen except the dear old captain, with whom she was a prime favourite. He gave Mrs. Ashe and herself the seats next to him at table, looked after their comfort in every possible way, and each night at dinner sent Katy one of the apple-dumplings made specially for him by the cook, who had gone many voyages with the captain and knew his fancies. Katy did not care particularly for the dumpling, but she valued it as a mark of regard, and always ate it when she could.

Katy never forgot the thrill that went through her when, after so many days at sea, her eyes first caught sight of the dim line of the Irish coast. An exciting and interesting day followed as, after stopping at Queenstown to leave the mails, they sped north-eastwards between shores which grew more distinct and beautiful with every hour—on one side Ireland, on the other the bold mountain lines of the Welsh coast. It was late afternoon when they entered the Mersey, and dusk had fallen before the captain got out his glass to look for the white, fluttering speck in his own window which meant so much to him. Long he studied before he made quite sure that it was there. At last he shut the glass with a satisfied air.

"It's all right," he said to Katy, who stood near, almost as much interested as he. "Lucy never forgets, bless her! Well, there's another voyage over and done with, thank God, and my Mary is where she was. It's a load taken from my mind."

The moon had risen and was shining softly on the river as the crowded tender landed the passengers from the *Spartacus* at the Liverpool docks.

"We shall meet again in London or in Paris," said one to another, and cards and addresses were exchanged. Then, after a brief delay at the Customs they separated, each to his own particular destination.

"Four-wheeler or hansom, ma'am?" said a porter to Mrs. Ashe.

"Which, Katy?"

"Oh, let us have a hansom! I never saw one, and they look so nice in *Punch*."

So a hansom cab was called, the two ladies got in, Amy cuddled down between them, the folding doors were shut over their knees like a lap-robe, and away they drove up the solidly paved streets to the hotel where they were to pass the night. It was too late to see or do anything but enjoy the sense of being on firm land once more.

"How lovely it will be to sleep in a bed that doesn't tip or roll from side to side!" said Mrs. Ashe,

"Yes and one that is wide enough and long enough and soft enough to be comfortable!" replied Katy. "I feel as if I could sleep for a fortnight to make up for the bad nights at sea."

Everything seemed delightful to her—the space for undressing, the great tub of fresh water which stood beside the English-looking washstand with its ample basin and ewer, the chintz-curtained bed, the coolness, the silence—and she closed her eyes with the pleasant thought in her mind, "It is really England and we are really here!"

CHAPTER V

STORY-BOOK ENGLAND

"OH, is it raining?" was Katy's first question next morning, when the maid came to call her. The pretty room, with its gaily flowered chintz, and china, and its brass bedstead, did not look half so bright as when lit with gas the night before; and a dim grey light struggled in at the window, which in America would certainly have meant bad weather coming or already come.

"Oh no, h'indeed, ma'am, it's a very fine day—not bright, ma'am, but very dry," was the answer.

Katy couldn't imagine what the maid meant, when she peeped between the curtains and saw a thick dull mist lying over everything, and the pavement opposite her window shining with wet. Afterwards, when she understood better the peculiarities of the English climate, she too learned to call days not absolutely rainy "fine," and to be grateful for them; but on that first morning her sensations were of bewildered surprise, almost vexation.

Mrs. Ashe and Amy were waiting in the coffee-room when she went in search of them.

"What shall we have for breakfast," asked Mrs. Ashe—"our first meal in England? Katy, you order it."

"Let's have all the things we have read about in books and don't have at home," said Katy eagerly. But when she came to look over the bill of fare there didn't seem to be many such things. Soles and muffins she finally decided upon, and, as an afterthought, gooseberry-jam.

"Muffins sound so good in Dickens, you know," she explained to Mrs. Ashe; "and I have never seen a sole."

The soles when they came proved to be nice little pan-fish, not unlike what in New England are called "scup." All the party took kindly to them; but the muffins were a great disappointment, tough and tasteless, with a flavour about them as of scorched flannel.

"How queer and disagreeable they are!" said Katy. "I feel as if I were eating rounds cut from an old ironing-blanket and buttered! Dear me! What did Dickens mean by making such a fuss about them, I wonder? And I don't care for gooseberry jam, either; it isn't half as good as the jams we have at home. Books are very deceptive."

"I am afraid they are. We must make up our minds to find a great many things not quite so nice as they sound when we read about them," replied Mrs. Ashe.

Amy's doll, Mabel, was breakfasting with them, and was heard to remark at this juncture that she didn't like muffins either, and would a great deal rather have waffles; whereupon Amy reproved her, and explained that nobody in England knew what waffles were, they were such a stupid nation, and that Mabel must learn to eat whatever was given her and not find fault!

After this moral lesson it was found to be dangerously near train-time; and they all hurried to the railroad station, which, fortunately, was close by. There was rather a scramble and confusion for a few moments; for Katy, who had undertaken to buy the tickets, was puzzled by the unaccustomed coinage; and Mrs. Ashe, whose part was to see after the luggage, found herself perplexed and worried by the absence of checks, and by no means disposed to accept the porter's statement, that if she'd only bear in mind that the trunks were in the second van from the engine, and got out to see that they were safe once or twice during the journey, and call for them as soon as they reached London, she'd have no trouble—"please remember the porter, ma'am!" However all was happily settled at last; and without any serious inconveniences they found themselves established in a first-class carriage, presently running smoothly at full speed across the rich English Midlands towards London and the eastern coast.

Their destination in London was Batt's Hotel in Dover Street. The old gentleman on the *Spartacus*, who had "crossed" so many times, had furnished Mrs. Ashe with a number of addresses of hotels and lodging-houses, from among which Katy had chosen Batt's for the reason that it was mentioned in Miss Edgeworth's *Patronage*. "It was the place," she explained, "where Godfrey Percy didn't stay when Lord Oldborough sent him the letter." It seemed an odd enough reason for going anywhere, that a person in a novel didn't stay there. But Mrs. Ashe knew nothing of London, and had no preference of her own; so she was perfectly willing to give Katy hers, and Batt's was decided upon.

"It is just like a dream or a story," said Katy as they drove away from the London station in a four-wheeler. "It is really ourselves, and this is really London. Can you imagine it?"

She looked out. Nothing met her eyes but dingy weather, muddy streets, long rows of ordinary brick or stone houses. It might very well have been New York or Boston on a foggy day, yet to her eyes all things had a subtle difference which made them unlike similar objects at home.

"Wimpole Street!" she cried suddenly, as she caught sight of the name on the corner, "that is the street where Maria Crawford in *Mansfield Park*, you know, 'opened one of the best houses' after she married Mr. Rushworth. Think of seeing Wimpole Street! What fun!" She looked eagerly out after the "best houses," but the whole street looked uninteresting and old-fashioned; the best house to be seen was not of a kind, Katy thought, to reconcile an ambitious young woman to a dull husband. Katy had to remind herself that Miss Austen wrote her novels nearly a century ago, that London was a "growing" place, and that things were probably much changed since that day.

More "fun" awaited them when they arrived at Batt's.

and exactly such a landlady sailed forth to welcome them as they had often met with in books—an old lady, smiling and rubicund, with a towering lace cap on her head, a flowered silk gown, a gold chain, and a pair of fat mittened hands demurely crossed over a black brocade apron. She alone would have been worth crossing the ocean to see, they all declared. Their telegram had been received, and rooms were ready, with a bright, smoky fire of soft coals; the dinner-table was set, and a nice, formal, white-cravatted old waiter, who seemed to have stepped out of the same book with the landlady, was waiting to serve it. Everything was dingy and old-fashioned, but very clean and comfortable; and Katy concluded that on the whole Godfrey Percy would have done wisely to go to Batt's, and could have fared no better at the other hotel where he did stay.

The first of Katy's "London sights" came to her next morning before she was out of her bedroom: she heard a bell ring and a queer, squeaking little voice utter a speech of which she could not make out a single word. Then came a laugh and a shout, as if several boys were amused at something or other; and altogether her curiosity was roused, so that she finished dressing as fast as she could, and ran to the drawing-room window, which commanded a view of the street. Quite a little crowd was collected under the window, and in their midst was a queer box raised high on poles, with little red curtains tied back on either side to form a miniature stage, on which puppets were moving and vociferating. Katy knew in a moment that she was seeing her first Punch and Judy!

The box and the crowd began to move away. Katy, in despair, ran to Wilkins, the old waiter, who was setting the breakfast-table.

"Oh, please stop that man!" she said. "I want to see him."

"What man is it, miss?" said Wilkins.

When he reached the window, and realised what Katy meant his sense of propriety seemed to receive a severe shock. He even ventured on remonstrance.

"H'I wouldn't, miss, h'if h'I was you. Them Punches

are a low lot, miss; they h'ought to be put down, really they h'ought. Gentlefolks, h'as a general thing, pays no h'attention to them."

But Katy didn't care what "gentlefolks" did or did not do, and insisted upon having Punch called back. So Wilkins was forced to swallow his remonstrances and his dignity, and go in pursuit of the objectionable object. Amy came rushing out, with her hair flying, and Mabel in her arms; and she and Katy had a real treat of Punch and Judy, with all the well-known scenes, and perhaps a few new ones thrown in for their special behalf, for the showman seemed to be inspired by the rapturous enjoyment of his little audience of three at the first-floor window. Punch beat Judy and stole the baby, and Judy banged Punch in return, and the constable came in, and Punch outwitted him, and the hangman and the devil made their appearance duly; and it was all perfectly satisfactory, and "just exactly what she hoped it would be, and it quite made up for the muffins," Katy declared.

Then, when Punch had gone away, the question arose as to what they should choose, out of the many delightful things in London, for their first morning.

Like ninety-nine Americans out of a hundred, they decided on Westminster Abbey; and indeed there is nothing in England better worth seeing, or more impressive, in its dim, rich antiquity, to eyes fresh from the world which still calls itself "new." So to the Abbey they went, and lingered there till Mrs. Ashe declared herself to be absolutely dropping with fatigue.

"If you don't take me home and give me something to eat," she said, "I shall drop down on one of these pedestals and stay there and be exhibited for ever after as an 'h'effigy' of somebody belonging to ancient English history."

So Katy tore herself away from Henry the Seventh and the Poet's corner, and tore Amy away from a quaint little tomb shaped like a cradle, with the marble image of a baby in it, which had greatly taken her fancy. She could only be consoled by the promise that she should soon come again and stay as long as she liked.

She reminded Katy of this promise the very next morning.

"Mamma has waked up with rather a bad headache, and she thinks she will lie still and not come to breakfast," she reported. "And she sends her love, and says will you please have a cab and go where you like; and if I won't be a trouble, she would be glad if you would take me with you. And I won't be a trouble, Miss Katy, and I know where I wish you would go."

Amy putting roses on Baby's tomb

"Where is that?"

"To see that cunning little baby again that we saw yesterday. I want to show her to Mabel—she didn't go with us, you know, and I don't like to have her mind not improved; and, darling Miss Katy, mayn't I buy some flowers and put them on the baby? She's so dusty and so old that I don't believe anybody has put any flowers for her for ever so long."

Katy found this idea rather pretty, and willingly stopped at Covent Garden, where they bought a bunch of late roses for eighteen pence, which entirely satisfied Amy. With them in her hand, and Mabel in her arms, she led the way through the dim aisles of the Abbey, through gates and doors, and up and down steps; the guide following, but not at all needed, for Amy seemed to have a perfectly clear recollection of every turn and winding. When the chapel was reached, she laid the roses on the tomb with gentle fingers, and a pitiful, reverent look in her grey eyes. Then she lifted Mabel up to kiss the odd little baby effigy above the marble quilt; whereupon the guide seemed altogether surprised out of his composure, and remarked to Katy:

"Little miss is an h'American, as is plain to see; no h'English child would be likely to think of doing such a thing."

"Do not English children take any interest in the tombs of the Abbey?" asked Katy.

"Oh, yes, m'm—h'interest; but they don't take no special notice of one tomb above h'another."

Katy could scarcely keep from laughing, especially as she heard Amy, who had been listening to the conversation, give an audible sniff, and inform Mabel that she was glad *she* was not an English child who didn't notice things, and liked grown-up graves as much as she did dear little cunning ones like this!

Later in the day, when Mrs. Ashe was better, they all drove together to the quaint old keep which has been the scene of so many tragedies, and is known as the Tower of London. Here they were shown various rooms and chapels and prisons; and among the rest the apartments where Queen Elizabeth, when a friendless young princess, was shut up for many months by her sister Queen Mary.

"If this is English History, I never mean to learn any more of it, and neither shall Mabel," she declared.

But it is not possible for Amy or anyone else not to learn a great deal of history simply by going about London. So many places are associated with people or events, and seeing the places makes one care so much more for the

371

people or the events that one insensibly questions and wonders. Katy, who had "browsed" all through her childhood in a good old-fashioned library, had her memory stuffed with all manner of little scraps of information and literary allusions, which now came into use. It was like owning the disjointed bits of a puzzle, and suddenly discovering that properly put together they make a pattern. Mrs. Ashe, who had never been much of a reader, considered her young friend a prodigy of intelligence; but Katy herself realised how inadequate and inexact her knowledge was, and how many bits were missing from the pattern of her puzzle. She wished with all her heart, as everyone wishes under such circumstances, that she had studied harder and more wisely while the chance was in her power.

October is not a favourable month in which to see England. Water, water is everywhere; you breathe it; you absorb it; it wets yours clothes and it dampens your spirits. Mrs. Ashe's friends advised her not to think of Scotland at that time of the year. One by one their little intended excursions were given up. A single day and night in Oxford and Stratford-on-Avon; a short visit to the Isle of Wight, where, in a country-place which seemed provokingly pretty as far as they could see it for the rain, lived that friend of Mrs. Ashe who had married an Englishman and in so doing had, as Katy privately thought, "renounced the sun"; a peep at Stonehenge from under the shelter of an umbrella, and an hour or two in Salisbury Cathedral—was all that they accompished, except a brief halt at Winchester, that Katy might have the privilege of seeing the grave of her beloved Miss Austen. Katy had come abroad with a terribly long list of graves to visit, Mrs. Ashe declared. They laid a few rain-washed flowers upon the tomb, and listened with edification to the verger, who inquired:

"Whatever was it, ma'am, that lady did which brings so many h'Americans to h'ask about her? Our h'English people don't seem to take the same h'interest."

"She wrote such delightful stories," explained Katy; but the old verger shook his head.

"I think h'it must be some other party, miss, you've confused with this here. It stands to reason, miss, that we'd have heard of 'em h'over 'ere in England sooner than you would h'over there in h'America, if the books 'ad been h'anything so h'extraordinary."

The night after their return to London, they were dining for the second time with the cousins of whom Mrs. Ashe had spoken to Dr. Carr; and as it happened Katy sat next to a quaint elderly American, who had lived for twenty years in London and knew it much better than most Londoners do. This gentleman, Mr. Allen Beach, had a hobby for antiquities, old books especially, and passed half his time at the British Museum, and the other half in sale-rooms and the old shops in Wardour Street.

Katy was lamenting over the bad weather which stood in the way of their plans.

"It is so vexatious!" she said. "Mrs. Ashe meant to go to York and Lincoln and all the cathedral towns and to Scotland; and we have had to give it all up because of the rains. We shall go away, having seen hardly anything."

"You can see London."

"We have—that is, we have seen the things that everybody sees."

"But there are so many things that people in general do not see. How much longer are you to stay, Miss Carr?"

"A week, I believe."

"Why don't you make out a list of old buildings which are connected with famous people in history, and visit them in turn? I did that the second year after I came. I gave up three months to it, and it was most interesting. I unearthed all manner of curious stories and traditions."

"Oh," cried Katy, struck with a sudden bright thought, "why mightn't I put into the list some of the places I know about in books—novels as well as history—and the places where the people who wrote the books lived?"

"You might do that, and it wouldn't be a bad idea, either," said Mr. Beach, pleased with her enthusiasm. "I will get a pencil after dinner, and help you with your list if you will allow me."

Mr. Beach was better than his word. He not only suggested places and traced a plan of sight-seeing, but on two different mornings he went with them himself.

With such a lot to see and to do, the last week sped all too swiftly, and the last day came before they were at all ready to leave what Katy called "Story-book England." Mrs. Ashe had decided to cross by Newhaven and Dieppe, because someone had told her of the beautiful old town of Rouen, and it seemed easy and convenient to take it on the way to Paris. Just landed from the long voyage across the Atlantic, the little passage of the Channel seemed nothing to our travellers, and they made ready for their night on the Dieppe steamer with the philosophy which is born of ignorance. They were speedily undeceived!

The English Channel has a character of its own, which distinguishes it from other seas and straits. It seems made fractious and difficult by nature, and set as on purpose to be a barrier between two nations who are too unlike to understand each other easily, and are the safer neighbours for this wholesome difficulty of communication between them. The "chop" was worse than usual on the night when our travellers crossed; and the steamer had to fight her way inch by inch. And oh, such a little steamer! And oh such a long night!

CHAPTER VI

ACROSS THE CHANNEL

DAWN had given place to day, and day was well advanced towards noon, before the stout little steamer gained her port. It was hours after the usual time for arrival; the train for Paris must long since have started, and Katy felt dejected and forlorn as, making her way out of the terrible ladies'-cabin, she crept on deck for her first glimpse of France.

The sun was struggling through the fog with a watery

smile, and his faint beams shone on a confusion of stone piers, higher than the vessel's deck, intersected with canal-like waterways, through whose intricate windings the steamer was slowly threading her course to the landing-place. Looking up, Katy could see crowds of people assembled to watch the boat come in—workmen, peasants, women, children, soldiers, custom-house officers, moving to and fro—and all this crowd were talking at once and all were talking French.

"Oh dear, what is the word for trunk-key?" she asked herself. "They will all begin to ask questions, and I shall not have a word to say; and Mrs. Ashe will be even worse off, I know." She saw the red-trousered custom-house officers pounce upon the passengers as they landed one by one, and she felt her heart sink within her.

But after all, when the time came, it did not prove so very bad. Katy's pleasant looks and courteous manner stood her in good stead. She did not trust herself to say much; but the officials seemed to understand without saying. They bowed and gestured, whisked the keys in and out, and in a surprisingly short time all was pronounced right, the baggage had "passed," and it and its owners were free to proceed to the railway station, which fortunately was close at hand.

Inquiry revealed the fact that no train for Paris left till four in the afternoon.

"I am rather glad," declared poor Mrs. Ashe, "for I feel too used up to move. I will lie here on this sofa, and, Katy dear, please see if there is an eating place, and get some breakfast for yourself and Amy, and send me a cup of tea."

"I don't like to leave you alone," Katy was beginning; but at that moment a nice old woman, who seemed to be in charge of the waiting-room, appeared, and with a flood of French which none of them could follow, but which was evidently sympathetic in its nature, flew at Mrs. Ashe and began to make her comfortable. From a cupboard in the wall she produced a pillow, from another cupboard a blanket; in a trice she had one under Mrs. Ashe's head and the other wrapped round her feet.

"Pauvre madame," she said. *"Si pâle! si souffrante! Il faut avoir quelque chose à boire et à manger tout de suite."* She trotted across the room and into the restaurant which opened out of it, while Mrs. Ashe smiled at Katy and said, "You see you can leave me quite safely; I am to be taken care of." And Katy and Amy passed through the same door into the *buffet*, and sat down at a little table.

Fortified with a satisfactory breakfast, Katy felt equal to a walk; and after they had made sure that Mrs. Ashe had all she needed, she and Amy (and Mabel) set off by themselves to see the sights of Dieppe. I don't know that travellers generally have considered Dieppe an interesting place, but Katy found it so. There was a really old church and some quaint buildings of the style of two centuries back, and even the more modern streets had a novel look to her unaccustomed eyes. At first they only ventured a timid turn or two, marking each corner, and going back now and then to reassure themselves by a look at the station; but after a while, growing bolder, Katy ventured to ask a question or two in French, and was surprised and charmed to find herself understood. After that she grew adventurous, and, no longer fearful of being lost, led Amy straight down a long street lined with shops, almost all of which were for the sale of articles in ivory.

Ivory wares are one of the chief industries of Dieppe. There were cases full, windows full, counters full, of the most exquisite combs and brushes, some with elaborate monograms in silver and colours, others plain; there were boxes and caskets of every size and shape, ornaments, fans, parasol handles, looking-glasses, frames for pictures large and small, napkin-rings.

Katy was particularly smitten with a paper-knife in the form of an angel with long, slender wings raised over its head and meeting to form a point. Its price was twenty francs, and she was strongly tempted to buy it for Clover or Rose Red. But she said to herself sensibly: "This is the first shop I have been into and the first thing I have really wanted to buy, and very likely as we go on I shall see things I like better and want more, so it would be foolish to do it. No, I won't." And she resolutely turned her back on the ivory angel, and walked away.

The next turn brought them to a gay-looking little market-place, where old women in white caps were sitting on the ground beside baskets and panniers full of apples, pears, and various queer and curly vegetables, none of which Katy recognised; fish of all shapes and colours were flapping in shallow tubs of sea-water; there were piles of stockings, muffettees, and comforters in vivid blue and red worsted, and coarse pottery glazed in bright patterns. The faces of the women were brown and wrinkled; there were no pretty ones among them, but their black eyes were full of life and quickness, and their fingers clicked with knitting-needles as their tongues flew equally fast in the chatter and the chaffer, which went on without stop or stay, though customers did not seem to be many and sales were few.

Returning to the station they found that Mrs. Ashe had been asleep during their absence, and seemed so much better that it was with greatly amended spirits that they took their places in the late afternoon train which was to set them down at Rouen. Katy said they were like the Wise Men of the East, "following a star," in their choice of a hotel; for, having no better advice, they had decided upon one of those thus distinguished in Baedeker's Guidebook.

The star did not betray their confidence; for the Hôtel de la Cloche, to which it led them, proved to be quaint and old, and very pleasant of aspect. The lofty chambers with their dimly frescoed ceilings, and beds curtained with faded patch, might to all appearances have been furnished about the time when "Columbus crossed the ocean blue"; but everything was clean, and had an air of old-time respectability. The dining-room, which was evidently of more modern build, opened into a square courtyard, where oleanders and lemon trees in boxes stood round the basin of a little fountain, whose tinkle and splash blended agreeably with the rattle of the knives and forks. In one corner of the room was a raised and railed platform, where, behind a desk, sat the mistress of the house, busy with her account-books, but keeping an eye the while on all that went forward.

The next day Mrs. Ashe, Katy and Amy toured the old city, rich in carvings and sculptures and traditions, and saw the Cathedral, the church of St. Ouen, the Palace of Justice, and the "Place of the Maid," where poor Jeanne d'Arc was burned and her ashes scattered to the winds.

Paris looked very modern after the peculiar quaint richness and air of the Middle Ages which distinguished Rouen. Rooms had been engaged for Mrs. Ashe's party in a *pension* near the Arc de l'Etoile, and there they drove immediately on arriving. The rooms were not in the *pension* itself, but in a house close by—a sitting-room with six mirrors, three clocks, and a pinched little grate about a foot wide, a dining-room just large enough for a table and four chairs, and two bedrooms. A maid called Amandine had been detailed to take charge of these rooms and serve their meals.

Dampness, as Katy afterwards wrote to Clover, was the first impression they received of "gay Paris." The tiny fire in the tiny grate had only just been lighted, and the walls and the sheets and even the blankets felt chilly and moist to the touch. They spent their first evening in hanging the bed-clothes round the grate and piling on fuel; they even set the mattresses up on edge to warm and dry! It was not very enlivening, it must be confessed. Amy had taken a cold, Mrs. Ashe looked worried, and Katy thought of Burnet and the safety and comfort of home with a throb of longing.

The days that ensued were not brilliant enough to remove this impression. The November fogs seemed to have followed them across the Channel, and Paris remained enveloped in a wet blanket which dimmed and hid its usually brilliant features. Going about in cabs with the windows drawn up, and now and then making a rush through the drip into shops, was not exactly delightful, but it seemed pretty much all that they could do. It was worse for Amy, whose cold kept her indoors and denied her even the relaxation of the cab. Mrs. Ashe had engaged a well-recommended elderly English maid to come every morning and take care of Amy while they were out; and with this respectable functionary, whose ideas were of a rigidly British type, and who did not speak a word of any language but her own, poor Amy was compelled to spend most of her time.

Katy looked at Amy's pale little face and eager eyes with a real heartache. Her rapture when, at the end of the long dull afternoons, her mother returned to her was touching. Paris was very *triste* to poor Amy, with all her happy facility for amusing herself; and Katy felt that the sooner they got away from it the better it would be. So, in spite of the delight which her brief glimpses at the Louvre gave her, and the fun it was to go about with Mrs. Ashe and see her buy pretty things, and the real satisfaction she took in the one perfectly made walking-suit to which she had treated herself, she was glad when the final day came, when the belated dressmakers and artistes in jackets and wraps had sent home their last wares, and the trunks were packed. It had been rather the fault of circumstances than of Paris; but Katy had not learned to love the beautiful capital as most Americans do, and did not feel at all as if she wanted that her "reward of virtue" should be to go there when she died! There must be more interesting places for live people, and ghosts too, to be found on the map of Europe, she was sure.

Next morning, as they drove slowly down the Champs Elysées, and looked back for a last glimpse of the famous Arch, a bright object met their eyes, moving vaguely against the mist. It was the gay red wagon of the Bon Marché, carrying bundles home to the dwellers of some up-town street.

Katy burst out laughing. "It is an emblem of Paris," she said—"of our Paris, I mean. It has been all Bon Marché and fog!"

"Miss Katy," interrupted Amy, "*do* you like Europe? For my part, I was never so disgusted with any place in my life!"

"Poor little bird, her views of 'Europe' are rather dark just now, and no wonder," said her mother. "Never mind, darling, you shall have something pleasanter by and by if I can find it for you."

"Burnet is a great deal pleasanter than Paris," pronounced Amy, decidedly. "It doesn't always keep raining there, and I can take walks, and I understand everything that people say."

All that day they sped southwards, and with every hour came a change in the aspect of their surroundings.

And when the long night ended and day roused them from broken slumbers, behold, the world was made over! Autumn had vanished, and the summer, which they thought fled for good, had taken its place. Green woods waved about them, fresh leaves were blowing in the wind, roses and hollyhocks beckoned from white-walled gardens; and before they had done with exclaiming and rejoicing, the Mediterranean shot into view, intensely blue, with white fringes of foam, white sails blowing across, white gulls flying above it, and over all a sky of the same exquisite blue, whose clouds were white as the drifting sails on the water below, and they were at Marseilles.

It was like a glimpse of Paradise to eyes fresh from autumnal greys and glooms, as they sped along the lovely coast, every curve and turn showing new combinations of sea and shore, olive-crowned cliff and shining mountain-peak. With every mile the blue became bluer, the wind softer, the feathery verdure more dense and summer-like. Hyeres and Cannes and Antibes were passed, and then, as they rounded a long point, came the view of a sunshine city lying on a sunlit shore; the train slackened its speed, and they knew that their journey's end was come and they were in Nice.

The place seemed to laugh with gaiety as they drove down the Promenade des Anglais and past the English garden, where the band was playing beneath the acacias and palm trees. On one side was a line of bright-windowed hotels and *pensions*, with balconies and striped awnings; on the other, the long reach of yellow sand-beach, where ladies were grouped on shawls and rugs, and children ran up and down in the sun, while beyond stretched the waveless sea. The December sun felt as warm as on a late June day at home, and had the same caressing touch. The pavements were thronged with groups of leisurely-looking people, all wearing an unmistakable holiday aspect; pretty girls in correct Parisian costumes walked demurely beside their mothers, with cavaliers in attendance; and among these young men appeared now and again the well-known uniform of the United States Navy.

"I wonder," said Mrs. Ashe, struck by a sudden thought, "if by any chance our squadron is here." She asked the question the moment they entered the hotel; and the porter, who prided himself on understanding "zose Eenglesh," replied:

"Mai oui, madame, za Americaine fleet is here; zat is, not here, but at Villefranche, just a leetle four mile away —it is ze same zing exactly."

"Katy, do you hear that?" cried Mrs. Ashe. "The frigates *are* here, and the *Natchitoches* among them of course; and we shall have Ned to go about with us everywhere. It is a real piece of good luck for us. Ladies are at such a loss in a place like this, with nobody to escort them. I am perfectly delighted."

"So am I," said Katy. "I never saw a frigate, and I always wanted to see one. Do you suppose they will let us go on board them?"

"Why, of course they will." Then to the porter: "Give me a sheet of paper and an envelope, please—I must let Ned know that I am here at once."

Mrs. Ashe wrote her note and despatched it before they went upstairs to take off their bonnets. She seemed to have a half-hope that some bird of the air might carry the news of her arrival to her brother, for she kept running to the window as if in expectation of seeing him. She was too restless to lie down or sleep, and after she and Katy had lunched, proposed that they should go out on the beach for a while.

"Perhaps we may come across Ned," she remarked.

They did not come across Ned, but there was no lack of other delightful objects to engage their attention. The sands were smooth and hard as a floor. Soft pink lights were beginning to tinge the western sky. To the north shone the peaks of the maritime Alps, and the same rosy glow caught them here and there, and warmed their greys and whites into colour.

"I wonder what that can be!" said Katy, indicating the rocky point which bounded the beach to the east, where stood a picturesque building of stone, with massive towers and steep pitches of roof. "It looks half like a house and half like a castle, but it is quite fascinating, I think. Do you suppose that people live there?"

"We might ask," suggested Mrs. Ashe.

Just then they came to a shallow river spanned by a bridge, beside whose pebbly bed stood a number of women who seemed to be washing clothes by the simple and primitive process of laying them in the water on top of the stones, and pounding them with a flat wooden paddle till they were white. Katy privately thought that the clothes stood a poor chance of lasting through these cleansing operations; but she did not say so, and made the inquiry which Mrs. Ashe had suggested, in her best French.

"*Celle-là?*" answered the old woman whom she had addressed. "*Mais c'est la Pension Suisse.*"

"A *pension*! Why, that means a boarding-house!" cried Katy. "What fun it must be to board there!"

"Well, why shouldn't we board there?" said her friend. "You know we meant to look for rooms as soon as we were rested and had found out a little about the place. Let us walk on and see what the Pension Suisse is like. If the inside is as pleasant as the outside, we could not do better, I should think."

"Oh, I do hope all the rooms are not already taken!" said Katy, who had fallen in love at first sight with the Pension Suisse. She felt quite oppressed with anxiety as they rang the bell.

The Pension Suisse proved to be quite as charming inside as out. The thick stone walls made deep sills and embrasures for the casement windows, which were furnished with red cushions to serve as seats and lounging-places. Every window seemed to command a view, for those which did not look towards the sea looked towards the mountains. The house was by no means full either.

382

Several sets of rooms were to be had; and Katy felt as if she had walked straight into the pages of a romance when Mrs. Ashe engaged for a month a delightful suite of three, a sitting-room and two sleeping-chambers, in a round tower, with a balcony overhanging the water, and a side window, from which a flight of steps led down into a little walled garden, nestled in among the masonry, where tall laurustinus and lemon-trees grew, and orange and brown wall-flowers made the air sweet. Her contentment knew no bounds.

"I am so glad that I came!" she told Mrs. Ashe. "I never confessed it to you before, but sometimes—when we were sick at sea, you know, and when it would rain all the time, and after Amy caught that cold in Paris—I have almost wished, just for a minute or two at a time, that we hadn't. But now I wouldn't not have come for the world! This is perfectly delicious. I am glad, glad, glad we are here, and we are going to have a lovely time, I know."

They were passing out of the rooms into the hall as she said these words, and two ladies who were walking up a cross passage turned their heads at the sound of her voice. To her great surprise Katy recognised Mrs. Page and Lilly.

"Why Cousin Olivia, is it you?" she cried, springing forward with the cordiality one naturally feels in seeing a familiar face in a foreign land.

Mrs. Page seemed puzzled rather than cordial. She put up her eye-glass and did not seem to quite make out who Katy was.

"It is Katy Carr, Mamma," explained Lilly. "Well, Katy, this *is* a surprise! Who would have thought of meeting you in Nice?"

There was a decided absence of rapture in Lilly's manner. She was prettier than ever, as Katy saw in a moment, and beautifully dressed in soft brown velvet, which exactly suited her complexion and her pale-coloured wavy hair.

"Katy Carr! Why, so it is!" admitted Mrs. Page. "It is a surprise indeed. We had no idea that you were abroad. What has brought you so far from Tunket—Burnet, I mean? Who are you with?"

"With my friend Mrs. Ashe," explained Katy, rather chilled by this cool reception. "Let me introduce you. Mrs. Ashe, these are my cousins, Mrs. Page and Miss Page. Amy—why, where is Amy?"

Amy had walked back to the door of the garden staircase, and was standing there looking down upon the flowers.

Cousin Olivia bowed rather distantly. Her quick eye took in the details of Mrs. Ashe's travelling-dress and Katy's dark-blue ulster.

"Some countrified friend from that dreadful Western town where they live," she said to herself. "How foolish of Philip Carr to try to send his girls to Europe! He can't afford it, I know." Her voice was rather rigid as she inquired:

"And what brings you here—to this house, I mean?"

"Oh, we are coming to-morrow to stay! We have taken rooms for a month," explained Katy. "What a delicious-looking old place it is!"

"Have you?" said Lilly, in a voice which did not express any particular pleasure. "Why, we are staying here too."

CHAPTER VII

THE PENSION SUISSE

"WHAT do you suppose can have brought Katy Carr to Europe?" inquired Lilly, as she stood in the window watching the three figures walk slowly down the sands. "She is the last person I expected to turn up here. I supposed she was stuck in that horrid place—what is the name of it?—where they live, for the rest of her life."

"I confess I am surprised at meeting her myself," rejoined Mrs. Page. "I had no idea that her father could afford so expensive a journey."

"And who is this woman that she has got along with her?"

"I have no idea, I'm sure. Some Western friend, I suppose."

"Dear me! I wish they were going to some other house than this," said Lilly discontentedly. "If they were at the Rivoir, for instance, or one of those places at the far end of the beach, we shouldn't need to see anything of them, or even know that they were in town! It's a real nuisance to have people spring upon you this way, people you don't want to meet; and when they happen to be relations it is all the worse. Katy will be hanging on us all the time, I'm afraid."

"Oh, my dear, there is no fear of that! A little repression on our part will prevent her from being any trouble. I'm quite certain. But we *must* treat her politely, you know, Lilly, her father is my cousin."

"That's the saddest part of it! Well, there's one thing, I shall *not* take her with me every time we go to the frigates," said Lilly decisively. "I am not going to inflict a country cousin on Lieutenant Worthington, and spoil all my own fun beside. So I give you fair warning, Mamma, and you must manage it somehow."

"Certainly, dear, I will. It would be a great pity to have your visit to Nice spoiled in any way, with the squadron here, too, and that pleasant Mr. Worthington so very attentive."

Unconscious of these plans for her suppression, Katy walked back to the hotel in a mood of pensive pleasure. Europe at last promised to be as delightful as it had seemed when she only knew it from maps and books, and Nice so far appeared to her the most charming place in the world.

Somebody was waiting for them at the Hôtel des Anglais—a tall, bronzed, good-looking somebody in uniform, with pleasant brown eyes beaming from beneath a gold-banded cap; at the sight of whom Amy rushed forward with her long locks flying, and Mrs. Ashe uttered an exclamation of pleasure. It was Ned Worthington, Mrs.

Ashe's only brother, whom she had not met for two years and a half.

"You got my note then?" she said, after the first eager greetings were over and she had introduced him to Katy.

"Note? No. Did you write me a note?"

"Yes; to Villefranche."

"To the ship? I shan't get that till to-morrow. No; finding out that you were here is just a bit of good fortune. I came over to call on some friends who are staying down the beach a little way, and dropping into look over the list of arrivals, as I generally do, I saw your names; and the porter not being able to say which way you had gone, I waited for you to come in."

"We have been looking at such a delightful old place, the Pension Suisse, and have taken rooms."

"The Pension Suisse, eh? Why, that was where I was going to call. I know some people who are staying there. It seems a pleasant house; I'm glad you are going there, Polly. It's first-rate luck that the ships happen to be here just now. I can see you every day."

"But, Ned, surely you are not leaving me so soon? Surely you will stay and dine with us?" urged his sister, as he took up his cap.

"I wish I could, but I can't to-night, Polly. You see I had engaged to take some ladies out to drive, and they will expect me. I had no idea that you would be here, or I should have kept myself free," apologetically. "To-morrow I will come over early, and be at your service for whatever you like to do."

"That's right, dear boy. We shall expect you." Then the moment he was gone: "Now, Katy, isn't he nice?"

"Very nice, I should think," said Katy, who had watched the brief interview with interest. "I like his face so much, and how fond he is of you!"

"Dear fellow! So he is. I am seven years older than he, but we have always been intimate. Brothers and sisters are not always intimate, you know—or perhaps you don't know, for all of yours are."

"Yes, indeed," said Katy, with a happy smile. "There is nobody like Clover and Elsie, except perhaps Johnnie and

Dorry and Phil," she added, with a laugh.

The remove to the Pension Suisse was made early the next morning. Mrs. Page and Lilly did not appear to welcome them. Katy rather rejoiced in their absence, for she wanted the chance to get into order without interruptions. There was something comfortable in the thought that they were to stay a whole month in these new quarters; for so long a time it seemed worth while to make them pretty homelike. So, while Mrs. Ashe unpacked her own belongings and Amy's, Katy who had a natural turn for arranging rooms, took possession of the little parlour, pulled the furniture into new positions, laid out portfolios and workcases and their few books, pinned various photographs which they had bought in Oxford and London on the walls, and tied back the curtains to admit the sunshine. Then she paid a visit to the little garden, and came back with a long branch of laurustinus, which she trained across the mantelpiece and a bunch of wallflowers for their one little vase. The maid, by her orders, laid a fire of wood and pine cones ready for lighting; and when all was done she called Mrs. Ashe to pronounce upon the effect.

"It is lovely," she said, sinking into a great velvet armchair which Katy had drawn close to the seaward window. "I haven't seen anything so pleasant since we left home. You are a witch, Katy, and the comfort of my life. I am so glad I brought you! Now, pray go and unpack your own things, and make yourself look nice for the second breakfast. We have been a shabby set enough since we arrived. I saw those cousins of yours looking askance at our old travelling-dresses yesterday. Let us try to make a more respectable impression to-day."

So they went down to breakfast, Mrs. Ashe in one of her new Paris gowns, Katy in a pretty dress of olive serge, and Amy all smiles and ruffled pinafore, walking hand in hand with her Uncle Ned, who had just arrived, and whose great ally she was; and Mrs. Page and Lilly, who were already seated at table, had much ado to conceal their somewhat unflattering surprise at the conjunction. For one moment Lilly's eyes opened into a wild stare of incredulous astonishment; then she remembered herself.

nodded as pleasantly as she could to Mrs. Ashe and Katy, and favoured Lieutenant Worthington with a pretty blushing smile as he went by, while she murmured:

"Mamma, do you see that? What does it mean?"

"Why, Ned, do you know those people?" asked Mrs. Ashe at the same moment.

"Do *you* know them?"

"Yes, we met yesterday. They are connections of my friend Miss Carr.'

"Really? There is not the least family likeness between them." And Mr. Worthington's eyes travelled deliberately from Lilly's delicate golden prettiness to Katy, who, truth to say, did not shine by the contrast.

She has a nice, sensible sort of face, he thought, and she looks like a lady, but for beauty there is no comparison between the two. Then he turned to listen to his sister as she replied:

"No, indeed, not the least; no two girls could be less like." Mrs. Ashe had made the same comparison, but with quite a different result. Katy's face had grown dear to her, and she had not taken the smallest fancy to Lilly Page.

Her relationship to the young naval officer, however, made a wonderful difference in the attitude of Mrs. Page and Lilly towards the party. Katy became a person to be cultivated rather than repressed, and thence-forward there was no lack of cordiality on their part.

"I want to come in and have a good talk," said Lilly, slipping her arm through Katy's as they left the dining-room. "Mayn't I come now while mamma is calling on Mrs. Ashe?" This arrangement brought her to the side of Lieutenant Worthington, and she walked between him and Katy down the hall and into the little drawing-room.

"Oh, how perfectly charming! You have been fixing up ever since you came, haven't you? It looks like home. I wish we had a *salon,* but mamma thought it wasn't worth while, as we were only to be here such a little time. What a delicious balcony over the water, too! May I go out on it? Oh, Mr. Worthington, do see this!"

She pushed upon the half-closed window and stepped out as she spoke. Mr. Worthington, after hesitating a moment, followed. Katy paused uncertain. There was hardly room for three on the balcony, yet she did not quite like to leave them. But Lilly had turned her back, and was talking in a low tone; it was nothing more in reality than the lightest chit-chat, but it had the air of being somewhat confidential; so Katy, after waiting a little while, retreated to the sofa and took up her work, joining now and then in the conversation which Mrs. Ashe was keeping up with Cousin Olivia. She did not mind Lilly's ill breeding, nor was she surprised at it. Mrs. Ashe was less tolerant.

"Isn't it rather damp out there, Ned?" she called to her brother; "you had better throw my shawl round Miss Page's shoulders."

"Oh, it isn't a bit damp!" said Lilly, recalled to herself by this broad hint. "Thank you so much for thinking of it, Mrs. Ashe, but I am just coming in." She seated herself beside Katy, and began to question her rather languidly.

"When did you leave home, and how were they all when you came away?"

"All well, thank you. We sailed from Boston on the 14th of October, and before that I spent two days with Rose Red—you remember her? She is married now, and has the dearest little home and such a darling baby!"

"Yes, I heard of her marriage. It didn't seem much of a match for Mr. Redding's daughter to make, did it? I never supposed she would be satisfied with anything less than a member of Congress or a Secretary of Legation."

"Rose isn't particularly ambitious, I think, and she seems perfectly happy," replied Katy flushing.

"Oh, you needn't fire up in her defence! You and Clover always did adore Rose Red, I know, but I never could see what there was about her that was so wonderfully fascinating. She never had the least style, and she was always just as rude to me as she could be."

"You were not intimate at school, but I am sure Rose was never rude," said Katy with spirit.

"Well, we won't fight about her at this late day. Tell me where you have been, and where you are going, and how long you are to stay in Europe."

389

Katy, glad to change the subject, complied, and the conversation diverged into comparisons of plans and experiences. Lilly had been in Europe nearly a year, and had seen "almost everything," as she phrased it. She and her mother had spent the previous winter in Italy, had taken a run into Russia, "done" Switzerland and the Tyrol thoroughly and France and Germany and were soon going to Spain, and from there to Paris, to shop, in preparation for their return home in the spring.

"Of course we shall want quantities of things," she said. "No one will believe that we have been abroad unless we bring home a lot of clothes. The *lingerie* and all that is ordered already; but the dresses must be made at the last moment, and we shall have a horrid time of it, I suppose. Worth has promised to make me two walking-suits and two ball-dresses, but he's very bad about keeping his word. Did you do much when you were in Paris, Katy?"

"We went to the Louvre three times, and to Versailles and St. Cloud," said Katy, wilfully misunderstanding her.

"Oh, I didn't mean that kind of stupid thing! I meant gowns. What did you buy?"

"One tailor-made suit of dark-blue cloth."

"My! What moderation!"

Poor Lilly! Europe to her was all "things." She had collected trunks full of objects to carry home, but of the other collections, which do not go into trunks, she had little or none. Her mind was as empty, her heart as untouched as ever; the beauty and the glory and the pathos of art and history and Nature had been poured out in vain before her closed and indifferent eyes.

Life soon dropped into a peaceful routine at the Pension Suisse, which was at the same time restful and stimulating. Katy's first act in the morning, as soon as she opened her eyes, was to hurry to the window in hopes of getting a glimpse of Corsica. She had discovered that this elusive island could almost always be seen from Nice at the dawning, but that as soon as the sun was fairly up, it vanished, to appear no more for the rest of the day. There was something fascinating to her imagination in the hovering mountain outline between sea and sky. She felt as if she were under an engagement to be there to meet it, and she rarely missed the appointment. Then, after Corsica had pulled the bright mists over its face and melted from view, she would hurry with her dressing, and as soon as was practicable, set to work to make the *salon* look bright before the coffee and rolls should appear, a little after eight o'clock. Mrs. Ashe always found the fire lit, the little meal cosily set out beside it, and Katy's happy untroubled face to welcome her when she emerged from her room; and the cheer of these morning repasts made a good beginning for the day.

Then came walking and a French lesson, and a long sitting on the beach, while Katy worked at her home letters and Amy raced up and down in the sun; and then towards noon Lieutenant Ned generally appeared, and some scheme of pleasure was set on foot. Mrs. Ashe ignored his evident *penchant* for Lilly Page, and claimed his time and attention as hers by right. Young Worthington was a good deal "taken" with the pretty Lilly; still, he had an old-time devotion for his sister and the habit of doing what she desired, and he yielded to her behests with no audible objections. He made a fourth in the carriage while they drove over the lovely hills which encircle Nice towards the north, to Cimiers and the Val de St. André, or down the coast towards Ventimiglia. He went with them to Monte Carlo and Mentone, and was their escort again and again when they visited the great warships as they lay at anchor in a bay which in its translucent blue was like an enormous sapphire.

Mrs. Page and her daughter were included in these parties more than once; but there was something in Mrs. Ashe's cool appropriation of her brother which was infinitely vexatious to Lilly, who before her arrival had looked upon Lieutenant Worthington as her own especial property.

"I wish *that* Mrs. Ashe had stayed at home," she told her mother. "She quite spoils everything. Mr. Worthington isn't half so nice as he was before she came. I do believe she has a plan for making him fall in love with Katy; but there she makes a miss of it, for he doesn't seem to care anything about her."

"Katy is a nice girl enough," pronounced her mother, "but not of the sort to attract a gay young man, I should fancy. I don't believe *she* is thinking of any such thing. You needn't be afraid, Lilly."

"I'm not afraid," said Lilly, with a pout; "only it's so provoking!"

Mrs. Page was quite right. Katy was not thinking of any such thing. She liked Ned Worthington's frank manners; she owned, quite honestly, that she thought him handsome, and she particularly admired the sort of deferential affection which he showed to Mrs. Ashe, and his nice ways with Amy. For herself, she was aware that he scarcely noticed her except as politeness demanded that he should be civil to his sister's friend but the knowledge did not trouble her particularly. Her head was full of interesting things, plans, ideas. She was not accustomed to being made the object of admiration, and experienced none of the vexations of a neglected belle. If Lieutenant Worthington happened to talk to her, she responded frankly and freely; if he did not, she occupied herself with something else; in either case she was quite unembarrassed both in feeling and manner, and had none of the awkwardness which comes from disappointed vanity and baffled expectations, and the need for concealing them.

Towards the close of December the officers of the flagship gave a ball, which was the great event of the season to the gay world of Nice. Americans were naturally in the ascendant on an American frigate; and of all the American girls present, Lilly Page was unquestionably the prettiest. Exquisitely dressed in white lace, with bands of turquoise on her neck and arms and in her hair, she had more partners than she knew what to do with, more bouquets than she could well carry, and compliments enough to turn any girl's head. Thrown off her guard by her triumphs, she indulged a little vindictive feeling which had been growing in her mind of late on account of what she chose to consider certain derelictions of duty on the part of Lieutenant Worthington, and treated him to a taste of neglect. She was engaged three deep when he asked her to dance; she did not hear when he invited her to walk; she turned a cold shoulder when he tried to talk, and seemed absorbed by the other cavaliers, naval and otherwise, who crowded about her.

Piqued and surprised, New Worthington turned to Katy. She did not dance, saying frankly, that she did not know how, and was too tall; and she was rather simply dressed in a pearl-grey silk, which had been her best gown the winter before in Burnet, with a bunch of red roses in the white lace of the tucker, and another in her hand, both the gifts of little Amy; but she looked pleasant and serene, and there was something about her which somehow soothed his disturbed mind, as he offered her his arm for a walk on the decks.

For a while they said little, and Katy was quite content to pace up and down in silence, enjoying the really beautiful scene—the moonlight on the bay, the deep, wavering reflections of the dark hulls and slender spars, the fairy effect of the coloured lamps and lanterns, and the brilliant moving maze of the dancers.

"Do you care for this sort of thing?" he suddenly asked.

"What sort of thing do you mean?"

"Oh, all this jigging and waltzing and amusement!"

"I don't know how to 'jig,' but it's delightful to look on," she answered merrily. "I never saw anything so pretty in my life."

The happy tone of her voice, and the unruffled face which she turned upon him, quieted his irritation.

"I really believe you mean it," he said; "and yet, if you won't think me rude to say so, most girls would consider the thing dull enough if they were only getting out of it what you are—if they were not dancing, I mean, and nobody in particular was trying to entertain them."

"But everything *is* being done to entertain me," cried Katy. "I can't imagine what makes you think that it could seem dull. I am in it all, don't you see—I have my share—— Oh, I am stupid, I can't make you understand!"

"Yes, you do. I understand perfectly, I think; only it is such a different point of view from what girls in general would take." (By girls he meant Lilly!) "Please do not think me uncivil."

"You are not uncivil at all; but don't let us talk any more about me. Look at the lights between the shadows of the masts on the water. How they quiver! I never saw anything so beautiful, I think. And how warm it is! I can't believe that we are in December and that it is nearly Christmas."

"How is Polly going to celebrate her Christmas? Have you decided?"

"Amy is to have a Christmas tree for her dolls, and two other dolls are coming. We went out this morning to buy things for it—tiny little toys and candles fit for Lilliput. And that reminds me, do you suppose one can get any Christmas greens here?"

"Why not? The place seems full of green."

"That's just it; the summer looks makes it unnatural. But I should like some to dress the parlour with, if they could be had."

"I'll see what I can find, and send you a load."

I don't know why this very simple little talk should have made an impression on Lieutenant Worthington's mind, but somehow he did not forget it.

" 'Don't let us talk any more about me'," he said to himself, that night when alone in his cabin. "I wonder how long it would be before the other one did anything to divert the talk from herself. Some time, I fancy." He smiled rather grimly as he unbuckled his sword-belt. It is unlucky for a girl when she starts a train of reflection like this. Lilly's little attempt to pique her admirer had somehow missed its mark.

Amy played on the beach the next afternoon, while Katy, in her favourite place on the beach, was at work on the long weekly letter which she never failed to send home to Burnet. She held her portfolio in her lap, and her pen ran rapidly over the paper.

She was suddenly interrupted by a crunching step on the gravel behind her.

"Good afternoon!" said a Voice. "Polly has sent me to fetch you and Amy in. She says it is growing cool."

"We were just coming," said Katy, beginning to put away her papers.

Ned Worthington sat down on the cloak beside her. The distance was now steel grey against the sky; then came a stripe of violet, and then a broad sheet of the vivid iridescent blue which one sees on the necks of peacocks, which again melted into the long line of flashing surf.

"Are you going?" said Lieutenant Worthington in a tone of surprise, as she rose.

"Didn't you say that Polly wanted us to come in?"

"Why, yes; but it seems too good to leave, doesn't it? Oh, by the way, Miss Carr, I came across a man to-day and ordered your greens! They will be sent on Christmas Eve. Is that right?"

"Quite right, and we are ever so much obliged to you." She turned for a last look at the sea, and, unseen by Ned Worthington, formed her lips into a "good night." Katy had made great friends with the Mediterranean.

The promised "greens" appeared on the afternoon before Christmas Day, in the shape of an enormous fagot of laurel and laurustinus and holly and box, orange and lemon boughs with ripe fruit hanging from them, thick ivy tendrils whole yards long, arbutus, pepper-tree, and great branches of acacia, covered with feathery yellow bloom. The man apologised for bringing so little. The gentleman had ordered two francs' worth, he said, but this was all he could carry; he would fetch some more if the young lady wished. But Katy, exclaiming with delight over her wealth, wished no more; so the man departed, and the three friends proceeded to turn the little *salon* into a fairy bower. Every photograph and picture was wreathed in ivy, long garlands hung on either side of the windows, and the chimney-piece and door-frames became clustering banks of leaf and blossom.

Mabel and Mary Matilda, and their two doll visitors, sat gravely round the table, in the laps of their little mistresses; and Katy, putting on an apron and an improvised cap, and speaking Irish very fast, served them with a repast of rolls and cocoa, raspberry jam, and delicious little

395

almond cakes. The fun waxed fast and furious, and Lieutenant Worthington, coming in with his hands full of parcels for the Christmas tree, was just in time to hear Katy remark in a strong County Kerry brogue:

"Och, thin indade, Miss Amy, and it's no more cake you'll be getting out of me the night. That's four pieces you've ate, and it's little shlape your poor mother'll git with you a-tossin' and tumblin' forenenst her all night long because of your big appetite."

"Oh, Miss Katy, talk Irish some more!" cried Amy.

"Is it Irish you'd be afther having me talk, when it's me own langwidge, and sorrow a bit of another do I know?" demanded Katy. Then she caught sight of the new arrival and stopped short with a blush and a laugh.

"Come in, Mr. Worthington," she said; "we're at supper, as you see, and I am acting as waitress."

"Oh, Uncle Ned, please go away," pleaded Amy, "or Katy will be polite, and not talk Irish any more!"

"Indade, and the less ye say about politeness the better, when ye're afther ordering the jantleman out of the room in that fashion!" said the waitress. Then she pulled off her cap and untied her apron.

"Now for the Christmas tree," she said.

It was a very little tree, but it bore some remarkable fruits; for in addition to the "tiny toys and candles fit for Lilliput," various parcels were found to have been hastily added at the last moment for various people. The *Natchitoches* had lately come from the Levant, and delightful Oriental confections now appeared for Amy and Mrs. Ashe; Turkish slippers, all gold embroidery; towels, with richly decorated ends in silks and tinsel;— all the pretty superfluities which the East holds out to charm gold from the pockets of her Western visitors. A pretty little dagger in agate and silver fell to Katy's share out of what Lieutenant Worthington called his "loot"; and, besides, a most beautiful specimen of the inlaid work for which Nice is famous—a looking-glass, with a stand and little doors to close it in—which was a present from Mrs. Ashe. It was quite unlike a Christmas Eve at home, but altogether delightful; and as Katy sat next morning on the sand, after service in the English church, to finish her home letter, and felt the sun warm on her cheek, and the perfumed air blow past as softly as in June, she had to remind herself that Christmas is not necessarily synonymous with snow and winter, but means the great central heat and warmth, the advent of Him who came to lighten the whole earth.

A few days after this pleasant Christmas they left Nice. All of them felt a reluctance to move, and Amy loudly bewailed the necessity.

"If I could stay here till it is time to go home, I shouldn't be home-sick at all," she declared.

"But what a pity it would be not to see Italy!" said her mother. "Think of Naples and Rome and Venice!"

"I don't want to think about them. It makes me feel as if I was studying a great long geography lesson, and it tires me so to learn it."

"Amy, dear, you're not well."

"Yes I am—quite well; only I don't want to go away from Nice."

"You only have to learn a little bit at a time of your geography lesson, you know," suggested Katy; "and it's a great deal nicer way to study it than out of a book." But though she spoke cheerfully she was conscious that she shared Amy's reluctance.

"It's all laziness," she told herself. "Nice has been so pleasant that it has spoiled me."

The next day brought them to Genoa, to a hotel once the stately palace of an archbishop, where they were lodged, all three together, in an enormous room, so high and broad and long that their three little curtained beds, set behind a screen of carved wood, made no impression on the space. There were no less than four sofas and double that number of arm-chairs in the room, besides a couple of monumental wardrobes; but, as Katy remarked, several grand pianos could still have been moved in without anybody's feeling crowded. On one side of them lay the port of Genoa, filled with crafts from all parts of the world, and flying the flags of a dozen different nations.

From the other they caught glimpses of the magnificent old city, rising in tier over tier of churches and palaces and gardens; while nearer still were narrow streets, which glittered with gold filigree and the shops of jewel-workers. And while they went in and out, and gazed and wondered, Lilly Page, at the Pension Suisse, was saying:

"I am so glad that Katy and *that* Mrs. Ashe are gone! Nothing has been so pleasant since they came. Lieutenant Worthington is dreadfully stiff and stupid, and seems quite different from what he used to be. But now that we have got rid of them it will all come right again."

"I really don't think Katy was to blame," said Mrs. Page. "She never seemed to me to be making any effort to attract him."

"Oh, Katy is sly!" responded Lilly vindictively. "She never *seems* to do anything, but somehow she always gets her own way. I suppose she thought I didn't see her keeping him down there on the beach the other day when he was coming in to call on us, but I did. It was just out of spite, and because she wanted to vex me; I know it was."

"Well, dear, she's gone now, and you won't be worried with her again," said her mother soothingly. "Don't pout so, Lilly, and wrinkle up your forehead. It's very unbecoming."

"Yes, she's gone," snapped Lilly; "and as she's bound for the east, and we for the west, we are not likely to meet again, for which I am devoutly thankful."

CHAPTER VIII

ON THE TRACK OF ULYSSES

"WE ARE going to follow the track of Ulysses," said Katy, with her eyes fixed on the little travelling-map in her guide-book. "Do you realise that, Polly dear? He and his companions sailed these very seas before us, and we shall see the sights they saw—Circe's Cape and the Isles of the Sirens, and Polyphemus himself, perhaps—who knows?"

The *Marco Polo* had just cast off her moorings, and was slowly steaming out of the crowded port of Genoa into the heart of a still rosy sunset. The water was perfectly smooth; no motion could be felt but the engine's throb. The trembling foam of the long wake showed glancing points of phosphorescence here and there, while low on the eastern sky a great silver planet burned like a signal-lamp.

"Polly dear," said Katy, who was in the highest spirits. "There is one delightful thing I forgot to tell you about! The captain says we shall stay in Leghorn all day tomorrow and we shall have plenty of time to run up to Pisa and see the Cathedral and the Leaning Tower. Now, that is something Ulysses didn't do! I am so glad I didn't die of measles when I was little, as Rose Red used to say!" She gave her book a toss into the air as she spoke, and caught it again as it fell, very much as the Katy Carr of twelve years ago might have done.

"What a child you are!" said Mrs. Ashe approvingly; "you never seem out of sorts or tired of things."

"Out of sorts! I should think not! And pray why should I be, Polly dear?"

Katy had taken to calling her friend "Polly dear" of late—a trick picked up half-unconsciously from Lieutenant

Ned. Mrs. Ashe liked it; it was sisterly and intimate, she said, and made her feel nearer Katy's age.

"Does the tower really lean?" questioned Amy—"far over, I mean, so that we can see it?"

"We shall know to-morrow," replied Katy. "If it doesn't, I shall lose all my confidence in human nature."

Katy's confidence in human nature was not doomed to be impaired. There stood the famous tower, when they reached the Place del Duomo in Pisa, next morning, look-

The very air seemed full of eager faces

ing all aslant, exactly as it does in the pictures and the alabaster models, and seeming as if in another moment it must topple over, from its own weight, upon their heads. Mrs. Ashe declared that it was so unnatural that it made her flesh creep; and when she was coaxed up the winding staircase to the top, she turned so giddy that they were all thankful to get her safely down to firm ground again. She turned her back upon the tower, as they crossed the grassy space to the majestic old Cathedral, saying that if she thought about it any more, she should become a disbeliever in the attraction of gravitation, which she had always been told all respectable people *must* believe in.

The guide showed them the lamp, swinging by a long, slender chain, before which Galileo is said to have sat and pondered while he worked out his theory of the pendulum. This lamp seemed a sort of own cousin to the attraction of gravitation, and they gazed upon it with respect. Then they went to the Baptistery to see Niccolo Pisano's magnificent pulpit of creamy marble, a mass of sculpture supported on the backs of lions, and the equally lovely font, and to admire the extraordinary sound which their guide evoked from a mysterious echo, with which he seemed to be on intimate terms, for he made it say whatever he would, and almost "answer back."

Their way to the hotel where they were to lunch led them through a narrow street inhabited by the poorer classes—a dusty street with high shabby buildings on either side and wide doorways giving glimpses of interior courtyards. As is usual in poor streets, there were swarms of children; and the appearance of little Amy with her long bright hair falling over her shoulders, and Mabel clasped in her arms, created a great sensation. The children in the street shouted and exclaimed, and other children within the houses heard the sounds and came trooping out. The very air seemed full of eager faces and little brown and curly heads bobbing up and down with excitement, and black eyes fixed upon big beautiful Mabel, who with her thick wig of flaxen hair, her blue velvet dress and jacket, feathered hat and little muff, seemed to them like some strange small marvel from another world. They could not decide whether she was a living child or a make-believe one, but they dared not come near enough to find out; so they clustered at a little distance, pointed with their fingers, and whispered and giggled, while Amy, much pleased with the admiration shown for her darling, lifted Mabel up to view.

At last one droll little girl with a white cap on her round

head seemed to make up her mind, and, darting indoors, returned with *her* doll—a poor little image of wood, its only garment a coarse shirt of red cotton. This she held out for Amy to see. Amy smiled for the first time since meeting the children and Katy, taking Mabel from her, made signs that the two dolls should kiss each other. But though the little Italian screamed with laughter at the idea of a *bacio* between two dolls, she would by no means allow it, and hid her treasure behind her back, blushing and giggling, and saying something very fast which none of them understood, while she waved two fingers at them with a curious gesture.

"I do believe she is afraid Mabel will cast the evil eye on her doll," said Katy at last, with a sudden understanding as to what this pantomime meant.

"Why, you silly thing," cried the outraged Amy: "do you suppose for one moment that my child could hurt your dirty old dolly? You ought to be glad to have her noticed at all by anybody that's clean."

The sound of the foreign tongue completed the discomfiture of the little Italian. With a shriek she fled, and all the other children after her; pausing at a distance to look back at the alarming creatures who didn't speak the familiar language. Katy, wishing to leave a pleasant impression, made Mabel kiss her waxen fingers towards them. This sent the children off into another fit of laughter and chatter, and they followed our friends for quite a distance as they proceeded on their way to the hotel.

All that night, over a sea as smooth as glass, the *Marco Polo* slipped along the coasts past which the ships of Ulysses sailed in those old legendary days which wear so charmed a light to our modern eyes. Katy roused at three in the morning, and, looking from her cabin window, had a glimpse of an island, which her map showed her must be Elba, where that war-eagle Napoleon was chained for a while. Then she fell asleep again, and when she roused in full daylight the steamer was off the coast of Ostia and nearing the mouth of the Tiber. Dreamy mountain-shapes rose beyond the far-away Campagna, and every curve and every indentation of the coast bore a name which recalled some interesting thing.

About eleven a dim-drawn bubble appeared on the horizon, which the captain assured them was the dome of St. Peter's, nearly thirty miles distant. This was one of the "moments" which Clover had been fond of speculating about; and Katy, contrasting the real with the imaginary moment, could not help smiling. Neither she nor Clover had ever supposed that her first glimpse of the great dome was to be so little impressive.

That night, the *Marco Polo* sailed into the Bay of of Naples, past Vesuvius, whose dusky curl of smoke could be seen outlined against the luminous sky, and brought her passengers to their landing-place.

They woke next morning to a summer atmosphere full of yellow sunshine and true July warmth. Flower-vendors stood on every corner, and pursued each newcomer with their fragrant wares. Katy could not stop exclaiming over the cheapness of the flowers, which were thrust in at the carriage windows as they drove slowly up and down the streets. They were tied into flat nosegays, whose centre was a white camellia, encircled with concentric rows of pink tea-rosebuds, ring after ring, till the whole was the size of an ordinary milk-pan; all to be had for the sum of ten cents! But after they had bought two or three of these enormous bouquets, and had discovered that not a single rose boasted an inch of stem, and that all were pierced with long wires through their very hearts, she ceased to care for them.

"I would rather have one Souvenir or General Jaqueminot, with a long stem and plenty of leaves, than a dozen of these stiff platters of bouquets," Katy told Mrs. Ashe. But when they drove beyond the city gates, and the coachman came to anchor beneath walls overhung with the same roses, and she found that she might stand on the seat and pull down as many branches of the lovely flowers as she desired, and gather wallflowers for herself out of the clefts in the masonry, she was entirely satisfied.

"This is the Italy of my dreams," she said.

With all its beauty there was an underlying sense of

danger about Naples, which interfered with their enjoyment of it. Evil smells came in at the windows, or confronted them as they went about the city. There seemed something deadly in the air. Whispered reports met their ears of cases of fever, which the landlords of the hotels were doing their best to hush up. An American gentleman was said to be lying very ill at one house. A lady had died the week before at another. Mrs. Ashe grew nervous.

"We will just take a rapid look at a few of the principal things," she told Katy, "and then get away as fast as we can. Amy is so on my mind that I have no peace of my life. I keep feeling her pulse and imagining that she does not look right; and though I know it is all my fancy, I am impatient to be off. You won't mind, will you, Katy?"

After that everything they did was done in a hurry. Katy felt as if she were being driven about by a cyclone, as they rushed from one sight to another, filling up all the chinks between with shopping, which was irresistible where everything was so pretty and so wonderfully cheap. She herself purchased a tortoise-shell fan and chain for Rose Red, and had her monogram carved upon it; a coral locket for Elsie; some studs for Dorry; and for her father a small, beautiful vase of bronze, copied from one of the Pompeian antiques.

"How charming it is to have money to spend in such a place as this!" she said to herself, with a sigh of satisfaction, as she surveyed these delightful buyings. "I only wish I could get ten times as many things and take them to ten times as many people. Papa was so wise about it! I can't think how it is that he always knows beforehand exactly how people are going to feel, and what they will want!"

Mrs. Ashe also bought a great many things for herself and Amy, and to take home as presents; and it was all very pleasant and satisfactory, except for that subtle sense of danger from which they could not escape and which made them glad to go. "See Naples and die," says the old adage; and the saying has proved sadly true in the case of many an American traveller.

Besides the talk of fever there was also a good deal of

gossip about brigands going about, as is generally the case in Naples and its vicinity. Something was said to have happened to a party on one of the heights above Sorrento; and though nobody knew exactly what the something was, or was willing to vouch for the story, Mrs. Ashe and Katy felt a good deal of trepidation as they entered the carriage which was to take them to the neighbourhood where the mysterious "something" had occurred.

It is a pity that the beautiful drive should have been wasted on Mrs. Ashe and Katy, but they were too frightened to half enjoy it. Their carriage was driven by a shaggy young savage, who looked quite wild enough to be a bandit himself. He cracked his whip loudly as they rolled along, and every now and then gave a long shrill whistle. Mrs. Ashe was sure that these were signals to his band, who were lurking somewhere on the olive-hung hillsides. She thought she detected him once or twice making signs to certain questionable-looking characters as they passed; and she fancied that the people they met gazed at them with an air of commiseration, as upon victims who were being carried to execution. Her fears affected Katy; so, though they talked and laughed, and made jokes to amuse Amy, who must not be scared or led to suppose that anything was amiss, and to the outward view seemed a very merry party, they were privately quaking in their shoes all the way, and enjoying a deal of highly superfluous misery. And after all they reached Sorrento in perfect safety; and the driver, who looked so dangerous, turned out to be a respectable young man, with a wife and family to support, who considered a plateful of macaroni and a glass of sour red wine as the height of luxury, and was grateful for a small gratuity of thirty cents or so, which would enable him to purchase these dainties. Mrs. Ashe had a very bad headache next day, to pay for her fright; but she and Katy agreed that they had been very foolish, and resolved to pay no more attention to unaccredited rumours or allow them to spoil their enjoyment, which was a sensible resolution to make.

Their hotel was perched directly over the sea. From the balcony of their sitting-room they looked down a sheer cliff some sixty feet high, into the water; their bedrooms opened on a garden of roses, with an orange grove beyond. Not far from them was the great gorge which cuts the little town of Sorrento almost in two, and whose seaward end makes the harbour of the place. Katy was never tired of peering down into this strange and beautiful cleft, whose sides, two hundred feet in depth, are hung with vines and trailing growths of all sorts, and seem all a-tremble with the fairy fronds of maiden-hair ferns growing out of every chink and crevice.

They made two different excursions to Pompeii, which is within easy distance of Sorrento. They scrambled on donkeys over the hills, and had glimpses of the far-away Calabrian shore, of the natural arch, and the temples of Pæstum shining in the sun many miles distant. On Katy's birthday, which fell towards the end of January, Mrs. Ashe let her have her choice of a treat; and she elected to go to the Island of Capri, which none of them had seen. It turned out a perfect day, with sea and wind exactly right for the sail, and for getting into the famous "Blue Grotto," which can only be entered under particular conditions of tide and weather. And they climbed the great cliff-rise at the island's end, and saw the ruins of the villa built by the wicked emperor Tiberius, and the awful place known as his "Leap," down which, it is said, he made his victims throw themselves; and they lunched at a hotel which bore his name, and just at sunset pushed off again for the row home over the charmed sea. This return voyage was almost the pleasantest thing of all the day. The water was smooth, the moon at its full. It was larger and more brilliant than American moons are, and seemed to possess an actual warmth and colour. The boatmen timed their oar-strokes to the cadence of Neopolitan *barcaroles* and folk-songs, full of rhythmic movement, which seemed caught from the pulsing tides. And when at last the bow grated on the sands of the Sorrento landing-place, Katy drew a long, regretful breath, and declared that this was her best birth-day-gift of all, better than Amy's flowers, or the pretty tortoise-shell locket that Mrs. Ashe had given her, better even than the letter from home, which, timed by happy accident, had arrived by the morning's post to make a bright opening for the day.

But all pleasant things must come to an end.

"Katy," said Mrs. Ashe, one afternoon in early February, "I heard some ladies talking just now in the *salon*, and they said that Rome is filling up very fast. The Carnival begins in less than two weeks, and everybody wants to be there then. If we don't make haste we shall not be able to get any rooms."

"Oh dear!" said Katy, "it is very trying not to be able to be in two places at once. I want to see Rome dreadfully, and yet I cannot bear to leave Sorrento. We have been very happy there, haven't we?"

So they took up their wandering staves again, and departed for Rome, like the Apostle, "not knowing what should befall them there."

CHAPTER IX

A ROMAN HOLIDAY

"OH dear!" said Mrs. Ashe, as she folded her letters and laid them aside, "I wish those Pages would go away from Nice, or else that the frigates were not there."

"Why, what's the matter?" asked Katy, looking up from the many-leaved journal from Clover over which she was poring.

"Nothing is the matter except that those everlasting people haven't gone to Spain yet, as they said they would, and Ned seems to keep on seeing them," replied Mrs. Ashe petulantly.

"But, dear Polly, what difference does it make? And they never did promise you to go at any particular time, did they?"

"N-o, they didn't; but I wish they would, all the same. Not that Ned is such a goose as really to care anything for that foolish Lilly!" Then she gave a little laugh at her own inconsistency, and added: "But I oughtn't to abuse her when she is your cousin."

"Don't mention it," said Katy cheerfully. "But really, I don't see why poor Lilly need worry you so, Polly dear."

The room in which this conversation took place was on the very topmost floor of the Hotel del Mondo in Rome. It was large and many-windowed; and though there was a little bed in one corner half-hidden behind a calico screen, with a bureau and washing-stand, and a sort of stout mahogany hat-tree on which Katy's dresses and jackets were hanging, the remaining space, with a sofa and easy-chairs grouped round a fire, and a round table furnished with books and a lamp, was ample enough to make a good substitute for the private sitting-room which Mrs. Ashe had not been able to procure on account of the near approach of the Carnival and the consequent crowding of strangers to Rome. In fact, she was assured that under the circumstances she was lucky in finding rooms as good as these; and she made the most of the assurance as a consolation for the somewhat unsatisfactory food and service of the hotel, and the four long flights of stairs which must be passed every time they needed to reach the dining-room or the street door.

The party had been in Rome only four days, but already they had seen a host of interesting things. They had stood in the strange sunken space with its marble floor and broken columns, which is all that is left of the great Roman Forum. They had visited the Colosseum, at that period still overhung with ivy garlands and trailing greeneries, and not, as now, scraped clean and bare and "tidied" out of much of its picturesqueness. They had seen the Baths of Caracalla and the Temple of Janus and St. Peter's and the Vatican Marbles, and had driven out on the Campagna and to the Pamphili-Doria Villa to gather purple and red anemones, and to the English cemetery to see the grave of Keats. They had also peeped into certain shops, and attended a reception at the American Minister's—in short, like most unwarned travellers, they had done about twice as much as prudence and experience would have permitted, had those worthies been consulted.

All the romance of Katy's nature responded to the fascination of the ancient city—the capital of the world, as it may truly be called. The shortest drive or walk brought them face to face with innumerable and unexpected delights. No matter what it was,—a bit of oddly-tinted masonry with a tuft of brown and orange wall-flowers hanging upon it, or a vegetable stall where endive and chicory and curly lettuces were arranged in wreaths with tiny orange gourds and scarlet peppers for points of colour, it was all Rome, and, by virtue of that word, different from any other place—more suggestive, more interesting, ten times more mysterious than any other could possibly be, so Katy thought.

This fact consoled her for everything and anything—for the fleas, the dirt, for the queer things they had to eat and the still queerer odours they were forced to smell! Nothing seemed of any particular consequence except the deep sense of enjoyment, and the newly-discovered world of thought and sensation of which she had become suddenly conscious.

The only drawback to her happiness as the days went on, was that little Amy did not seem quite well or like herself. She had taken a cold on the journey from Naples, and though it did not seem serious, that, or something, made her look pale and thin. Her mother said she was growing fast; but the explanation did not quite account for the wistful look in the child's eyes and the tired feeling of which she continually complained. Mrs. Ashe, with vague uneasiness, began to talk of cutting short their Roman stay and getting Amy off to the more bracing air of Florence. But meanwhile there was the Carnival close at hand, which they must by no means lose; and the feeling that their opportunity might be a brief one made her and Katy all the more anxious to make the very most of their time. So they filled the days full with sights to see and things to do, and came and went; sometimes taking Amy with them, but more often leaving her at the hotel under the care of a kind German chambermaid, who spoke pretty good English and to whom Amy had taken a fancy.

The roof, which Amy had chosen as a play-place, covered the whole of the great hotel, and had been turned into a sort of upper-air garden by the simple process of gravelling it all over, placing trellises of ivy here and there, and setting tubs of oranges and oleanders and boxes of gay geraniums and stock-gilly-flowers on the balustrades. A tame fawn was tethered there. Amy adopted him as a playmate; and what with his company and that of the flowers, the times when mother and Katy were absent from her passed not unhappily.

Katy always repaired to the roof as soon as they came in from their long mornings and afternoons of sightseeing. Years afterwards, she would remember with contrition how pathetically glad Amy always was to see her. She would put her little head on Katy's breast and hold her tight for many minutes without saying a word. When she did speak it was always about the house and the garden that she talked. She never asked any questions as to where Katy had been, or what she had done; it seemed to tire her to think about it.

"I should be very lonely sometimes if it were not for my dear little fawn," she told Katy once. "He is so sweet that I don't miss you and mamma very much while I have him to play with. I call him Florio—don't you think that is a pretty name? I like to stay with him a great deal better than to go about with you to those nasty-smelling old churches, with fleas hopping all over them!"

So Amy was left in peace with her fawn, and the others made haste to see all they could before the time came to go to Florence.

Katy realised one of the "moments" for which she had come to Europe when she stood for the first time on the balcony, overhanging the Corso, which Mrs. Ashe had hired in company with some acquaintances made at the hotel, and looked down at the ebb and surge of the just-begun Carnival. The narrow street seemed humming with people of all sorts and conditions. Some were masked, some were not. There were ladies and gentlemen in fashionable clothes, peasants in the gayest costumes, surprised-looking tourists in tall hats and linen dusters, harlequins, clowns, devils, nuns, dominoes of every colour—red, white, blue, black; while above, the balconies bloomed like a rose-garden with pretty faces framed in lace veils or picturesque hats. Flowers were everywhere wreathed along the house-fronts, tied to the horses' ears, in ladies' hands and gentlemen's button-holes, while vendors went up and down the street bearing great trays of violets and carnations and camellias for sale. The air was full of cries and laughter, and the shrill calls of merchants advertising their wares—candy, fruit, birds, lanterns, and *confetti*, the latter being merely lumps of lime, large or small, with a pea or a bean embedded in each lump to give it weight. Boxes full of this unpleasant confection were suspended in front of each balcony, with tin scoops to use in ladling it out and flinging it about. Everybody wore or carried a wire mask as protection against this white, incessant shower, and before long the air became full of a fine dust, which hung above the Corso like a mist, and filled the eyes and noses and clothes of all present with irritating particles.

Pasquino's Car was passing underneath just as Katy and Mrs. Ashe arrived—a gorgeous affair, hung with silken draperies, and bearing as symbol an enormous egg in which the Carnival was supposed to be in act of incubation. A huge wagon followed in its wake, on which was a house some sixteen feet square, whose sole occupant was a gentleman attended by five servants, who kept him supplied with *confetti*, which he showered liberally on the heads of the crowd. Then came a car in the shape of a steamboat, with a smoke-pipe and sails, over which flew the Union Jack, and which was manned with a party wearing the dress of British tars. The next wagon bore a company of jolly maskers equipped with many-coloured bladders, which they banged and rattled as they went along. Following this was a troupe of beautiful circus-horses, cream-coloured with scarlet trappings, or sorrel with blue, ridden by ladies in pale-green velvet laced with silver or blue velvet and gold. Another car bore a bird-cage which was an exact imitation of St. Peter's, within which perched a lonely old parrot. This device evi-

411

dently had a political signification, for it was alternately hissed and applauded as it went along. The whole scene was like a brilliant, rapidly-shifting dream; and Katy, as she stood with lips apart and eyes wide open with wonderment and pleasure, forgot whether she was in the body or not—forgot everything except what was passing before her gaze.

Exactly opposite them was a balcony hung with white silk, in which sat a lady who seemed to be of some distinction; for every now and then an officer in brilliant uniform, or some official covered with orders, and stars, would be shown in by her servants, bow before her with the utmost deference, and after a little conversation retire, kissing her gloved hand as he went. The lady was a beautiful person, with lustrous black eyes and dark hair, over which a lace mantilla was fastened with diamond stars. She wore pale-blue with white flowers, and altogether, as Katy afterwards wrote to Clover, reminded her exactly of one of those beautiful princesses whom they used to play about in their childhood and quarrel over, because every one of them wanted to be the Princess and nobody else.

"I wonder who she is," said Mrs. Ashe in a low tone. "She might be almost anybody from her looks. She keeps glancing across to us, Katy. Do you know, I think she has taken a fancy to you."

Perhaps the lady had; for just then she turned her head and said a word to one of her footmen, who immediately placed something in her hand. It was a little shining bon-bonniére, and, rising, she threw it straight at Katy. Alas, it struck the edge of the balcony and fell into the street below, where it was picked up by a ragged little peasant girl in a red jacket, who raised a pair of astonished eyes to the heavens, as if sure that the gift must have fallen straight from thence. Katy bent forward to watch its fate, and went through a little pantomime of regret and despair for the benefit of the opposite lady, who only laughed, and, taking another from her servant, flung with better aim, so that it fell exactly at Katy's feet. This was a gilded box in the shape of a mandolin, with sugar-plums tucked cunningly away inside. Katy kissed both her hands in acknowledgement for the pretty toy, and tossed back a bunch of roses which she happened to be wearing in her dress. After that it seemed the chief amusement of the fair unknown to throw bonbons at Katy. Some went straight and some did not; but before the afternoon ended, Katy had quite a lapful of confections and trifles—roses, sugared almonds, a satin casket, a silvered box in the shape of a horse-shoe, a tiny cage with orange blossoms for birds on the perches, a minute gondola with a *marron glacée* by way of passenger, and, prettiest of all, a little ivory harp strung with enamelled violets instead of wires. For all these favours she had nothing better to offer, in return, than a few long-tailed bonbons with gay streamers of ribbon. These the lady opposite caught very cleverly, rarely missing one, and kissing her hands in thanks each time.

"Isn't she exquisite?" demanded Katy, her eyes shining with excitement. "Did you ever see anyone so lovely in your life, Polly, dear? I never did. There, now! She is buying those birds to set them free, I do believe."

It was indeed so. A vendor of larks had, by the aid of a long staff, thrust a cage full of wretched little prisoners up into the balcony; and "Katy's lady," as Mrs. Ashe called her was paying for the whole. As they watched she opened the cage door and with the sweetest look on her face encouraged the birds to fly away. The poor little creatures cowered and hesitated, not knowing at first what use to make of their new liberty; but at last one, the boldest of the company, hopped to the door, and with a glad exultant chirp flew straight upwards. Then the others, taking courage from this example, followed, and all were lost to view in the twinkling of an eye.

"Oh, you angel!" cried Katy, leaning over the edge of the balcony and kissing both hands impulsively. "I never saw anything so sweet as you are in my life. Polly dear, I think carnivals are the most perfectly bewitching things in the world. How glad I am that this lasts a week, and that we can come every day! Won't Amy be delighted with these bonbons! I do hope my lady will be here tomorrow."

How little she dreamed that she was never to enter that

balcony again! How little can any of us see what lies before us till it comes so near that we cannot help seeing it, or shut our eyes, or turn away!

The next morning, almost as soon as it was light, Mrs. Ashe tapped at Katy's door. She was in her dressing-gown, and her eyes looked large and frightened.

"Amy is ill," she cried. "She has been hot and feverish all night, and she says that her head aches dreadfully. What shall I do, Katy? We ought to have a doctor at once, and I don't know the name even of any doctor here."

Katy sat up in bed, and for one bewildered moment did not speak. Her brain felt in a whirl of confusion; but presently it cleared, and she saw what to do.

"I will write a note to Mrs. Sands," she said. Mrs. Sands was the wife of the American Minister, and one of the few acquaintances they had made since they came to Rome. "You remember how nice she was the other day, and how we liked her; and she has lived here so long that of course she must know all about the doctors. Don't you think that is the best thing to do?"

"The very best," said Mrs. Ashe, looking relieved. "I wonder I did not think of it myself, but I am so confused that I can't think. Write the note at once, please, dear Katy. I will ring your bell for you, and then I must hurry back to Amy."

Katy made haste with the note. The answer came promptly in half an hour, and by ten o'clock the physician recommended appeared. Dr. Hilary was a dark little Italian to all appearance; but his mother had been a Scotchwoman, and he spoke English very well—a great comfort to poor Mrs. Ashe, who knew not a word of Italian and not a great deal of French. He felt Amy's pulse for a long time, and took her temperature; but he gave no positive opinion, only left a prescription, and said that he would call later in the day, and should then be able to judge more clearly what the attack was likely to prove.

Katy augured ill from this reserve. There was no talk of going to the Carnival that afternoon; no one had any heart for it. Instead, Katy spent the time in trying to recollect all she had ever heard about the care of sick people.

All night Amy grew worse, and when Dr. Hilary came next day, he was forced to utter plainly the dreaded words "Roman fever." Amy was in for an attack—a light one he hoped it might be—but they had better know the truth and make ready for it.

Mrs. Ashe was utterly overwhelmed by this verdict, and for the first bewildered moments did not know which way to turn. Katy, happily, kept a steadier head. She had the advantage of a little preparation of thought, and had decided beforehand what it would be necessary to do "in case." Oh, that fateful "in case"! The doctor and she consulted together, and the result was that Katy sought out the *padrona* of the establishment, and without hinting at the nature of Amy's attack, secured some rooms just vacated, which were at the end of a corridor, and a little removed from the rooms of other people. There was a large room with corner windows, a smaller one opening from it, and another, still smaller, close by, which would serve as a storeroom or might do for the use of a nurse.

When all was ready, Amy, well wrapped in her coverings, was carried down the entry and laid in the fresh bed with soft pillows about her; and Katy, as she went to and fro, conveying clothes and books and filling drawers, felt that they were perhaps making arrangements for a long, hard trial of faith and spirits.

By the next day the necessity of a nurse became apparent, and in the afternoon Katy started out in a little hired carriage in search of one. She had a list of names, and went first to the English nurses; but, finding them all engaged, she ordered the coachman to drive to a convent where there was hope that a nursing-sister might be procured.

Their route lay across the Corso. So utterly had the Carnival with all its gay follies vanished from her mind that she was for a moment astonished at finding herself entangled in a motley crowd, so dense that the coachman was obliged to rein in his horses and stand still for some time.

There were the same masks and dominoes, the same picturesque peasant costumes which had struck her as so gay and pretty only three days before. The same jests and merry laughter filled the air, but somehow it all seemed out of tune. The sense of cold, lonely fear that had taken possession of her killed all capacity for merriment; the apprehension and solicitude of which her heart was full made the gay chattering and squeaking of the crowd sound harsh and unfeeling. The bright colours affronted her dejection; she did not want to see them. She lay back in the carriage, trying to be patient under the detention, and half shut her eyes.

A shower of lime-dust aroused her. It came from a party of burly figures in white cotton dominoes, whose carriage had been stayed by the crowd close to her own. She signified by gestures that she had no *confetti* and no protection, that she "was not playing," in fact; but her appeal made no difference. The maskers kept on shovelling lime all over her hair and person and the carriage and never tired of the sport till an opportune break in the procession enabled their vehicle to move on.

The convent was propitious, and promised to send a sister next morning, with the proviso that every second day she was to come back to sleep and rest. Katy was too thankful for any aid to make objections, and drove home with visions of saintly nuns with pure, pale faces full of peace and resignation, such as she had read of in books, floating before her eyes.

Sister Ambrogia, when she appeared next day, did not exactly realise these imaginations. She was a plump little person, with rosy cheeks, a pair of demure black eyes, and a very obstinate mouth and chin. It soon appeared that natural inclination, combined with the rules of her convent, made her theory of a nurse's duties a very limited one.

In fact, all that Sister Ambrogia seemed able or willing to do, beyond the bathing of Amy's face and brushing her hair, which she accomplished handily, was to sit by the bedside telling her rosary, or plying a little ebony shuttle in the manufacture of a long strip of tatting. Even this amount of usefulness was interfered with by the fact that Amy, who by this time was in a semi-delirious condition, had taken an aversion to her at the first glance, and was not willing to be left with her for a single moment.

"I won't stay here alone with Sister Embroidery," she would cry, if her mother and Katy went into the next room for a moment's rest or a private consultation; "I hate Sister Embroidery! Come back, Mamma, come back this moment! She's making faces at me, and chattering just like an old parrot, and I don't understand a word she says. Take Sister Embroidery away, Mamma, I tell you! Don't you hear me? Come back, I say!"

The little voice would be raised to a shrill scream; and Mrs. Ashe and Katy, hurrying back, would find Amy sitting up on her pillow with wet, scarlet-flushed cheeks and eyes bright with fever, ready to throw herself out of bed; while, calm as Mabel, whose curly head lay on the pillow beside her little mistress, Sister Ambrogia, unaware of the intricacies of the English language, was placidly telling her beads and muttering prayers to herself. Some of these prayers, I do not doubt, related to Amy's recovery, if not to her conversion, and were well meant: but they were rather irritating under the circumstances!

CHAPTER X

CLEAR SHINING AFTER RAIN

WHEN the first shock is over and the inevitable realised and accepted, those who tend a long illness are apt to fall into a routine of life which helps to make the days seem short. The apparatus of nursing is got together. Every day the same things need to be done at the same hours and in the same way. Each little appliance is kept at hand; and, sad and tired as the watchers may be, the very monotony and regularity of their proceedings give a certain stay for their thoughts to rest upon.

But there was little of this monotony to help Mrs. Ashe and Katy through with Amy's illness. Small chance was there for regularity of exact system; for something unexpected was always turning up, and needful things were often lacking. The most ordinary comforts of the sick-room, or what are considered so in America, were hard to come by, and much of Katy's time was spent in devising substitutes to take their places.

Was ice needed? A pailful of dirty snow would be brought in, full of straws, sticks, and other refuse, which had apparently been scraped from the surface of the street after a frosty night. Not a particle of it could be put into milk or water; all that could be done was to make the pail serve the purpose of a refrigerator, and set bowls and tumblers in it to chill.

But the greatest trial of all was the beef-tea. It was Amy's sole food, and almost her only medicine; for Dr. Hilary believed in leaving Nature pretty much to herself in cases of fever. The kitchen of the hotel sent up, under that name, a mixture of grease and hot water, which could not be given to Amy at all. In vain Katy remonstrated and explained the process. In vain did she go to the kitchen herself to translate a carefully-written recipe to the cook, and to slip a shining five-franc piece in his hand, which, it was hoped, would quicken his energies and soften his heart. In vain did she order private supplies of the best of beef from a separate market. The cooks stole the beef and ignored the recipe; and day after day the same bottleful of greasy liquid came upstairs, which Amy would not touch, and which would have done her no good had she swallowed it all. At last, driven to desperation, Katy procured a couple of stout bottles, and every morning slowly and carefully cut up two pounds of meat into small pieces, sealed the bottle with her own seal ring, and sent it down to be boiled for a specified time. This answered better, for the thieving cook dared not tamper with her seal; but it was a long and toilsome process, and consumed more time than she well knew how to spare—for there were continual errands to be done which no one could attend to but herself, and the interminable flights of stairs taxed her strength painfully, and seemed to grow longer and harder every day.

At last a good Samaritan turned up in the shape of an American lady with a house of her own who, hearing of their plight from Mrs. Sands, undertook to send each day a supply of strong, perfectly-made beef-tea from her own kitchen for Amy's use. It was an inexpressible relief, and the lightening of this one particular care made all the rest seem easier of endurance.

Another great relief came, when, after some delay, Dr. Hilary succeeded in getting an English nurse to take the places of the unsatisfactory Sister Ambrogia and her substitute, Sister Agatha, whom Amy, in her half-comprehending condition, persisted in calling "Sister Nutmeg-Grater." Mrs. Swift was a tall, wiry angular person, who seemed made of equal parts of iron and whalebone. She was never tired; she could lift anybody, do anything; and for sleep she seemed to have a sort of antipathy, preferring to sit in an easy-chair and drop off into little dozes, whenever it was convenient, to going regularly to bed for a night's rest.

Amy took to her from the first, and the new nurse managed her beautifully. No one else could soothe her half so

419

well during the delirious period, when the little shrill voice seemed never to be still, and went on all day and all night in alternative raving or screaming, or, what was saddest of all to hear, low pitiful moans. There was no shutting in these sounds. People moved out of the rooms below and on either side, because they could get no sleep; and till the arrival of Nurse Swift, there was no rest for poor Mrs. Ashe, who could not keep away from her darling for a moment while that mournful wailing sounded in her ears.

Somehow the long, dry Englishwoman seemed to have a mesmeric effect on Amy, who was never quite so violent after she arrived. Katy was more thankful for this than can well be told; for her great underlying dread—a dread she dared not whisper plainly even to herself—was that "Polly dear" might break down before Amy was better, and then what *should* they do?

She took every care that was possible of her friend; She made her eat; she made her lie down. She forced daily doses of quinine and port-wine down her throat and saved her every possible step. But no one, however affectionate and willing, could do much to lift the crushing burden of care, which was changing Mrs. Ashe's rosy fairness to wan pallor and laying such dark shadows under the pretty grey eyes. She had taken small thought of looks since Amy's illness. All the little touches which had made her toilette becoming, all the crimps and fluffs, had disappeared; yet somehow never had she seemed to Katy half so lovely as now in the plain black gown which she wore all day long, with her hair tucked into a knot behind her ears. Her real beauty of feature and outline seemed only enhanced by the rigid plainness of her attire, and the charm of true expression grew in her face. Never had Katy admired and loved her friend so well as during those days of fatigue and wearing suspense, or realised so strongly the worth of her sweetness of temper, her unselfishness and power of devoting herself to other people.

"Polly bears it wonderfully," she wrote to her father, "she was all broken down for the first day or two, but now her courage and patience are surprising. When I think how precious Amy is to her, and how lonely her life would be if she were to die, I can hardly keep the tears out of my eyes. But Polly does not cry. She is quiet and brave and almost cheerful all the time, keeping herself busy with what needs to be done; she never complains, and she looks—oh, so pretty! I think I never knew how much she had in her before."

All this time no word had come from Lieutenant Worthington. His sister had written him as soon as Amy was taken ill, and had twice telegraphed him, but no answer had been received, and this strange silence added to the sense of lonely isolation and distance from home.

So, first one week and then another wore themselves away somehow. The fever did not break on the fourteenth day, as had been hoped, and must run for another period, the doctor said; but its force was lessened, and he considered that a favourable sign. Amy was quieter now and did not rave so constantly, but she was very weak. All her pretty hair had been shorn away, which made her little face look tiny and sharp. Mabel's golden wig was sacrificed at the same time. Amy had insisted upon it, and they dared not cross her.

One day, Katy, coming in from a round of errands, found Mrs. Ashe standing erect and pale, with a frightened look in her eyes, and her back against Amy's door, as if defending it from somebody. Confronting her was Madame Frulini, the *padrona* of the hotel. Madame's cheeks were red, and her eyes bright and fierce; she was evidently in a rage about something, and was pouring out a torrent of excited Italian, with now and then a French or English word slipped in by way of punctuation, and all so rapidly that only a trained ear could have followed or grasped her meaning.

"What *is* the matter?" asked Katy in amazement.

"Oh, Katy, I am so glad you have come!" cried poor Mrs. Ashe. "I can hardly understand a word that this horrible woman says, but I think she wants to turn us out of the hotel, and that we shall take Amy to some other place. It would be the death of her—I know it would. I never, never will go, unless the doctor says it is safe. I oughtn't to—I couldn't; she can't make me, can she, Katy?"

"Madame," said Katy—and there was a flash in her eyes before which the landlady rather shrank—"what is all this? Why do you come to trouble madame while her child is so ill?"

Then came another torrent of explanation which didn't explain; but Katy gathered enough of the meaning to make out that Mrs. Ashe was quite correct in her guess, and that Madame Frulini was requesting, nay, insisting, that they should remove Amy from the hotel at once. There was plenty of apartments to be had now that the Carnival was over, she said—her own cousin had rooms close by— it could easily be arranged, and people were going away from the Del Mondo every day because there was fever in the house. Such a thing could not be, it should not be— the landlady's voice rose to a shriek, "the child must go!"

"You are a cruel woman," said Katy indignantly, when she had grasped the meaning of the outburst. "It is wicked, it is cowardly, to come thus and attack a poor lady under your roof who has so much already to bear. It is her only child who is lying in there—her only one, do you understand, madame?—and she is a widow. What you ask might kill the child. I shall not permit you or any of your people to enter that door until the doctor comes, and then I shall tell him how you have behaved, and we shall see what he will say." As she spoke she turned the key of Amy's door, took it out and put it in her pocket, then faced the *padrona* steadily, looking her straight in the eyes.

"Mademoiselle," stormed the landlady, "I give you my word, four people have left this house already because of the noises made by little miss. More will go. I shall lose my winter's profit—all of it—all; it will be said there is fever at the Del Mondo—no one will hereafter come to me. There are lodgings plenty, comfortable—oh, so comfortable! I will not have my season ruined by a sickness; no, I will not!"

Madame Frulini's voice was again rising to a scream.

"Be silent!" said Katy sternly; "you will frighten the child. I am sorry that you should lose any customers, madame, but the fever is here and we are here, and here we must stay till it is safe to go. The child shall not be moved till the doctor gives permission. Money is not the only thing in the world! Mrs. Ashe will pay anything that is fair to make up your losses to you, but you must leave this room now, and not return till Dr. Hilary is here."

Where Katy found French for all these long coherent speeches, she could never afterwards imagine. She tried to explain it by saying that excitement inspired her for the moment, but that as soon as the moment was over the inspiration died away and left her as speechless and confused as ever. Clover said it made her think of the miracle of Balaam; and Katy merrily rejoined that it might be so, and that no donkey in any age of the world could possibly have been more grateful than was she for the sudden gift of speech.

"But it is not the money—it is my prestige," declared the landlady.

"Thank heaven! Here is the doctor now," cried Mrs. Ashe.

The doctor had, in fact, been standing in the doorway for several moments before they noticed him, and had overheard part of the colloquy with Madame Frulini. With him was someone else, at the sight of whom Mrs. Ashe gave a great sob of relief. It was her brother at last.

When Italian meets Italian then comes the tug of expletive. In five minutes Madame Frulini was, metaphorically speaking, on her knees, and the doctor standing over her with drawn sword, making her take back every word she had said and every threat she had uttered.

"Prestige of thy miserable hotel!" he thundered; "where will that be when I go and tell the English and Americans—all of whom I know, every one!—how thou hast served a country-woman of theirs in thy house! Dost thou think thy prestige will help thee much when Dr. Hilary has fixed a black mark on thy door? I tell thee no; not a stranger shalt thou have next year to eat so much as a plate of macaroni under thy base roof! I will advertise thy behaviour in all the foreign papers—in *Figaro*, in *Galignani*, in the *Swiss Times*, and the English one which

423

is read by all the nobility, and the *Heraldo* of New York, which all Americans peruse——"

"Oh, doctor—pardon me—I regret what I said—I am afflicted——!"

Having thus reduced Madame Frulini to powder the doctor now condescended to take breath and listen to her appeals for mercy; and presently he brought her in with her mouth full of protestations and apologies, and assurances that the ladies had mistaken her meaning, she had only spoken for the good of all; nothing was farther from her intention than that they should be disturbed or offended in any way, and she and all her household were at the service of "the little sick angel of God." After which the doctor dismissed her with an air of contemptuous tolerance, and laid his hand on the door of Amy's room. Behold, it was locked!

"Oh, I forgot!" cried Katy, laughing, and she pulled the key out of her pocket.

"You are a hee-roine, mademoiselle," said Dr. Hilary. "I watched you as you faced that tigress, and your eyes were like a swordsman's as he regards his enemy's rapier."

"Oh, she was so brave, and such a help!" said Mrs. Ashe, kissing her impulsively. "You can't think how she has stood by me all through, Ned, or what a comfort she has been."

"Yes, I can," said Ned Worthington, with a warm, grateful look at Katy. "I can believe anything good of Miss Carr."

"But where have *you* been all this time!" said Katy, who felt this flood of compliments to be embarrassing; "we have so wondered at not hearing from you."

"I have been off on a ten-days' leave to Corsica for moufflon-shooting," replied Mr. Worthington. "I only got Polly's telegrams and letters the day before yesterday, and I came away as soon as I could get my leave extended. It was a most unlucky absence. I shall always regret it."

"Oh, it is all right now that you have come!" his sister said, leaning her head on his arm with a look of relief and rest which was good to see. "Everything will go better now, I am sure."

"Katy Carr has behaved like a perfect angel," she told her brother when they were alone.

"She is a trump of a girl. I came in time for part of that scene with the landlady, and upon my word she was glorious! I didn't suppose she could look so handsome."

"Have the Pages left Nice yet?" asked his sister, rather irrelevantly.

"No—at least they were there on Thursday, but I think that they were to start to-day."

Mr. Worthington answered carelessly, but his face darkened as he spoke. There had been a little scene in Nice which he could not forget. He was sitting in the English garden with Lilly and her mother when his sister's telegrams were brought to him; and he had read them aloud, partly as an explanation for the immediate departure which they made necessary and which broke up an excursion just arranged with the ladies for the afternoon. It is not pleasant to have plans intererfered with; and as neither Mrs. Page nor her daughter cared personally for little Amy, it is not strange that disappointment at the interruption of their pleasure should have been the first impulse with them. Still, this did not excuse Lilly's unstudied exclamation of "Oh, bother!" and though she speedily repented it as an indiscretion, and was properly sympathetic, and "hoped the poor little thing would soon be better," Amy's uncle could not forget the jarring impression. It completed a process of disenchantment which had long been going on; and as hearts are sometimes caught at the rebound, Mrs. Ashe was not so far astray when she built certain little dim sisterly hopes on his evident admiration for Katy's courage and this sudden awakening to a sense of her good looks.

But no space was left for sentimental match-making while still Amy's fate hung in the balance, and all three of them found plenty to do during the next fortnight. The fever did not turn on the twenty-first day, and another weary week of suspense set in, each day bringing a decrease of the dangerous symptoms, but each day as well marking a lessening in the childish strength which had been so long and severely tested. Amy was quite conscious now, and lay quietly, sleeping a great deal and speaking seldom. There was not much to do but to wait and hope; but the flame of hope burned low at times, as the little life flickered in its socket, and seemed likely to go out like a wind-blown torch.

Now and then Lieutenant Worthington would persuade his sister to go with him for a few minutes' drive or walk in the fresh air, from which she had so long been debarred, and once or twice he prevailed on Katy to do the same; but neither of them could bear to be away long from Amy's bedside.

Intimacy grows fast when people are thus united by a common anxiety, sharing the same hopes and fears day after day, speaking and thinking of the same thing. The gay young officer at Nice, who had counted so little in Katy's world, seemed to have disappeared, and the gentle, considerate, tender-hearted fellow who now filled his place was quite a different person in her eyes. Katy began to count on Ned Worthington as a friend who could be trusted for help and sympathy and comprehension, and appealed to and relied upon in all emergencies. She was quite at ease with him now, and asked him to do this and that, to come and help her, or to absent himself, as freely as if he had been Dorry or Phil.

He, on his part, found this easy intimacy charming. In the reaction of his temporary glamour for the pretty Lilly, Katy's very difference from her was an added attraction. This difference consisted, as much as anything else, in the fact that she was so truly in earnest in what she said and did. Had Lilly been in Katy's place, she would probably have been helpful to Mrs. Ashe and kind to Amy so far as in her lay; but the thought of self would have tinctured all that she did and said, and the need of keeping to what was tasteful and becoming would have influenced her in every emergency, and never have been absent from her mind.

Katy, on the contrary, absorbed in the needs of the moment, gave little heed to how she looked or what anyone was thinking about her. Her habit of neatness made her take time for the one thorough daily dressing—the

426

brushing of hair and refreshing of clothes which were customary with her; but, this tax paid to personal comfort, she gave little further heed to appearances. She wore an old grey gown, day in and day out, which Lilly would not have put on for half an hour without a large bribe, so unbecoming was it; but somehow Lieutenant Worthington grew to like the grey gown as a part of Katy herself.

The grey gown played its part during the long, anxious night when they all sat watching breathlessly to see which way the tide would turn with dear little Amy. The doctor came at midnight, and went away to come again at dawn. Mrs. Swift sat grim and watchful beside the pillow of her charge, rising now and then to feel pulse and skin, or to put a spoonful of something between Amy's lips. The doors and windows stood open to admit the air. In the outer room all was hushed. A dim Roman lamp, fed with olive-oil, burned in one corner behind a screen. Mrs. Ashe lay on the sofa with her eyes closed, bearing the strain of suspense in absolute silence. Her brother sat beside her, holding in his one of the hot hands whose nervous twitches alone told of the surgings of hope and fear within. Katy was resting in a big chair near by, her wistful eyes fixed on Amy's little figure seen in the dim distance, her ears alert for every sound from the sick-room.

A faint stir of wind and a little broadening of the light roused Katy from a trance of half-understood thoughts. She crept once more into Amy's room. Mrs. Swift laid a warning finger on her lips; Amy was sleeping, she said with a gesture. Katy whispered the news to the still figure on the sofa, then she went noiselessly out of the room. The great hotel was fast asleep; not a sound stirred the profound silence of the dark halls. A longing for fresh air led her to the roof.

There was the dawn just tingeing the east. The sky, even thus early, wore the deep, mysterious blue of Italy. A fresh *tramontana* was blowing, and made Katy glad to draw her shawl about her.

Faint rumblings of wheels and here and there a curl of smoke, showed that Rome was waking up. The light insensibly grew upon the darkness. A pink flush lit up the horizon.

A footstep startled her. Ned Worthington was coming over the roof on tiptoe, as if fearful of disturbing somebody. His face looked resolute and excited.

"I wanted to tell you," he said in a hushed voice, "that the doctor is here, and he says Amy has no fever, and with care may be considered out of danger."

"Thank God!" cried Katy, bursting into tears. The long fatigue, the fears kept in check so resolutely, the sleepless night just passed, had their revenge now, and she cried and cried as if she could never stop, but with all the time such joy and gratitude in her heart! She was conscious that Ned had his arm round her and was holding both her hands tight; but they were so one in the emotion of the moment that it did not seem strange.

"How sweet the sun looks!" she said presently, releasing herself, with a happy smile flashing through her tears; "it hasn't seemed really bright for ever so long. How silly I was to cry! Where is dear Polly? I must go down to her at once. Oh, what does she say?"

CHAPTER XI

NEXT

LIEUTENANT WORTHINGTON'S leave had nearly expired. He must rejoin his ship; but he waited till the last possible moment in order to help his sister through the move to Albano, where it had been decided that Amy should go for a few days of hill air before undertaking the longer journey to Florence.

It was a perfect morning in late March when the pale little invalid was carried in her uncle's strong arms, and placed in the carriage which was to take them to the old town on the mountain slopes which they had seen shining from far away for so many weeks past. Spring had come in her fairest shape to Italy.

When once the Campagna with its long line of aqueducts, arches, and hoary tombs, was left behind, and the carriage slowly began to mount the gradual rises of the hill. Amy revived. With every breath of the fresher air her eyes seemed to brighten and her voice to grow stronger. She held Mabel up to look at the view; and the sound of her laugh, faint and feeble as it was, was like music to her mother's ears.

Amy wore a droll little silk-lined cap on her head, under which a downy growth of pale-brown fuzz was gradually thickening. Already it showed a tendency to form into tiny rings, which to Amy, who had always hankered for curls, was an extreme satisfaction. Strange to say, the same thing exactly had happened to Mabel; her hair had grown out into soft little round curls also; Uncle Ned and Katy had ransacked Rome for this baby-wig, which filled and realised all Amy's hopes for her child. On the same excursion they had bought the materials for the pretty spring suit which Mabel wore, for it had been deemed necessary to sacrifice most of her wardrobe as a concession to possible fever-germs. Amy admired the pearl-coloured dress and hat, the fringed jacket and little lace-trimmed parasol, so much that she was quite consoled for the loss of the blue velvet costume and ermine muff which had been the pride of her heart ever since they left Paris, and whose destruction they had scarcely dared to confess to her.

So up, up, up they climbed till the gateway of the old town was passed, and the carriage stopped before a quaint building, once the residence of the Bishop of Albano, but now known as the Hôtel de la Poste. Here they alighted, and were shown up a wide and lofty staircase to their rooms.

Such enormous rooms as they were! It was quite a journey to go from one side of them to another. The floors were of stone, with squares of carpet laid down over them, which looked absurdly small for the great spaces they were supposed to cover. The beds and tables were of the usual size, but they seemed almost doll furniture because the chambers were so big. A quaint old paper, with an enormous pattern of banyan-trees and pagodas, covered the walls, and every now and then betrayed, by an oblong of regular cracks, the existence of a hidden door, papered to look exactly like the rest of the wall.

These mysterious doors made Katy nervous, and she never rested till she had opened every one of them and explored the places they led to. One gave access to a queer little bathroom. Another led, through a narrow dark passage, to a sort of balcony or loggia overhanging the garden. A third ended in a dusty closet with an artful chink in it from which you could peep into what had been the bishop's drawing-room, but which was now turned into the dining-room of the hotel. It seemed made for purposes of espial; and Katy had visions of a long line of reverend prelates with their ears glued to the chink, overhearing what was being said about them in the apartment beyond.

Before he left them Lieutenant Worthington had a talk with his sister in the garden. She rather forced this talk upon him, for various things were lying at her heart about which she longed for explanation; but he yielded so easily to her wiles that it was evident he was not averse to the idea.

"Come, Polly, don't beat about the bush any longer," he said at last, amused and a little irritated at her half-hints and little feminine *finesses*. "I know what you want to ask; and as there's no use making a secret of it, I will take my turn in asking. Have I any chance, do you think?"

"Any chance!—about Katy, do you mean? Oh, Ned, you make me so happy!"

"Yes; about her, of course."

"I don't see why you should say 'of course'," remarked his sister, with the perversity of her sex, "when it's only five or six weeks ago that I was lying awake at night for fear you were being gobbled up by that Lilly Page."

"There was little risk of it," replied her brother seriously. "She's awfully pretty and she dances beautifully, and the other fellows were all wild about her, and—well, you know yourself how such things go. I can't see now what it was that I fancied so much about her. I don't suppose I could have told exactly at the time; but I can tell without the smallest trouble what it is in—the other."

"In Katy? I should think so," cried Mrs. Ashe emphatically; "the two are no more to be compared than—than—well, bread and syllabub! You can live on one and you can't live on the other."

"Come now, Miss Page isn't so bad as that. She is a nice girl enough, and a pretty girl, too,—prettier than Katy; I'm not so far gone that I can't see that. But we won't talk about her, she's not in the present question at all; very likely she'd have had nothing to say to me in any case. I was only one out of a dozen, and she never gave me reason to suppose that she cared more for me than the rest. Let us talk about this friend of yours; have I any chance at all, do you think, Polly?"

"Ned, you are the dearest boy! I would rather have Katy for a sister than anyone else I know. She's so nice all through—so true and sweet and satisfactory."

"She is all that and more; she's a woman to tie to for life, to be perfectly sure of always. She would make a splendid wife for any man. I'm not half good enough for her; but the question is—and you haven't answered it yet, Polly—what's my chance?"

"I don't know," said his sister slowly.

"Then I must ask her; and I shall do so to-day."

"I don't know," repeated Mrs. Ashe. " 'She is a woman, therefore to be won': and I don't think there is anyone ahead of you; that is the best hope I have to offer, Ned. Katy never talks of such things; and though she's so frank, I can't guess whether or not she ever thinks about them. She likes you, however, I am sure of that. But, Ned, it will not be wise to say anything to her yet."

"Not say anything! Why not?"

"No. Recollect that it is only a little while since she looked upon you as the admirer of another girl, and a girl she doesn't like very much, though they are cousins. You must give her time to get over that impression. Wait a while, that's my advice, Ned."

"I'll wait any time if only she will say yes in the end. But it's hard to go away without a word of hope, and it's more like a man to speak out, it seems to me."

"It's too soon," persisted his sister. "You don't want her to think you a fickle fellow, falling in love with a fresh girl every time you go into port, and falling out again when the ship sails. Sailors have a bad reputation for that sort of thing. No woman cares to win a man like that."

"Great Scott! I should think not! Do you mean to say that is the way my conduct appears to her, Polly?"

"No, I don't mean just that; but wait, dear Ned, I am sure it is better."

Fortified by this sage counsel, Lieutenant Worthington went away next morning, without saying anything to Katy in words, though perhaps eyes and tones may have been less discreet. He made them promise that someone should send a letter every day about Amy; and as Mrs. Ashe frequently devolved the writing of these bulletins upon Katy, and the replies came in the shape of long letters, she found herself conducting a pretty regular correspondence without quite intending it. Ned Worthington wrote particularly nice letters. He had the knack, more often found in women than men, of giving a picture with a few graphic touches and indicating what was droll or what was characteristic with a single happy phrase. His letters grew to be one of Katy's pleasures; and sometimes, as Mrs. Ashe watched the colour deepen in her cheeks while she read, her heart would bound hopefully within her. But she was a wise woman in her way, and she wanted Katy for a sister very much; so she never said a word or looked a look to startle or surprise her, but left the thing to work itself out, which is the best course always in love affairs.

Little Amy's improvement at Albano was something remarkable. Mrs. Swift watched over her like a lynx. Her vigilance never relaxed. Amy was made to eat and sleep and walk and rest with the regularity of a machine; and this exact system, combined with the good air, worked like a charm. The little one gained hour by hour. They could absolutely see her growing fat, her mother declared.

She had gained so much before the time came to start for Florence that they scarcely dreaded the journey; but it proved worse than their expectations. They had not been able to secure a carriage to themselves, and were obliged to share their compartment with two English ladies, and three Roman Catholic priests, one old, the others young. The older priest seemed to be a person of some consequence, for quite a number of people came to see him off, and knelt for his blessing devoutly as the train moved away. The young ones Katy guessed to be seminary students under his charge.

At last the train, steaming down the valley of the Arno, revealed fair Florence sitting among olive-clad hills, with Giotti's beautiful Bell-tower, and the great, many-coloured, soft-hued Cathedral, and the square tower of the old Palace, and the quaint bridges over the river, looking exactly as they do in the photographs; and Katy would have felt delighted, in spite of dust and fatigue, had not Amy looked so worn out and exhausted. They were seriously troubled about her, and for the moment could think of nothing else. Happily the fatigue did no permanent harm, and a day or two of rest made her all right again. By good fortune, a nice little apartment in the modern quarter of the city had been vacated by its winter occupants the very day of their arrival, and Mrs. Ashe secured it for a month, with all its conveniences and advantages, including a maid named Maria, who had been servant to the just-departed tenants.

Maria was a very tall woman, at least six feet two, and had a splendid contralto voice, which she occasionally exercised while busy over her pots and pans. It was so remarkable to hear these grand arias and recitatives proceeding from a kitchen some eight feet square that Katy was at great pains to satisfy her curiosity about it. By aid of the dictionary and much persistent questioning, she made out that Maria in her youth had received a partial training for the opera; but in the end it was decided that she was too big and heavy for the stage, and the poor "giantess," as Amy named her, had been forced to abandon her career, and gradually had sunk to the posi-

433

tion of maid-of-all-work. Katy suspected that heaviness of mind as well as of body must have stood in her way; for Maria, though a good-natured giantess, was by no means quick of intelligence.

"I do think that the manner in which people over here can make homes for themselves at five minutes' notice is perfectly delightful," cried Katy, at the end of their first day's housekeeping. "I wish we could do the same in America. How cosy it looks here already!"

It was indeed cosy. Their new domain consisted of a parlour in a corner, furnished in bright yellow brocade, with windows to south and west; a nice little dining-room; three bedrooms, with dimity-curtained beds; a square entrance-hall, lighted at night by a tall slender brass lamp whose double wicks were fed with olive-oil; and the aforesaid tiny kitchen, behind which was a sleeping-cubby, quite too small to be good fit for the giantess. The rooms were full of conveniences—easy-chairs, sofas, plenty of bureaus and dressing-tables, and corner fireplaces like Franklin stoves, in which odd little fires burned on cool days, made of pine cones, cakes of pressed sawdust exactly like Boston brown bread cut into slices, and a few sticks of wood thriftily adjusted, for fuel is worth its weight in gold in Florence. Katy's was the smallest of the bedrooms but she liked it best of all for the reason that its one big window opened on an iron balcony over which grew a Banksia rose-vine with a stem as thick as her wrist. It was covered just now with masses of tiny white blossoms, whose fragrance was inexpressibly delicious and made every breath drawn in their neighbourhood a delight. The sun streamed in on all sides of the little apartment, which filled a narrowing angle at the union of three streets; and from one window and another, glimpses could be caught of the distant heights about the city—San Miniato in one direction, Bello Sguardo in another, and for the third the long olive-hung ascent of Fiesole, crowned by its grey cathedral towers.

It was astonishing how easily everything fell into train about this little establishment. Every morning at six the

English baker left two small sweet brown loaves and a dozen rolls at the door. Then followed the dairyman with a supply of tiny leaf-shaped pats of freshly-churned butter, a big flask of milk, and two small bottles of thick cream with a twist of vine leaf in each by way of a cork. Next came a *contadino* with a flask of red Chianti wine, a film of oil floating on top to keep it sweet. People in Florence must drink wine, whether they like it or not, because the lime-impregnated water is unsafe for use without some admixture.

Dinner came from a *trattoria*, in a tin box, with a pan of coals inside to keep it warm, which box was carried on a man's head. It was furnished at a fixed price per day—a soup, two dishes of meat, two vegetables, and a sweet dish; and the supply was so generous as always to leave something towards next day's luncheon. Salad, fruit, and fresh eggs Maria bought for them in the old market. From the confectioner's came loaves of *pane santo*, a sort of light cake made with arrow-root instead of flour; and sometimes, by way of a treat, a square of *pan forte da Siena*, compounded of honey, almonds and chocolate—a mixture as pernicious as it is delicious, and which might take a medal anywhere for the sure production of nightmares.

Amy soon learned to know the shops from which these delicacies came. She had her favourites, too, among the strolling merchants who sold oranges and those little sweet native figs dried in the sun without sugar, which are among the specialities of Florence. They, in their turn, learned to know her and to watch for the appearance of her little capped head and Mabel's blonde wig at the window, lingering about till she came, and advertising their wares with musical modulations, so appealing that Amy was always running to Katy, who acted as housekeeper to beg her to please buy this or that, "because it is my old man, and he wants me to so much."

"But, chicken, we have plenty of figs for to-day."

"No matter; get some more, please do. I'll eat them all, really, I will."

And Amy was as good as her word. Her convalescent appetite was something prodigious.

435

There was another branch of shopping in which they all took equal delight. The beauty and the cheapness of the Florence flowers are a continual surprise to a stranger. Every morning after breakfast an old man came creaking up the two long flights of stairs which led to Mrs. Ashe's apartment, tapped at the door, and, as soon as it opened, inserted a shabby elbow and a large flat basket full of flowers. Such flowers! Great masses of scarlet and cream-coloured tulips, and white and gold narcissus, knots of roses of all shades, carnations, heavy-headed trails of wistaria, wild hyacinths, violets, deep crimson and orange ranunculus, *giglios*, or wild irises—the Florence emblem, so deeply purple as to be almost black—anemones, spring-beauties, faintly-tinted wood-blooms tied in large nosegays, ivy, fruit blossoms—everything that can be thought of that is fair and sweet. These enticing wares the old man would tip out on the table. Mrs. Ashe and Katy would select what they wanted, and then the process of bargaining would begin, without which no sale is complete in Italy. The old man would name an enormous price, five times as much as he hoped to get. Katy would offer a very small one, considerably less than she expected to give. The old man would dance with dismay, wiring his hands, assure them that he should die of hunger, and all his family with him, if he took less than the price named; he would then come down half a franc in his demand. So it would go on for five minutes, ten, sometimes for a quarter of an hour, the old man's price gradually descending, and Katy's terms very slowly going up, a cent or two at a time. Next the giantess would mingle with the fray. She would bounce out of her kitchen, berate the flower-vendor, snatch up his flowers, declare that they smelt badly, fling them down again, pouring out all the while a voluble tirade of re-proaches and revilings, and looking so enormous in her excitement that Katy wondered that the old man dared to answer her at all. Finally, there would be a sudden lull. The old man would shrug his shoulders, and, remarking that he and his wife and his aged grandmother must go without bread that day since it was the signora's will, take the money offered and depart, leaving such a mass of flowers behind him that Katy would begin to think that they had paid an unfair price for them and to feel a little rueful, till she observed that the old man was absolutely dancing downstairs with rapture over the good bargain he had made, and that Maria was black with indignation over the extravagance of her ladies!

"The Americani are a nation of spendthrifts," she would mutter to herself, as she quickened the charcoal in her droll little range by fanning it with a palm-leaf fan; "they squander money like water. Well, all the better for us Italians!" with a shrug of her shoulders.

"But, Maria, it was only sixteen cents that we paid, and look at those flowers! There are at least half a bushel of them."

"Sixteen cents for garbage like that! The signorina would better let me make her bargains for her. Già! Già! No Italian lady would have paid more than eleven sous for such useless roba. It is evident that the signorina's countrymen eat gold when at home, they think so little of casting it away!"

Altogether, what with the comfort and quiet of this little home, the numberless delightful things that there were to do and to see, and Viessieux's great library, from which they could draw books at will to make the doing and seeing more intelligible, the month at Florence passed only too quickly, and was one of the times to which they afterwards looked back with most pleasure. Amy grew steadily stronger, and the freedom from anxiety about her after their long strain of apprehension was restful and healing beyond expression to both mind and body.

Their very last excursion of all, and one of the pleasantest, was to the old amphitheatre at Fiesole, and it was while they sat there in the soft glow of the late afternoon, tying into bunches the violets which they had gathered from under walls whose foundations antedate Rome itself, that a cheery call sounded from above, and an unexpected surprise descended upon them in the shape of Lieutenant Worthington, who, having secured another fifteen days' furlough, had come to take his sister on to Venice.

"I didn't write you that I had applied for leave," he explained, "because there seemed so little chance of me getting off again so soon; but as luck had it, Carruthers, whose turn it was, sprained his ankle and was laid up, and the Commodore let us exchange. I made all the capital I could out of Amy's fever; but upon my word, I felt like a humbug when I came upon her and Mrs. Swift in the Cascine just now, as I was hunting for you. How she has picked up! I should never have known her for the same child."

"Yes, she seems perfectly well again, and as strong as before she had the fever, though that dear old Goody Swift is just as careful of her as ever. She would not let us bring her here this afternoon, for fear we should stay out till the dew fell. Ned, it is perfectly delightful that you were able to come. It makes going to Venice seem quite a different thing, doesn't it, Katy?"

"I don't want it to seem quite different, because going to Venice was always one of my dreams," replied Katy, with a little laugh.

"I hope at least it doesn't make it seem less pleasant," said Mr. Worthington, as his sister stopped to pick a violet.

"No, indeed, I am glad," said Katy; "we shall all be seeing it for the first time, too, shall we not? I think you said you had never been there." She spoke simply and frankly, but she was conscious of an odd shyness.

"I simply couldn't stand it any longer," Ned Worthington confided to his sister when they were alone. "My head is so full of her that I can't attend to my work, and it came to me all of a sudden that this might be my last chance. You'll be going north before long, you know, to Switzerland and so on, where I cannot follow you. So I made a clean breast of it to the Commodore; and the good old fellow, who has a soft spot in his heart for a love-story, behaved like a brick, and made it all straight for me to come away."

Mrs. Ashe did not join in these commendations of the

Commodore; her attention was fixed on another part of her brother's discourse.

"Then you won't be able to come to me again? I shan't see you again after this!" she exclaimed. "Dear me! I never realised that before. What shall I do without you?"

"You will have Miss Carr. She is a host in herself," suggested Ned Worthington. His sister shook her head.

"Katy is a jewel," she remarked presently; "but some-

Amy and Mabel sat on his knee, they were all very happy together

how one wants a man to call upon. I shall feel lost without you, Ned."

The month's housekeeping wound up that night with a "thick tea" in honour of Lieutenant Worthington's arrival, which taxed all the resources of the little establishment. Maria was sent out hastily to buy *pan forte da Siena* and *vino d'Asti*, and fresh eggs for an omelette, and chickens' breasts smothered in cream from the restaurant, and artichokes for a salad, and flowers to

439

garnish all; and the guest ate and praised and admired; and Amy and Mabel sat on his knee and explained everything to him, and they were all very happy together. Their merriment was so infectious that it extended to the poor giantess, who had been very pensive all day at the prospect of losing her good place, and who now raised her voice in the grand aria from "Orfeo," and made the kitchen ring with the passionate demand *"Che fara senza Euridice?"* The splendid notes, full of fire and lamentation, rang out across the saucepans as effectively as if they had been footlights; and Katy, rising softly, opened the kitchen door a little way that they might not lose a sound.

The next day brought them to Venice. It was a "moment," indeed, as Katy seated herself for the first time in a gondola, and looked from beneath its black hood at the palace walls on the Grand Canal, past which they were gliding. Some were creamy white and black, some orange-tawny, others of a dull delicious ruddy colour, half-pink, half-red; but all, in build and ornament, were unlike palaces elsewhere. High on the prow before her stood the gondolier, his form defined in dark outline against the sky, as he swayed and bent to his long oar, raising his head now and again to give a wild musical cry, as warning to other approaching gondolas. It was all like a dream. Ned Worthington sat beside her, looking more at the changes in her expressive face than at the palaces. Venice was as new to him as to Katy; but she was a new feature in his life also, and even more interesting than Venice.

They seemed to float on pleasures for the next ten days. Their arrival had been happily timed to coincide with a great popular festival which for nearly a week kept Venice in a state of continual brilliant gala. All the days were spent on the water, only landing now and then to look at some famous building or picture, or to eat ices in the Piazza with the lovely façade of St. Mark's before them. Dining or sleeping seemed a sheer waste of time! The evenings were spent on the water too; for every night, immediately after sunset, a beautiful drifting pageant started from the front of the Doge's Palace to make the tour of the Grand Canal, and our friends always took a part in it. In its centre went a barge hung with embroideries and filled with orange-trees and musicians. This was surrounded by a great convoy of skiffs and gondolas bearing coloured lanterns and pennons and gay awnings, and managed by gondoliers in picturesque uniforms. All these floated and shifted and swept on together with a sort of rhythmic undulation, as if keeping time to the music, while across their path dazzling showers and arches of coloured fire poured from the palace fronts and the hotels. Every movement of the fairy flotilla was repeated in the illuminated water, every torch-tip and scarlet lantern and flake of green or rosy fire, above all the bright full moon looked down as if surprised. It was magically beautiful in effect. Katy felt as if her previous sober ideas about life and things had melted away. For the moment the world was turned topsy-turvy. There was nothing hard or real or sordid left in it; it was just a fairy tale, and she was in the middle of it as she had longed to be in her childhood. She was the Princess, encircled by delights, as when she and Clover and Elsie played in "Paradise"—only this was better; and, dear me, who was this Prince who seemed to belong to the story and to grow more important to it every day?

Fairly tales must come to ending. Katy's last chapter closed with a sudden turn-over of the leaf when, towards the end of this happy fortnight, Mrs. Ashe came into her room with the face of one who has unpleasant news to communicate.

"Katy," she began, "should you be *awfully* disappointed, should you consider me a perfect wretch, if I went home now instead of in the autumn?"

Katy was too much astonished to reply.

"I am grown such a coward, I am so knocked up and weakened by what I suffered in Rome, that I find I cannot face the idea of going on to Germany and Switzerland alone, without Ned to take care of me. You are a perfect angel, dear, and I know that you would do all you could to make it easy for me, but I am such a fool that I do not dare. I think my nerves must have given way," she continued half-tearfully; "but the very idea of shifting for

441

myself for five months longer makes me so miserably homesick that I cannot endure it. I dare say I shall repent afterwards, and I tell myself now how silly it is, but it's no use—I shall never know another easy moment till I have Amy safe again in America and under your father's care.

"I find," she continued, after another little pause, "that we can go down with Ned to Genoa and take a steamer there which will carry us straight to New York without any stops. I hate to disappoint you dreadfully, Katy, but I have almost decided to do it. Shall you mind very much? Can you ever forgive me?" She was fairly crying now.

Katy had to swallow hard before she could answer, the sense of disappointment was so sharp; and with all her efforts there was almost a sob in her voice as she said:

"Why, yes, indeed, dear Polly, there is nothing to forgive. You are perfectly right to go home if you feel so." Then with another swallow she added: "You have given me the loveliest six months' treat that ever was, and I should be a greedy girl indeed if I found fault because it is cut off a little sooner than we expected."

"You are so dear and good not to be vexed," said her friend, embracing her. "It makes me feel doubly sorry about disappointing you. Indeed I wouldn't if I could help it, but I simply can't. I *must* go home. Perhaps we'll come back some day when Amy is grown up, or safely married to somebody who will take good care of her!"

This distant prospect was but a poor consolation for the immediate disappointment. The more Katy thought about it the sorrier did she feel. It was not only losing the chance —very likely the only one she would ever have—of seeing Switzerland and Germany; it was all sorts of other little things besides. They must go home in a strange ship with a captain they did not know, instead of in the *Spartacus*, as they had planned, and they should land in New York, where no one would be waiting for them, and not have the fun of sailing into Boston Bay and seeing Rose on the wharf, where she had promised to be. Furthermore, they must pass the hot summer in Burnet instead of in the cool Alpine valleys; and Polly's house was let till October. She

442

and Amy would have to shift for themselves elsewhere. Perhaps they would not be in Burnet at all. Oh dear, what a pity it was, what a dreadful pity!

Then, the first shock of surprise and discomfiture over, other ideas asserted themselves; and as she realised that in three weeks more, or four at the longest, she was to see papa and Clover and all her dear people at home, she began to feel so very glad that she could hardly wait for the time to come. After all there was nothing in Europe quite so good as that.

"No, I'm not sorry," she told herself; "I am glad. Poor Polly! It's no wonder she feels nervous after all she has gone through. I hope I wasn't cross to her! And it will be *very* nice to have Lieutenant Worthington to take care of us as far as Genoa."

The next three days were full of work. There was no more floating in gondolas, except in the way of business. All the shopping which they had put off must be done, and the trunks packed for the voyage. Everyone recollected last errands and commissions; there was continual coming and going and confusion. And Amy, wild with excitement, popping up every other moment in the midst of it all, to demand of everybody if they were not glad that they were going back to America.

Katy had never yet bought her gift for old Mrs. Redding. She had waited, thinking continually that she should see something more tempting still in the next place they went to; but now, with the sense that there were to be no more "next places," she resolved to wait no longer, and with a hundred francs in her pocket, set forth to choose something from among the many tempting things for sale in the Piazza. A bracelet of old Roman coins had caught her fancy one day in a bric-à-brac shop and she walked straight towards it, only pausing by the way to buy a pale-blue iridescent pitcher at Salviate's for Cecy Slack, and see it carefully rolled in sea-weed and soft paper.

The price of the bracelet was a little more than she expected, and quite a long process of bargaining was necessary to reduce it to the sum she had to spend. She

443

had just succeeded, and was counting out the money, when Mrs. Ashe and her brother appeared, having spied her from the opposite side of the Piazza, where they were choosing last photographs at Naga's. Katy showed her purchase and explained that it was a present "for of course I should never walk out in cold blood and buy a bracelet for myself," she said, with a laugh.

"This is a fascinating little shop," said Mrs. Ashe. "I wonder what is the price of that queer old châtelaine with the bottles hanging from it."

The price was high; but Mrs. Ashe was now tolerably conversant with shopping Italian, which consists chiefly of a few words repeated many times over, and it lowered rapidly under the influence of her *troppo*'s and *é molto caro*'s, accompanied with telling little shrugs and looks of surprise. In the end she bought it for less than two-thirds of what had been originally asked for it. As she put the parcel in her pocket, her brother said:

"If you have done your shopping now, Polly, can't you come out for a last row?"

"Katy may, but I can't," replied Mrs. Ashe. "The man promised to bring my gloves at six o'clock, and I must be there to pay for them. Take her down to the Lido, Ned. It's an exquisite evening for the water, and the sunset promises to be delicious. You can take the time, can't you, Katy?"

Katy could.

Mrs. Ashe turned to leave them, but suddenly stopped short.

"Katy, look! Isn't that a picture?"

The "picture" was Amy, who had come to the Piazza with Mrs. Swift, to feed the doves of St. Mark's, which was one of her favourite amusements. These pretty birds are the pets of all Venice, and so accustomed to being fondled and made much of by strangers that they are perfectly tame. Amy, when her mother caught sight of her, was sitting on the marble pavement, with one on her shoulder, two perched on the edge of her lap, which was full of crumbs, and a flight of others circling round her head. She was looking up and calling them in soft tones.

The sunlight caught the little downy curls on her head and made them glitter. The flying doves lit on the pavement, and crowded round her, their pearl grey and rose-tinted and white feathers, their scarlet feet and gold-ringed eyes, making a shifting confusion of colours, as they hopped and fluttered and cooed about the little maid, unstartled ever by her clear laughter. Close by stood Nurse Swift, observant and grimly pleased.

The mother looked on with happy tears in her eyes. "Oh, Katy, think what she was a few weeks ago, and look at her now! Can I ever be thankful enough?"

She squeezed Katy's hand convulsively and walked away, turning her head now and then for another glance at Amy and the doves; while Ned and Katy silently crossed to the landing and got into a gondola. It was the perfection of a Venice evening, with silver waves lapsing and lulling under a rose and opal sky, and the sense that it was their last row on those enchanted waters made every moment seem doubly precious.

I cannot tell you exactly what it was that Ned Worthington said to Katy during that row, or why it took so long to say it that they did not get in till after the sun was set, and the stars had come out to peep at their bright, glinting faces reflected in the Grand Canal. In fact, no one can tell; for no one overheard, except Giacomo, the brown yellow-jacketed gondolier, and as he did not understand a word of English he could not repeat the conversation. Venetian boatmen, however, know pretty well what it means when a gentleman and lady, both young, find so much to say in low tones to each other under the gondola hood, and are so long about giving the order to return; and Giacomo deeply sympathetic, rowed as softly and made himself as imperceptible as he could—a display of tact which merited the big silver piece with which Lieutenant Worthington "crossed his palm" on landing.

Mrs. Ashe had begun to look for them long before they appeared, but I think she was neither surprised nor sorry that they were so late. Katy kissed her hastily and went away at once—"to pack," she said—and Ned was equally undemonstrative; but they looked so happy, both

445

of them, that "Polly dear" was quite satisfied and asked no questions.

Five days later the parting came, when the *Florio* steamer put into the port of Genoa for passengers. It was not an easy goodbye to say. Mrs. Ashe and Amy both cried, and Mabel was said to be in deep affliction also. But there were alleviations. The squadron was coming home in the autumn, and the officers would have leave to see their friends, and of course Lieutenant Worthington must come to Burnet—to visit his sister. Five months would soon go, he declared; but, for all the cheerful assurance, his face was rueful enough as he held Katy's hand in a long tight clasp while the little boat waited to take him ashore.

After that it was just waiting to be got through with till they sighted Sandy Hook and the Neversinks—a waiting varied with peeps at Marseilles and Gibraltar, and the sight of a whale or two and one distant iceberg. The weather was fair all the way, and the ocean smooth. Amy was never weary of lamenting her own stupidity in not having taken Marian Matilda out of confinement before they left Venice.

"That child has hardly been out of the trunk since we started," she said. "She hasn't seen anything except a little bit of Nice. I shall really be ashamed when the other children ask her about it. I think I shall play that she was left at boarding-school and didn't come to Europe at all! Don't you think that would be the best way, Mamma?"

"You might play that she was left in the State prison for having done something naughty," suggested Katy; but Amy scouted this idea.

"She never does naughty things," she said, "because she never does anything at all. She's just stupid, poor child! It's not her fault."

The thirty-six hours between New York and Burnet seemed longer than all the rest of the journey put together, Katy thought. But they ended at last, as the *Lake Queen* swung to her moorings at the familiar wharf, where Dr. Carr stood surrounded with all his boys and girls just as they had stood the previous October, only that now there were no clouds on anybody's face, and Johnnie was skipping up and down for joy instead of grief. It was a long moment while the plank was being lowered from the gangway; but the moment it was in place, Katy darted across, first ashore of all the passengers, and was in her father's arms.

Mrs. Ashe and Amy spent two or three days with them, while looking up temporary quarters elsewhere; and so long as they stayed all seemed a happy confusion of talking and embracing and exclaiming, and distributing gifts. After they went away things fell into their customary train, and a certain flatness became apparent. Everything had happened that could happen. The long-talked-of European journey was over. Here was Katy at home again, months sooner than they expected; yet she looked remarkably cheerful and content! Clover could not understand it: she was likewise puzzled to account for one or two private conversations between Katy and papa in which she had not been invited to take part, and the occasional arrival of a letter from "foreign parts" about whose contents nothing was said.

"It seems a dreadful pity that you had to come so soon," she said one day when they were alone in their bedroom. "It's delightful to have you, of course; but we had braced ourselves to do without you till October, and there are such lots of delightful things that you could have been doing and seeing at this moment."

"Oh, yes indeed!" replied Katy, but not at all as if she were particularly disappointed.

"Katy Carr, I don't understand you," persisted Clover. "Why don't you feel worse about it? Here you have lost five months of the most splendid time you ever had, and you don't seem to mind a bit! Why, if I were in your place my heart would be perfectly broken. And you needn't have come either; that's the worst of it. It was just a whim of Polly's. Papa says Amy might have stayed as well as not. Why aren't you sorrier, Katy?"

"Oh, I don't know! Perhaps because I had so much as it was—enough to last all my life, I think, though I *should* like to go again. You can't imagine what beautiful pictures are put away in my memory."

"I don't see that you had so awfully much," said the aggravated Clover; "you were there only a little more than six months—for I don't count the sea—and ever so much of that time was taken up with nursing Amy. You can't have any pleasant pictures of *that* part of it."

"Yes, I have, some."

"Well, I should really like to know what. There you were in a dark room, frightened to death and tired to death, with only Mrs. Ashe and the old nurse to keep you company—Oh yes, that brother was there part of the time! I forgot him——"

Clover stopped short in sudden amazement. Katy was standing with her back towards her, smoothing her hair, but her face was reflected in the glass. At Clover's words a sudden deep flush had mounted in Katy's cheeks. Deeper and deeper it burned as she became conscious of Clover's astonished gaze, till even the back of her neck was pink. Then, as if she could not bear it any longer, she put the brush down, turned, and fled out of the room; while Clover, looking after her, exclaimed in a tone of sudden comical dismay:

"What does it mean? Oh, dear me! Is *that* what Katy is going to do next?"

THE END